I0760886

NERO AND SPORUS

S.P. SOMTOW

SPECIAL EDITION
DIPLODOCUS PRESS · 2025

ISBN:
paperback: 978-1940999-93-7
hardcover: 978-1940999-94-4

0 9 8 7 6 5 4 3 2 1
First Edition

I started writing this novel
because in so many ways
it's the story of my adopted son Mikey
he too went from a homeless orphan
to hobnobbing with royals and myth makers
he too changed his gender
almost as frequently as his clothes
he too had visions and dreams
of gods and demons
and he too was destroyed by them

No one your life touched
will ever forget you.

CONTENTS

Nero and Sporus

BOOK ONE

DELICATUS

Nero and Sporus · 12

Sol omnibus lucet
The sun shines on everybody

— Petronius

I

GODDESS

Chains and the sea….

Hold still. The rouge has to be even.

It seems I will end as I began, my feet chained to a wall, and a roar in my ears. Though then it was the ocean, and now it is a crowd. Both hungry, both eager to swallow up souls.

Don't talk so much. Wait. Let me finish your lips first.

My life begins with the wooden wall and the roaring sea. To remember further back is to be in hell, and so I won't. Though snatches of it have haunted me all along. Burning villages. Blood. A crucifixion at a crossroads, an auction in an agora.

Smudged!

Don't be all nervous. You have time to finish this. And I … I feel like talking. You must let me. There are things I wish I could tell someone. Especially now, when I'm about to enter the next plane of my existence.

I've been a refugee. I've been a slave boy. I've been an empress. I've mated with two gods, and soon I'll be a god myself. And all before my twentieth birthday.

Again! Should I mix the rouge myself? Hold still.

Does it matter?

We all know how this will end.

Demeter's daughter, spirit of spring, Proserpina the fair, comes forth among the flowers, trees and meadows. The earth opens up, and from the gates of Hades itself emerges Pluto, Lord of the Dead, with his three-headed hound in tow. Violently he seizes the maiden, drags her onto his chariot, kicking and screaming, quirting his skeletal horses down into the bowels of the earth as the flowers begin to wilt, as the fruit falls and rots on the barren ground, as the leaves turn brittle and yellow, as cold envelops the world.

You know how Ceres-Demeter searches the desolate world. How the plants mourn, how the soil turns to stone and can no longer sustain life, how men and animals begin to starve for lack of sustenance. You know Proserpina's mother descends to the depths of hell where her daughter is now queen. How she pleads with the dark god until he relents. How Proserpina is tricked into eating six seeds of a pomegranate … and so must live six months of the year in the dark realm of the dead. How the earth blooms again when she returns, how the earth dies she when returns to the cold.

I shall act out that drama. With all the violence that entails.

Such is the command of Himself the Divine Vitellius, my Emperor and my God. This, he has told me, shall be how I atone for my infamy. Not that I ever *chose* infamy. It chose me.

If you are going to be of ignoble birth, don't be beautiful. You will come to a bad end. As I already have. The Rape of

Proserpina is merely the garnish.

This being the Roman *ludi,* of course, Proserpina doesn't come back. No one comes back from such an outing. Oh, perhaps the odd gladiator, if the mob loves him, if he sticks it out long enough to earn the wooden sword. People like me, we are not the main course. We're but a kind of amuse-bouche in between the serious fights, and we don't get to ask for a thumbs-up.

Doubtless, the "actor" chosen to play Pluto will be some priapic monstrosity selected for sole purpose of leaving me as ripped and bloody as possible before the chariot drags me round and round and the crowds cheer each bump, each jolt. Doubtless some savage from Germania or Nubia.

No point in imagining every second of your agony in advance, Divinity. You'll have plenty of time to enjoy it in the flesh, if you see what I mean.

Impudent slave!

Look who's talking!

I know. I am one to talk. I was once lowlier than you, and soon shall be again. So let me talk. In a few hours, my voice will be stilled forever. And you, junior assistant cosmetic artist of the imperial household, sent to make me beautiful for the last time by the Grace of none other than Himself the Divine Vitellius, third emperor in this year of many emperors but perhaps not the last … you will go back to painting the faces of the mighty, being slapped around from time to time, and dying like a shriveled old dog on the master's country estate.

You called me *Divinity* just now, not just in deference to the role I will play today, but because I have been a God. And I have mated with a God. Or Gods. And let me tell you, the Gods are no better in bed than ordinary men.

Lift up the mirror.

I want my eyelids gold … real gold dust, bound with the

boiled bones of horses. It doesn't matter if it blocks my pores. It will not be for long.

And the kohl-rimmed eyes ... they must be black. My eyelashes *will* be seen even by the plebeians!

Oh, such a decrepit stage for my final performance. Big, the Circus Maximus, but strangely déclassé. They have everything here from chariot races to executions, gladiators to Greek theater. One day some Emperor will build a proper venue. Not this dusty space that hasn't been repaired in a century or two. When I was Empress I sometimes told Lucius, the one you call Nero, he should peel off some of the domestic budget he set aside for his Golden House to build a proper amphitheater for games. Doesn't look like I will live to see such a colosseum. It would be nice to die in a venue worthy of my godhead.

Hold still!

I *am* holding still. I mean, you do have me chained up.

Chained up, just like the day I first came to Rome.

... chains and the sea...

Still, Divinity!

... chains and the sea...

This place is rooted to the ground, but it reminds me of that ship. Me, chained in the hold with a few dozen others. Scrawny. The roar of the sea, the roar of the crowd ... the bite of the chains on my thin skin ... here the walls are moist with sweat and tears ... there they were damp from the brine of the sea. The smell of the ocean, the sweaty smell of human misery ... it is the same. This cell of stone, that cell of wood ... the twin imprisonments of my life's journey.

I'm going to talk ... I'm going to tell all of it. To pass the time before they call me out. Someone should know about my life. In times to come, *someone* must surely speak of Sporus, my journey from slave boy, fellator of senators, to Empress of

Rome, to Goddess of Spring, to Queen of the Dead.

II

PIRATE

A village? ... You ask if I recall ... a village?

Before the chains and the sea, no clear memories. No memories at all.

In dreams, I can see a sun-drenched village. A clear blue sky. A woman in the woods, me tugging at the edge of her tunic. Her eyes ... clear, green, her face furrowed, lined.

The woods in the foothills, village in the plain.

Smoke tendrilling up from thatched huts.

Savoring the stillness.

Now and then, the song of a thrush. We are picking mushrooms. I look at my mother and ... I don't know ... her eyes ... I remember. I remember the eyes. The warmth.

... or was it a palace?

Am I in the bath, being oiled, feet dangling in the tepidarium, my mother idly sipping a goblet of Lesbian wine from a painted kylix? I see the winecup so clearly but am I remembering from somewhere else, from the home of the sybaritic Gaius Petronius?

Is the song a slave girl from Nubia, singing some nonsense from her native land, from the atrium as she cleans? Am I prince or peasant?

Only my mother's eyes are the same.

My mother's eyes … and the screaming.

At first I think it's a lot of thrushes. It's high-pitched and thick and faint, a distant wall of keening. It takes a while to realize the entire village is screaming. And burning. They're not thrushes but the dying, each pinprick shriek a sound-smear in the clear bright sky.

They're coming through the forest, clanging their shields and banging on trees like hunters driving out game. I don't see faces, only soulless eyes. They catch me. They catch my mother. They swing her, brain her against a tree-trunk, and the sound of smashing skull on hardwood is indelibly seared in my memory —

Or is it? Are the dead-eyed savages striding through the atrium, spearing the men and lassoing the women — and is it the brick wall where my mother's brains are smeared? — Oh, I am confused — I have lost my past. Oh, I have invented so many pasts for myself, they all have merged into a confused tapestry — but all these pasts converge in a single place —

A line of pathetic creatures, barely human, shackled, being urged on by the ones with the dead eyes. Single file. The ones too sick to walk, they urge on with blows, or just let them go limp and be dragged along by those still clinging to life. And the line goes on and on, and me with them, and I don't even know who I have been chained to. I just know that we walk and walk, and after some days it is all downhill so we slip and slide and knock our shins on sharp stones and slither in mud, and we walk through a nightmare landscape, past burning villages, dead bodies putrefying, and then we are shoved, still chained but now only by twos or fours, onto rickety boats, and thence onto a ship.

A *ship!*

I have never seen a ship. I've never seen the sea, let alone *smelled* the sea.

There's awe. There's pain, overwhelming pain, not just from the blows, not just from the lashing, but hunger, thirst, and heartache. The wind of the waves and the dry heaves because you want to vomit but there is nothing to throw up.

Being completely ignored. No one to answer questions. To ask is to be beaten. I haven't even heard my own language yet. I don't know where I am going. We are jammed in the hold. It's chaos.

The ship begins to move. We can barely see in the hold. There's one smoky lamp. I do not know if it is day or night. I listen to murmurings. I think that we are slaves.

Only a few days have gone by but I'm already not sure where it is I came from. I've walled off the past. It's how my mind is, I think. I build compartments, and I throw away the key. You'll see … it's how I will survive through lightning transformations. I am like some kind of insect. I suffer unspeakable pain and I emerge as someone completely different … not even the same species, any more than a caterpillar is a butterfly.

Later, I will read about transformations in an old book by Publius Ovidius Naso, in a language which in that moment I have yet to learn. He says, *Omnia mutantur, nihil interit.* He means something like "Everything changes … yet nothing perishes." But he is wrong. Because you can't change back.

Everything is *always* perishing. Your soul, your identity isn't some unchanging shard of light within that is never affected by the outside world.

And that very first afternoon on the ship, my first metamorphosis begins in earnest. The dead-eyed people took off my chains. A woman came to me and led me by the hand, up rickety steps into the sunlight. She made me remove every remaining rag that still clung to me, glued by blood and sweat and dried mucus.

Carefully, she washed me, combed my hair, scrubbed me with olive oil, and scraped the oil away with a strigil. "There you are," she said at last. She had a kind of tenderness. I could understand her, though she formed her words differently from what I was used to.

I said, "Are you my new mother?"

She laughed and said words in a foreign language. Then she said, laughing, "Mother! I'm a pirate."

She held up a polished plate of brass and I saw myself. I had never seen myself before, did not know who stared back up at me. The boy in the mirror was scrawny, pale, with straggly, blond hair.

I had big eyes.

"The eyes," she said. "The eyes do the selling." She brushed on a little kohl. "Try to smile."

I managed a wan smile.

"You'll do."

They left me like that. Naked, oiled, and lightly brushed with perfume. My eyes were brightened with a little kohl. I was not chained, but there was nowhere to go. I watched the open sea. In the distance, big fishes leaped. I allowed myself a moment of pleasure.

"They are not fish," said a voice. "A pod of dolphins."

Startled, I turned. I saw a man in a kind of armor — assembled from bits and pieces. One eye was dead and hard, like all the other captors on this ship. The other eye was missing.

"You can stare," he said.

He came closer, put a callused hand on my shoulder. "I need to study the dolphins. Usually they are our friends, but sometimes they mean danger. They speak, in their own way."

He bends to look at my face. He turns my face this way and that.

I am passive. I am shaking.

"You're a good one," he said. "Where are you from?"

"You speak like me."

"One of many languages. But you will learn another soon. Two, if you fetch the right price."

"Am I for sale?"

"The world is for sale, child, and you are owned without even knowing it."

"And who are the owners?"

"Only the gods. They're all completely uninterested in the human race, sitting in their sky palaces. None of them will do anything. They will leave the world to fester in its own shit. Only one god lives in the real world. And he's the most troublesome one of all."

I did not understand any of that.

"You are a prime piece of merchandise," he says. "But the useful life of a delicatus is brief. You'll flower for a day, and then — poof — you will be too old. Learn to read and write. Be useful. Or they'll sell you to some filthy lupanar when they're done with you."

"What is a delicatus?" I said.

He shook his head. "I suppose I will have to break you in," he said, and there was a twinge of sadness in his voice, regret, almost. Then he took me into a private cabin, and subjected me to the most painful, most humiliating, most soul-destroying acts, beyond anything I imagined possible. In that hour, he broke me, and I searched my mind in vain for any trace of anyone I had ever been.

I sat on the floor, bleeding, weeping, and he said softly, "Save your tears. You still own your tears. Do not give them away."

"After what you did —!" I said, crying even more disconsolately.

"That was just business, boy," he said. "I meant no harm. And you will see by tomorrow, there is no permanent damage; I owe that much to the client. But now that I've shattered your identity, let's give you a new one. Did you come from a village, an innocent flower of the field? Were you actually a prince, scion of some barbarous nation?"

"I don't know."

"Find a good past. A colorful past can really up the bidding," he said. "Prince, I think."

I dried my eyes with my arm.

"And we must give you a name."

"I *have* a name!"

But in that moment, I could not recollect it.

"Ah, ah, you must have a name."

"You haven't told me yours," I said. Although he had used me like a rag.

"You do not need my name," he said. "It would only be another burdensome memento of a past you should forget. You, however … your fate could be to serve in a great house … and to be cast away. Or it could be to serve and worm your way upwards, learn skills, become a freedman, even own an entire stable of delicati. You are a seedling — and I hope you will not be cast on stony ground."

He peered at me with his one eye. "A seedling! You will be called *Sporos*. That is Greek, a civilized language; the Romans will undoubtedly coarsen it to Sporus."

My captor pulled me up and pushed me out onto the deck. I was still naked, still bleeding a little.

The sun's beginning to set. The wind is cool. Dolphins are leaping, more agitated now.

"Are they telling us something?" I asked him.

One-eye leaned over the edge and stared into the distance, where the dolphins breached against the face of the sun. When he turns back his eye seems bloodshot. "Romani!" he shouts. "Outrun them!"

I hear it now. Faint but regular. Oars slapping on the water. The thud of a drum. Hundreds of oars maybe.

And I see the ships. Three of them. Bearing down on us. Swiftly.

Cacophony broke loose around me. Another drumbeat from below deck, frantic. Oars too, but on this ship they hit the water almost randomly, not synchronized. The drum accelerated. We were moving away from the Romans.

"Lock up the slaves!" someone screamed. Someone was bolting down the entrance to the hold. In the confusion no one saw me, a naked, helpless boy, cowering. I could hear the captives shrieking, bewildered, in the dark, from below. Pirates were readying weapons. The drumming reached fever pitch.

But we were getting away, weren't we? The Romans would not catch up. I would be sold. There was no escape. One-eye stalked about, barking orders.

Then I turned toward the prow and saw that another ship was almost on top of us. We were about to be rammed. I could see the corvus being lowered. I heard the crash as the corvus landed. I heard screaming. I heard trampling, disciplined, relentless. Fire-arrows were raining down now. The Romans' boots banging, a terrifying, steady rhythm. I saw the one-eyed pirate brandishing a sword, roaring.

So you were rescued! How exciting! The Roman army plucked you from the mouth of hell! I do love an adventure, but you must hold still. We want to make sure your audience sees you. Even the ones in the uppermost tiers, the women, the slaves. Now, tell me more about the rescue.

Was that a rescue?

Or was it something worse?

III

CRUCIFIXION

Chains and the sea …

Hold still. The rouge has to be even.

How much longer?

A while. There is a mass crucifixion going on.

Oh, who?

Some cult that forbids worshipping the Emperor.

It serves them right, then. How boring. I've seen so many. But you never forget your first, do you. When criminals are crucified en masse in the arena, it is entertainment of course. The display crosses let people in the stands get a better view of the faces.

But when it's not a show, it's often quite banal. Except, perhaps, to the crucified.

In what people are already calling the "good old days", they dipped them in pitch as well, and set them ablaze, and they burned through the night like human torches … though the screams did not last long.

The good old days, really, don't we all agree! A singing emperor and a burning city. Legend! And to think that you — you — *were debauched by a God!*

You forget ... I am going to *be* a God soon.

You are. So hold still. The eyes must be perfect.

The Romans escorted the pirate vessel close to shore. We were sorted into pirates and cargo. Cargo was catalogued from most valuable to least: first came statues, works of art, jewelry, last mundanities like amphoras of olive oil; we were worth less than the art, but was that surprising? Human life is brief — art is eternal.

The pirates were shackled. We were chained. No one had thought to find me any clothes, but I was wearing a lot of dirt and blood — other people's, I am sure. There were other people with no clothes. Slaves don't really need clothes. I was chained next to the woman who had made me beautiful — beautiful enough to be savagely violated. She did not look at me. I wondered whether she knew what had happened to me ... how much she had known beforehand. We squatted on the sand. The pirates did not squat. They were chained with their arms between poles, and were made to stand; when one looked like he was going to fall over, he got a whack of the flagellum, and stayed standing.

Where we landed, the beach was just a strip; beyond, on higher ground, were grassy areas alternating with boulders. The sky was a brilliant blue. Later I will think of this place as Greece, but really it could have been another part of the empire.

A man walked up and down the rows of merchandise. Next to him, a wizened little man was making notes on a wax tablet. The man's armor was polished, his plumes bright red; he did not look at all like someone who had just been in a sea-battle. He moved, in a leisurely way, from object to object, murmuring to the scribe, who said repeatedly, *"Ita, Centurio, ita, centurio,"* nodding as he scribbled. I had heard the word *centurio* before. He was a centurion, a commander of a hundred men.

They were getting nearer. He spoke to one captive, then another. I said, "Sir, are we being rescued?"

He clapped his hands and had my chains struck off. I had not expected to be understood but he spoke to me in my own language. "It depends on what you mean by rescue," he said.

He put his hand on my shoulder. He motioned and someone brought me a tunica. It was torn, but I'd never felt such soft fabric against my skin.

"How do you know my language?" I asked him.

"On the campaigns," he said. "Come, you pretty little thing. You already have that sadness that people like you always have, the sadness hiding behind every smile. Did one of these pirates hurt you?"

I nodded.

"Come, point him out."

He led me to the pirates and I soon pointed out the leader. The single eye was not so dead now. I saw — no, *smelled* – his terror. The Centurion beckoned with his finger and two soldiers pulled him out. They began dragging him up the slope, to a patch of elevated ground.

"Come with me," the Centurion said to me.

On the incline, soldiers were cutting up tree trunks, making crude crosses. This wasn't the fine workmanship you see in the arena, perfectly straight pieces of wood teased and scraped into the right shape. These were just tree trunks, slightly trimmed, no finishing. And not the display crosses that you can see in Rome, either. The criminal soldiers threw the one who had hurt me on the ground and started tying his arms to one of the crosses.

"Did he hurt you very much?" said the Centurion.

I nodded again.

"Right then." My captor was strangely compliant; I expected him to struggle, but was calm, almost like a sacrificial animal. The Centurion knelt down and I knelt with him. A soldier produced a monster of a nail, placed it spike down against the man's wrist. Then he gave me his hammer. I hefted it.

"Go on," said the Centurion. "You're with the grownups now. Aim well and drive the nail home."

I swung. The pain must have been unimaginable. The pirate tensed, jerked; blood spurted; but he did not cry out at all. I suppose he did not want to give me the satisfaction. I swung again and I think he fainted.

"Good lad," the Centurion said. He held me as his underlings finished the job and did the other wrist, and the feet as well. The sound the bone made, cracking … you never forget something like that.

The Centurion lifted me up and made me watch as they hoisted the pirate into an upright position. The one who had quoted Ovid to me looked at me dully. His eyes were empty. If his body was not dead already, his soul was no longer inside him.

I vomited, all over the nearly new tunica. "It's all right, lad. No one has the stomach for it at first." He wiped me off. "Did you get any satisfaction?"

I closed my eyes, remembering. "I don't think so."

I looked around and saw that it was a kind of routine process, tying, hoisting, tying, hoisting. There was a lot of screaming. Presently it was like a little grove of dying men, groaning, wheezing. Their screams gradually becoming dull.

A few scavenger birds were beginning to gather.

"We don't usually use nails normally," the Centurion said. "That was a little treat, just for you. It's a mercy, really; he'll bleed out a lot quicker than these others."

***

The crucifixions had been done in a very orderly way, the crosses planted at regular intervals, and the soldiers showed little emotion; it was just a job.

And then they fed us.

Bread, olives, diluted wine.

We had had almost nothing for days. We sat on the beach and looked up at the forest of the dying, savoring our bread.

The Centurion was kind. He called me to his side and sat me by a fire. He didn't speak to me for a while, but instead to some companions, discussing the coming voyage, supply logistics, things I did not understand. He looked at my meager portion of bread and gave me a small piece of dried meat. Then, incredibly, an apple.

Looking around the makeshift encampment, I saw that many of the soldiers had a boy as a companion. They would bring their masters food. When their master reached out, a cup of wine would be ready without their even asking. The boys were silent shadows. I could see myself in a role like that. I didn't think I would mind him touching me.

I would have liked to know how he had learned my language "on campaign" — who he had fought, what action he had seen. Was he a Roman at all or had he once been what I was? Something, I sensed, had damaged him. That is why he felt empathy for me. We had this in common, though my wounds were fresher. My past had been pushed behind a wall. In my present, he was the first person I felt close to. I asked him what his name was. I didn't tell him my own name, nor could I bring myself to tell him the name the pirate had given me.

He said, "You can call me Marcus, I suppose."

"Will I live with you now? Will I go on campaign with you? Will I learn languages?"

He laughed. "I am not your owner."

"But I would go of my own free will," I said.

"Lad … you don't have any free will. You're destined for my betters, I'm afraid."

"But … didn't you come to punish the pirates, to rescue us?"

"Yes … the cargo has been rescued," he said. "The state has confiscated it and it will all be auctioned off properly, not in some sordid contraband market."

"We are not to be freed?"

"Where would you go? You are a pretty thing and you will adorn some noble house — not some whorehouse in the suburra. You could accumulate a decent peculium, and once you lose your looks there's no reason you shouldn't be able to buy your freedom."

"But you unchained me! You treated me almost like … a son. Marcus, let me stay with you!"

He looked away. "A centurion may not marry," he said, "and the term of service is at least twenty-five years. A boy is better suited than a wife for these rough campaigns, and a slave is more practical; the prohibition on marriage keeps us wedded to the legion."

"Can't you buy me?"

"On nine hundred sesterces a year? You're worth ten times that at least. I hardly dare put my hand on your shoulder for fear of bruising your skin."

"Don't you love me?"

"So young, already so good at the game! Love is for the gods," he said. "We're only people. What we have is duty, desire, and hope. And if I gave you hope, I am sorry. I didn't mean to. You just reminded me of … something. Someone."

"The pirate said that there is also a human who is a god."

And Marcus fished a coin from a pouch. It was large, polished brass. I saw a portrait of a comely, slightly pudgy man. Marcus held it up to the flickering firelight. He handed it to me and I gazed at the portrait, the first time I ever saw the face of Nero Claudius Caesar Augustus Germanicus.

"Keep it," he said. "Let's call it my contribution to your peculium. A fragment of your future freedom."

***

Your Emperor. Your God. And for a time —

My husband.

The first, alas, of many.

And the reason I've been chosen for today's apotheosis … a mythic drama that will be acted out before the gaze of twenty thousand hungry pairs of eyes … the reason I've been chosen to play the Queen of Hell. No figure is more tragic than an empress fallen from her throne. Oh, Divinity! What times we had!

But you could not have known any of that at the time.

No. All I knew was that Marcus had me chained up again, and we were loaded back into the hold of a ship bound for Ostia. I did not see him again on that voyage.

I think that for an afternoon I was in love. That would never happen again. I had learned my lesson.

IV

WAREHOUSE

They laughed when I gawked at Ostia.

"Whatever barbarous hamlet you came from," said the little Greek accountant, who was watching over us as we were offloaded, "compared with Ostia, is as Ostia compared to Rome."

Ostia is a port. A town with walls! There are streets lined with shophouses, crammed with people, and merchandise moving all day and all night (in Rome the carts only come out at night). The sounds! Grinding carts. Dirty water being sloshed into the streets. Music of pipes and drums. Cries of merchants. The trudging of soldiers' caligae.

The people! People of hues I had never imagined. People in outlandish costumes. Now I can identify them, then they were a blur, the smells of delicious food and shit mingling in the streets as they marched us to the warehouse district; for we were merchandise, not to be housed with the people.

It was a room with high, barred windows that seemed to be at street level; we must be underground. Our chains were generous in length, allowing us to move about quite a bit, and our hands were free. As prisons went — I would learn this eventually from observation and experience — this one was luxurious. After all, we were not being punished. Indeed, we had done nothing wrong, except for misplacing our personhood.

It must have been next to a laundry, because the stench of urine was beyond belief. Every morning a slave from the laundry came to collect our piss as well.

They only fed us once a day, refilling the water and the lone amphora of very weak wine; the bread was stale but plentiful. And all the rats we could catch and roast over the open fire we kept going on the stone floor — a plentiful source of meat.

There was even a running water lavatory on one end, with four openings you could sit over, and our chains were long enough to reach it. But they had to teach me how to use it, and to this day I'd rather squat to shit, and I long to clean myself with leaves and not with a sponge someone else has used before me.

The toilet and the food made this a truly upscale slaves' warehouse. I've since learned how lucky I was.

You've experienced other prisons.

Including this one. You'd think that an actor could be allowed to prepare to play a god in a slightly more luxurious chamber than this!

The woman who had cleaned me up to be raped was with us. So were others who had been with me on the pirate ship, but the numbers were depleted each day. A few died and were removed. Each day brought new captives, and the sick and dying were removed, as well as some healthy ones. I did not understand the reason.

The woman had a name: Spider. Perhaps it was a nickname. She was, she told me, a weaver. She taught me to say the name: a-RAKH-nê … she had been named in Greek, the language, she told me, of civilized people. "But you must learn Latin, too. At least a few words. Enough to avoid being thought slow-witted."

It seemed she spoke from experience, and that this was not her first time being sold. Her previous owners were Greeks in Cappadocia, a cloth merchant family; the master had been bankrupted and forced to make a quick sale; he had not realized that the buyer was a front for pirates.

"Why do I have to learn two languages?"

"Because you are not going to be sweeping floors or chopping onions," said Spider. "It's true that the lords and masters only speak Latin to the slaves and the lower classes. But among themselves, they affect to speak Greek. They think it makes them seem more refined."

If they already owned the whole world, why did they need to seem more refined? Who were they trying to impress?

"So ... your master is called the *dominus*. But when you talk to him, say *domine*. And he will have a wife, even if his taste runs more to your sort. You will call her *domina*. You're not a person, so they can do anything they want to you. In the end, you're just like a table, or a jug of wine. If you find a good house, they may even say they love you. They will expect your love, of course. They've paid for it. And eventually, if you're thrifty and thoughtful, your peculium will grow and you can even buy back your personhood. And if you're not too shopworn, you could go into business. You could even be a slave dealer; ex-slaves know the business better than anyone. But for now, learn to speak. Sometimes your tongue will be the only thing that saves you from a beating."

"A beating."

"In your case, your tongue may have other uses, too. Keep it agile, and don't do something that will get it cut off."

***

I hoped to see the centurion again, but I only saw the little Greek, who was a linguist as well as an accountant — that was how he could understand me. He would supervise the deliveries and the removals. From time to time he would have us weighed, and write the results down on his tablet. I understood more and more of what he said but did not dare say anything.

Days came and went. I learned that the tall, black-as-the-night ones were from a territory well south of the empire, and that they were warriors who often made fierce gladiators. The shaggy blond ones often were from Germania, and had a pungent odor, perhaps from anointing themselves with deer fat. There were those called Celts, and there were Scythians, and Jews ... but few of the prisoners save Spider spoke my language — and none of the new additions did. I had come from the very end of the known world.

The day came when they called out Spider to be removed.

I burst into tears and said, "You take me too! She like mother for me!"

Some of the slaves laughed. I'd made a fool of myself with my bad grammar.

The Greek stopped and peered at me. *"Latine loqueris?"* he said.

"I'm learning. You take her, I no learn no more."

"Greek?"

"Skatá!"

They were all laughing, even the black warriors from the other end of the world. I felt humiliated.

The Greek had a tripod brought in and he sat down. They pulled Spider out and threw her down in front of him. They spoke for a long time; I could not make out all the words, but it seemed that she was telling him something of my story, and something of her own.

After that conversation, he motioned for his assistants to take away about a dozen, but Spider stood there for a moment.

"What happened? What did he say?"

"You're a valuable piece of property," she said. "I'm not. But he is letting me say goodbye at least."

I said to the Greek, "Don't take care — I be more valuable — she teach me speak more good."

"Don't massacre the tongue of the muses," he said in my own language. "I will teach you better than she could. It will hurt, but you will thank me."

And then they took her away. The pirate, the centurion, and now my surrogate mother. I was alone again.

***

I see you became accustomed to losing anyone you felt attached to.

What do you care? Finish the makeup.

I'm sorry. You distracted me with your story.

But you are right. And so was the centurion Marcus, when he told me not to love.

I was learning this lesson very quickly.

But yourself! You mustn't give up loving yourself.

Loving myself? Perhaps I never have.

V

MIRROR

Spider left me a gift. I suppose she must have found it when collecting her things: everything she owned would belong to her master when she was sold, so she must have talked the Greek into letting me have it.

It was the warped brass plate in which I had first seen my own face.

The Greek, who had a name, it turned out — Aristarchos — treated me better than I expected. He moved me out of the holding area and into a real room. I had never had one of those before, not even when I was free. The room was little more than a cupboard, but it had a raised concrete bed covered with straw and a woolen blanket, and a little oil lamp with an erotic scene. I was still in the warehouse district, but I was not caged with a hundred others.

I could read at night, and Aristarchos made me read *every* night. None of this "Greetings, master! My name is Sporus!" that the average traveller might learn. He said, "You're not going to be the kitchen help. They'll expect you at parties, with society. If someone quotes Ovid to you, and compares you to the virginal Proserpina gathering flowers in the valley, her dress torn by accident to reveal her breast to the predatory God of Hell … you must be swift to answer, snappily: 'usque adeo est properatus amor.' If you say 'Sorry, I beg your pardon, I don't understand,' they will take you for a dumb slave, and you'll have a bloody bottom with nothing to show for it. But understand the art of poetry … seduce the mind, don't just stir the patrician penis … you'll survive, you will even prosper. To a slave, all sex is rape, for even the possibility of consent is forbidden. So you must have the master think you, for a moment, his equal."

"Why would he want that?"

"They all fantasize about that. That all those around them love them, would serve out of sheer devotion without the constant specter of the lash. You must feed that fantasy. You must play whatever role you are given, play as if your life depends on it. But always know it is only a role. It is not you. You must not forget what you are."

"A slave?"

"On an even deeper level," said Aristarchos, "you're still a human being."

***

Deep into the night, I would pore over the scrolls I had been lent. Worlds were opening up, but in those worlds I was at best half-blind. There were mysteries. The Latin language, the words all categorized, marching in strict military rows, each with its proper ending, walking down its proper pathway … you could say things with a clarity I didn't know language could express. And Greek, so similar in its structures, so different in application! A language designed for ambiguity, where a single change in one vowel in a word could add layers of doubt, hope, or desire; a language with a different dialect for every species of poetry. I found the language very hard, to be sure, but it entranced me.

Removed from the dehumanizing cage of the warehouse, given no chores except my studies, there were times when I didn't think about my enslavement much. The food was simple: porridge, bread, olives, an occasional bit of meat. But I do not think I ate so well in my old life.

Each day my Latin improved. I stumbled over endings and genders, but the verbs had a relentless logic. You could tell why the people who spoke this language ruled the world.

After a time, I could speak after a fashion, and without too barbarous an accent. My Greek, though, not so much; Aristarchos despaired of my ever understanding the second aorist, or the middle voice.

But I was lonely.

I tried to inquire about Spider, to see if she had been sold nearby … no one knew anything. My tutor was not my friend. He had a job to do. Sometimes, just in case I forgot that we weren't friends, he'd treat me to a touch of the strap when I couldn't decline some demonstrative pronoun. But he never drew blood, and I could see it saddened him to beat me. So, I suffered without complaint, thinking that at least I had good food and a real bed, and who knew how long that could last?

***

Then there were other lessons. Deportment. I had to stand, walk, and sit with grace. This I took to easily. I had been raised by women.

There was the *kithara.* A Greek instrument very conducive to seduction. A single note, once plucked, hung in the air like a lover's sigh.

In addition, there was the *Ars Amatoria* — more Ovid, you see — though my tutor's instruction on this was more theoretical than physical. He never laid a hand on me in that way. I thought that either he really was worried about damaging this "fragile" piece of merchandise, or he was one of those rare individuals without any taste for the same sex whatsoever. People like that do exist … trust me, I've seen everything.

He taught me the different customs among the peoples of the empire; how in Rome the quality of *virtus* or manliness was ascribed only to the penetrator, regardless of who was being penetrated, which meant that well brought up Roman men only exercised their *virtus* on slaves or members of the lower classes, unlike in Greece where love formed a real part of such a relationship; for Romans, it was power over an underling that was the motivating force. He would go on to describe the mating customs among the Celts, the Scythians, the Numidians, the Parthians, and it was all rather exotic but also a bit dull.

When I nodded in those lessons, he didn't punish me. I only got the strap for missing my conjugations.

***

And one day, after beating me, he took me to the public baths. It was, I supposed, by way of apology. He told me it was a small place, not like the palatial baths in the city. But it was the most overwhelming experience of my life till then. First, the baths themselves — the scorching caldarium, the soothing tepidarium, the bracing frigidarium where slaves kept shovelling in snow brought in from distant hills — a shock to my body but afterwards, I felt so pure, so refreshed. The fact that there was an institution like this, just to keep clean. The hawkers with refreshments. The attendants who seemed to double as prostitutes, sneaking off to the shadows with their clients.

Then there were the bathers — the men, at any rate, for

women used the waters at a different hour — some arriving in rags, others in togas, yet underneath we were all the same — senator or fruit vendor. For a time, they left those identities behind and immersed themselves and were at peace.

"And this," Aristarchos said, "is what it means to be civilized. Forget the towering columns, the roads that criss-cross the whole world. Everywhere they go — in Gaul, in Hispania, in Africa, the Romans build baths."

We walked back through the market; I held his belongings for him, and before we got back, he bought me an apple.

Not long after that, I went to Aristarchos's study and found him oddly limping about. One arm was bruised. "What happen?" I asked him.

"*Happened, happened,*" he said.

"How can you correct my grammar when you're in pain?"

"It's nothing," he said. "My master was in a bad mood."

It was only in that moment that I realized that Aristarchos was a slave too, like me. I suppose I should have known. He didn't seem to have a home, or a wife, and his room was in the warehouse area. He was small man, but he seemed ageless. I must have stared at him oddly, because he said, not unkindly, "I suppose you've only just figured it out."

"But … you move about freely. You're not chained up. You go where you please. You could even run away." He laughed bitterly.

"Child … Rome runs on slavery. Our hands and feet and backs build the temples and palaces and aqueducts, of course. But it's the minds of slaves that balance their books, tutor their children, and keep their estates from being mismanaged. Only the lowest are in chains of iron, but there are many other kinds of chains. Why am I still a slave? I'm a wonderful accountant, and I can expound on literature and art at the best of dinner parties, but I cannot manage my own peculium."

I hoped I would do better. Any abuse could be endured if freedom lay at the end of the path.

"Now, Sporus, tomorrow you and I will soon be parting ways. Oh, do not look sad! I know you think you can't get to know anyone before they disappear from your life, but this will end soon. I have made a financial arrangement with the steward of a great house. He will pay a price that is acceptable to my master, as the agent of the state which in principle acquired you as contraband when the pirate ship and its cargo were seized. Even I will benefit; I have taught you well enough to replenish my peculium. Until the next time I get drunk and gamble," he added ruefully. "Or wake up in a brothel, having lost everything."

"What great house?" I asked him. "Is it the Emperor?"

"Ha! It seems like only yesterday that you knew of nothing but a few huts and forests and now you're talking about the Emperor! No, but I assure you, you will almost certainly see your God in person. I have heard that he visits this great house on occasion."

I couldn't resist. Seeing him like this, afflicted yet still thinking of my welfare, I went up to him and hugged him, as though he were my own father, whom I had never known.

"Haven't I told you not to love anyone?" he said brusquely. But he didn't rebuff my embrace.

Looking into his eyes, I could intuit that there was another reason why he had not tried to use me in that way. He had finely honed features. Though his eyes were lined, his face had a delicacy to it, a boyish quality; it was that in him that had seemed ageless. And I suddenly understood ... "Where I'm going," I said, "you've already been, haven't you?"

He didn't answer. I went on ... "And your inability to hold on to your peculium ... it's got something to do with that, hasn't it? There's a darkness that gnaws at you, deep inside. That is always telling you you're no more than ... an object."

Aristarchos said, "You have seen."

Like the plate of warped bronze Spider had given me, this man, too, was a mirror. We were each other's mirror, gazing across the gulf of time.

But mirrors can deceive. "I'll never be defeated," I said. "I'll do what I did to my previous life — I'll wall it away, untouchable, forever. I won't lose my soul."

***

Your life, on the other hand…

Oh, be quiet. Will this makeup never be done?

Patience, goddess. What does time mean to an immortal?

I'm not an immortal *yet.*

But after your performance, your masterpiece, you will be….

VI

MARKET

Nothing is as pointless as the chatter of slaves.

I've heard that saying so many times during the past four reigns. Yet here I am, chattering to a slave, pouring out my deepest inner pain as one might pour a libation from the dregs of a loving-cup.

Say what you will, Goddess. Tomorrow I'll be making someone else up. These scenes from mythology — fabulae crepidatae *— have become all the rage in our entertainment ... dare I call it such ... industry. Tomorrow I'll do Hercules ripping up his wife and children ... or Medea cutting up her little brother into pieces and throwing him overboard. You're getting it easy, being raped to death; my makeup will make you such a delicate flower that the crowd might even root for you, and beg whatever monstrous Gaul or Nubian they've assigned to play Pluto to spare you ... who knows, you might even get a thumbs up. Not.*

You're quite the chatterbox.

Only because you're not telling me more.

Show me a mirror.

Must I?

Oh! I am hideous! You have made me a clown, not a goddess.

Because, Your Divinity, you must shine even in the uppermost rows of the Circus, where the slaves sit. As for where the Emperor sits, he's probably already acquainted with your face — and other parts of your anatomy.

Oh, you lowly little hairdresser ... how well you know how to hurt a girl. Just to shut you up ... I will tell what happened next.

***

The next day, I was summoned to Aristarchos's room and told to strip. Two hefty men flanked the accountant. They were both twice my size and amply proportioned. One of them took my tunica and tossed it into a brazier. I started to panic. Surely these men were not here to ... soften me up for my next master! ... a whimper escaped my throat, but Aristarchos laughed. Presently two women came in — they too were giantesses — and between them they carried a wooden chest topped with a gold ornament of lions' heads facing in opposite directions. When they opened the chest I saw ... cloth. And a glint of gold.

Aristarchos said, "Didn't we pick the barbarian prince story?"

"We haven't picked a story."

"A slave with your looks must come with a story. I thought you knew that."

"I came from a village at the edge of the world."

"No, no, a palace. A palace at the edge of the world."

The two men began pouring olive oil on me and rubbing me

down. I confess it felt good. Sensual. Not like being shoved about like a feelingless doll. I was embarrassed and looked for something to conceal my obvious pleasure. Aristarchos laughed again. "You can keep a little of the coyness," he said. "They will find it endearing. But it's good to see they haven't completely destroyed your ability to feel."

When they were through with the anointing, they scraped the oil off with strigils, leaving my skin tingling. "And now they will dress you," said my tutor. And one of the women beckoned me with a finger. She reached into the chest and pulled a garment of a material so soft and diaphanous it seemed to have been woven from spider-webs, making me think of the woman who had been like a mother to me for a short time.

When the garment touched my skin it was more like a caress.

"I can see," the woman said, "you have never felt the touch of silk before." She launched into a fantastical tale about how this fabric is woven from the sputum of caterpillars....

Meanwhile the other woman — did I forget to say? — though they were a matched pair, those impressive women, one of them was pale as snow and even her eyes were bleached and a little pink, while the other was so black, her skin was almost a shiny, deep blue, like a night sky in the moonlight. Had they scoured the earth for such a pair? Surely the Romans could bring to life any marvel a poet could dream of. They were pleasingly plump and I found myself daydreaming about returning to infancy and suckling at one of their generous bosoms.

In short, being cleaned and dressed was humiliating in a different way from when people were chaining me up and beating me. Luckily, once I had on the silk tunica, and a blue chlamys also of silk which was fastened with a fibula of real gold, I no longer betrayed any arousal.

"You look like a proper, aristocratic Greek boy," Aristarchos said, "perhaps from the north, with your hair color."

"Is this to help with the story about my being a captured prince?"

Aristarchos said, "Greece, motherland of culture, hasn't had an aristocracy in a century or two; the best of us are slaves now." And he looked away. I think he had a tear in his eye. "But no," he said. "You're not being decked out like a prince for some special show. Where you are going, everything and every*one* is beautiful. From the house slaves to the gardener, there is nothing in that house that is not purest elegance."

***

I found myself being carried in a litter, with Aristarchos accompanying me. The litter-bearers moved swiftly, in tandem, and with a kind of precision that made the ride far smoother than an oxcart. The curtains were drawn and I didn't see much — though I heard and smelled plenty.

The smells of Ostia! Human sweat, perfume, bread baking in ovens open to the streets, but through it all the smell of shit — horse, ox, human — pervading everything.

"Rome will smell worse," Aristarchos said.

"I want to look," I said, putting my hand on the curtain.

"Yes, yes, but not here. I don't want you to see —" It was too late. I was peeking out and we were just passing a slave auction. It was a small square with a temporary auction platform set up, and salesmen yelling out from all four corners of the platform, several auctions running at the same time, and bids frantically coming from all sides.

I saw a burly man with wild, orange hair, being prodded and poked by a potential buyer.

"A Celt," said Aristarchos.

I saw a boy and girl my own age being twirled around like a matched pair of dolls. I heard a barker call out: "One hundred sesterces! Do I hear two? Three hundred sesterces!" I would have thought a year's supply of bread and wine to be a high price, but I heard higher, too.

You could tell the slaves from the free people in just two ways. They were naked. Some were not even chained. Perhaps they were already domesticated, not war captives, or born into slavery and so knew nothing else. I thought I saw Spider, but I could not be sure. It must be her, surely. She looked at me. She seemed to be about to say something, but her keeper shoved her up to the block.

I heard another barker shout "Five thousand! Fifty-five hundred!" and I saw that the object being sold was someone little different from me. Young, and extremely frightened. But exquisite. This might indeed be the captive princeling that I was pretending to be. And his price was going up and up.

"Close the curtain!" Aristarchos whispered.

"Why is he so expensive?" I said.

I think he met my eye. I am not sure, he was so distant. I wouldn't forget the look in his eye very easily. Hot tears spurted, wetting my cheeks.

"Pueri delicati are highly desired by the best families," Aristarchos said. "After a while, the barker might have to stop counting in sesterces and move up to denarii. Perhaps even aurei. Or the numbers will go off the end of the scribe's tablet."

"How much was paid for me?"

"I don't know," he said. Though perhaps he did, and simply did not want me to get an inflated sense of myself. "Draw the curtain."

I would have done so immediately, but at that moment, some blood spattered on my face. The litter had been moving and my eyes were level with someone's crucified feet. They had used nails. I looked up at the wretch. The cross was low. This was the moment when, his lungs collapsing from the asphyxiation, he had sort of crumpled up and expired, straining at the nails to produce a few final spurts of blood. A bird was sitting on his shoulder, pecking at an eye.

Quickly, I closed the curtain.

But the thing that struck me the most was this: a main was dying in agony in the middle of the street ... and no one was even stopping to look. It was a sight so commonplace that people were just going about their business.

***

They'll look at you *all right. You're such a celebrity.*

And somehow, it's more satisfying to watch awful things happen to a celebrity. I was their Empress for a while. Was I not loved? Nero was loved, though it is no longer fashionable to say so.

We never talk about past Emperors. If we did, we could end up where you've ended up, reenacting one of the great moments of myth or history.

Thank you for reminding this goddess of her fate.

I'm sure you don't need reminding. But at least, for the more subtle entertainment value of your life's story, you have an attentive audience of one. So carry on, Daughter of Demeter.

Let me tell you what happened when I closed the silken curtain...

VII

OXCART

And what happened when you closed the curtain?

So you *do* want me to go on.

Of course I do. You're the least boring job I've had since the Kalends.

... in essence, nothing. I drew the curtains closed, and I shut out the world with its noise, squalor, beauty, and pain. And we went on in silence for a while longer.

Until I asked, suddenly realizing that I hadn't actually asked ... "Are we going to Rome?"

He said, "Who is there in this empire who is *not* going to Rome? Rome is the center of the world."

The outskirts of Ostia are a scant five *mille passuum* from the outskirts of Rome. I thought I would be riding by litter all the way, but at the inland boundary of Ostia we were switched to an oxcart. For the rest of the afternoon, things were arriving and being loaded into the cart; for I was just one of the pieces of costly merchandise that had been listed for delivery to my new master's house. It was a marvel that I was still not chained up. Though where would I have run to?

Other carts joined us as well. Presently there was a convoy, but mine was first in the line. A line of slaves came bearing more and more goods.

There were large amphorae filled with wine and olive oil. There were bolts of cloth. There was a monkey in a cage. There was another slave, too, a strapping specimen in a loincloth. Perhaps a gladiator. He was quite heavily chained, and snarled and snapped like a wild beast. He spoke in grunts. There was also a sloe-eyed woman, quite exotic-looking.

Aristarchos kept making notes on his tablet.

There was glassware, exquisitely transparent in iridescent hues. There were wine cups — Greek ones, painted with all manner of mythical or erotic imagery. Some showed voluptuous women, some boys like me, with the legend *ho pais kalos* … yes, I was already starting to pick out a word or two. And a silver one as well, in which I saw, for the first time, what exactly it was that a *puer delicatus* did, for the cup depicted in relief, a person much like me, nude, reclining on a couch and being subjected to the attentions of a man in a toga; the cup left little to the imagination. I looked at it and I was very afraid.

I looked at Aristarchos, who was climbing off the cart now that I had been deposited with the cargo. I think there was a tear in my eye, and he did not look directly at me; I fear there may have been one in his, as well.

He stood by the side of the cart, his face peering up past the wooden edge, still not meeting my gaze. He said softly, "It's not a bad life. You will taste a lot of rare viands that ordinary mortals can't dream of trying. You'll know the private nicknames of senators and poets. And if there is pain, it can be dulled by poppy juice, or by a tea made from willow bark; the steward will know how to find such things. And no one will strike you, at least not enough to draw blood. No one would dare to damage your skin. Did I say the steward? You will meet him soon, and I must finally leave you."

He turned, but before doing so he tossed me a coin. "Another bit of change for your peculium," he said.

And he walked away without so much as a *vale.* Perhaps it would have been too painful.

I looked at the coin. It was a sestertius and it was shiny and big, fresh from the mint. And by now, I could read the legend:

NERO CLAVD CAESAR AVG GER PM TRP PP

A bold portrait: a young man with chubby cheeks, quite a jaw on him; a bit of a sneer; a long neck. I compared it with the other coin in my pouch. The new one was larger and less shiny. Marcus had only given me a dupondius, worth half, and made of bright orichalcum, not bronze.

I was alone again, and two military men were riding up to us.

To my great joy, one of them was the centurion who had been kind to me after the sea-battle with the pirates.

"Marce!" I called out.

He ignored me, and went on talking to his companion.

I started to call his name again, but the other soldier gave me a clout with his quirt. It stung but left no mark — he had been skillful.

"Impudent cunt!" he said. To Marcus, he said, "Shall I kill the *cinaedus*, sir?"

Marcus waved him away. Some soldiers on foot came up and took their places in front of and behind the cart. Marcus's torso loomed over me and his horse stuck its head in the cart, perhaps looking for a snack among the bags of fruit. He glared at the handful of people in the cart until they all cast their eyes down ... all but me. Then his demeanor changed quite abruptly. He winked at me, and said, "Your Latin has improved."

"Oh! You notice me say 'Marce' and no 'Marcus,'' I said in

my best barbarian accent.

He laughed. "Infelicities are charming from your lips," he said. "Though if you were in school, you'd get a proper lashing."

I said, "But Aristarchos said if I don't speak proper Greek and Latin I will be a miserable failure."

"I doubt that," he said. "But you could always say nothing at all. That could also be seen as adorable. Perhaps they will think you are a mute, and they will start spilling their secrets. The cost of your silence could add considerably to your peculium … as would the price of your blabbing!"

"How will I know if I should tell or not tell?"

"If you are right, you will survive. If not —" A throat-slitting gesture. "And I am sure you will understand why I cannot behave towards you as I did when we were at sea. Society would not approve, not here, at the center of the world."

"What's a *cinaedus?"* I asked him.

"You'll know soon enough," he said.

"Centurion!" One of the soldiers was approaching. 'We are ready to escort the cargo into the city."

Marcus immediately became stern again, and acting as though I did not exist. His subordinate saluted him. The foot soldiers formed and began a slow, precise march. Their footfalls on the flat Roman road were a percussive accompaniment to our journey. The carts groaned under the weight of merchandise. My teeth rattled with each turn of the iron wheels.

After what seemed an age of jogging and bumping we reached the walls of the city, just before sunset.

We stopped.

At that stage, Marcus returned, and when we were alone, I asked what the matter was.

"We have to wait until the tenth hour," he said. "No wheeled vehicles in Rome until night. Rome is not a grand place of wide avenues. It started as a village, and the streets are as they were eight hundred years ago. Traffic would bring Rome to its knees if carts and pedestrians shared the roads."

And so came a time of waiting. I had not emptied my bowels and I was feeling desperate. I would have gone by the roadside, but I did not know if that was the kind of thing that got you a beating.

I was weary. I think I was asleep when we started to move again. But coming half awake, I did see the mother of all cities, steeped in gloom. We passed tall wooden structures reeking of human waste. From an open doorway, a fat prostitute jiggled and beckoned.

Wood gave way to concrete and stone. Temples in the starlight, their steps half lit, half shadowed. A statue of a goddess. A triumphal archway, then down another alley. A link-boy, torch aloft, guided litter-bearers through the street, so narrow that it seemed the opposing walls might bend and touch. The streets not straight but often veering in odd directions. And now, the carts strained as we moved uphill. Soldiers helped to push. I had heard that Rome has seven hills, but had not *felt* that.

Even so, the regular thud of the soldiers' caligae lulled me, made me drift off to sleep. I dreamed….

***

Of what?

Am I to take nothing private to the grave?

Suit yourself.

I dreamed of a village.

I dreamed of a palace.

My many pasts were weaving into some new fantasy.

***

When I awoke again it was because the pounding of the military escort's boots on the road abruptly stopped.

There was a wall. We had practically collided with it. In the dark, the wall went beyond the edge of my vision in both directions.

Marcus rode up to me. "This is your home now," he said. Then he rode away.

All I could feel now was terror.

VIII

STORYTELLER

There was, as I have said, a wall. The wall itself was nothing fancy. Indeed, in the light of uplifted torches, I saw that the wall was quite filthy. It even had graffiti, including a crude sketch of a woman tied to a stake, being ravaged by wolves — a common enough sight, I was to learn, in the arena, for the Romans are as cruel as they are civilized.

And in the wall was an ordinary door, which opened. At once came well-trained slaves, all wearing identical tunicae, each knowing exactly what to do as they unloaded the carts and carried the precious objects do into the house.

A tall, thin old man in a tunic and a woollen himation emerged. He looked hither and thither and spotted me. "Come down from there," he said. "He'll want to look at you right away."

Marcus was nowhere to be seen.

The man motioned for a boy to hold up a torch. He looked me over very thoroughly. My teeth. Even felt my privates, perhaps to make sure I had any.

"You'll do," he said. "I'll take you in directly."

"Shouldn't I —" I looked imploringly; he must have known I needed to relieve myself.

"Yes, yes, boy. We have a private shitter. Take care of yourself. We need to make the right impression." He turned to the slaves. "Everything is to be taken to the storage rooms for cataloguing and checking against the master list. Yes, slaves, too. Except this one."

I climbed out and he pushed me forward by the neck. I found myself in the doorway. With some trepidation, I stepped inside the house. A huge black man guarded the door. He was naked, and his feet were chained ... though I noticed that the other end of the chain was not actually attached to anything. The chain was just for show.

"Is this the new one, Croesus?" he asked the tall man.

"Don't be impertinent," came the reply. To me he said, "The latrina is to your left. When you are done, go straight to the triclinium. Follow the chatter and you will find it by yourself. Hop to it."

I looked up.

First ... it was a house of the utmost simplicity. I don't know what I was expecting — probably a lot of gold, ornate decorations, colorful statues. Fidgety mosaics and garish murals. But no. Instead there was the impression of spaciousness. The ceiling of the hall was high; a wide stairway led to an upper level.

The foyer was bare except for the masks of dead ancestors. There were columns and past them you could see the atrium, again laid out with simple elegance, with just a single statue of a young boy, very archaic looking — I learned later it was a thousand years old and pilfered from Greece. Above the garden was only starlight. I knew they were unloading the carts, and carrying things inside, but all I had eyes for was this magnificent emptiness.

The toilet was remarkable in that it had but a single opening, allowing you to defaecate in solitary splendor. Surely that, and not the opulent simplicity of the hallway, was what proved how rich the master of this house must be.

The floor of the latrina was a mosaic of an ocean scene. Neptune with his trident, sea creatures — shellfish, squid, a giant octopus all done with such cunning it seemed I was sitting at the ocean's edge.

A torch burned in a bracket, lighting up the bucket with the sponge on a stick with which to clean myself. I was just swabbing at my rear when I heard a voice. I almost jumped out of my skin because there was some kind of acoustic effect that made it sound almost as though the speaker were sitting alongside me.

It came from a nearby room. It was a rounded, modulated voice, and it was telling a story, and it was the most extraordinary Latin I had ever heard — for it was clearly of the utmost literary quality, yet it was also plain-spoken, as common folk talk, so even I could catch the gist of it ...

"'Erras,' inquit, 'Encolpi, si putas contingere posse, ut ante moriaris....'

I translated as best I could into my own language: 'You're wrong, Encolpius, if you think I'm gonna let you get away with dying before me, I'm going to kill myself. I've been looking for a sword. If I hadn't found you, I'd have thrown myself off a cliff ...'"

I was taking a crap in the palace of a rich stranger — why, this personal toilet was as large as my village home had been — listening to the most astonishing tale, in the most beautiful, powerful language. The story went on. It seemed to be about a lovers' quarrel, between a master and slave, but there was more to it than master and slave because it seemed that the slave was adept at acting the dominus, and presently the slave was pretending to cut his own throat with a razor he knew to be blunted, inflaming his possessor's passion still further....

I knew I should hurry.

At that moment, a large man stumbled into the latrina, accompanied by a young slave. I could not see him that clearly in the light from the one torch and in any case he had drawn his toga over his face.

"I thought this toilet was supposed to be private," he said.

"It is, domine," said the slave. He gestured at me to finish my business.

"Wipe your arse at once," the man growled. "Or I'll puke on your head." His slave held up a feather and was about to tickle his throat. In a minute, my fine silk tunica was going to be hurled on.

Hurriedly, I cleaned myself up and left the lavatory through another door. As soon as I closed it, that mellifluous voice returned, narrating more of the tale. It was even louder now, bouncing off the four walls of the atrium, amplified and echoing on marble surfaces.

I found myself in the cloister that ran all the way around the atrium. It was dark save for the occasional lit torches, but I could hear that voice, and the story he told was riveting. I presently found myself at the entrance to a triclinium. A dozen guests reclined on couches. Shyly, I stood at the opening, not wanting this miracle of storytelling to cease.

I looked at the narrator, who was reading from a scroll. He wore simple dress — simple as the house itself, yet bespeaking immense wealth — a plain, white toga, though it was the finest wool, a cloak dipped in purple held in place by a gold fibula. He wore a wreath. Was this the emperor himself? Surely not ... this was not the pudgy face on the two coins in my pouch. This was someone quite refined-looking, a man in his forties, perhaps, who had taken great pains with his grooming and makeup.

On the table were dishes I could never even imagine. Giant stuffed birds and the heads of unknown beasts. Fruits I had never seen. The guests had not seen me come in, so entranced were they by their host's narration.

Two naked boys, with little wings strapped on, were tending to the guests, sitting first in one lap then another, or being idly stroked, like kittens. They giggled, they smiled, they purred. Was this to be my job in this household?

The host went on: *"And Eumolpus, the poet, had not bothered to interrupt our death-scene ...* ah, but I see someone else has."

The two *pueri delicati* looked up at me. Beautiful they were indeed, and yet — their eyes looked daggers. I stared at the ground, not daring to meet their gaze. Had I arrived in some kind of competition, where boys too knowing for their age played games to curry favor with a fickle master? I knew that my terror on entering the house was justified.

"Who is this bewitching creature?" said the master of the house. "Croesus, do tell."

"But you already know, master," said the steward in Greek. For that was who the thin old man was. He had suddenly appeared behind me as though by magic. "Approach him, you little brat," he hissed at me.

The dominus crooked a finger. Awkwardly, I came closer.

"You speak Latin?" he said.

"Ita, domine."

"Greek?"

"Me not talking Greek so good, master."

"From *your* lips, child, that travesty sounds like Sappho!"

And then he said to the others: *"Eros daut' etinaxen emoi phrenas, anemos kat oros drysin empeson."* And, as they all applauded, he translated it into Latin, looking into my eyes: *"Eros shook my heart, like a mountain wind that sweeps down on an oak-tree."* And I admit I blushed ... I mean, my cheeks went hot and cold and I shivered all over. He motioned for me to come closer.

He sat me on the couch next to him. "Off with this girlish silk," he said to me, and ripped my tunica away so quickly I had not time to get even more embarrassed. Dipping a cloth in a kylix of resinated white wine, he wiped my face. "Nor does your face need painting. I did not buy you to be a whore." The resin stung my nostrils. I sneezed. "We already have enough of those in this house. Be still. I shall not eat you. Not tonight, anyway," he added, then, seeing that I was about to burst into tears, he relented. Sensing there was kindness in him, I hugged him, and shed more tears into his expensive cloak. "There, there," he said, patting my back. He unclasped his cloak — which I know cost more than I did — and put it around my shoulders. "Perhaps you'd care for a peacock's brain?" And then he started feeding me from a platter on the table.

I had not eaten anything since morning. I swallowed the entire brain; I would later learn that this morsel was worth as much as a week's bread for some peasant.

I did not even know my master's name.

But I was emboldened, and I said, "That story you were telling ... is it true? Who are Giton, and Encolpius, and Eumolpus?"

"We all have an epic inside us," my master said, "though we do not always have the leisure to write it. In my case, I daresay I shall not live to finish it."

***

You were sold to Gaius Petronius Arbiter?

You guessed.

Who would not have guessed it by now? And to think you heard his writing from his own lips — while crapping, no less! His unfinished epic is a legend. And even more so, the letter he wrote to the Emperor Nero before he committed —

Don't speak ill of my husband.

Ex-husband! You've had two others.

And none to hold a candle. Let me tell you what else Petronius said.

***

For indeed, as I was to learn by morning, I was now the property of Petronius Arbiter, one of the most celebrated wits in history. A man whose entire life was a poem. A man whose taste in music, painting, sculpture, poetry, drama, and the art of love, was such that the Emperor called him his *arbiter of elegance.* But it was not until I left his service that I was to appreciate just how important he was.

But now, the man whose name I did not yet know was saying, "My nephew, Vinicius, wrote me a letter in which he said the resemblance is uncanny. What do you all think? Lucan?"

A dour man on a nearby coach said, "Uncanny, indeed, uncanny."

"Seneca?"

Another, even more dour, muttered something.

I heard others, mumbling the same thing.

"Excuse me, *domine,*" I said. "I am just an impertinent boy but ... who is it I resemble so uncannily?"

Petronius said, "Resemblance is, indeed the issue. I think that it is just about exact. Exact, of course —" he gave me a playful prod — "there are some anatomical anomalies. But why have perfection when you can have *better* than perfect? I would not be surprised, Sporus, if the one person who is to judge just how *uncanny* the resemblance is ... were to prefer you to the real thing."

We all heard footsteps. Tottering, unsteady. A man stood at the entrance to the triclinium, his arm on the shoulder of a slave. It was the man who had been vomiting in the lavatory not long before. Now, in the light of many torches, I saw his features more clearly. He was broad-faced, broad-shouldered, and his hair resembled an upside-down wine bowl. His slave was wiping the last specks of vomitus from his lips.

It amused me to notice that he was using the same sponge that I had earlier used to wipe my posterior.

"Now," said Petronius, "stand up. Pull my purple himation about your shoulders. Here, I'll fix the fibula. Stand up straight and majestic. Put your arms out in a supplicatory gesture and whisper seductively 'Otho, Otho.'"

I got up from the couch and did what I was told. It was, I suppose, my theatrical debut.

"Marcus Salvius Otho," said Gaius Petronius Arbiter. "Who is it that you see before you?"

"Otho, Otho," I said.

The guests drew a collective breath. Something was going on in their minds. Not for the last time in my life, I was playing a role that my audience understood well, but meant nothing to me.

Marcus Salvius Otho looked at me for a long time. He squinted. He peered. He whispered into his slave's ear and the slave whispered something back. He *transformed*. I swear, he actually sobered up on the spot. He became a different person. Heroic, perhaps. A little henpecked as well. He stared at me, he saw *me,* just as I was ... and yet there was someone else here too, someone whose outward soma I was borrowing, though perhaps my soul was still my own.

He gazed at me through this miasma of epiphany and disbelief. “Poppaea?” he whispered.

Then he fainted.

IX

SYMPOSIUM

Although Marcus Salvius Otho had collapsed onto the floor, slaves still managed to drag him to an empty couch. They loosened the folds of his toga, daubed his face with cold water, and the two *delicati* took turns stimulating him in various ways, but he seemed to have passed out for the night.

"We shall ignore him," said Petronius, "but at least now we know that our Sporus is the real thing ... he can even fool the husband."

"But who is Poppaea, *domine*?" I asked.

I don't know why, but it seemed permissible to address my lofty master almost as though I were not his property. I had already learned that this was not the usual way things went in the Romans' world.

"You're not very slavish," Petronius said. "Most would look at the floor, and wince if spoken to, to ward off the inevitable slap. You were not born a slave. Perhaps you *are* a captive prince ... I believe that was the story we were sold on ... along with an unnecessary doubling of the price."

"Nevertheless, *domine,*" I persisted, "Who *is* she?"

"Before I answer," Petronius said, "let me explain something. Tomorrow, before breakfast, Croesus will take you to the back and give you ten lashes, for all your saucy back talk — that is not appropriate to my *dignitas* as your master. But I will tell him not to damage your skin, so it will not hurt much. And you do need to learn that, kind as I am, I do own you. Every piece of you. Your pretty little mouth, your radiant hair, your weasley excuse for a *phallos,* and even your empty little mind which I shall hope to fill with thoughts as beautiful as your body. I am not saying this to hurt you, child; I am just telling you the simple truth, the way the world works. For I, too, have a master. And when he whistles, I too must dance. So learn to be more circumspect, especially in front of guests."

Seneca scoffed. "You're too softhearted, Petronius."

"Let him be," Lucan said. "He is eccentric in how he treats his belongings, but it works. His slaves adore him. Do yours?"

"The love of a slave is innate hypocrisy. It's fear, made palatable with an excess of sweet sauce."

"By Juno! Am I not to rule in my own house?" Petronius said. "Summon the steward!"

Croesus was there, kneeling, and I had not even seen him come in. That's how the slaves were in the house — never visible until the moment they were needed. It was an art I would need to master.

"Croesus," Petronius said, "I've sentenced the new boy to ten lashes."

"Very good, *domine,*" he said without any visible emotion.

"However, seeing that he is something of a chatterbox, I'll give him until dawn to talk me out of it."

"A veritable Solomon!" said a bearded young man with a covered head.

"Whoever that might be," Petronius said, beckoning me to sit beside him once more, and stuffing another peacock's brain into my mouth, though the heavy admixture of garum and honey in the sauce was too confusing to my tongue.

"An ancient king of my old country," said the young man.

"And you, too, are now a king, young Agrippa, since your father was murdered while watching the games in Caesarea," Seneca said. "Yet you do not rule. You just sit around in Rome, frittering away your private treasury, while our praefectus handles law and order."

Petronius said, "You're as Roman as we are, Marcus Julius Agrippa, known to the subjects you haven't seen in ages as King Herod the not-so-Great . But we are in a Symposium, and you must recite poetry."

Slaves poured more wine. The *delicati* moved from couch to couch.

"Where is the Lady Poppaea?" I asked, since if I was to be "lightly" beaten in the morning, I might as satisfy all my questions.

"There are no ladies here," Petronius said. "I told you, it's a Symposium, not a dinner-party. A sober evening of edification and poetry."

"But there's a lady over there," I said, indicating one. Looking again, I saw that it was not a lady at all, but a rather grotesquely made-up elderly gentleman, his face completely white with lead paint.

The guests all began laughing. I had made a fool of myself so many times that evening that I wanted to shrivel up into the floor.

"Sit," Petronius said. "We'll have more poetry." A slave served wine from a dipper of purple crystal.

Presently it was Lucan's turn to begin a recitation, and although my master's eyes were opened, his mind seemed vacant. It seemed he understood the art of sleeping through a full performance without ever appearing to drift. I, however, did start to fall asleep. It had been a day of changes, and in this bewildering household, I had no idea of my true place. I was sitting, practically in the lap of the master of the house, who presently, slightly stirring, made me try a lark's tongue, then a young dormouse roasted in honey, all delicacies I could barely dream of; yet I knew I was going to be whipped in the morning. Who were these people, who could torment you and lavish sweetmeats on you, all in one breath?

"So this is what it means to be rich," I said. "Slaves everywhere, and all-night banquets."

"This isn't a banquet," Petronius said. "It's just a symposium. Soon, you'll see what a real banquet is. If you think this is extravagant ... and I am by far the most refined and tasteful of those I know. Why ... in my book, I describe *such* a banquet — but you shall read it for yourself. Once you are properly trained. Because at the moment, you are a ravishment to the eye, but to the ear ... that is another matter. That fool of a tutor has taught you almost nothing. And as for the *ars amatoria* ... of that you know nothing and you will need at least some rudiments if you're going to have a successful career — and help me recoup my investment.."

There came a familiar voice from the doorway of the triclinium: "Uncle!"

And I was amazed to see that it was my friend — if a slave could be said to *have* friends — Marcus, the centurion.

"I've done the whole inventory, Uncle," he said. "You are now the owner of some of the most beautiful things in Rome."

He had interrupted Seneca in mid-narration, but some in the company seemed actually relieved. Though I knew more Latin than Greek, I hadn't understood much of it.

To the guests, Petronius said, "You know, of course, my nephew Marcus Vinicius. Most beloved by the gods, and always in the heart of his extremely doting Uncle, Gaius Petronius Arbiter. Quite the soldier, for so young a man. About to be raised to *tribunus*, I understand, though he entered the Divine Emperor's service as a mere centurion, wishing to taste an ordinary soldier's rough life, the Gods alone know why. And, being my nephew, he also has exquisite taste in poetry."

I was beginning to have an inkling of the complexity of this aristocrat whom I'd had the audacity to think of as a friend.

"My slave," said Petronius, "reminds me of the true purpose of this evening's gathering. It's time to get to the real business of our symposium. What will the topic of tonight's discourse be?"

"Love," said the old man garbed as a woman.

"Tragedy," said Seneca the tragedian.

"Democracy," said Lucan. The guests at the party gasped.

"All of these subjects flirt with destiny," Petronius said. "You, Lucan, will probably be ordered to commit suicide one of these days; I doubt you'll live to see thirty, if you keep pining for the Republic. And as for tragedy, we're surrounded by it; why wallow? And love — well, just look at *you,*" he said to the man in a stola. "Can you do a better job than Plato?"

"I have a subject," said Marcus Vinicius, and he got me from his uncle's couch, led me by the hand to the centre of the circle, and slipped off the purple cloak that had been my only covering. "Let's talk about beauty." To me, he whispered, "Just stand there, looking a little stand-offish, unattainable. Be their muse. Yes, let them stare. You're an object. But at least you're a valuable one."

He let go. I was the center of attention.

Behind me was the door to the triclinium. In front was the couch where my master sat. Behind him there was a mural, women dancing among trees.

To hide my embarrassment, I looked at the trees in the murals. I started to count the leaves. They were so realistically rendered that it was easy to imagine myself in that grove as well, dancing among the nymphs.

"May I begin," said Marcus, "by quoting a poem by Asklepiades, where he says *ei kathyperthe labois khrysea ptera...* imagine if you had golden wings and a quiver on your silvery shoulders ... if you stood next to Cupid in all his splendor ... could his mother Venus tell you apart? ..." He winked at me, and then it was someone else's turn to discuss the nature of beauty. Which they did at length, quoting poets to prove their points. Their topics ranged from fragility to impermanence, from spirituality to physicality, and then, too, they would discuss every piece of my anatomy as though I weren't even there.

Agrippa spoke next, and he chose to speak some odd, guttural language. He translated it, though: *"Your lips drop sweetness as the honeycomb, my bride; milk and honey are under your tongue* ... It is from our holy scriptures," he said. "You did ask me who Solomon was. And before you ask, these words describe a woman." A few oohs and aahs at this anomaly.

"Your religious texts seem rather erotic," said Lucan, "not unlike Ovid. Are your gods fertility gods?"

"We only have one," Agrippa said.

"Heavens, only one," Seneca said. "No wonder we crushed you. Hardly seems fair. Now, as for fair, consider young Sporus's eyelashes..."

They went on in this vein for a while, eulogizing my eyes,

my nose, my smile, and many words were expended on my buttocks, while I stood stiffly, feeling quite humiliated.

And presently Otho began twisting and murmuring, and it was clear he was about to emerge from his stupor. One of the slaves emptied a jug filled with water chilled with snow — *that* must have been expensive — on his head. He sat up all at once. He saw me. He interrupted the chorus of encomiums, crudely calling out "Poppaea! Poppaea!" and shambling off the couch to enfold me in his beastly, fat, vomit-stained arms. He did not quite make it and fell, prostrate at my feet, with a groan.

The audience applauded. "With the fewest words," Seneca said, "he has said the most! What delicious irony, to praise the absent love while staring at the one organ she does not possess!" They were all laughing, and I still had no idea who Poppaea might be.

"He has won!" cried Lucan. "No one else shall be the victor!"

"Indeed. His rhetoric has outdone you all," Petronius said. The slaves pressed a laurel wreath on Otho's head and lifted him up — half pushed, half pulled him back to his couch. He had passed out again.

The guests began to get ready to leave, with slaves adjusting their clothing, straightening their togas, pinning their cloaks, and presenting them with little gifts as souvenirs of the evening. And presently there was no one left but myself, Marcus Vinicius, and a snoring Marcus Salvius Otho.

Marcus (my Marcus) said, "We'd better put him in the guest cubiculum."

"Sporus will bring his breakfast in the morning," Petronius said.

"I'd love to see Otho's face when he looks upon our Poppaea sober. But I need to go back to the castra. I shall leave you with your latest acquisition." And he left, without even bothering to glance at his uncle's property.

I was still standing there, feeling a strange combination of emotions: a warmth, even a kind of pride, that so many wealthy men had been singing my praises, but also a stark terror because I had been in this house for only a few hours, and knew I was completely at the mercy of one man.

Slaves were snuffing out the lamps and carrying away the half-eaten remains of the cena. "You can attend me in the bath," he said, "and in the bedchamber, for the rest of the night, though I daresay it is coming up to dawn. You'll have plenty of time to convince me not to have you beaten."

He had not forgotten! At these words my fear became so palpable that I almost threw up ... what with the rich foods and the unaccustomed amount of wine that had been fed me. For was this not the reason I had been purchased — so that some rich lord could brutalize me in degradation and pain?

"What's the matter, Sporus? You're shaking like a leaf." He called to his steward. "Croesus — take the creature to the cubiculum and instruct him."

Instruct me? Had I not had enough instruction in my role from that crucified pirate? "No, domine, no!" I exclaimed as the terror seized hold of me completely and I broke down in a paroxysm of weeping.

X

CUBICULUM

There now," said my master. "Tears *can* be a way to avoid the whip, but when a master has a bit of cruel streak, tears might encourage *more* whipping...."

Croesus took me by the shoulder ... quite roughly, after the tenderness which his owner had shown me ... and marched me away, while Petronius sipped at a posset that one of his women had just poured for him.

First, Croesus took me to the slaves' quarters. They were not as ghastly as the place in Ostia where we had been warehoused, but they were a reminder that I hadn't yet attained the status of being fully human.

The slaves were housed in dormitories in a damp basement. There was an area where slaves were tending a furnace that seemed to be designed to conduct heat upstairs. This room was like a little hell. The slaves were drenched in sweat, working in loincloths that were completely soggy. I felt very fortunate not to be forced to work there.

Croesus had his own room, which was quite roomy — and held some valuable objects, like some scrolls, a little statue of some god — but also a selection of whips. The rest of the quarters were cramped indeed — each cell held up to a dozen; the beds were raised rectangles of concrete next to which each slave's meagre belongings were held in a small wooden box. I shared a room with the other delicati — the two who had looked at me with such disdain when I'd first stumbled into the triclinium.

My belongings were few, and they had already been deposited by my sleeping space; and the two boys were already searching through them, holding up the mirror. Luckily they had not opened my peculium; I would have to find a good hiding place.

"Your companions in debauchery," Croesus said, sounding very disapproving. "They are called Hyacinth and Hylas."

Hylas was olive-skinned and green-eyed, and smirked at me. Hyacinth, to my amazement, looked as though he could have come from my village. In fact, he immediately spat at me, and hissed in my own language, "Filthy whore."

"You're one to talk!" I said. He merely laughed. Yet it was a relief to hear my own language, even in derision.

"You favorite one now," Hylas said in strangely accented Greek, "but in two years you feeding the ducks in dominus's farm."

Hyacinth said to me, "You've got a tongue. Use it wisely." I did not like the way that sounded at all. The two of them laughed at me.

In my own tongue I asked him, "Are you from a village? Is it near the sea? Do you remember your parents?"

"I should punch you in the face," he answered. "What village? I'm a fucking prince."

"Me too," I said.

And suddenly we both laughed, and for a moment I thought we might be friends. "Don't speak our language in front of anyone." He made a dismissive gesture to Hylas. "That one doesn't count. He's barely verbal, and anyway he can keep a secret. If they knew we had a secret way of communicating … they'd sell me. Not you! After all, they have you now, the new, improved me, anyway. I'm just about over the hill."

"That's ridiculous," I said. "You … you're beautiful."

"But for how much longer? I'm thinking I'll ask Croesus to take me to have me cut. I'd have a few good years left if I did."

"Cut?"

The two laughed again, but this time it was edgy.

"A few good years," said Hyacinth, "if I survive the operation. Half don't."

Hylas had been going through my things again. "Nice mirror," Hylas said. "Think me keep it."

"Stop being mean," Hyacinth said.

And at that moment, Croesus came back for me.

***

First I was brought to the master's private bath. Gaius Petronius was already soaking and I realized that we were directly above the hellish basement where slaves had been toiling to stoke the furnace.

I entered the water and was shocked at the heat. No wonder the room beneath us seemed like the depths of infernum itself. My master beckoned. I did not know what to do exactly, so I waded in and began by rubbing his back. He sighed in pleasure. I continued, using my hands to gently massage his arms, as Aristarchos had taught me. Petronius did not demand anything more titillating than that; he merely sat with his eyes closed, occasionally murmuring something in Greek. I wondered whether later on, in the bedchamber, I would be subjected to less savory predations. This kept me on edge. How could he not sense my unease? Or was it simply normal to him, that a slave must always be in fear?

At length, Petronius stood up and went to a marble stool, where he sat, not saying a word, while I wiped him down with a soft cloth, rubbed him down with perfumed olive oil, and scraped him with a strigil. Again, he did not say a word to me.

Then the master took me by the hand and led me to the cubiculum. We were both naked, and my anxiety was now practically at the breaking point. Surely I could not stave off my fate much longer.

I was surprised once more to see that there were others in the room. There were two women on the bed — the same giantesses who had come to prepare me for delivery to this house. They, too, were completely unclad. They shifted position so that Petronius could get between them, but made no move to accommodate me.

"Stand right there," Petronius said. "In front of my bed. I want to look at you while I write my novel."

Then, one of the women, the darker, pulled out a writing tablet and a stylus from under the bed, The other offered him wine in a rhyton of precious, rainbow-fringed glass. All I did was stand there. Two slaves held up a damask veil behind me, and another fanned the veil, not to cool me, but to create a billowing effect.

And my dominus wrote on the tablet, looking at me as he wrote: *"Dum haec loquimur, puer speciosus, vitibus hederisque reditimus, modo Bromium, intendum Lyaeum Euhiumque confessus* ... 'as we were conversing, a gorgeous boy with grapeleaves and ivy in his hair brought grapes in a basket, imitating Bacchus in ecstasy, dreaming, full of wine ...'" He went on in this vein for some time, composing as he wrote. Now and then he told me to turn around. "You are the perfect model for my Giton," he said. "I just have to hope your looks can be distilled by my stylus into words. Turn again, smile a little.

Are you tired? Share some of my wine."

"Who is Giton, domine?" I asked him.

"A slave. And in my book, a supreme object of desire."

"I thought books were about gods and kings and heroes."

"I have a different vision. I am creating a book that on occasion talks as ordinary people talk, yet also at times soars like the finest classic poetry — a book that talks about art and literature in the same breath as raunchy sex acts and lust and sweat and gluttony and cupidity and treachery and the worst exemplars of human slime … and the beauty of young love. A book that dwells as much among slaves as among the gods … but which treats them as human beings and not simply as comic relief as in the comedies of Plautus."

While he said all this, I must add, the two women were alternately performing various acts upon him, including "swallowing the serpent" and "polishing the tail." Yet Gaius Petronius Arbiter seemed quite bored by it all, having eyes only for me.

"And I am in this book, domine?"

"Be quiet and let me write. More wine, Euphrosyne."

The slave took a break from her ministrations to ply him with more, and also shuffled over to where I was stiffly standing, and gave me a few sips from the same rhyton.

"Crook your elbow a little … now smile."

I did my best.

My master said, "Others may find you are the spitting image of Poppaea Sabina, most ravishing, most monstrous of women. To me, however, you are precisely Giton, the boy in my story, the boy two young men fight over; a boy who is a slave, yet enslaves all who see him; that's you."

I looked at my master, who was writing intently; there were tablets strewn about the bed and I knew he would have to send them off to be properly transcribed. It was tiring to stand so long; I tried resting my weight on first one foot, then another.

Petronius peered at the tablet, then at me. His eyes were piercing. He saw more than my outside. I think he could see everything I had suffered. I loved him, then, because he seemed to know who I was, and because of all the people I had met this evening, he was the one who did not see me as a mere thing to be owned … ironic, because he did, in fact, own me.

Eventually I could see dawn steal in through the drapes.

Petronius dismissed the attendants, had them gather up the tablets, and told them to take them to the scribe. Then he gestured for me to come to the bed.

This must be the moment, I thought. *My fantasy is over. Now comes reality, ripping into my rear end.*

I lay down meekly. My lord and master turned me so that my back was to him, and hugged me like a doll. "You are soft," he said. He stroked my hair for a while. And he fell into a deep sleep.

I lay wide awake, not daring to hope that my fate in this mansion was not to be painfully violated by the master, but simply to be admired, perhaps even loved, as a favorite toy is loved. It was a better destiny than I had been told to expect, and I wondered how long it would last.

His gentleness and consideration were such that I even felt a little regret that he had not wanted more; I had never wanted to be touched by someone before, but now I felt a little surge of feeling. Was I happy? I do not know, but with so much unhappiness before and after, perhaps I should treasure this memory as a time when I was less victim, and more muse.

And thus it was that he began to snore, making it impossible to sleep. He was deafening — so were my thoughts, racing, wondering whether I had finally reached home.

***

Touching! You lived happily ever after with a rich, mad poet!

You know I did not. You know that I rose much higher than to be the plaything of a senator.

But you have no titillating tales of the private life of the most famous libertine of our times?

Most famous, perhaps, but not so much of a voluptuary as many others I was fated to encounter. You see, he did not even bother to have sex with me. He saw me as something quite other than a convenient hole to plug.

***

And thus it was that I lay awake until it was broad daylight, when Croesus entered the room and pulled me off the master's bed.

"You are to serve Lord Otho's breakfast," he said. "Oh, and I am to beat you."

"But the dominus said —"

"You are going to ask me to wake him up to ask whether he has countermanded his order? I will get whipped myself! Better your back than mine. Come quickly. Let's get it over with. I'll hurt you as little as I can get away with, and I won't leave any marks."

XI

MARCUS SALVIUS OTHO

Croesus had barely touched me, and to be sure he had used the strap with a very gentle hand, before one of the cleaning slaves came down to tell us that Marcus Salvius Otho was awake.

"Well," Croesus said, untying me from the post, "you can't very well serve breakfast while covered in welts."

I took a tray into the guest cubiculum, where Otho lay sprawled out on a huge couch, one that could easily fit three or even more. Doubtless, this room was designed for an orgy. The murals showed Jupiter in particularly concupiscent aspects. On one wall, he chased Leda, in the guise of a swan, though displaying a remarkably human set of genitalia. In another, he chased the nymph Europa. But the wall directly at the head of the bed showed Jupiter snatching Ganymede from the shores of Troy, with golden Ilium's walls in the background and Mount Ida in the distance, and fluffy clouds overhead.

"Your breakfast, domine," I said. On the tray were olives, figs, bread, and a cup of wine. I set it down beside the couch and prepared to leave, but Otho grabbed my slender wrist with a plump hand and pulled me down to the bed.

"When I have breakfast in the home of Petronius," he said, "the slave generally feeds me." The way he was looking me up and down, I did not think he would be content with a few figs. Clearly the servus was being served along with the prandium. Perhaps I could get away with being one of the trimmings, rather than the main course.

It did not seem likely.

"Poppaea," Otho murmured in a husky simulacrum of an erotic sigh.

"I am Sporus," I said softly. Otho slapped me soundly, catching me by surprise so I barked in pain, remembering my position just in time.

"You are whoever I say you are, Poppaea, my Poppaea," said Otho. He pulled me closer and he began — I cannot say it more delicately — to slobber. His breath was odious — morning breath combined with sour wine. I closed my eyes and tried to think of my peculium.

Otho took me into his embrace. I was fainting from the stench.

At that moment, however, there was a rescue ... of sorts.

My ravisher suddenly dropped me. I sank down onto the bed. I couldn't really move much, because I was pinned down by the weight of Otho's thighs.

"Oh," Otho said, "good morning, my darling." He was not speaking to me.

I looked up from and saw, in the doorway ... myself.

I knew who it was because I had already seen myself in that

piece of mirror that was one of my only belongings.

Myself, that is, with hair elaborately coiffed, wearing a silken stola embroidered with gold thread, held at the shoulder by a fibula in the shape of a Cupid with little diamonds in its eyes.

The Lady Poppaea Sabina, I presumed.

She stared at me, and I at her.

One of the wealthiest noble ladies in the known world, and me, the lowliest of the low, and we were the proverbial two peas in a pod.

"What monstrous obscenity have you found this time?" said the Lady Poppaea Sabina.

Her voice — strident in rage — was nevertheless sheer music.

Her eyes — flashing with the fury of Jove's thunder — were the most sensuous I had ever seen.

I thought ... *Do I really look like that, too? Am I that beautiful?*

"I can explain," Otho said.

"I am sure you cannot," said the Lady Poppaea, bearing down, her palm raised up as if to deliver a resounding slap.

She sat down at the edge of the bed and motioned for Otho to get off me. I wanted to run away, but I knew that I would have to wait for these high-and-mighty aristocrats to dismiss me.

"I'm perfectly aware that I'm the most desirable trophy wife in all of the empire," Poppaea said. "Yet you've taken it on yourself to get yourself an improved model, I see. With certain ... special attachments, I imagine. And doesn't talk back, either. Entirely compliant ... or made so with a dose of the strap."

She tugged me closer, so my eye was level with hers. "What's your name, slave? You must be a slave. No freeborn lad who looks like you would willingly lie with my piggy of a husband."

"Oh don't be so tiresome, dear," Otho said. "I just woke up. Sporus, give my wife some figs."

"I'm not being tiresome. You've humiliated me in the worst possible way — denigrating the one thing I can't do anything about — the fact that I don't have a penis." She turned to me. "See it from my point of view, Sporus. All my beauty, my intelligence, my wealth ... and I have to play the devoted Roman matron to this effete fat *thing.*"

"Only in public, darling. In private, you can dally with anyone you wish."

"Externally," said Poppaea. "I'm sure you don't want any bastards planted inside me."

"But we have a way to solve this now, my dear. Don't you see? Sporus is a godsend. I finally have a way to bring myself to —"

***

Thus it was that I performed my first role in service to Gaius Petronius Arbiter, and it was an ignominious one. First, the Lady Poppaea Sabina disrobed and lay down on the bed. Then I lay next to her, face down, with my buttocks elevated by a cunning arrangement of pillows, to facilitate what Otho was planning.

There was a lot of slobbering. Luckily I did not have to see Otho's face. He squashed my slender body, grunting repulsively. "My love," he said. "My Queen, my Empress, my Goddess."

Poppaea whispered in my ear. "You'd better moan," she said. "It will go faster if he thinks you're reciprocating."

I tried a few half-hearted moaning sounds and Otho instantly became even more aggressive. I screamed, and it was definitely not from pleasure. But the scream got him into a heightened state of excitement. He started pounding away, and presently worked himself up to near-climax. Then he slid off me, landing right on top of his wife, as I rolled off the cubiculum.

I shook myself, got up, and stared down at the bed where Otho was belaboring Poppaea with a couple of perfunctory thrusts. He was able to discharge into his decidedly bored lady wife. He finished, got up, and ordered me to bring him the wine cup.

It was the strangest lovemaking — if it could be called that — I had ever witnessed, let alone been a party to. "Well," he said, "that was lovely. Did you enjoy it, dear?"

"As much as I enjoy the attentions of one of my dogs," she said.

I pulled on my tunica and helped the Lady Poppaea back into her clothes. An attendant entered the room and began to do her hair. When she was dressed, you could not tell what a strange act she had just participated in.

Marcus Salvius Otho got dressed as well, with the help of some slaves who appeared, it seemed, out of nowhere.

No one cleaned me up, of course. I straightened my tunica and hair as best I could. Otho had not actually penetrated me, but I had thought I was going to get killed, such was the violence of his passion. Yet now, that passion spent, he seemed like a perfectly bland, uninteresting person.

“Well, my dear,” he said, “that certainly changes things. I imagine, with this little thing as an incentivizer, I could even father a child on you.”

“This little thing, as you put it,” said Poppaea, “belongs to someone else. And after this morning’s sorry showing, I doubt the little thing’s for sale. You need to realize that they’re not just objects, you know. Slaves, I mean. They do scurry off to their masters and tell them everything. By the end of today, Petronius will know a lot more about you than he knew yesterday."

Wild-eyed, Otho looked first at me, then at his wife. "He planned this!" he said.

"In politics," said the Lady Poppaea Sabina, "you figure out the opposition's weak spot. And yours, my dear, is that though you may love your wife, you do not love her vagina."

"I'm only human," said Otho.

Poppaea laughed. She pulled me to me and gave me a kiss on the cheek. "Cheer up, boy," she said. "I may help you fill up your peculium yet. Though I've half a mind to have you whipped, just to wipe that smirk off your face. Do you know how difficult it has been to get my husband to perform his ... ah ... duty?"

To Otho, she said, "Now, sit up straight and behave. We are going to say goodbye to our host now. You've overstayed your welcome by passing out drunk at his symposium. And, heavens, the Emperor wants a private cena with you tonight! He's planning to sing you his new song! You've got at least three hours of hot soak, oiling, scraping, perfuming, and beard-trimming before you can face a vocal recital from Himself the Divinity, Pater Patriae, Pontifex Maximus!"

And with that, she pushed her husband out into the hall.

I followed at a discreet distance and caught Otho remonstrating with my master.

I had caught his eye, so I couldn't slink away. He beckoned me with a crooked finger.

"You don't look well," Petronius said. "I'm afraid I forgot to cancel your whipping. You should tell Croesus that it is perfectly all right to wake me in the morning on any occasion that I've sentenced you to lashes the day before and forgotten to commute. He will say he wouldn't dare wake me, but insist." I knew that insisting was not my place, and that Croesus had beaten me as lightly as he dared, so I decided it would be best to keep silent.

I bowed my head, preferring, perhaps, that my master not know the true extent of my humiliation that morning — not the beating, but being treated as some kind of surrogate wife. I felt pity for Poppaea, even though I hardly had the right to feel pity for someone so much more privileged than I — but for all that privilege I sensed she was as trapped as I was.

Otho had been trying to interrupt this conversation and he continued, "Name your price, Petronius. You know I'm good for it. Besides, the boy *loves* me! You should have heard him moan!"

You should have seen Poppaea roll her eyes.

Petronius patted me on the head. "It'll take more than money," he said, "to part me from my Giton. I am as devoted to him as he is to me. *Serva me, servabo te,*" he added, and kissed me on the cheek.

"Poets' drivel," Otho said. "Slaves don't really serve anything but their own self-preservation."

"There, there," Petronius said, patting my cheek again, trying to reassure me. "I'm not going to sell you."

Poppaea looked at both of us, then said, with an evil gleam in her eye, "But you *would* consider giving him away, wouldn't you?"

XII

POPPAEA SABINA

The Lady Poppaea was not wrong. Petronius did not sell me, but he did make a deal. A deal he had every right to make, and he did his best to let me have a share in it. A deal I did not like, but which I could hardly refuse, since my master had gone out of his way to see that I would benefit.

I would be sent to the home of Marcus Salvius Otho twice a month, on whichever days that the medicus deemed the Lady Poppaea Sabina would be most likely to conceive. I would have to participate in the strange ritual where I was the object of desire, yet the lady was the object to be inseminated. Otho pledged not to damage me in any way, and to avoid any kind of painful penetration; his enjoyment of my charms was to be purely intercrural. Two guards, hand-picked by Marcus Vinicius, would escort me there and back. I would be returned to the home of my master before dawn.

For this peculiar service, I would collect from the Lord Otho the princely sum of three denarii, of which I would add one to my peculium, and hand over two to Croesus, who would note it all down in the house records.

It did not seem like a bad arrangement. My function was solely as a facilitator. I did not need to have any kind of relationship with "the piggy husband," as the Lady Poppaea called him.

Unfortunately, Otho was never quite able to stick to the no-damage clause. No matter what he had agreed to, I drove him mad, it seemed. The first night I returned to the domus Petronii bleeding and in tears. Maddened by pain and disillusionment, I charged straight into my master's cubiculum and threw myself at him, sobbing. Croesus came right behind me, wielding a strap, but it was too late; I had aroused the one known throughout Rome for sleeping all day and carousing all night.

Croesus immediately prostrated himself abjectly at the foot of the bed. "Master," he said, "I don't know how I let this happen ... I have not dared awaken you in three decades of service ... beat me within an inch of my life, Gaius Petronius, but I beg you, don't sell me!"

My master was barely awake while all this was going on, but he gradually became aware of a whimpering old slave on the floor and a weeping young one in his arms. He looked at Croesus, and then at me, and — thank the gods — he began laughing. It was a throaty laugh, rich and not unkind, and amazingly, he got me laughing, too. But his demeanor grew serious when he saw blood on my tunica.

"This was not my intention," he said.

"I appreciate that you did not want me hurt —"

"Oh, well, there's that, but it's only common sense. When you borrow a precious object, you don't return it all bloody. If he'd *bought* you, he'd have done what he liked, I suppose. I hope he tipped you."

"He did, domine. I received three denarii plus an extra as."

"One miserable as to salve a bleeding arse! I've a mind to charge him for a full replacement. Not that I'd actually replace you, of course."

A strange mixture of genuine concern and complete callousness. That was how it was, to be master and slave. That is how the relationship is. I never delude myself anymore.

***

Well, you're not a slave anymore. You're an ex-empress, about to be a god.

And death comes to slaves and empresses alike.

But not gods.

Somehow, I don't believe it. Where I come from, the gods are mortal. Oh, they live a very long time, far longer than any human being, and yet there will come a time when they fight the ultimate darkness, and the darkness wins. As it always does.

Where do you come from? You never said.

One barbarian village is much like another. What difference does it make?

It will take some time for your hair to conform to the shape I have designed. If I bore you, I can leave for a while, as I can't go on with your makeup until the hair is firmed up.

Do I have to sit here? Perhaps the guard can take me on a little tour? Where do they keep the lions? I love cats.

Oh, the lions. Come. I will walk with you, and you can tell me more scandalous tales, perhaps over a haunch of Christian.

The Christians! I had a run-in with them, too. But that is much later. For now, the stately homes of two wealthy noblemen were all I had seen of the grandeur of Rome.

***

I had at least a fortnight before my next session at the house of Otho. I spent the time in improving my languages; I yearned to speak as eloquently as my master, who could leap from vaulting poetry to coarse vulgarity in the confines of one sentence. Latin is a language of incredible precision — Greek, on the other hand, revels in ambiguity and veiled revelations. My speaking improved by leaps and bounds because each night, my master read to me from his novel-in-progress, and the adventures of Encolpius, Ascyltus, and Giton were not just exciting, but lessons in every level of the Latin language, from the exalted to the obscene.

As for my roommates, Hylas and Hyacinth, they calmed down considerably when they realized I wasn't about to deprive them of their jobs. The master held symposia almost every other night, and at those, I was rarely trotted out; Hylas and Hyacinth collected the tips. At normal dinners, with fewer guests, my master made me chief cupbearer and my duties were more like Ganymede in Olympus than a by-the-hour boy in a lupanar. Late into the night, Petronius would read to me, or speak to me, or rather *at* me, about life at court, about the Emperor's wild poetry, and about how he had to neither flatter nor demean, and the fine line he had to walk to keep Himself the Divinity's favor.

At length, the time came for another visit to the house of Otho. As before, two legionaries escorted me and my litter was carried downhill a little way, through winding, irregular streets — it was not far. This time, with the worst to expect already in my mind, I was able to gaze at the scenery.

Unless he is as rich as my master, a Roman lives on the street — he eats, defecates, shops, copulates in dark corners, and strolls over to the public baths to clean up after all of it, through a labyrinth where no streets are marked and where no one gives directions. The litter was not just for comfort, though of course it did protect against the odors of the open gutter and the occasional projectile turd.

One of the most striking aspects of the city streets by day was the sheer color and variety of the graffiti. Sexual boasts, poems praising gladiators, and religious slogans like "fuck the Christians" were on the walls, as well as political advertisements, hopefuls running for quaestor or tribune.

Though I was a slave, the fact that was carried on a litter by a matched team of slaves meant that people assumed I *was* somebody. Later I was to learn that all sorts of slaves are somebodies ... many of them run the empire's finances, shape political actions, and influence the very visions of the great. For now, I pretended to be important. When I stepped into the atrium of Marcus Salvius Otho, my fantasy could continue because the house servants deferred to me, fed me well, and made sure I was bathed and perfumed before being led to my fate.

Knowing what to expect now, I was able to manipulate my buttocks and thighs so that I always managed to avoid being speared on the senatorial member. This actually seemed to inflame him all the more. I felt as though I was being probed by an elephant's trunk. Taking the Lady Poppaea's advice to heart, I moaned, perhaps more convincingly than the previous time, because Otho's heavings became ever more suffocating.

Meanwhile, the Lady Poppaea Sabina lay languidly, her flesh cool as snow, sipping from a kylix of resinated Lesbian wine.

When the necessary moment came for Otho's *coitus* to become *interruptus,* I swiftly slid off the cushions and allowed the Lord to breach the Lady, who had smoothed the way with a lubricious infusion of olive oil. He came, I think, rather copiously, and immediately began snoring.

"Help me get out from under this lump," said the Lady Poppaea Sabina. I hopped over to her side and helped pull her free. Otho rolled to the edge of the bed, leaving the Lady Poppaea Sabina and me practically on top of each other and, I was embarrassed to discover, rendering me considerably more excited than I had been by her boorish husband.

"Oh!" Poppaea said, giggling. This was the first emotion I'd seen in her all evening. "I didn't realize you were able to actually ... *enjoy* ... it."

"I didn't, either."

"After last time, I supposed you traumatized for life."

"Very nearly, domina."

"I certainly was," she said. "Can you imagine anything more awful than to be me, the most glamorous, most beautiful, richest, cleverest woman in all Rome — being wedded to someone who doesn't even like women?"

"I wouldn't know, my Lady."

"With all that heaving and grunting, I'm as dry as a papyrus in Egypt," she said. "But perhaps *you* could ... no. I'd be taking advantage of a dear friend."

"You can command me anyway you like, domina."

"I mean Petronius, silly. You're just a toy. And yet ... I've often wondered what kind of a lover I would be, if I had a little *phallos* of my own."

Suddenly, the advice of Hyancinth, my compatriot and colleague in depravity, came back to me. "You've got a tongue. Use it wisely."

I did.

How wise it was I do not know, but in mere moments, the Lady Poppaea Sabina was shrieking in ecstasy. "Oh! Oh! Remind me to send Petronius a brace of my cook's legendary stuffed geese!" she murmured in between moans. (As I was otherwise engaged, I was unable to respond.) At length she reached some kind of climax, and as she lay panting, I plied her with another cupful of retsina. She turned to order some attendant, kneeling in a corner, to send along the brace of geese and a jar of figs along with my litter. She then reached into a pouch next to the lectus. "I haven't any change, and I don't suppose you can change an aureus," she said, sighing, tossing me a gold coin. I had never seen one. I tried to refrain from gawking. "You deserve it, for the momentary pleasure you brought an old woman."

"Old!" I cried. "You must be joking, domina."

"Sporus," she said — I remember sitting straight up at the shock that she remembered my name — "I'm seven years older than Piggy, and seven times more intelligent, and at least seven times as rich. I don't *like* my husband. He's not my first, and I promise you, he won't be my last. I have my eye on a much bigger prize."

"Who?" I asked, in all innocence.

"Oh, someone I knew in my childhood as Lucius. Lucius Domitius Ahenobarbus." She pointed to the gold coin in my hand.

"You mean the Emperor!" I said. Even a lowly slave like me knew by now the birth name of Himself the Divinity, Nero Claudius Caesar Augustus Germanicus, Imperator, Pater Patriae, Pontifex Maximus, and so on so forth. One wouldn't presume to call the Divinity by his human childhood name unless one actually *was* a childhood playmate.

"Perhaps you didn't even think a woman like me could hope to marry the Emperor, who is, after all, already married, and to his stepsister at that, Octavia, the daughter of his uncle, the Emperor Claudius."

"I don't normally think about such things at all. I'm a slave, remember?"

"I know what you're thinking," she said to me. "But I have a plan. And I have an edge."

"An edge?" I asked her.

"A secret weapon. I have you," she said, her eyes sparkling.

XIII

WEDDING-GIFT

I returned to my master's house more confused than ever. I gave the geese to Croesus, who told me that the slaves' quarters would sing my praises for such largesse; when I told him that the Lady Poppaea had meant Petronius to have them, he laughed it off. "We don't share tips with the dominus," he said.

About my other tip, the golden aureus, I was in a panic. I did not dare show it to anyone, because I didn't want people picking through my peculium.

In fact, I trusted my master, who technically owned my peculium anyway, more than any of the slaves of the household. And so I slipped into his bedroom — I knew he would not have awoken — and, after folding my clothes neatly at the foot of the lectulus, I slid in beside him, meaning to ask him first thing when he woke up.

It was past noon when I felt him stir; he had hugged me close to him, as a child might a doll; he had a unique scent, part perfumed olive oil part old wine, that filled my nostrils. I opened my eyes to see him looking down at me.

"My Giton," he said. "I gave no command for you to be sent to my bed after coming back from Otho's house." He stroked my hair and added, "But at least you're not in tears, and you haven't left any bloodstains on my bed."

I told Petronius that the Lady Poppaea had given me a whole aureus, since she had no change. "Should I give it to you, *domine?* It doesn't seem right for a slave to carry gold on him."

Petronius laughed. "Our Supreme Lord and God, Himself the Divinity, once bet four hundred thousand sesterces on a single roll of dice! That's four thousand of those things. Once the Late and Unlamented Caligula spent ten million sesterces on a banquet. You're going to be rich long before you're free. If I ever even agree to your manumission; why would I ever let such a lovely thing go?"

"You will soon enough, domine, when I start to lose my looks. Everyone says so."

"Your looks will live on in my book, Sporus," said Petronius Arbiter.

I did not tell him about the Lady Poppaea's imperial ambitions. Perhaps I should have. He might have warned me off, or protected me a little better; then again, in the end he could not even protect himself.

***

I'm getting a bit impatient. We all want to hear about Nero. After all, ever since the day they decreed damnatio memoriae *upon him, we no longer hear all those wild stories of indulgence and decadence. In fact, we can't get anyone to talk about Himself the Late Divinity at all. And they're chipping his name off all the big monuments.*

Why do you think *I'll* tell you anything?

Because you're going to die anyway.

True enough. I will tell you one thing. There has been a massive campaign to blacken Nero's name, though less than a year has passed. But I was with him. I was the one to whom he whispered his last words. Not some senator or trusted guard, and certainly not his mistress Actë, though she has since dined out on many a scandalous story.

Remember, too, that there was never an official senatorial decree of *damnatio.* No one is going to be arrested for talking about him. Allowing a kind word once in a while is not going to lead to being strung up on a cross.

He may have murdered his mother and kicked his wife to death, but remember that he lowered your taxes.

I don't pay taxes, silly. I'm a slave.

Fair enough.

He was a monster to some. Indeed, he had my balls cut off. And yet, he loved me.

As much as a god is capable of love.

***

And yet my first sight of the most powerful man in the universe was not edifying. It seemed that my master was invited — not too willingly — to a banquet at the home of a man named Tigellinus. Now this Tigellinus was the commander of the Praetorian Guard, I heard. He had power. Marcus Vinicius had dropped his name a few times. This banquet was going to be attended by Rome's elite.

"I hate these affairs," Petronius said. "I'm told there will be a wedding. In that case, perhaps lavish gifts will be distributed to the guests. Your duty will be to wait in an anteroom with the other slaves and, should I receive such a gift, to carry it out to my litter. It won't do to carry such a thing myself … I'll need a pretty young thing to do the carrying. I've got appearances to uphold."

"Couldn't one of the other boys do it, domine?"

"Of course, Sporus, but I am fond of your company! I shall get out of this hideous obligation all the more quickly, if I know you're going to be accompanying me in the litter going home. I'll need to unload a year's worth of scandalous gossip, and you're too loyal, too discreet, and too innocent, to go selling information."

"I wouldn't know who to sell it to, master."

I had a bad feeling, but a slave has no say. It was a long journey; Tigellinus's house was all the way on the Palatine, and mostly uphill for the litter-bearers. I could not really believe that my master would bring me along just to carry something that he might not even receive. Or that he was merely fond of my company.

But a slave has no say.

When we finally reached this home, which was by no means the palatial wonder I expected, we could see that it was surrounded by guards, and that all sorts of swords, daggers, and even little knives that could barely peel an apple had been temporarily held on a table just inside the entrance. Someone was being very strict about security.

We slaves were inspected very thoroughly and indeed somewhat roughly handled. A burly centurion even looked up the back of my tunica. Then I and the litter-bearers were sent to a large waiting room with stairs that seemed to lead down to a dungeon-like slaves' quarters, with a soldier guarding the door.

My master joined a stream of guests and I was able to look at my new surroundings. This room was a madhouse. Petronius would never abide a mess like this, and litter-bearers usually waited in the street anyway; they were probably glad of being inside, for it promised to be a long banquet indeed.

There were teams of litter-bearers, most of them matched — they were all Numidians, all Germans, all Nubians, all Britons, all superb physical specimens, well-oiled and not wearing much clothing, as if their owners wanted to show off every inch of what they possessed. Other teams were clearly thrown together with little care: paunchy with scrawny, hairy with bald, and uncoordinated dress; these probably had owners more interested in getting where they were going than any kind of ostentatious display, or perhaps really important people who preferred to travel anonymously.

There were slaves like me, basically there to ornament their owner, to carry things, or perhaps to provide a quick orgasm on the long ride back. I sat for a while, listening to the chatter; I had not heard so many languages in one room since being penned up in Ostia.

I didn't want to draw attention, so I squeezed myself into a corner, put my head between my knees, and waited.

At length, a man loomed over me and spoke to me in my native language. "Don't often see one of *us,*" he said.

I didn't answer.

"It's all right, boy," he said. "When we talk, no one will listen. That's because where we come from, the Empire does not really extend; only the pirates do. I would love to hear news of our country. I have been here … a long time."

I looked at him. He was one of the unmatched litter-bearers. He must have noticed my curiosity, because he started to explain. "My master is a Stoic," he said. "He's not into ostentation."

"What's a Stoic?"

"It's a philosophy, a way of life. Personally, it is not that different from what I believe. I am a Christianos."

"What's that?"

"I would love to tell you, but this is not the time."

We were interrupted by sounds from the basement. Someone was being whipped, and was screaming. The cries were more animal than human; I could not even tell if it was a man or a woman.

"This is a strict house," said my compatriot. "Someone is always being whipped down there. You, on the other hand, you don't carry yourself like someone who is afraid of the flagellum."

"I've had a few beatings," I said, though I was almost embarrassed to admit how few.

"My master has been to your house," he said. "I saw you once, in the distance. My master is the tragic poet, Seneca. He once wrote, *Divitae bonum non sunt.*" Which I could interpret now as something like, "Material things aren't the one good thing in life."

He saw me before? It must have been at the symposium then, the day I first laid eyes on Gaius Petronius Arbiter. "If you need to speak our language," he said, "find a pretext to send a message to the house of Seneca, or look for me when my master visits yours … I think he plans to come on the Kalends, for a poetry reading. My name is Viridian. Well, my real name is …" And he spoke a name in my native tongue.

I wasn't interested. I wanted my past walled off. I was subsisting in a strange half-world, learning every day, as a baby learns. I did not want to be shackled by the past when I was already chained up in the present. I tried to brush off this conversation and asked him where I could relieve myself.

"They are strict in this house," Viridian said. "There is an amphora down the hall to the left, on this side of the peristyle. This house does its own laundry, so they need to collect every drop of piss they can. Ten lashes if you go in the bushes."

"They beat other people's slaves?"

"No master is going to quibble about ten," he said.

He pointed the way and whispered something to the guard, who motioned me through. But, as seemed to always happen to me when I went for a piss in an unfamiliar mansion, I made a wrong turn, and I found myself standing in a doorway.

What I saw was so strange I could not look away. I was looking into a triclinium, but it was far grander than the one in Petronius's house. Indeed, where I was standing was a black marble pedestal in the shape of a Corinthian column, on which was perched a more-than-life-sized bust of the Emperor. I knew him from the coins. On the aureus, the portrait was particularly clear.

No one could see me, in the shadow of a column. But I saw —

First, a lectus had been laid out in the center of the room. Around it, guests on couches, decked out in fine fabrics and glittering baubles, had abandoned their dinner to stare at the couch. I recognized the Lady Poppaea, and Marcus Salvius Otho and even my friend, Marcus Vinicius ... and everyone else must have been just as lofty as those patricians. A rhythmic music on drums, double-flutes and finger cymbals was rousing the guests to fever pitch as they observed the goings-on.

A woman in a *tunica recta* — dressed as a bride, that is — crouched on her hands and knees. The *zona,* which should have symbolized virginity in such wedding garments, was not double-knotted but loosened, and the back of her tunica was hitched up, exposing her buttocks. Rearing above her was a sweat-drenched, bearded man wearing a golden wreath and nothing else, and he was pumping away at the woman's posterior as the guests chanting *Feliciter! Feliciter!* and quaffed wine from oversized cups.

The woman was shrieking and moaning in a what was almost a parody of erotic exaltation. The guests were cheering and calling out the groom's name now: *Pythagoras! Pythagoras!*

As I stared, the exhibition mounted to a climax and the bride was clawing at the air — and then, a lusty scream escaped her throat and a spasm shook her — and then her wig flew into the air and right onto my face!

Panicking, I looked up. As the wig slid down to the floor, the bride looked straight at me. We saw each other clearly. And, as I looked away — looked at *anything* rather than the egregious spectacle in front of me — my gaze fell on the bust I stood next, and I realized who that woman was.

And the woman cried out: "Lo! The God Hymen himself comes down from heaven to bless this sacrament!"

At that moment, there was a hand on my shoulder. I was about to scream, but another hand closed my mouth and yanked me away. It was Viridian.

He marched me down the peristyle. I said, "But I haven't pissed yet — and I'm about to burst!"

"Too late. Your master sent for you."

And there he was, Gaius Petronius Arbiter. In a splendid toga and wreath, displaying not the slightest dishevelment. He was furious. I had barely registered his expression of rage when I felt the sting of his slap on my cheek. "Domine!" I cried out.

I knew I deserved the slap, and much more. For a slave is property; when a slave misbehaves, it's the owner who looks the fool.

But Petronius's anger dissipated quickly. "I tire of the banquet, and I have slipped away," he said. "There are at least twenty more courses … post-coital sweetmeats, I suppose. They will all be in a stupor by dawn; no one will miss me. Carry this."

He threw a bag at me. It was small, but heavy. I didn't doubt that whatever it contained must be solid gold. I peeked in the bag and it appeared to be a gold statuette of the God Hymen — such irony!

Petronius pushed me toward the door, stopping for a moment to pick up his dagger from the attendant.

***

"Master —" I began, as the litter began to move bumpily downhill, led by a link-boy with a torch.

"I was going to tell you the gossip," Petronius said, "but it looks like you've seen it for yourself. And lived it, as well!"

"Domine," I said, "I was only trying to find the pee-bucket for the house laundry."

"And I suppose you're going to go all over my nice litter now," Petronius said.

"Domine —" I braced for another slap.

"My slaves piss and shit where they please, it seems." He called out to the head bearer. "Toilet break!" The litter came to a stop at a steep angle. My master parted the curtain slightly and said, "Do your business, boy."

I lifted my tunica and urinated into the night … splash, trickle, plink, straight into the gutter … the only sound on the Palatine, in the deep darkness.

"A ritual asperging from the God of Marriage himself!" Petronius said. "Shall I quote Catullus? *Hymen O Hymenaee, Hymen ades O Hymenaee!"*

"You mock me, my Lord." I put my mentula back in my tunica. We moved off. "And yet, I would really love to know —"

"I'm sure you would!"

"The bride tonight — was that really the Emperor?"

"The gods may assume any form," said my master. I did not realize he was joking. So he laughed heartily, slapping me on the shoulder a few times. His humor was infectious and I laughed too.

Then he stopped, and I stopped, too. I could sense his eyes on me in the dark.

"My Giton," he said. "You will speak of this to no one. *On pain of death!* Did the Emperor get a good look at your face?"

"I … think so, domine."

"Then you are doomed," said Gaius Petronius Arbiter.

XIV

DORMOUSE

Doom, however, was not imminent.

In fact, the next day was much like any other, a routine day. As were several days to follow. Days of learning how to comport myself, how to modulate my voice to land precisely the spoken tones that Roman aristocrats found delicate and seductive, of learning which wines went with which foods, of tasting for the first time strange sea creatures, and desserts cooled with mountain snow.

Days of becoming more proficient in the languages of the world into which I had been thrust. Of the subtleties of Greek, whose different genres of literature are written in distinct dialects.

Nights I often fell asleep in the bed of my master, not realizing in my innocence that it was a presumptuous overreach for a slave to do so without being commanded. But it was only because, drunk on Greek poetry and wine, I did not have the strength to crawl back to the tiny cell I shared with Hylas and Hyacinth.

To tell the truth, sleeping with Hylas and Hyacinth was not as bad as it seemed it would be, the first night I was there. Hylas, who was not very verbal in *any* language, was a boy who endured life rather than living it. Hyacinth, on the other hand, always wanted to talk.

Late at night, he often waited up for me.

One night, with Hylas snoring very loudly, he said, "I'd like to go speak to our gods. Will you come?"

I said, "They won't listen."

"They *have* to, Sporus. I've grown a whole digitus just in the time you've been here. I need help."

We stole into the atrium in the moonlight wearing only subligacula, for the night was warm. Slaves should not really be seen unless called for, but tonight was not a party night and there was no one there. It was a simple garden, with an archaic herm at one end mounted on a column, and a statue of Cupid ... a real antique, for the paint had worn almost completely white, and the youth stood stiffly, in an angular way, not like the smooth natural curves of a modern statue.

"Which will it be?" I whispered. "The battered herm or the weathered God of Love?" For neither of those gods was worshipped in our villages. Rather it was trees, rocks, and streams ... nothing that looked human.

But gods, everywhere in the world, are alike in one thing. If you're going to bargain with them, you have to pay in pain. If not your own, then some other creature's.

Hyacinth, of course, didn't have power over other creatures, in order to make them suffer on his behalf. I thought he would do something symbolic, like hack off a hank of hair, or cut himself and drip some blood onto the hungry earth. Instead, he pulled a dormouse from his pouch.

It was fat, having already spent the last month running around aimlessly in its fattening jar.

"The master will have your hide," I said, whistling. "Cook's been fattening them up for the Emperor."

"I'm desperate," he said. The moon lit up his pale features. Sweat clung to his face ... or were they tears?

He held up the dormouse in clasped hands. He said, "Moon, you see everything that happens in the night. Murder, stealth, thievery, sickness, death ... and love. They call me Hyacinth here, but I have a secret name too, which I will only utter in your presence." He then whispered something. That was the custom in our village, too, keeping one's true name secret.

Hyacinth then said, "I beg you, by the sacred moonlight that bathes me, do not let me grow another digitus. Don't let my voice drop to the bark of a grown man. Keep me on the cusp of manhood. Or I'll have nothing left. I'll end up in the fields, or in the mines, or chained to an oar."

"Don't be ridiculous," I mumbled. "Our master's not like that."

"Yes, but he's walking a fine line," Hyacinth grated. "This game of simultaneously flattering and ridiculing the Emperor ... he's going to make a false step, and we'll all be on the auction block." He held up the dormouse and, putting both hands around its fat neck, prepared to throttle it. "I offer you the life of this dormouse," he said, "in exchange for your favor."

But this drama was to no avail. The creature squirmed and slipped from Hyacinth's grasp. It ran into the grass and Hyacinth got down on his hands and knees to catch it, but it scampered away. "Help me grab it!" he said. But for a moment the sight of this desperate boy pursuing a rodent in the grass, in the moonlight, in only a loincloth, was outlandishly comical. I almost laughed, but I caught myself in time.

In a moment, I was on the ground too, scrabbling after this surprisingly nimble dormouse. My loincloth snagged on the pedestal of the herm. Somehow Hyacinth's, too, had got lost in the grass. I knew we'd never escape the whip no matter what and it was in desperation that drove us ... "Fuck you. You *made* me lose the mouse," Hyacinth said, and punched me. I punched back. In moments we were wrestling. And then we *were* laughing. And weeping. The absurdity. The life-and-death ridiculousness of our situation. But suddenly —

"Look! Let go! There it is!"

I pointed. The dormouse had reached the edge of the atrium. It was about to spring up onto the walkway. Hyacinth stretched out his hand and dived for it.

Instead, the dormouse ran right into someone else's hands. We both looked up. Hylas held a flaming torch above us, and kneeling on the ground, having deftly caught the mouse, was Croesus, who, holding it gingerly by the tail, dropped it back into its fattening-jar.

"Downstairs, this very second," he said. I had never heard so much menace uttered so softly. "Both of you. Don't forget to gather up your undergarments. Sporus, your subligaculum is wrapped around the herm." I was close to pissing myself. "Hylas, bring a whip. A real one."

***

We stood in Croesus's chamber. We had not even had time to get dressed. Croesus had in his hand not one of the rods he used for administering light punishments, but something that could rip off skin with a single swipe.

In one corner, Hylas was still holding the torch. He wasn't even in trouble, but he was shaking.

"I'm in a very awkward position," Croesus said. "Stealing from the master is bad enough, but these mice were being fattened for Himself the Divinity, who likes to show up at the most inconvenient of times. Theoretically, this isn't just a flogging. You ought to be crucified."

The punishment seemed so extreme as to be unimaginable. My mind went blank, because it was better not to think at all than to contemplate that kind of death.

"Kill me if you like," Hyacinth said tonelessly. "I haven't got a life left anyway. But don't hurt Sporus. He was just keeping me company. And the dominus likes him. *Loves* him."

"The dominus," said Croesus, "had a favorite vase once. It was an original by Polygnotos, not a copy. It showed a beautiful young man making love to an Athenian hetaira. It was four hundred years old. It was the most beautiful thing in this house. The dominus *loved* it. Just as he loves you, Sporus. This did not prevent the master from smashing it to bits one evening in a fit of rage. The next day, he wept over it. But the vase was still smashed. You, Sporus, are beautiful, but it is not the eternal beauty of an ancient Greek vase."

And now, I was truly terrified. I said, "Croesus, I am innocent and if I die from this, it will be a misfortune but, as you say, soon forgotten. But Hyacinth ... he stole the dormouse because he wanted to make a worthy sacrifice to our moon-god ... because he was afraid of losing his looks, afraid of no longer being able to please Petronius. Honestly, his motives were pure. Just one rodent in exchange for being able to give another year or two of pleasure to this household. Surely he should not die for loving his master too much!"

Croesus studied me for a long time. He fiddled with the whip. I have said that I almost pissed myself. I am ashamed to say that in that moment, I actually did.

And Croesus began laughing. "You came up with that entire argument?" he said. "Not even in your native language? You could be a Cicero come back from the dead, if you could only conjugate a few more verbs properly! Wait till I tell the dominus!"

"You're not *going* to tell the dominus," I said. "Remember? Or else ... him and me ... *crucifixi!"*

It is to this incident, perhaps, that I owe my reputation for being able to talk my way out of things.

***

And yet, here you are. You didn't talk your way out of this.

No, I did not. How much longer until my farewell performance?

Still time to tell more dirty secrets. But don't speak of slaves; it's vulgar. Speak of Emperors and Gods.

But you're a slave yourself.

Yes. I want to know of other worlds, other strata of our world. I want to dream. I want fantasies.

Is that why you work in the Circus?

I work here because my master is Editor of these games. How would I get to choose where I work?

But you *can* choose your dreams.

Yes.

***

It was now extremely late, close to the time of *gallicinium.* Soon it would be light. I stood there, my legs wet from my terror. Hyacinth was frozen like a statue, and Croesus was still laughing. Eventually, Hylas laughed too, though whether it was because he saw the humor, or because he thought he would be promoted to chief delicatus, I am not certain.

"Assuming that this does not go beyond this room," Croesus said at last, "what is it, Hyacinth, that you want?"

"I want to be castrated," he said.

I gasped.

"Sporus, wipe yourself off. What a waste of perfectly good piss. We have a lot of laundry in this house!" I nodded, looked for a cloth. "Now, Hyacinth, why on Earth would you want that? You might not even survive the operation. And this is Rome, you know. We're not in some barbaric oriental kingdom like Parthia. We don't just keep eunuchs around just for the fun of it."

"I want to prolong ... what I am. If I lose it, I'll just end up scrubbing toilets. Or worse."

"There is nothing sadder than an ageing eunuch," Croesus said.

"I'll die young," he said.

At that moment, there was commotion upstairs. One of the women came rushing down the stairs. "Alert!" she cried. "The Emperor! No more than half an hour. A runner came to warn us."

"By the Gods! He must not have slept yet," Croesus said. "Hyacinth, Hylas, get washed and perfumed. The girls will take longer, so rouse a few *now.* The new one from Nubia. He likes a touch of ebony. And a German. You, Hyacinth," he said, glaring, "are fortunate we caught that dormouse."

The boys went off to get ready. I hadn't received any orders so I followed Croesus into the anteroom, where the entire household was gathered. Croesus was barking orders as though he were running the military. Fresh garum from the cellar. The basting-honey for the mice. Slaves to stand in attendance in the hall. Fresh lamps in the triclinium. Tallow candles, braziers, torches set into brackets; it would almost be like daylight. But hadn't Croesus forgotten something?

"I had better wake the dominus," I said softly.

"No," Croesus said. "You had better not."

"But I'm the only one who can."

"Not this time, child," Croesus said. "I have received very

specific orders about what to do with you, should the Emperor make a surprise visit. You are not to show your face. You are not to make a sound. You are not even to breathe. On no account is Himself the Divinity to know that you even exist. Otherwise — let me make this clear — otherwise, it is *I* who will be whipped. To death."

XV

DIVINITAS

My curiosity has always been my bane.

Everyone has always presumed to control me by fear, but curiosity always gets the better of me; for what happened next I had only myself to blame.

I was not locked up in my cell. Croesus had not seen fit to chain me. I saw all the household slaves go upstairs, hastening to dust and burnish and polish in the minutes before the Emperor would arrive.

I sat on the floor pondering the imponderable: *Why?* Why was I doomed because Himself the Emperor had caught sight of me? Hadn't he mistaken me for the God Hymen? What had the Lady Poppaea Sabina called me — her secret weapon?

What could be the harm of observing from a distance?

It was foolish of me. In the past months I had been lulled into believing that my life was somehow charmed — despite my lowly condition. In spite of having barely escaped the lash on many occasions, it seems I couldn't help myself. And so, after giving a little time so that the entire household would being making their obeisance to the Emperor, finding myself completely alone in the slaves' quarters, I decided to slip up to the atrium, trusting that no one would notice me. Which they did not.

Himself the Divinity was holding court in the atrium, seated on a golden throne which he must have brought with him, and the entire household was in attendance — on their faces, on the ground. It was, as I have said, not yet dawn. Some slaves held torches aloft, but they were intended to illuminate personages of importance, not some sneaky child. I had emerged right behind the throne.

There was a large wooden chest, with the lid open, right behind the Emperor. I thought I could crouch behind it, but I heard soldiers' caligae somewhere behind and in a slight panic, I crawled into the box. A guard did walk past. And slammed the lid shut before he went on his way.

The smell inside the box was ... well, if could multiply tenfold the stench of cats about to mate ... but I was trapped. To my amazement, the chest I was trapped in had breathing holes, which afforded a perfect view of what was happening in the atrium. I was not too pleased to see what must have been the previous occupant of the box. It was like a cat, but bigger. Like a leopard, but more sleek. It had a collar with a silver chain which was being held by hands that I knew well ... the hands of the Lady Poppaea Sabina.

"It is called a cheetah," she was telling my master, all the while idly stroking the animal, which was alternately growling and baring its teeth. "Isn't it just darling! I rescued him from the Circus. So kind of Himself to let me keep it."

She and Petronius were sitting on either side of the Emperor, and although the entire household were present, my master and the Lady Poppaea were the only people aside from Himself who mattered.

Prostrating before the Emperor was not something one did automatically, but it had recently become the fashion to require it, at least for members of the lower classes. My tutor once told me that although Emperors are deified after they die, since Caligula, they've come to enjoy this kind of obsequy even before being officially declared Gods by the senate. It did seem to be overdoing it, and presently even the Emperor became a bit irritated at looking at a sea of backs. He said to Petronius, "They don't have to worship all the time, you know. We're en famille here."

"I'm sorry, Divinitas," said my dominus. "I rather thought you'd enjoy the novelty of having your inner godlike nature recognized outwardly."

"Ah," said Nero, "it's true that you alone of my friends appreciates me."

"Divinitas, we all do."

"When you say *we,* my dear Petronius," said the Emperor, "you assume that I have more than one friend."

"And do you not, Divinitas?"

"I'm your friend too," Poppaea said softly.

"Get rid of the attendants," said Nero. "Poppaea and I wish to speak to you of ... delicate matters."

Petronius clapped his hands. The slaves all left the atrium.

Now, as Himself was not in the throes of carnal congress, I managed to get a clearer view than last time. He was young, and did not have the jowls and chin he later acquired. I must say that he was at that time an attractive man, and not just because he possessed unlimited power. He also had a beautiful speaking voice, speaking Greek in a formal, archaic way, modulating the tones so that each utterance was like a melisma in an endless melody.

Those who now think him a monster will not admit it, but he had charisma.

"You plan to try out a new poem on me?" Petronius said, waving away the household.

"Later. Later. No, no, I want to discuss ... marriage."

"But Divinitas, you already have a wife ... not to mention a species of husband."

"Oh, Pythagoras ... that was just a whim, really. He knows it. He was just indulging me. Mad, really, that party at Tigellinus's. We were all drunk. I should divorce the man, really, but that would give too much validation to the wedding."

"Divinitas," Petronius said, "how is your Trojan Ode coming?"

"We won't rush the muse." Himself looked at Poppaea, waved a languid hand. "Poppaea ... state secrets."

The Lady Poppaea took the cheetah's leash. "I'll take a stroll and frighten the slaves a bit, then," she said.

When she was out of earshot, Himself said to my master, "I'm going to marry her, you know." He picked up a dormouse by the tail and started sucking the honey sauce, wiping his lips with a fold of his purple garment, which alone was worth the price of a modest mansion.

"Marriage? Is that your state secret, Divinitas?"

I saw the Emperor's face in the torchlight. What glittered in his eyes was a thing I could never possess — certainty. Which came with absolute power.

I could see that Petronius felt an obligation now to "fix" things. "That will be a scandal, Caesar," he said, "though as a God, you must know that Gods have a tendency not to mind scandals."

"Take care, Gaius." The menace was muted, but I could see my master adjust his thinking quickly. "You're my arbiter of taste, Petronius! Tell me this is not madness! I'm besotted, bewitched ... bewilderingly so. For as you know, I normally have perfect control of my emotions, and do nothing on a whim."

"Indeed not, Divinity," Petronius said. "You are quite rational, for a God. Though we mortals sometimes cannot perceive it ... that is our fault alone."

There he was, steering the ship of his wit so carefully between the Scylla of flattery and the Charybdis of condescension!

"But ... Divinity ... she *is* married. And more to the point, so are you, and the Lady Octavia is a direct link to the founder of this Julio-Claudian Dynasty ... dare I say it, more direct than your Divine Mother's." The Emperor's face clouded, but only briefly.

"I suppose I could have them killed," Nero said.

"As a God, you can do anything you like," said my dominus, "but ... the Lady Octavia is popular."

"I'll just send them away, then. Out of sight, out of mind."

"The Lady Poppaea is, indeed, beautiful. But she has already been your mistress for some time, has she not?"

"Oh, but she's more than that. Look at her, walking through the garden with that wild animal. It eats out of her hand! If anyone can tame me, and I am not willingly tamed ... it's her. She *must* become Empress."

"Then you will do whatever you think fit, Divinitas, to achieve that will. For you *are* Rome, and Rome always gets what she wants."

"Very well," said the Emperor. He gestured at the shadows.

I was getting more and more uncomfortable in the confined

space of this box, and I needed to get out soon — or I would be sharing the space with a vicious feline. I tried not to breathe. The Lady Poppaea's cheetah become excited suddenly, and practically dragged her toward the box. I could smell the animal's foul breath as he sniffed at the breathing hole. I'm sure he saw me as a meal. "Calm down, Hercules!" said the Lady Poppaea. "If you don't behave, I'll have to put you back in the box."

Luckily the animal listened to its mistress and, whimpering, returned to heel. "Your private business discussed?" she said to the Emperor ... and, I realized now, her lover.

"One other thing," the Emperor said. "You've recently acquired a most delightful puer delicatus, I hear. I want him."

My world fell apart. Petronius's house, if not Olympus, was as close to heaven as a slave could hope for in the real world. I may have gasped. No one noticed. Maybe they just thought it was one of the night-creatures in the garden.

"Of course, Divinity," Petronius said. "All I possess is yours."

He clapped his hands and Croesus appeared as if by magic. "Bring Hylas and Hyacinth," he said. The two boys emerged ... also as if by magic.

"Don't be afraid, boys," Petronius said. "The Emperor won't bite."

"Well," the Emperor chuckled, "not right now, at any rate."

Poppaea said, "He has been known to tie people up, dress up as a wild animal, and voraciously attack their genitals, after which they are dispatched by the Praetorian Guard."

The two boys looked horrified. There was, of course, no escape.

"Neither is the one I told you about, dearest," Lady Poppaea said. "They don't look a bit like me."

"Come forward." Anxiously, Nero got out of his throne and

approached them before they could approach him. He held up a torch himself, peering into their faces. "Not in the slightest," he said. "Be off with you."

The boys scampered away. Relieved, I am sure.

"I'm not making it up," said the Lady Poppaea.

"What are you hiding from me, Gaius Petronius Arbiter?" the Emperor said, stroking my master's cheek, as a cat toys with a mouse.

"Some of the boys have been sent on to Antium," he said. "We're taking the household there ahead of the heat and stench of summer."

The Emperor nodded. "Wise as always, Gaius," he said. "I'll come and collect him when we move the court. Though, to be honest, I might have completely forgotten the whole thing by then."

"The whims of the Gods are truly inscrutable, Divinitas," said Petronius.

"I will keep you guessing. Poppaea, come."

The Emperor called for his litter. But Poppaea tarried a moment. "I shall follow," she said. "I have a few secrets of my own to talk over with Petronius."

The Emperor left the atrium. All sorts of slaves, soldiers, a pair of bucina-players and a drummer, emerged from the shadows, and prepared to escort him back. Two burly Nubians carried out the throne. My master was alone with Poppaea and a cheetah.

Poppaea said to Petronius. "So, you've hidden him. It's a pity. I so wanted to have him as a little bit of spice in our ... nightly entertainments. Spice, you know, is what he craves the most, and the spicier the better. Having little Sporus on hand is the most convenient way for the beautiful and extremely feminine Poppaea Sabina to grow the occasional penis. But I'll come up with other diversions. Well done knowing we were on our way. Spies in the palace?"

My master did not answer.

"It doesn't matter," she said. "Octavia will be disposed of, and so will Otho. Without any fuss. No need to stoop to assassinations; just, as the Divinitas said ... out of sight, out of mind. But you'll do your part, of course. Your honeyed tongue can make black look like white, and you'll mollify any critics. You'll keep the politicians in line. And most importantly, the poets. They'll all follow your lead."

"I see."

"But I need you to promise to do your part. You'll be richly rewarded, I'm sure. Imagine, if you will, scenes from the Satyricon painted on the walls of Nero's new palace ... or Trimalchio's banquet immortalized as a comic drama!"

"My work is its own reward, Lady Poppaea, and I'm wealthy enough; apart from a predilection for late nights of drinking and whoring, I follow more the Stoic philosophy."

"Well ... we understand each other, I think ... as two snakes, circling the same mouse."

And they both laughed.

Poppaea said, "Oh! Hercules! You sweet little pussy-wussy, it's time for you to get back in your little boxie-woxie!"

I was doomed. I could smell the cheetah and now I could feel his paws on the lid. Which Poppaea opened. My life was over.

Poppaea and my dominus were looming above the box. I was an insignificant boy in a loincloth, shrinking away from a blow ... or a mauling.

"Antium!" Poppaea was cackling.

My master shrugged. "That is the most troublesome boy I have ever owned," he said. "I've half a mind to put you in with the cat and lock the chest."

"Beat me, domine," I said, "Beat me as hard as you want,

but don't give me away. I want to be part of your household forever. The pirates took away everything, my family, my whole world. You're my world now." I could feel hot tears spurting. "I love you, domine, I really do," I said. I put my arms around his knees and held him tight, trying to manipulate my grovelling so that my lips were hovering over just the right spot.

"This is rich," said the Lady Poppaea Sabina. "Don't beat him, he's far too amusing. And whatever you do, don't cut off his tongue. Though I imagine you already know that."

"Oh, I do," said Gaius Petronius Arbiter. Though in truth, he had never forced anything into my mouth that I had not accepted with willingness and gratitude.

"Keep him for now," Poppaea said. "You'll need a good wedding gift."

XVI

CLAUDIA OCTAVIA

So you staved off the Emperor's attentions for a while.

Not for ever, as is well known. But it is true that he was always easily distracted. I would not lay eyes on him again until my master took me to Antium, to escape the oppressive humidity of the Roman summer.

From one kind of humidity to a worse, I suppose!

You could say that.

And were you, in fact, the wedding gift for the Coronation of the Lady Poppaea?

Let me tell it at my own pace.

I will. Though I'm not the one with only a day to live.

***

Though we had managed to keep the Emperor's hands off me, at least for a while, the same could not be said for the plump and sweaty hands of Marcus Salvius Otho, which roved more aggressively with every visit. Fortunately, I was able to figure out how to drive him to such heights of lust that he would tire out quickly and fall into a deep sleep.

Each session with Otho would be followed by a less frenetic time with the Lady Poppaea, whose company I was beginning to enjoy, in a strange way. The one characteristic they shared, of course, was complete selfishness with regard to pleasure; I was there to facilitate their desires, not to fulfill any of my own; for what needs could a slave possibly have, except the need to eat, sleep, and avoid the lash?

But while Otho grabbed me and gripped me and groped me, groaning and moaning, I was just a thing to him, a thing that conveniently resembled his wife yet possessed the appendages he craved. The Lady Poppaea was different. Although she was equally inconsiderate to me when pleasuring herself, once she was satisfied, she talked to me, even confided in me.

She told me so much that I could have held her destiny in my hands, except that I knew a slave's word cannot be held true in a court of law without having been tortured to extract that word. The Romans used us for everything, even, in their way, loved us, but they feared us, too.

And one morning, after a night of such confidences, Poppaea announced she was taking me to visit someone. It pleased her to have me sit with her as she enjoyed some bread, wine, and olives, with Hercules the cheetah at her feet. Occasionally she would toss me an olive and have me catch it in my mouth. My hands were not free since it took all my strength to grip the chain that kept Hercules at heel. She would also toss the animal a hunk of flesh from time to time — a tidbit of mouse or a leftover peacock's brain. I was a pet animal, like Hercules, but could perform many more tricks.

I have to admit that Hercules was growing on me. He actually let him pet him and he would nuzzle up, rub up against my leg … once I was convinced he would not start nibbling or gnawing, I was content to let him, though he was a bit rank, as wild animals tend to be.

"Oh don't worry, Sporus," the Lady Poppaea said. "I've already sent word to your master and he has said you need not be home until supper. And you're so good with Hercules! I don't trust anyone else to hold his leash. You will relish this visit, I am sure. It's someone I talk about all the time."

"Who, domina?" I said.

"I'll tell you later."

"Why, domina, are we visiting this person?"

"To gloat."

***

Our destination was the Oppian Hill (I heard the litter-bearers chattering before we climbed on board — the lady, the cat, and me) and I had heard that the Emperor himself lived there, so I was apprehensive. When the Lady Poppaea saw, she patted me on the head. "I won't let the Big, Bad Emperor see you," she said. "Anyhow, where we are going, the Emperor would *never* set foot in a million years. We are about to visit one of the people he hates the most."

I could imagine Himself hating many people. I did not wish to speculate, and the journey to the Oppian was up and down and winding, so I tried to make myself small. We found ourselves at the side entrance of what appeared to be a sprawling estate. It was, indeed, the Imperial Palace … not the Golden House you know today, but still vast. I realized that the likelihood of bumping into Himself the Divinity was small indeed.

The Lady Poppaea's litter was waved through more than one gateway, the sentries all appearing to recognize it. Or perhaps they recognized Hercules, peering through the curtain with slightly bared teeth.

At length we reached a kind of anteroom and the Lady

Poppaea, the cheetah, and I stepped out of the litter. She motioned me to hover in the background. It was all I could to hold on to Hercules, as there were a few peacocks strutting about. In the room, slaves were scurrying about, throwing dresses into chests, packing up jewels and statuettes, all in great haste. Directing them was a stately woman with extremely tall hair, simply but expensively attired in silk.

She barely glanced at Poppaea, and not at all at the cheetah, let alone me. She merely moved quietly about the room, quietly commanding her slaves, who obeyed her swiftly and noiselessly.

Presently a slave brought the Lady Poppaea a jar of water. No wine. The other lady did not address us. It was a kind of game between her and Poppaea. Whoever acknowledged the other first would lose. I could see, however, that there was a great deal waiting to be said between them. The Lady Poppaea had brought me for a reason, not just to lead her pet on a leash. It seemed that she was too high and mighty to speak first. So, I approached the woman. The cheetah caused a bit of sensation and her slaves stifled screams as they tried to go about their business.

"Domina," I said.

"Impertinence!" said Lady Poppaea, slapping my face. At the exact same moment, the grand lady said, "Let him speak!"

I rubbed my cheek. If it was just for show, I wondered why she had to hit me quite so hard.

"I never realized you had a twin, Poppaea," said the Lady. "You should have dressed up that way. So … child … are you a true twin, or do you have a penis?"

"He has, for the time being, Octavia. How much longer, I do not know."

Octavia! This statuesque, very proper woman was no less than the Empress of Rome, the Lady Claudia Octavia.

I fell to the ground, almost losing my grip on Hercules's leash.

"Such nonsense. Get up, you snivelling brat. Your mistress has come to gloat. I know it. She won't have the pleasure. I will not speak to her."

"You needn't prostrate yourself to the Lady Claudia Octavia, you silly boy. She's in disgrace. Being sent off to exile on some remote island. Not sure which island, but it's *very* remote … and *small.* Smaller than this room, I would imagine."

"Let's take a look at you, you little freak of nature," Lady Octavia said, pulling me to my feet … the cheetah snarled. "Oh, Hercules, darling," said the Lady, who obviously knew the creature. "Let go the little boy." She called one of her women. "Lavinia, get one of the guards to come in and hold the leash for a while. One of those big hairy Germans. Or a pretty tall black one. One of each, better."

Two guards came in and took the cheetah off my hands. They stood at some distance, between two Corinthian columns.

"Tell the former Empress that I do not gloat … no more than one would expect. I'm not unnecessarily cruel. It's a fact that you have to be sent away, but it is no more than required by my ambitions. No, I'm not cruel. Selfish, yes. Not cruel."

The Lady Claudia Octavia did not look at the Lady Poppaea Sabina. Instead, she stared straight into my eyes. "Tell your mistress," she said, "that she is entering the demon's lair. No cheetahs … he is a creature far more monstrous. His enemies don't even dare say his name … rather, they take the numerological *gematria* to reduce NERON KAISAR to the number Six Hundred and Sixty-Six. People think that he imagines himself a God, even before the senate has deified him … but he *is* a God. To enter his presence is to be consumed alive. He is the God of Death. Only another God can mate with him and live."

"Tell the ex-Divinitas," Poppaea said to me, "that bloated fantasies about mythical beings can't hide the simple fact that she is simply too *boring* to be Empress."

"Kindly inform Her Incoming Imperial Majesty," said the Lady Octavia, "that I may be boring, but I am the who carries the bloodline of the Julio-Claudian Dynasty. Divorcing me delegitimizes his birthright. He may be worshipped now, but he won't be after he's dead."

"And what *is* there after he is dead? What does it matter?" Poppaea said, accidentally addressing the Lady Octavia in person and thus, as it were, losing the competition. Suddenly aware of this, she stopped herself. "We should leave," she said to me. "Go and get Hercules."

"I haven't finished," Octavia said, seizing my shoulders. "You tell that ... *whore* that I am the one loved by the Roman rabble. The people look at me and see past doddering Claudius, past twisted Caligula, past that dull pervert Tiberius, and they see in my eyes Germanicus, the beloved, Augustus, the moral, and Julius Caesar, who left three hundred sesterces to every plebeian in his will. Divorcing me also divorces him from the right to be Emperor. The mob loves *me*. And without the mob, where is power? So, Nero is bundling me off in secret. Not to some island, as she insists, but to Campania. Doubtless she'll whisper in his ear and I'll end up on an island. Or I'll be killed. But the people's love for me won't be killed as easily. Nor their hatred for *you*," she added, finally turning to stab her finger in Poppaea's face.

The two of them stood like that, two frozen Furies, personifications of sheer rage.

Then, suddenly, they both started laughing.

"Enough drama," said the Lady Octavia. "Have a drink.

I'm not long for this world ... and neither are you, Poppaea. I don't really envy you."

"Well it will have been glorious while it lasted. And maybe I'll be tough to kill. Like Nero's mother. How many tries did it take? Tsk-tsk!"

"He rigged her ship to collapse and drown her, and she managed to swim ashore," Octavia said, laughing.

"And installing a machine in her ceiling to drop tiles on her while she slept!"

"And poisoning her *three* times, only she guessed in advance and swallowed an antidote first...."

"Finally, faking her suicide."

I wondered why an Emperor needed to go to such lengths to kill someone, even his own mother. Later I would learn far more than I ever needed to know, about the labyrinthine love-hate between mother and son, and from his own lips.

"All right," Octavia said at last. "It's a sad thing we're not still children. Do you remember ..."

"Stealing the old tutors' tunicae from the bathhouse? Seeing them run howling down the street?" Poppaea giggled.

"Pouring the pepper in Nero's dormice! Ah! That slave got whipped to death for our prank," Octavia said, cackling. "I've had a good run. And now, I'm off to obscurity, stale bread, and the loom."

"It's a pity."

"I forgive you," said the Lady Octavia. "That's what you want, isn't it?"

***

On the journey back to our side of the hill, I asked the Lady Poppaea if the Lady Octavia was her friend.

She said, "Childhood is a magic time."

I said, "You won't need me any more. Whatever it is you

were planning to get the Emperor, it worked."

"That's true, Sporus," she said. "While we were whiling away the morning at the Oppian Hill, Otho will already have packed. He is being made governor of Lusitania."

"Where's that?"

"Somewhere, you know, with wild tribes, warriors rubbing themselves with bear fat. The Celts are quite into buggery; Diodorus wrote that their warriors lie on the skins of animals, with 'a catamite on either side.' He'll be in heaven, the poor dear."

"So will his wife," I said softly.

"I shall be a goddess. There it is. It's a pity about Octavia, but goddesses need sacrifices."

It would be some time before I laid eyes on the Lady Claudia Octavia once more. And it would be in the form of a decapitated head, delivered to the Empress Poppaea in a golden casket.

XVII

HYACINTH

When I arrived, I was certain I would finally get that whipping I had avoided all these months. I had been all over the city, from Poppaea's villa to the apartments of the Empress herself, and after witnessing that altercation, all was not over, for Poppaea was not about to drop me off on her way back; Romans do not cater to the convenience of slaves, even those they are fond of.

At the home of Marcus Salvius Otho, it seemed that Poppaea's soon-to-be ex-husband had not yet departed. He was packing up everything that was not nailed down. Greek vases, statues, even the household lares and penates were being bundled into carts.

"You can't take those," Lady Poppaea was shrieking as she stepped from the litter. "Who will protect us?" She started slapping one of the slaves who was carrying a bulky statue.

The confused boy dropped the statue and it cracked. Poppaea screamed and a steward hustled the unfortunate lad off for a whipping. His screams punctuated the ensuing conversation.

They would not move the carts out of the city until nightfall, now, thanks to the legal provision against wheeled traffic during daylight.

Otho looked at me, his eyes beady with concupiscence. "One final sojourn in my wife's pretty little forest," he said.

"He's not your wife, you bastard," Poppaea said.

But Otho ripped my tunic and violated me right in the vestibule. I was screaming, the whipped boy was screaming from another room, and Poppaea was screaming, while Otho mercilessly had at me. He climaxed very quickly, then flung me to the floor like old laundry. I lay there whimpering while husband and wife quarrelled.

"I don't see why you're complaining," Poppaea was saying. "Lusitania's an excellent posting."

"It's practically Britannia," Otho said, "and I don't like garum."

"You'll learn to. By the time you get home, you'll have fish sauce running in your veins," Poppaea sniggered.

"Bitch!"

"Look who's talking," Poppaea. "You practically ripped that boy a new arsehole. And his old one won't be any use for days."

It is easy to forget that, however generous and compassionate and loving they are when they've a mind to it, they still don't think of you as a human being. I was sobbing on the cold stone floor, and no one cared.

"Remember, Poppaea darling, that the higher you rise, the more hideous your fall will be. And if the likes of you can become an Empress, then *I* could be an Emperor one day — and when I do, I'll have you in the arena, being raped to death by wolves."

"Oh, you do so terrify me, you spineless little *cinaedus.*"

"You dare call me that! You know I always take the active role in intercourse."

"You've never taken *any* role, to my knowledge," Poppaea said. "At least not with me."

He slapped her face.

"Bold, aren't you? You forget I'm the Empress."

"Not quite."

"And I won't forget how you brazenly speculated about becoming Emperor yourself! That, my darling, is treason. You could be thrown off the Tarpeian Rock for that, and you know I have the Emperor's ear."

"You do not! You only have his cock!"

"That is all one needs," said the Lady Poppaea Sabina, smiling sweetly. And finally saw me, weeping on the marble. "Don't be tiresome, Sporus," she said to me, pulling me to my feet.

"I'm in pain, domina."

"There, there." She clapped her hands and her steward appeared from behind a curtain. "Send the boy home, will you? And give him a tip. A *big* tip. I've really worn him out today, not to mention he'll probably catch a dose of the strap when he Petronius finds out he's almost a day late."

The steward bowed and led me out. I could still hear the soon-to-be-divorced couple shrieking at each other when I reached the front door. I was soon alone in the Lady Poppaea's private litter with the curtains drawn, with a heavy pouch of silver denarii to count.

The words of Marcus Salvius Otho were prophetic, were they not? For he did *become Emperor. For a day or two at least.*

Yes, and even such as I became Empress, too, *twice!* — so

you could say I was twice the goddess Poppaea ever was. And my violent death will be witnessed by more than twice as many people as Poppaea's ignominious end.

What a distinction!

Quiet.

Hear that menacing sound, like a cat's purr, only deeper, hungrier? They're delivering some fresh lions.

Haven't they run out of Christians yet?

Fresh batch.

Let's go and visit. Come on. I'm not exactly going to run away, not with my feet shackled like this.

***

I had resigned myself to more pain when I finally crossed the limen of my master's house. Though it was still daylight, there was a pall. Slaves looked at me and looked away. I saw Croesus go by and he did not even see me. I saw my master in the atrium and went to prostrate myself.

"Domine," I knelt at his feet, trying to frame an excuse for why I was so late getting home. "Domine, the Lady Poppaea made me go with her to gloat at the Empress on her way to exile."

Petronius did not seem at all interested. "Go to the slaves' quarters," he told me. "They'll tell you all about it. Leave me alone."

I slunk away and went down to the basement. Outside my cell, there were many members of the household gathered. I pushed through to the open door and saw Hyacinth on his pallet. His lower body was drenched in blood. A thin sheet covered his loins but it was dripping. Hyacinth was shaking and losing blood and I knew he was going to die.

I immediately realized what had happened.

Croesus came now, and the others fell back a little. I turned on him. "You let him have it done!" I was angry and I didn't care if he knew. "You didn't care about risking his life!"

"Sporus," Hyacinth said, so softly I had to strain to hear, "I used my peculium."

The other slaves were murmuring about how no one knew, how Hyacinth had sneaked away in the middle of the night and gone to some street surgeon who worked on slaves and criminals. I lay down next to Hyacinth and tried to warm him. Warm, sticky blood seeped into my tunica.

"By the time we knew," Croesus said, "he had already lost so much blood…."

"What about a doctor?" I said.

"I sent Hylas to fetch one."

"Some butcher from the market?"

Croesus said, "No, no. The best the household budget will stretch to. I haven't dared to ask the dominus for more because the boy did this on his own initiative. Meaning he damaged the master's property."

"What, he'll punish him for injuring himself?"

"No … no … he'll punish *us* for breaking something so precious."

Again, for me alone to hear, Hyacinth said, "Send me to our gods, Sporus. I don't want to rot in a Roman cave. I want to go whole to my Skyfather." He used a name for the chieftain of the gods that I had not heard since the village. When I heard that name, the tears started to come, and I couldn't stop them.

I ran from the room to seek out Petronius. I found him burning incense by the herm in the atrium garden. "Domine, domine," I said, "can't we do something?"

"Did Croesus not summon a doctor?"

"He has, but not a *proper* one." I knelt at his feet once more, just as I had when I begged him not to send me away. I clasped his waist, I buried my face in his groin. "We have to save him," I said.

"Come," he said. "This time your pretty head against my manhood is not going to work. This is Ananke … it is fate, my Giton."

He raised me to my feet and kissed me gently on the forehead.

"I did not want to see him at first. I keep no broken vases in my house, no shattered statues … some do, because they are old things found in Greece and redolent with ancient magic … I don't like to look at things that cannot be fixed. But your tears move me, Sporus."

The dominus and I went down to the slaves' quarters. It was clear that Petronius did not know his way down there in the basement, even though it was his own house. The odor disturbed him, too, though he did not mention it. I led him by the hand to my cell; he had not bothered to know where I slept, when I was not sleeping in his room.

When Petronius entered, the slaves, unbidden, knelt; even Hyacinth struggled to perform an obeisance, but the effort was too much for him and he slumped back. I rushed to his side. But he was already breathing his last.

"He loved you, domine," I said, not hiding my anger. "He did this to himself so you wouldn't throw him away." I glared at my master, heedless of any chastisement, while the other slaves shrank back, appalled at my audacity.

Then I knelt next to the cement bed and kissed Hyacinth on the lips, with that act drawing away his soul and setting him free.

Gaius Petronius Arbiter did not order me whipped. In fact, he said nothing at all, at first. And then, softly, so I was the only one who heard, "What right did he have to love me? No freeborn ever loved me enough to die for me."

And he turned abruptly and began to walk away.

At that moment, Hylas arrived with the doctor. He looked at me, and he looked at Hyacinth, and he knew. The doctor, seeing the dominus, bowed deeply and scurried away.

"I'll send for the libitinarius," Croesus said, but the dominus wasn't even listening.

"What's that?" I whispered.

"The undertaker. It costs sixty sesterces to dispose of a dead slave."

"But he told me wants a real funeral. He wants to go back to the Skyfather. With no pieces missing."

"Sporus, don't offend the master. In his way he is grieving. But you know how he is. He won't look at a broken vase."

I didn't care. I caught up with the dominus by the stairs. "Ah, Sporus," he said. "Don't you dare do anything like that."

"I wouldn't dream of it, domine."

"This unpleasantness … it fouls the air. I will have to bring in a priest for a purification ceremony. The house will reek of incense and oils. I think I shall pack up early for the summer. Cheer up, my Giton. You will love Antium. The breezes, the gentle sun … you can swim in the sea. Your lovely skin will turn to bronze. Come to bed, Sporus. I don't want to wrestle with any of my women tonight. I want to hold you like a doll."

I knelt again, not caring if I offended. "Domine! Hyacinth asked me to ensure him a proper burial."

"Very well, then," Petronius said abstractedly. "We'll have the libitinarius stash him in the family columbarium. I never go there. It's somewhat distant from the city walls but I'll tip him extra."

"Master, he asked me to send him to *his* gods." Frustrated, I pulled out the huge pouch of silver that the Lady Poppaea's steward had given me. "Please, domine. The lady paid me well, because she took me with her to gloat over Claudia Octavia, and then her husband was very rough with me on his way out the door. I can pay for the funeral."

Petronius looked at the pouch. Took it, hefted it, then loosened the string. He saw it was mostly silver, with even the glint of an aureus or two ... not one orichalcum in the whole bag.

"You would do this for him?"

And I heard the unspoken question: *But what would you do for me?*

"Don't you realize what a big piece of your freedom this is?" he said.

"I'm not an accountant. I'm just your puer delicatus."

"All right then," he said. "See to it."

He kept the money.

It was an important lesson. Hyacinth and I were like statues and vases. We were not people. Petronius loved me, indulged me ... but he still owned me. And on some level, because he owned every inch of me, because he had the right to do anything he wanted to any part of me ... he also feared me. Because the love of a thing you own is not the love a human being feels. It is a love whose roots are in fear. And fear always begets fear.

It was in that moment that I swore to myself: *I will be free.*

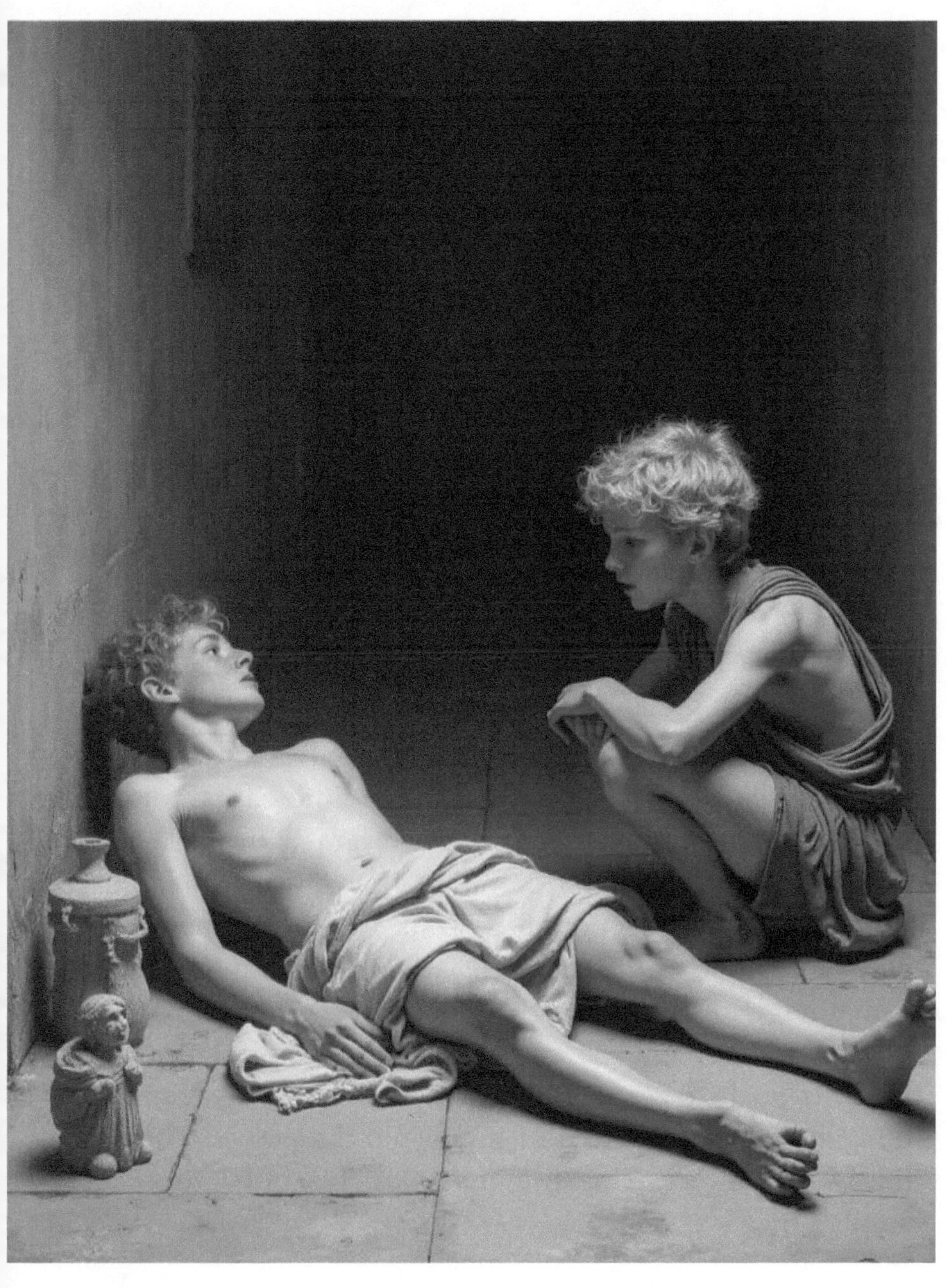

XVIII

ANTIUM

To speak of Antium is to speak of heaven, I suppose. Antium, Elysium on Earth, playground of the wealthy. And from Petronius's villa it was only a few steps to the sea. The villa stood a little way off from the gargantuan Villa Neronis, separated by a wall of rock, and with its own little cove. The harbor itself, hidden from our view by a bend in the shoreline, was close enough to walk to. The air was clear ... there were none of the foul smells that rise from the Aventine in summer and suffocate the city and spread pestilence.

Petronius loved to be surrounded by beautiful things and this was such a place. But I was mourning Hyacinth, so I didn't run along the sand or jump into the waves. The others did. I sat on a rock. The strangeness of Hyacinth's funeral still haunted me.

***

Why, what are funerals like in your country? Are they very exotic? Slave girls sacrificed on a burning boat? A well-loved puppy buried alive in the dead one's arms? Brains removed through the nostrils and stored in a jar?

Exotic? Not to me.

You never even told me the name of your country.

It is far from Rome. And I don't want to think of it. Thinking about it when we said goodbye to Hyacinth was painful ... though it was three emperors ago ... it hurts more than anything else.

I am from Bithynia.

Never heard of it.

***

My dominus had said, "It's to your credit that you would delay your own freedom to give your friend the rites he would have wished for. I could simply pay it myself, as a favor to a much loved slave, but then I would not be granting your desire the dignitas it deserves. But I have only two conditions. First, no matter what your native customs are, I don't want you chopping off your hair or wandering around glumly. If you have to do the Greek thing with the rending of garments and the shrieking and wailing, keep it discreet and put on some makeup if I have guests. Also, we don't keep dead bodies in the house overnight, so anything you do, have Croesus first arrange for the libitinarius to take away and store the body elsewhere."

In the village where I lived, dead people stayed in the home for many days; we talked to them, made much of them, sat beside them and told them stories ... making sure that old wrongs were righted ... before an old man who spoke for our Skyfather came to take us to some hilltop, open to the embrace of heaven. After the burning, we scatter the ashes from the highest point in the vicinity.

But I did not say goodbye properly, because the Romans were anxious to purify the house. And Rome is a hilly place, but there are no hilltops open to the sky, for the best hilltops have palaces and mansions on them. It was difficult to find anyone of our people who knew the ways, or could speak the words as our village shaman might have done.

One person who helped me was Marcus Vinicius. He even found the woman called Spider for me; she was working at a lupanar, not as a prostitute, of course, for she was long past the age of marketing her womanhood; she was the one who collected the guests' money and exchanged it for spintriae, little bronze tokens with depictions of various sex acts on the obverse. Useful to show the whores what was to be expected, since often they did not even speak Latin.

"It's dull enough work," she said, "and the girls are a sorry lot. The boys aren't much better. Your friend must have imagined that life, and felt it was worth the risk to do what he did."

Hyacinth lay in the cart, packed in snow and ice — the ice was what had used up almost all of Lady Poppaea's tip, as by the time it gets to Rome you've already lost half of it, and snow is a delicacy when honeyed spiced syrups are dribbled over it — But with the heat ... I knew Hyacinth would want to look beautiful until the last minute.

"We had best be going," Marcus said, as he had paid for only that evening of Spider's time. We were gathered in front of Petronius's front door, waiting for sunset so that we could leave the city by cart. Of the household, only Hylas came. Spider had found the right shaman ... he had been working as a doorman at one of the houses where they keep their doormen chained to the front post ... he had a fugitive brand on his forehead. He spoke no Latin or Greek, and had been much mistreated, as so often happens to those assumed to be idiots. But speaking to me in our own language, he was full of tales and he had spoken to the gods on many occasions; his words made me weep, even more than the spectacle of my dead friend packed in snow and ice in the glow of a Roman sunset.

Our sad processional moved slowly. The military escort was something Hyacinth would never have dreamed of when he was alive, but it was something Marcus's rank could command. Two hired link-boys with torches walked ahead. We passed the Circus Maximus, huge and gloomy. We moved through the slums in the Aventine and stopped at the Ostia Gate; we continued on foot to the designated high mountain....

But Mount Testaceus was not even a real hill, though it loomed up ahead as we walked in the moonlight. It had become a hill because this was where people had thrown their used amphorae for the last seven hundred years. It had plenty of vegetation, of course; trees' roots had worked their way through centuries of smashed wine-jugs. In the air hung the stale smell of old wine, laced with a whiff of human vomit. Our caligae crunched on the piles of potsherds.

I would be laying my friend to rest in a rubbish dump.

It was a bitter thing, more bitter because those who were in the position of being *domini* were trying so hard to give us room for our feelings. Each act of generosity came with an unconscious undertone of condescension, yet I had to take whatever I was given.

***

So there I was, in the glowing sunlight of Actium, my mind permeated with dark memories. I watched Hylas leaping up and down and wading near the shore. Petronius's women, too, were there, naked and of every hue, splashing each other and laughing.

In the distance I could see my master walking with the steward Croesus, deep in conversation. He stopped to look at the women, and at Hylas, and then at me. He summoned me with a crook of a finger and I went to him.

"Let me look at you," he said in a quizzical way.

"Domine," I said, "you speak as if you will never see me again."

"Oh," he said. "I will see you. But perhaps not in quite the same light as before."

It was a kind of inkling, then, of what the dominus was fond of quoting to me from the poet Virgil: *Tempus inreparabile fugit.* "What are you saying to me, domine?" I asked him. "Why not in the same light? Did I offend you in the matter of Hyacinth?"

"No, no, my Giton."

He put his arm around me and gently squeezed my bare back, which was already getting a little red from the sunlight. My skin's imperfection seemed to irk my dominus a little. But he drew me close and kissed me, very gently, on the lips, and again on the forehead, like a favorite child or puppy. My master always smelled of honey, with a subtle hint of frankincense. It was always comforting to fall asleep beside him.

"You should run along inside and have them put a poultice on that," he said. "I need you to look perfect tomorrow."

"Why, domine? Where are we going?"

"Look behind you. Looming over us on the hill."

I did. The sprawling Villa Neronis, the seaside residence of the Emperor, sat astride the precipice. "We are going to dinner tomorrow."

"Surely ... not me, master! You've told me I have to make myself scarce, and not let the Emperor see me."

"I'm afraid it's an imperial order. The Lady Poppaea Sabina has specifically requested you. No longer the Lady Poppaea Sabina, but the Augusta."

"A slave at a royal banquet, and not there to serve?"

"We are all slaves," Petronius said, "when it comes to Divinitas. But you shall help me; you will carry my scroll, and look pretty so people do not weary of just my voice droning on and on. For I am to give a private reading of the Trimalchio scene from the book I have been writing, the *Satyricon.* This scene describes the most overblown banquet in all of history ... yet my wildest imaginings will be as nothing compared to the feast we are going to be attending. Many would willingly die to see what we will see. So, this 'little something' at the Villa Neronis. It's an invitation that cannot be refused. It's a 'small affair with just a few friends.' That's what Himself has decided to call it. It's a wedding banquet."

"No, master, not that!"

"No, my delicatus, don't clasp my knees and beg again. I can't let you hide in a cat-box this time. I may not be able to do anything at all to prevent what will happen ... without risking ... *everything.*"

"You mustn't risk anything, master," I said. No, I thought, not for a favorite vase. Or would he smash it rather than give it away? For he *was* going to give me away. That *had* to be it.

Troubled, perhaps, my master turned to Croesus. "About the papers I asked to be drawn up, Croesus," he began ... and I could tell that I was being dismissed.

***

My mind was a blur as I walked back to my rock. After all, whose wedding could the Emperor be celebrating but his own wedding to the Lady Poppaea? Poppaea who had engineered the banishment of the Lady Claudia Octavia — a scion of the true blood of Augustus — and the dismissal of Lord Otho to rule some faraway province? And had Poppaea not demanded *me* as a wedding gift? Was this why my master was looking at me with such regret? Was I the favorite vase that must be given away? Or would he rather smash me to pieces than let someone else have me?

Would I now be another decoration in Lady Poppaea's home ... the home of an Empress? A woman with infinite power over the whole world, let alone my insignificant self?

"You. Come in this water," I heard Hylas call. "Warm. Good."

But I demurred, plunging instead into the ocean of memory ... thinking of Hyacinth, lying on the crude bier, surrounded by broken wine pots. I brushed away the last pieces of ice. There was no breeze to scatter the stench of vinegar and old puke.

Into his hands, I placed the small pouch that contained what he had had cut off. He had to be whole to go to the embrace of Skyfather. Hylas bent down to put a loaf of bread and some olives beside the body. "You eat good in sky," he said softly.

I placed next to his face the mirror fragment that Spider had once given me.

She looked oddly at me, as if to say, How could you give away my gift to you?

I said to her, "This piece of mirror showed me myself for the first time. But now, I don't think I need to see myself anymore. But Hyacinth ... he wanted to stay young and beautiful a little longer. Now it'll be forever. But me, I don't have a self that I yearn to see. I'm whatever other people see, nothing more. I am their mirror. I don't need to *have* a mirror anymore."

I stayed silent for the rest of the funeral. Hylas spoke a few words in broken Latin. The wise old man spoke a great deal, but his words were arcane, and though it was my mother tongue, the language seemed more and more alien to me. Even Spider spoke, warmly, like a mother.

When Hyacinth was consumed in the flames, I climbed the mountain of smashed pots to its highest point, to scatter the ashes at the sky, to make it easy for the gods to reach down and scoop him to their bosom.

But I still said nothing. It was not grief that prevented me from speaking, nor was it regret at the shortness of the time I had spent with him. It was anger. And envy. Hyacinth had gone somewhere where perhaps he could be happy. And he had left me behind.

And now, sitting in the golden sunset at the shore of Antium, even more unsure of my future than I was when a pirate captured and sold me ... now I felt the anger even more keenly. And the utter helplessness.

XIX

PRAEFECTUS

A little event, for a few close friends?"

***

I cannot wait for you to tell me of the party! What a spectacle it must have been! The extravagance! The decadence!

Did you ever read my master's book, *Satyricon?* It does not begin to describe what we saw. There must have been a thousand people at this little gathering, though, to be sure, a lot of them were there to serve: the cupbearers, each one more beautiful than Ganymede, the pageboy of the King of Heaven; the dancing girls, somersaulting over silver chargers piled with exotic roasted animals, the water-organ, the duelling orchestras from opposite sides of the hall ... the jugglers, the fire-eaters, and matched pairs of armed men fighting to the death, mostly ignored by the guests ... and in the center of it all, on a dais raised above the rest ... *Himself, the Divinitas, the Master of the World.* A Greek *kithara* in his arms, strumming now and then, while beautiful women and boys fed him the most delicate of morsels.

He wasn't this bloated lump you see on the last coins of the reign, you know. He was pretty; almost beautiful. No, beautiful is not too strong a word. The presentation ensured that. His radiance illuminated all the world, in the flickering of a thousand torches. The jowls, the scowl, they all came later.

It was then, perhaps, that the Emperor first laid eyes on you properly ... and you so seduced him with your siren wiles that eventually you became Empress?

Hardly that. If anyone was seduced, it was me. Not my Emperor, my God. For it takes a lot of hard work ... and a great deal of bad luck ... to win the love of a living God.

***

Reaching the Villa Neronis was easy, if strenuous; Petronius's own villa was tucked away in a cove, invisible from the royal enclave but actually easily accessible by steps cut into the cliff. It was too steep for a litter, but close enough on foot. Gaius Petronius brought a very small entourage; two slaves to hold the scroll of *Satyricon,* which was kept in a glazed amphora slung over their shoulders; me, to look pretty and adoring when the dominus read, and for some reason I could not yet fathom, Croesus.

When we entered the Villa Neronis, we had to pass through several colonnades, and to be looked over by impressive guards at each post. The uniforms became grander at each station. Finally we approached a throne room through a portico lined with the greatest art treasures stolen from the greatest fallen empires of the past, from Babylon to Egypt, and what seemed to be the complete statuary of a couple of plundered Greek temples.

And this was only the Emperor's *country* house.

Not the *Golden House* that was to come.

There were, as it were, several circles of guests, orbiting the Emperor, presumably the farther away being the less favored. The couch we were directed to was directly in front of Himself, in the inner circle. On the uppermost level were the Divinitas, the Lady Poppaea Sabina, with Hercules crouching at her feet, a sturdy-looking Nubian in the background holding onto his leash; there was Tigellinus, in whose house I had once been, and Pythagoras, who had once serviced the royal posterior in public, but was now relegated to standing behind the Divinitas with a tray of olives. I also saw Lucan, and was surprised he seemed to be enjoying higher favor than my master; though of course, he was younger and prettier.

We were to dine directly beneath the gaze of Himself the Divinity, meaning I would be seen at all times. And I was not naked, the normal garb of the puer delicatus. Petronius had made me wear a blindingly white tunic with a fresh, heady scent of urine, having just come from the laundry. Counteracting the fragrance of piss was the fact that my hair had been slathered with a pomatum composed of bear fat, laced with attar of roses.

When we arrived, a bevy of dark beauties from some far unconquered country were leaping and dancing to drums and choral singing in an exotic language full of clicks. Right in front of the Emperor, two hefty amazons were wrestling in a trough of mud. In the distance, an orchestra of bucinae and tubae squalled and screeched to the pounding of a tympanum.

As we took our seats, one woman warrior was having her neck broken, and the entire trough, with the other standing triumphant and sweaty, was carried off; the violent entertainment was replaced by a bard with a lyre. The bard sang a song by the immortal Sappho, one I had before in the house of Petronius:

As a mountain wind
Sweeps down upon an oak-tree
Love shook my heart

The haunting, antique melismata echoed in the hall and at once the shrieking brass and thudding percussion from the other end seemed to fade so that it sounded like a throbbing heartbeat. Still magical after six hundred years, the Aeolic cadences of the Lesbian poetess hung in the air, and gossip was silenced.

After the poetry, the actual nuptials were almost perfunctory. A priest came in, the Empress and Emperor recited the ritual formula:

Ubi tu Gaius, ibi ego Gaia …
Where thou art Gaius, I am Gaia.

There was general applause and cheering, but the feast could not have been interrupted for more than a few moments, for as soon as the applause ended, the bucinae blared and pies the size of chariot wheels were brought in; a chef at each table slashed them open and songbirds burst out of every one of them, filling the air with trilling melodies and, it must also be said, raining down droppings upon our heads. This was received with more applause … even the hapless guests who happened to have been shit upon took it all in good fun, though their laughter may have been laced with fear of the Emperor's displeasure.

"This wedding's nothing," a voice piped up from the next

table down, on the next circle beyond ours. "When I was posted to Judaea, now *those* people had weddings that lasted for days! People think of the Jews as crude barbarians, but they certainly knew how to have a good time, when they weren't revolting!"

Petronius and I looked over. It was an old man in a somewhat frayed toga. The entire table, in fact, was occupied by such old men, some in military uniform. My dominus said to me, "That man used to be the praefectus of Judaea, a very long time ago. I thought he was dead. I see that entire table is populated with several generations of generals. Look ... Galba ... Vitellius ... Vespasianus ... they're probably plotting a coup."

He waved at the man who had been speaking. "Didn't know you were still alive, Pilatus," he said.

"I've been living in retirement for thirty years," he said. "But I might make a comeback."

Petronius laughed, and whispered to me, "He was recalled in disgrace, but with a change of Emperors, disgrace became oblivion."

Pilatus turned away from us and continued to regale his companions. "They're constantly revolting," he said, "as Vespasianus here knows. And they have a folk belief that a king will arise and drive us away from the land, which, apparently, their God gave them. I had to crucify at least one of these messiahs every week! There was one my wife rather liked, although he gave her nightmares...."

I became aware that the Lady Poppaea was standing between our table and the praefectus's as he started to speak of a cannibalistic, blood-drinking sect he called *Chrestianoi.* "Totally godless," he was saying. "Won't even worship the Emperor! Can you imagine!"

At length the Lady Poppaea seemed to find the old men's

war stories tiresome, and turned to us.

Or, rather, to me. She looked at me, very pointedly, and Hercules was pulling at the Nubian's leash; the cheetah wanted me to pet him.

"I'm glad you came," she said to me. "Even though your favorite fat rapist is all the way in Lusitania."

"I could hardly not bring him," Petronius said. "An imperial invitation is a divine command."

To my alarm, I saw that Another was looking at me, too. Himself the Divinity, from his lofty vantage point, was scrutinizing me through a giant emerald held up to a squinting eye.

"Indeed," said the Lady Poppaea. "Oh! Petronius, too," she added, almost as an afterthought.

"My lady," he said.

"I see you've brought your wedding gift," she said to Petronius, "just as I requested."

I looked at my master in alarm. Was I going to be handed over right now, in front of a thousand people, gift-wrapped in my piss-pungent brand new tunic?

The Lady took my hand and pulled me up from the couch. "Shall I take him up to the Emperor now? I trust you've brought the deed of gift?" I looked past her to the Emperor. I could not help myself. He was truly the center of the universe.

Petronius waved Croesus over. He had a little scroll in his hand. Poppaea cackled. My heart sank.

"Divinity," said my master, bowing almost to the floor, "I do have a gift for Himself, one worthy of greatness. But I won't in fact be presenting him with this boy."

"You are reneging on your promise?"

"I did say I would give you my slave, Lady Poppaea. But Sporus is not my slave," he said, unrolling the scroll. "As you will see from this little document, the articles of manumission went into effect yesterday. Sporus is free."

I broke into tears. I fell prostrate and kissed my master's feet.

XX

LIBERTAS

I was shaken. And shaking, too, because when I got up off the floor, I was a different person … a different *species,* indeed, for I was no longer an object, but a human being. Yet I felt no different. At least, not in that moment.

An omelette with peacocks' brains and honey was being carried in, accompanied by another fanfare on brass and tympanum.

Poppaea Sabina had not ceased to look, rather, glare at me, and I could see she was already seeing this defeat as a temporary annoyance. She did not fly into a rage. What she said, however, was bone-chilling. "I am not my husband. He's a passionate creature, quick to have a tantrum and to cry afterwards about his friend he accidentally had beheaded in a fit of pique. I'm more of a … cold, slow, heartless, vengeance-minded kind of woman. So I will say only this to you, Petronius Arbiter: you know very well how this will end. Not immediately, because we are civilized people, by the Gods; we've managed to crawl our way into the Ninth Century since Romulus and Remus. We are Romans, cheerfully falling on our swords or slitting our wrists at the merest whisper of a stain to our honour. So, what are you really telling us, Petronius Arbiter? And is it worth it?"

"There is no guile. Sporus is a much-loved member of my household. I'm even letting him keep his peculium. I'll set him up in one of the hideous slum apartments I own in the suburra, or he'll just remain in my service and living in my household."

"And what will he do? What he did for me and Otho? Diminishing returns, you know. The older he gets, the cheaper."

"You're wrong, Divinity. And I only dare to contradict you because we've known each other so long. Sporus is coming along very nicely in languages, and if he ever loses his looks he could do well managing a library, interpreting for diplomats, negotiating with foreign merchants, and what have you. He's already as bright as Croesus."

"And as rich?" said the Lady Poppaea, making the usual joke about Croesus's name.

"One day, perhaps," my master said. "But it is his choice. He may go into the service of the Divinity if he wishes. He may choose. That is what freedom means."

"You silly man," said Poppaea. "We are all slaves … even the Emperor."

"Indeed," said Petronius Arbiter, "you are perceptive, Divinity."

"Let's listen to some more of what old Pilatus has to say," said the Lady Poppaea, and she leaned against the back of our couch, just within earshot of where the generals were telling their war stories.

"Is it true, Pilatus," she said, "that the Chrestianoi kill and eat babies?"

"Oh, far more appalling than that!" he said, laughing. "They practise licentious *orgia,* which they call love-feasts, in the catacombs, in the dark, amongst the decaying corpses. But they do worse than eating babies ... they actually eat the flesh of their god."

"A delicacy, I should think, if you could ever get it."

"But everyone hates them, and of all the silly oriental cults in Rome, theirs is one of the dullest, though they do give me some recognition for having crucified their leader, some madman."

It seemed that the other military men found him tedious, and had their own stories to tell, more recent and more bloody, for they soon started talking over him.

"I have something even more scandalous," said General Vitellius, "another subversive poem by Antistius Sosianus that has been discovered, comparing the Divinitas unfavorably to the faeces of a goose. The Emperor should never have spared his life...."

***

You saw Vitellius! You laid eyes on him who is now Himself the Divinity, the fourth Emperor we have had in a single year!

How was I to know? He was just some general. I barely glanced at this Vitellius, and perhaps I should have, since it was he who eventually condemned me to die in this ignominious theatrical display....

Ah, he was the Emperor who was to be your undoing.

Indeed. Well, he was fat.

***

It was Petronius's turn to perform, and I followed him to the Emperor's dais. My master opened up the scroll of his book and began to read. In this passage from his unfinished manuscript, Petronius spoke of a freedman named Gaius Pompeius Trimalchio Maecenatianus, who was throwing the most extravagant, tasteless, vulgar banquet one could imagine.

Gaius Petronius's voice was quite singular; though his narrative voice was deep, he modulated his tones, now sounding like the handsome Encolpius, now the simpering wife, Fortunata, now the brash, self-aggrandising Trimalchio. You could taste the pigs' carcasses into which were sewn living birds that the guests had to run about catching ... a dish for every sign in the zodiac ... hares with feathers stuck in their backs to represent Pegasus ... meat carvers who wielded their knives with the panache of a secutor with a gladius in the arena. It all came magically alive, just with words. Although the chamber was huge, conversation became hushed. A thousand people were hanging on my master's words. And there I was, holding the scroll open, displaying myself in my tunic of virginal whiteness to a God - to the only God who mattered in the real world.

The food and spectacle of Petronius's novel may not have been as epic as the Emperor's banquet, but his words unlocked more colors, textures and sounds than could be found in ten such banquets. The reading had the effect of making the feast we were at, in all its extravagance, seem drab and devoid of color. Petronius did not just use the elegant language of an Ovid or the metaphoric flights of Sappho. His palette also made liberal use of gutter talk, the slang of prostitutes, the gruffness of soldiers, the patois of unlettered slaves.

And in the Emperor's eyes I saw not just admiration, but also ... resentment. And I also saw that my master did not care. He had deliberately stepped over a line, as surely as Julius Caesar had when he crossed the Rubicon a hundred years ago, setting in motion events that would bring the Republic crashing down.

The Lady Poppaea Sabina had not been wrong. My master had the air of someone who has seen his own death.

Finally Petronius's reading came to an end and there was thunderous applause. The Divinitas, too, applauded languidly. The Empress clapped her hands a few times, and yawned.

"Brilliant, Petronius," said Nero. "You truly are a marvel. Of course, you quite overshadowed my own little meal."

"Perhaps so," said Petronius, walking a very careful tightrope. "But if our audience were to hear one of *your* compositions now, my own little recitation will pale into insignificance."

"I do have a little something planned," said the Emperor.

"I await with bated breath, Divinitas. But meanwhile…."

With a flourish, Petronius motioned for his slaves to bring the special amphora that was made to hold the scroll, and they laid it at the Emperor's feet.

"A tasteful presentation, as usual," said Himself the Divinity, "but Poppaea gave me to understand that the wedding gift was going to include the boy."

"The Divine Empress must not have realized, Divinitas, that I've actually given this delicatus his freedom. I regret that I'm unable to give that which I don't possess."

"Well, then I'll accept the freely given gift from the hands of the gift itself," said the Emperor, whom one did not, of course, contradict.

What was I to do? I had been free for only an hour. Would I now have to declare myself a slave again? Lady Poppaea had a look of triumph, and she launched into the Medusa-like cackle I'd heard her use on her ex-husband. "Choose, you silly child," she said, "and mind you make the right choice, because your master's fate lies in your answer!"

I was going to stand my ground. I was going to say that, no matter what, my loyalty was to my former dominus. I know that's what he wanted me to say. "I should really be your enemy, Petronius," said the Emperor, "but you're simply not important enough."

But at that moment, a steward came to whisper in the Empress's ear. Her cackling became shriller, even more raucous. "You've been upstaged, Petronius!" she said. "I have received an even better wedding gift than a twin sister with a penis."

More blaring bucinae now, and a dozen soldiers marched in lockstep into the room, escorting an enormous, covered platter wrought in gold.

"I'll deal with you later," said the Emperor to Petronius, and our party backed away, stepped down to our level, leaving the amphora with Petronius's precious creation unattended and forgotten.

To the beat of the tympanum, and the erotic wailings of double-flutes, the soldiers approached. As my master and his entourage, including me, returned to their places, the platter was set in front of the two Divinitates. It took two soldiers to lift the cover.

Squealing with delight, the Empress of Rome seized her gift and held it aloft ... by the hair. There were scattered screams and titters ... no applause, and for that I thanked the gods that there was still a shred of human decency in this depraved crowd. But the collective gasp of the crowd had a kind of vampiric hunger to it.

It had been packed with salt for the journey, but I still recognized the decapitated head of the Lady Claudia Octavia, who had once been Empress of Rome, the most direct in the tortuous line of the Julio-Claudian family … descended through Julius Caesar from Aeneas himself, and through him from the goddess Venus.

I was sitting so close I could hear the flies.

Then spoke Nero Claudius Caesar Augustus Germanicus. "Time, I think," he said, "to clear the air. I shall perform an ode I have composed, quite apposite, I think, for it honors the ancestry of the late Empress … *my* ancestry … for I am the adopted son of Claudius, son of Germanicus, son of … all the way back to the Prince Aeneas, son of Venus, who fled the burning fires of Troy. Let what I sing to you be a paean not only of death, but of rebirth. For Rome, like the phoenix, ever springs up from its own ashes, does it not?"

A hush fell over the room. It was as profound as the silence that accompanied by dominus's recitation. But where that silence came from fascination, from the seductive storytelling in my master's *Satyricon*, this was a silence birthed in stark terror.

"Before I begin," said Himself the Divinity, "I shall quote the immortal Virgil, who said, *'Infandum, regina, iubes renovare dolorem' — 'O Queen, you bid me renew unspeakable grief.'* You, my adoring public, shall decide whether the Queen I address is the late Augusta, or the current one."

A long, pregnant pause.

He was about to touch a finger to the *kithara* when another messenger arrived. Nero waited. He did not, apparently, want his opening chord to be ruined by some jarring message. The messenger was unbathed and had obviously been riding at top speed. He lurched through the guests and up to Himself without ceremony, and gave his message so quietly that perhaps not even Poppaea heard it.

Nero stood. "We are moving this banquet to Rome," he

said. "Poppaea, see that all the guests accompany us. Tell the army to mobilize every chariot, every oxcart. We're leaving right away."

"Now, my Lord?" she said. "There's another thirty-seven courses. Whatever for?"

"I'm told there's a better venue for my world premiere," he said.

The whispers became a roar and I caught a word here and there, and this is how I learned that Rome was burning.

XXI

PER IGNEM

It is forty-three *mille passuum* from Antium to Rome, thus four or five hours even at a trot. For a time, our procession was able to keep up this clip, for the Praetorians rode ahead, driving the riff-raff off the road. But as we approached the city, our caravan slowed to a crawl, even with an Emperor, for even armed soldiers cannot easily ram through a torrent of panicking plebeians.

We could feel the heat even before we could see the city. Three miles from Rome along the Via Appia, the journey became really tough going. Petronius and I and our small party were crammed into a horse-cart with several other poets, most of them drunk.

The Praetorians rode ahead at a steady trot, lashing people out of the way in the wake of Himself, resplendent on a golden chariot whose driver was dressed as Icarus … the cart I was in was not far behind. Riders, with torches held aloft, escorted our convoy.

But by now all the traffic was in the opposite direction, a sea of refugees, carrying all their possessions. Weeping, wailing, snivelling children, old men, pack animals ... none of the able-bodied men, for doubtless they were helping the vigiles to put out the fire. We moved as swiftly as we could.

Our party had suffered considerable attrition since leaving Antium. While few would think to openly contradict the Divinity's commands, it was clear that some hoped that in the pandemonium, Himself would not notice an absence or two. Yet the road was still packed with the guests who had not dared refuse, in their carts or on horseback, and with vehicle after vehicle piled high with luxury foods. Sweetmeats were packed tightly into snow. Other carts contained the stacked carcasses of creatures yet to be roasted. Cages with squawking peacocks waiting to be brained. Amphorae filled with live lampreys. Hares, turtles, monkeys, any exotic creature that could be eaten ... all were part of our procession. From time to time, the band of bucinae blared away.

The heat we felt first, but now came the glow, too. The horizon was ablaze. The wind seared our faces. Our caravan circumvented the closest gate and went right, around the Servian Wall until it reached the Porta Esquilina, mounting the city, as it were, from the rear.

We snaked up the Esquiline. The sky glowed, but the wind and smoke were being borne away from us, that is until we reached the valley and had to start climbing once more, this time the Palatine.

And now, the full majesty and terror hove into view as we reached the summit. The building we reached was at the edge of the imperial complex. There were already people gathered, members of the household, and the Praetorians began barking commands. Couches were brought in. We were gathering on a huge veranda that overlooked the burning city.

It was madness, but slaves were scurrying like rats to have the banquet continue uninterrupted after hours of trekking through the night. Musicians set up in one corner. A golden throne, illuminated by four naked slaves with flaming torches, was set up, dangerously close to the edge. Himself the Divinity leaped from his chariot and was carried to his seat of honor, another slave carrying the kithara on a cushion woven with rose-colored silk and spun gold threads.

A lower throne accommodated the now Divine Poppaea Sabina, who sat, Hercules on a leash at her feet, being fanned by no less a personage than Pythagoras, whom I had once seen getting married to, and publicly consummating that marriage with, Himself the Divinity in a wig and wedding dress. Poppaea, it seemed, superseded all previous unions, of either gender.

Now came Tigellinus, the all-powerful right-hand man, with a contingent of Praetorians. They arrayed themselves in lines to protect the Emperor and the guests.

If I had hoped that our group would cower in the background, I hoped in vain. The Emperor beckoned for the gang of poets to sit upon the closest couches and though I tried to avoid his gaze, I could not avoid that of Herself, who summoned me with a crooked finger.

I took my place at the feet of my former master, now patron.

He whispered to me to come closer and I knelt, nestling next to his toga. "Welcome, Gaius Petronius Gaii Libertus Sporus," he said, and I heard my post-*manumissio* name uttered for the first time. Did I feel any different? Hardly. My dominus was my dominus. I did not think the bond could be severed, unless one of us should die.

Once enough wine had been poured, and enough tidbits had been set out, Himself, the Divine Nero Claudius Caesar Augustus Germanicus, Fifth God to rule the Eternal City, stood, and struck a few notes, tuning his instrument. He cleared his throat.

No one touched any tidbits.

He stood practically at the very ledge. Below, the city was in flames, as far as the eye could see. In the distance, the slums. Of course! The wooden structures, squeezed together, were tinder; the suburra was always burning. But the fire was creeping closer. More than the anticipation of the Divinity's performance was the gnawing dread we all felt.

First, he spoke. "Rome," he said, "is like the phoenix, flaming as it traverses the vault of heaven, ever created anew in the fire of death and rebirth. My ancestor, Aeneas, son of Venus, fled from the fires of Troy, bearing his aged father on his back, to found a new Rome in the heart of Latium. But I do not flee the flames. I race toward them, open-winged, bearing in my arms not an aging parent, but the entire people of Rome … *Rome* … not withered, paraplegic Anchises, but the beautiful youth Ganymede, another Trojan Prince, another of my venerable, ancient lineage, my great, great, many times great-uncle … he has come to life in the arms of Jupiter, awakened to godhood by my holy seed. For tonight, I am every one of my ancestors. Tonight, I am all the gods. Rome, like Minerva, shall burst fully armed from my head, filled with wisdom, grace, and ultimate truth. Do not think I am mixing my metaphors, children! All things are one. All the universe is one. All paths lead to me. I am the past and the future, and I am the eternal present."

"He's gone mad," my *patronus* whispered, for my ears alone.

Himself continued: "I shall sing of the dawn of the world. Of the age of bronze, when men were heroes and there were no modern weapons of fire-quenched Seric steel … no weapons that could rain down destruction on whole cities as there are in our modern times, the Eighth Century since the founding of Rome, a millennium since the Fall of Ilium."

But I could not measure time in millennia. I was still a boy, though I had lived a lifetime of sorrow already. I did not really understand the words. They spoke of myths and realities beyond my limited existence, and I only felt their import, not their meaning.

Above, the bright stars shone.

The Emperor began to sing.

You must understand ... I have said this many times ... that in those days, the Emperor was beautiful. His eyes were captivating. The jowls, the jagged furrows that came from his later insecurity about his own divinity, from his constant fear of plots and assassinations, they were not there. In that moment, he was the empire's idol, the golden child who had come to sweep away the parsimonious fussiness of the old cuckold Claudius, the insanity of Caligula, the moral depravity of Tiberius, and the severity of Augustus. He was the new world.

He sang of the flames, as he stood above the flames.

His was not a trained voice. His Greek was quaint, antiquated, and I did not really understand much of the Aeolic tongue, the dialect for lyric poetry. But when he sang, he *was* Cassandra, wailing in vain at her unbelieved prophecy, he *was* Hecuba, weeping as she mourned her fifty sons, he *was* the faithful Andromache, being carried off to be raped by Neoptolemus, a mere boy, fired by revenge and bloodlust. These ancient women were real to him ... and he made them real to us.

I did not need to understand the words. This man, who owned the world, sang to me of the things I had experienced myself ... the burning of my village ... the enslavement ... the chains ... the violations ... the hopelessness. Surely, I was as innocent as they come, for it seemed that he sang to me, that he knew my ache, my pain.

Nero's song blended with the keening of the wind. The distant crash of collapsing buildings were the drumbeats … no, the heartbeats. At this distance, a hundred thousand screams blended into a soft drone, a sympathetic vibration that cradled his arching melismas and spun his voice into a celestial fabric … the substance of the universe itself.

Did anyone else hear what I heard, see what I saw? I could not tell. My eyes and ears were for him alone. I felt suspended in time.

Then, the wind shifted.

Smoke was billowing around us. An acrid stench, like charred flesh and incense and offal all at once, seeped into the air, poisoning the smell of wine and fine viands. The fire was creeping towards the Palatine. Slowly, inexorably. We stood in a haze that was glowing … searing.

And still he sang.

But the people around us were panicking. They could not go anywhere or risk the Emperor's wrath, but they feared for their lives.

And still the Divinity sang, and still I watched him, barely seeing the growing chaos around me.

The wind was stronger now, blowing smoke about the veranda, making it curl around the Corinthian columns of the portico behind us, making the audience cough, the slaves' arms unsteady as they tried to hold up their torches. One of the torch-women collapsed from the smoke. One of the Praetorians casually kicked her off the ledge. Sickness could not be allowed to mar the perfection of the Divinity's vision.

At last, the sound ended. But I went on staring at him.

A thought surfaced unbidden in my mind. A hopeless dream. A crazy joy that was as dark as the deepest despair. *I must have him,* I thought.

Around me I heard voices. "We can't leave this balcony. We can't go anywhere. We're completely surrounded by fire. We are trapped here until they put it out."

More wine was being poured. If people were indeed trapped, they were all going to drink themselves into a stupor. The building behind us, no doubt, had toilets, though probably no running water, as the aqueduct was probably being diverted to douse the fire. There was enough food in the banquet to last for days. But how many days would it take for the flames to die?

In one corner, some of the guests were already making love right there in the open. What else was there to do? Who knew whether the fire would reach the very summit of the Palatine?

Slowly, Himself the Divinity sat back down on his throne.

You see, I did not seduce the Emperor with my wiles. Only an overpainted whore like you would think in those terms.

On that day, Himself, the Divine Nero Claudius Caesar Augustus Germanicus, was still the best to have ascended the throne since the Julio-Claudians wrested control of the known world from the Senate, and reduced the Republic to a rabble of frightened yes-men. He was handsome. He was a poet, a singer, an actor — to be sure, this was hardly palatable to the sober patricians, for they were professions more proper to the Greeks, who despite having given Rome all its culture were still at root an enslaved race — but these things made him beloved of the people. He was generous. He had become Emperor at the age of only sixteen. He had begun his reign by promising to end corruption and to listen to the Senate. He had tried to abolish taxes completely — when that failed, he had regulated taxes and established stricter supervision. He had passed a law allowing slaves to protest their treatment to the local magistrate. Indeed, he had his deviant proclivities, but who in Rome did not? The people loved a bit of scandal. They loved that his love life played out in the public arena, an entertainment for the masses as absorbing as gladiatorial combat, chariot, or *damnatio ad bestias.*

On the day Rome burned, he was still only twenty-five.

The aura of the years when he had ruled with moderation and justice still clung to him. And he was beautiful, beardless, slender. He was godlike.

But that night, when he sang, the sublimity of his music, the splendid cadence of his words, did not put out the flames.

Instead, the gods willed that the flames turn towards the Palatine, threatening to consume even him. He had not commanded the wind and the flames.

In that moment, deep inside, I think he must have known for the first time that, though he was godlike, he was not a god. That must have been a terrible discovery for him.

So terrible it propelled his downward slide into depravity and darkness.

Yet in that moment, who was I to know anything?

In that moment, in my first day of freedom, I was made a slave again. In that moment, with all the volcanic passion that only an adolescent can feel, utterly, unconditionally, recklessly, and stupidly, I was in love.

XXII

NYMPHIDIUS SABINUS

As the fire consumed the night, there was nothing to drink but wine, and no water with which to dilute it. The heat … the wine … I must have dozed off.

And when I slept I had strange dreams. Borne by the wind, floating over the flames of Troy, sheltered from the fiery sun by the sheltering wings of a giant eagle. In my dream I was Ganymede and my abductor was the God of Love.

When I awoke, it was dawn. The July sun was barely up, but it beat down. Himself the Divinity's throne was unoccupied, and some guests appeared to have managed to slip away in his absence.

Below us, the fire raged, unabated; though some areas were completely gutted, others were flaring up anew. There did now seem to be a few possible pathways down from our vantage point, one of them more or less the way we came; another, more steep, led through what seemed to be a completely burnt-out sector of the city. The chorus of screams that had underscored the Emperor's ode had softened … now it was barely a whisper in the wind. But I knew people were still dying.

I had fallen asleep at the feet of my patronus, my head against his knee. At first I was conscious only of the heat … the harsh sunlight, the blast from the burning city. It looked like about the third hour, for the sun had not even reached its zenith, and already we were soaked in sweat. I forced myself to stand and looked around. Many of the aristocrats had already divested themselves of their clothing and some were rubbing themselves down with the melted snow from the troughs where snails and oysters had been chilled the previous night.

Now, some of the Praetorians were walking about, prodding and poking. One of them pulled the head of Octavia from a platter of pork. He and his friends were laughing. Another soldier, with a comical display of discretion, wrapped it in a military cloak and secreted in a nearby wine jar.

As noon approached, Himself and the Empress emerged onto the portico of the building behind us. I gasped. Somehow, amid the chaos, the Divinity had managed to spend time in the bath. He had been oiled and perfumed and wore only a cloak, fastened with a bronze fibula in the shape of a phallus. The fabric was only perfunctorily wrapped about the imperial torso. And I was still in love, so my feelings last night were not some delirium brought on by wine.

A soldier presented the Empress with yesterday's gift. She peeked into the amphora and seemed disgusted by the smell. She waved it away.

The Emperor made his way to his throne and she followed. He waved his hand and the guests fell silent.

"You may all go home," he said. "Those of you who still have homes, that is. If you can find a way off this hilltop. You may all go home … *except …"*

Behind him came the terrifying Praefectus of the Praetorians, Tigellinus and his co-praefectus, Nymphidius.

Tigellinus said — he had a gravelly, unpleasant voice — "Senators and military officers to remain."

"Yes," Nero said. "We will have to make some logistical plans to ease the city's agony. We will need the senators and soldiers. Experienced heads and all that. And military discipline. Tigellinus, you must organize the vigiles to put out the fires."

"Easier said than done, Divinitas," said the praefectus. "There aren't enough vigiles. It is impossible to divert the aqueducts. There is a simple solution, but many will not like it."

"What might that be, Tigellinus?" said the Lady Poppaea, with the kind of sweet smile that makes men shrivel with dread. But not Tigellinus.

"Any neighborhood that cannot be saved," Tigellinus said, "we just burn the rest of it down. A good clean ending. The burning will stop when there is nothing left to burn."

"Yes, yes," Nero said. "Swift and clean. Like a surgeon."

Those who overheard this immediately began talking amongst themselves. Even though I could not take my eyes off the Emperor, I heard my master whisper, "This won't look good."

"I should send everyone else away," Tigellinus said. "In particular the artists, as their delicate sensibilities may balk at some of what must be discussed."

"Yes," said Himself. "Tell them, Tigellinus."

Tigellinus beckoned; Nymphidius came to his side. And presently it was Nymphidius who was dispatched to give the order to disperse.

Good, I thought. *My patronus and I can go and see if anything remains of our home.* Petronius's mansion with its beautiful sculptures, its priceless vases … I shuddered, trying not to think of all that my former dominus might have lost. I saw

Croesus hovering about, gathering up Petronius's things. I looked across the valley. The fire was not dying down.

This Nymphidius — he theoretically shared the praefectus position with Tigellinus, yet always seemed to be the trained bulldog, not the mastermind — strutted officiously among the somewhat depleted ranks of dinner guests. He stopped here and there to pick at a tidbit here and there — a honeyed mouse embryo, a peacock's brain on a stick. He acted as if he owned the place. And wherever he thrust himself, people stepped back. He was not liked.

At length he returned to where I and my patronus were gathering our belongings. Nearby were the likes of Lucan and Seneca … all the literary circle of Himself the Divinity. He saw that we were preparing to depart and he peered at all of us. On my former master, on the poets — the handsome young one and the dour one … and last, at me.

"Everyone must leave the banquet now, unless you're a senator or a military officer," he said. "Do as I say, in the name of my ancestors!"

"His ancestors?" I heard someone whisper.

"He's a freedwoman's child, who fancies his mother was raped by Caligula," someone replied.

I do not know if Nymphidius heard. His eyes reflected nothing.

Not content to just leave, it was the poet Lucan who said, "We're all poets here."

"Literature, eh?" he said. "But the Divinitas is rather fond of literature, is he not?"

But he was not looking at the poets. He was gazing at me. And the *way* he was staring at me chilled me. Not that I wasn't used to being stared at. I was used to being mentally undressed, being the object of someone's random fantasies. Often, when I had been put on display by my master, I was not dressed at all, and I had been told so often that I was beautiful that it had no meaning for me.

So when a man or woman disrobed me with their eyes, I thought little of it. But Gaius Nymphidius Sabinus was not disrobing. He was disembowelling. His look made my skin crawl. I looked away.

Presently, I heard him speak again. "The Divinity has now informed me that literary figures, and their entourages, will remain as well. This coming time will not just be a time for dealing with a catastrophe. There will be a need for feeding the hungry and housing the homeless. But —"

"Well said, Nymphidius," came the voice of Himself. He was so close I could have reached out to touch him. I smelled his perfume. Between being aroused by the heady fragrance, and recoiling from the Praefectus, I was, to say the least, confused. "But," said the Emperor, "as you so rightly point out, we most deal not only with practicalities, but aesthetics. That's why I need my artists as well."

"This means you," said Nymphidius, apparently to the entire ensemble of poets. But his eyes were only on me.

And mine were only on the Emperor.

XXIII

AVERNUS

So you're telling me that this icon of debauchery and cruelty was actually some kind of paragon, a … excuse the expression … a God?

Wait! You're leaping ahead, and vapid as the rest of them, you've already forgotten that the Infamous One was once the most popular of Emperors. And if Himself were still on the throne, would you be getting me ready for a spectacular death, a mythic reenactment to entertain the feckless mob?

True enough. Still, you had a good run.

And a short one.

You've had enough happen in your life for someone four times your age.

Yes. Soon, I will be twenty years old.

The Fates have had your thread pinched off from the time you were born. I don't think you will elude it. So you might as well look as beautiful as possible. Hold still. You smudged your kohl.

From weeping, remembering the moment when I was an innocent, and innocently in love.

Come. The mob, as you call them, must be able to see the beauty of the goddess from the topmost tier of the Circus Maximus. Once glance from your divine eyes must be enough to still their mutterings.

On the second day of the blaze, having dismissed most of the banqueters and hangers-on, nothing much was done. Himself merely sat, surveying the spectacle, and now and then receiving ever-more alarming reports of the damage.

Now and then he paused to sing a little, accompanying himself. All the songs he sang were tragic, but the most plangent was Niobe, mourning the loss of her children. Fourteen strophes and fourteen antistrophes, one of each for each of her slain sons and daughters; he outdid even the first night's performance about the Fall of Troy. When he sang, all conversation was naturally silenced — this was not merely from politeness, but also fear, for Nero's cruelest guard dogs stood ready to punish the slightest discourtesy.

We were hungry. Even the palace was running out of supplies. We were dirty and scruffy — for only the Emperor and Empress had been able to bathe. The communal lavatory had a queue and exuded a stench that could not even be masked by a liberal fumigation of frankincense pilfered from the imperial altar.

On the third day, Himself decided that we should all descend the hill and inspect for ourselves the scale of the disaster. "Money!" he cried. "Bring treasure chests and jugs and amphorae! Hunt through the trunks for trinkets. Aurei and denarii only — no bronze!"

A flurry of activity, in and out of the building behind us. I had not seen that much money in my life. I think that perhaps even the wealthiest in the gathering had not. The Emperor's concept of a *trinket* could pay the rent on a room in the suburra for a year or two.

I roused myself, knowing that we would finally be able to

see what had become of the real world.

Himself summoned Tigellinus to him and whispered a few words. The praefectus barked out a new command. "By the gracious will of the Divinitas," he said, "you shall all enter the private caldarium within. He makes his *sanctum sanctorum* available for you mortals."

Himself the Divinity said, "Yes, indeed. It won't do at all for a manifestation from High Olympus to appear like a bevy of bedraggled dinner guests. We must pull ourselves together."

"Indeed," Lucan said, obsequiously falling to his knees, "you shall appear from the sky as redeemer of the world, personally hauling the plebeians back up from the gaping maw of Avernus."

"With the Divine Poppaea, indeed, as redemptrix," the Emperor remarked, without even a twinge of irony.

Petronius whispered to me, "I don't think I've ever heard a mythological allusion so mangled and abused."

Tigellinus said: "Right then! Groups of twenty! Disrobe quickly! The caldarium is inside, to the left, just past the public shitting chamber! No amorous activities please, Himself is in a hurry. And don't piss in the water. There are jars for that and the imperial laundry will be collecting."

We were all disrobing right there on the balcony: masters and attendants, slaves and millionaires, for the Romans are obsessed with bathing, and we were all caked with sweat, dried sauces, old wine, and vomit. The guests fairly charged into the building atop the hill which was little more than a private shelter for the Emperor or a few guests who would climb all this way for the view; it was not equipped for Imperial banquets.

When I and my master followed the guests to the building, Nymphidius stopped me as Petronius ascended the steps. Petronius turned and said, "Our group is fewer than twenty."

"He will go when I say," Nymphidius said. He laid a gnarled hand on my shoulder. You must realize what a state I was in. He was a Praetorian, a *chief* among Praetorians. I could suddenly feel a warm spurt between my legs. I was shaking. I was naked and I was terrified.

"Waste of good piss," Nymphidius said. "You know there's a fine for that."

And then he took me by both shoulders and pushed me up the steps.

The caldarium was already crammed; the command for "groups of twenty" had been ineffective, as people were so desperate to feel cleansed with warm water that they had rushed into the pool, not even bothering to scrape off the accumulated detritus of what was now a three-day party … three days and counting. Nor was the water hot. It was closer to a tepidarium.

"What are you waiting for?"

I turned and saw that Nymphidius was completely naked, save, perversely, for his helmet. He shoved me into the water and plunged in after. I became self-conscious. Everyone was watching me. Everyone from senator to cupbearer. And no one more than Nymphidius Sabinus, who stood so close to me I could feel him, ramming into my side like a truncheon, his eyes boring into me. I was terrified. But I dared not show fear now. I stared right back at him and saw insensate, insatiable hunger in his eyes. This was a man for whom nothing could ever be enough.

A foul-smelling steam enveloped us. Panicking, I considered climbing out of the pool. Then I caught a glimpse of Petronius, not far from me, the way blocked by a mass of overfed nobility. I elbowed my way through, and heedless of propriety and my lowly position, I clung to him fiercely, as tightly as if were in his bed, having a nightmare.

I could hear Nymphidius cackling like a malevolent fishwife.

"Sporus," said Petronius, "Remember you're a freedman now."

"I don't want to be free," I whispered.

"Yes, my Giton," he said, "you do."

"That man … why does he frighten me so much?"

"You have an instinct, that's why. You know bad men right away. You don't know this, but I observe you sometimes, in order to pick out the bad apples in my own orchard."

"This place — it's like Avernus, the lake of noxious fumes, the gateway to the country of the dead," I said, remembering when he had read to me from Virgil, the part when Aeneas visits his departed comrades.

"We'll be home soon," Petronius said.

"If we even have a home," I said. "All those beautiful things … gone, perhaps."

"Does it matter? I'll buy more," said my patron. "But I'll never be able to buy another Sporus."

At that moment, a consort of tubae and bucinae sounded and Himself entered the chamber. A dozen slaves carried armfuls of tunicae, some purple-bordered togas for the senators, stolae in bright colors.

The Emperor announced, "Some new clothes to replace the shabby vestments you've just cast off. If I am going scatter all sorts of treats to the mob, I might as well make sure my nobles look the part. Jupiter and Juno need a proper entourage of Olympians, not a ragtag band of dissolute voluptuaries." He surveyed our group. Hercules, strutting behind Poppaea, his leash barely controllable by a frightened little Nubian, growled. Nero said, "There seem to be fewer of you than I had hoped. Tigellinus, did not the senators, the military, and the poets all remain behind?"

"Yes, Divinity. So I instructed."

"If anyone has slipped away, contrary to my direct order, make sure that the blasphemy is appropriately dealt with."

"What fun," Nymphidius smirked. "Perhaps my new little friend would like a front row seat at the proceedings?"

For he had sidled back up to me, and was endeavoring to slide a stubby finger into my posterior. I squirmed and clung to my former master even more tightly. Quicky, I climbed out of the caldarium and allowed a slave to wrap a toga praetexta about my shoulders. It was a woolen garment, and warm, too warm. A freeborn youth, a Roman citizen, who has not yet attained his majority, is privileged to wear the purple stripe. It was far above my station.

"... But you wear it well." Petronius had read my thoughts. "It suits you. You'll soon get used to the different way your two arms feel, the one encumbered, the other free to gesticulate."

We were assembling on the portico. I tried to stay out of Nymphidius's sight. Flute players began a keening, erotic melody, weaving in and out above the beat of a small drum. Nude boys sang and girls strewed flowers as the procession began. The heat, trapped in the valley, burned our faces; and it had been but minutes since we had bathed.

My master whispered to me, "Himself believes Himself to be the God, descending from lofty Olympus to redeem the city from its fiery apocalypse. He is arrogant. He is narcissistic. And yet, he needs their love. He is hungry for love. He consumes it, indiscriminately, thoughtlessly. But what will he give back? O Sporus, I've seen the way you look at him. He has charisma. A dangerous charisma. But Sporus, my beautiful child, do not love a god. You will be incinerated."

I wondered whether my lord and master, who had given me the gift of being able to see beauty, who had saved me at some risk to his own self … whether he might not be a little jealous.

"You gave me freedom," I said.

"Yes, and now you are free to choose a long, productive old age, or to go down like Icarus, like Phaëton, flying too close to the sun."

The toga felt unnaturally warm. I was already beginning to sweat.

"We will have to see that you can be granted citizenship," Petronius said. "You will wear that garment without feeling lost inside it You'll go further if I can get the Emperor to grant you *civitas*. But he'll have to have you in his field of vision."

A foul wind sprang up. The stench from the bath chamber filled the air, mingled with the incense they had been burning to hide the odor, and blending with the smell of charring wood and flesh that was carried upward on the wind. We started down the portico steps, toward the steep pathway that led down the hill.

"You said," my patron said, "that the bath was like Avernus, the stinking lake that leads to the underworld. Be prepared, my son. The place we are going to now is like the place beyond Avernus. It is hell itself."

I followed. I was filled with dread. There was going to be death down there. Destruction on an unimaginable scale. And yet there was something else, a glimmer of joy. That was what I tried to think of as we descended to darkness.

Petronius had called me his son.

XXIV

SCAPEGOAT

It was, indeed, a descent into Hades. Our convoy, freshly bathed, dressed in gaudy clothes, perfumed, followed the Emperor's litter down the steep, narrow path ... down toward where the flames were raging still.

Some of the party had whited their faces and rouged their cheeks. As we reached the upper circle of the infernum, the lead paint of their faces glowed with reflected fire. The first flat area we reached had been burnt out, though in the middle distance, there were more flames. Further off still, the fire was still burning strongly. Screams echoed from every side. The clearing was jammed with people. Some were dead and charred, some half burned, others sitting, dazed, or crawling about. The delegation from heaven halted, and Himself got out of his litter; a small rug was laid out on the ashes, and a curule produced for him to sit on.

The apparition of a glittering, bejewelled Imperial court in the midst of this vista of destruction and misery did not provoke immediate adulation, though I am sure Himself the Divinity expected nothing less. The sight was fantastical and jarring. Overwhelming, all the suffering — the crying babies, the groaning wounded. Dead and dying people everywhere. Charred severed limbs. Crawling, barely recognizable as human, those of Emperor's subjects who still lived were more animal than human, and the divine visitation was so far outside their realm of pain that we seemed to belong to a different reality altogether.

The Divinitas cleared his throat. No one acknowledged him. At length, he clapped his hands for the band to play a fanfare. Petronius and I, the whole poets' group, crept further down, and now we were seated right behind the throne. I could hear everything that was said. The Lady Poppaea turned and winked at me. Tigellinus and Nymphidius stood on either side of the Emperor. Dancers moved, awkwardly avoiding piles of ash.

Nero raised his hand and the musicians gurgled to a halt. "My children," he said, "I, the God, have heard your cries. I have descended from on high to bring you solace. Attend to my words!"

Then he called for his kithara, plucked a few notes, cleared his throat again, and began to sing. It was a song of unspeakable anguish, Hecuba lamenting over the ashes of Troy. As his voice had soared over the burning city below, now it blended with the shrieks of the dying.

Yes. It was beautiful. But my heart was sinking. This could not possibly be what Rome needed at this moment.

Surely the Divinitas could not know ... could not understand ... real suffering. I remembered my own village burning. The forced march to the sea. The chains. The beatings, the pirate captain "breaking me in." What could the Divinitas be thinking? These people had lost *everything*. There were not ghosts from Homer and Virgil.

There are times when a song cannot salve the heart.

Nero's public was not moved. Even he could see that, used as he was to constant fawning. He paused and beckoned to the Praetorians, and then he went on singing. Soldiers came forward with bags full of gold. They began tossing them into the throng. You would expect them to become like hungry wolves, diving for the gold, but this provoked little reaction. I saw a toddler reach out to pick up a coin, but its mother snatched back his hand; the aureus had fallen into hot ash.

Hesitantly, one of the wounded took a coin. Others turned to scold him. What was the problem? The Emperor went on singing.

Andromache mourning the death of the great Hector at the hand of Achilles, wailing over her child Astyanax, his brains dashed out against the walls of Troy by Neoptolemus, Achilles's son … who would soon make her his concubine. Polyxena, sacrificed to assuage Achilles's hungry ghost. And through it all, preternaturally beautiful Helen, gliding through the desolation, untouched by it all. The performance should have wrung tears in any theater, but this was no theater.

Presently, Tigellinus grew tired of the audience's inattention. He pulled out a little quirt and started to lash the nearest in the crowd. "Don't you recognize your Emperor and God? Show some respect!" And he set a ring of Praetorians to protect the Emperor, all ready with swords and whips, to wring obeisance from them.

Cowed, they huddled in a pathetic mass prostration. Surely the Emperor must stop singing now! But he did not. He went to the very end of the song, and all the way the soldiers scattered gold and trinkets, and the plebeians, their eyes dead and desolate, did not pick them up.

Once Himself the Divinity finished singing, he handed his

kithara to an attendant. I saw his face. The flash of anger, certainly. But there was something else in his eyes … it was haughtiness, it was disdain … but also … he had the look of a rejected lover who wonders what he did wrong. *The Emperor is vulnerable,* I thought. *And he's lonely.*

He addressed the crowd directly.

"People of Rome," he said. "I've seen your suffering. I have come down from my home in the clouds. I've brought gold. I've brought coins and precious stones and rare objects. I am Jupiter and you are the beautiful Danaë, drifting on a sea of destruction. I shall rain down on you in a shower of gold, as Jupiter did. See, see — the glittering power of my love for you! I shall lift all of you out of this degradation. Out of your terrible suffering will come a Rome of gold and marble … together we shall build Neropolis."

Neropolis! But *Rome* was the urbs aeterna, in its eighth century since it was built on this spot by Romulus and Remus.

I thought I heard someone whisper the word *hubris.* But maybe it was just the wind. Less than a thousand paces away, fire was still blazing.

A tiny voice spoke up. "We can't eat gold!"

"Who said that?" Tigellinus said. He motioned for the guard to find the speaker. They dragged her in, not gently. It was a little woman in a torn red tunic. The sheerness of the crimson fabric, the painted cheeks, the heavy kohl that lined her eyes, all betrayed her profession. The whores must be out in force. The guards thrust her down on the hot ground.

"Do you dare contradict the Divinitas?" he said, and slapped her a few times. Her nose was bloodied, but she was defiant. She got up off the ground and looked her Emperor in the eye.

"Divinitas," she said bitterly. "Give us bread. The granaries are in cinders. All the gold in the world won't feed us if there's nowhere to buy food."

"Yes," came another shout. "We need food."

"Food! Food!" others shouted. The guards used the lash, but they would not stop. "Bread! Bread!"

"My children! Do not be disheartened. I'll find you grain. We're putting out all the fires. We will rebuild."

"You're not putting out the fire," came another voice, an old man. "The vigiles are burning down *more* sectors of the city."

"What!"

"A necessity, Divinitas," said Tigellinus. "There are neighbourhoods that are best levelled to the ground. If we don't destroy them, a random wind could spread the fire all the way to the Palatine."

"To my house?" Nero cried.

My house, I thought. *As large as most cities, and as yet mostly untouched by the flames.*

"Your house!" said the prostitute. "You're burning our houses so you can rebuild your own?"

A collective gasp came from the crowd ... and from our people, too. The woman had said the thing that must not be said. And the mob wasn't turning on her. In fact some of them took up her cry. "Arsonist! Incendiary!" And then people were saying other things. "You killed your mother! You killed your wife!"

"Shall I fetch the archers, Divinitas?" Tigellinus said. "You don't need subjects like these."

Nero was dithering. "More deaths?"

Petronius spoke up. "Divinitas, half the city has perished in the fire already. What is an Emperor without subjects? You don't need more corpses today. You need—"

"Oh, you are so right, Gaius Petronius," said the Emperor. "Always you bring me to my senses. You are the only one who brings order to my chaotic existence. You calm the tempest in my soul."

Tigellinus said, "They are exaggerating, Divinitas. Our men have only torched a couple of districts. Mostly slums anyway."

"You may stop now, Tigellinus. No more destruction. Don't kill anyone. Except traitors, of course." For the woman who had defied the Emperor was already being hustled away by the guards.

"Perhaps you should show her clemency, Divinitas," Petronius said. "The mob is in an ugly mood. They could ... turn against us."

"We have to give them something. They're calling *me* an arsonist — the father of the country, the one who labors without reward on their behalf! We must give them somewhere else to direct their anger."

"They don't need destruction — they need distraction," said the poet Lucan, and the Emperor let out a little giggle at his clever turn of phrase.

"Food, first of all," said Petronius.

"And if there's no food, then what?"

"Entertainment," Nymphidius said.

"Someone to blame," said Himself, and I could see that he meant that person must on no account be Himself. "Find one quickly."

"A scapegoat," said Poppaea.

"Yes, yes. Tigellinus — those men who set fire to those slums — have them crucified."

"Oh, hardly, Divinitas," said Tigellinus. "You can't execute the very people who put you on the throne."

"Don't be impertinent, Tigellinus," said Poppaea, who obviously feared the Praetorians far less than her husband. "He was just joking. My Divine husband ... Pontius Pilatus gave me an idea, when he was going on and on about his past glories at the banquet."

"That washed-up old windbag?"

"He told me of a group of people here in the city that nobody likes. Targeting them would deflect the mob's anger ... and also supply endless fodder for our city's flagging entertainment sector. And no one will miss them. They're just another cult from the east."

"Poppaea ... you are quite brilliant. What are they called, these convenient victims?"

"I'm not sure. But I see Pilatus skulking about over there. I'm sure he'll tell you all about it."

There was a glint in the Emperor's eye. As I looked at him, I realized that the passionate, unconditional love for Himself that I had been feeling a mere two days ago was already starting to fray. It was giving way to more complex feelings. For I still loved him, but I was also beginning to understand him.

That was one of the consequences of being free. I could see past whether someone would have me beaten, would violate me, or at best, not even see me in the room ... I could see who people really were. I could see beyond my own state of being chattel. Two days ago I saw perfection. Today I saw insecurity. All called him Divinitas, yet deep inside, he knew he was no god.

Falling in love, falling out of love ... and I had not even exchanged two sentences with Himself, he who owned the known world.

XXV

NEROPOLIS

Of the Christiani, or Chrestianoi, or whatever they were called, the less said the better; they were a reviled and radical sect, and if *someone* needed to be sacrificed for the preservation of Roman values and civilization, why not? Nobody actually *knew* any of these people. The day that Himself made the decision, no one could be found to disagree, and the Praetorians were immediately dispatched to make it so. But the scale of it ... that was something we did not expect. Nor the speed with which it began.

For my patron and me, and for our household as a whole, it was far more pertinent that somehow, Petronius's home had survived.

The fire had burnt itself out less than a hundred paces from the edge of his home. Farther up the hill, the villas were more or less intact, but looking downhill, the street was a wasteland. A dog was worrying at the corpse of slave. An old woman in a torn stola crouched and wept in the shadow of a broken column.

"The gods must love you," I told Petronius, as the door slave opened the front portal.

"It's you they love, Giton," said my patronus, "for my time will come quite soon."

"How can you say this?" I said.

As I was about to step inside, we heard the old woman, who had come up to the threshold and was screaming curses.

"Dead! Look around you! All dead! And your master is to blame!"

Petronius took an aureus from a pouch and handed it to her. Her eyes widened. "Control yourself, woman," he said. "We did not do this."

"The fire swept uphill all the way from the suburra," Croesus said. "It was the wind, the will of the gods."

She sputtered. "You are the favorite of Himself, the only God who matters — the Incendiary — and it was his Praetorians that flattened this house! Not the wind! They only spared your villa because you are Gaius Petronius Arbiter! The favorite of the Divinitas!"

"The *gods* do not love me," Petronius said to me. "You see it now, don't you? Only *one* god in particular, and he's fickle."

The old woman had been a slave in the villa two dwellings downhill. As the doomsayer of the morning, she was appropriately named Cassandra. She told us how Praetorians had come, not to put out the flames, but to level the house. Her dominus and domina being somewhat old-fashioned, and having no estates in the country to escape to, had killed themselves to avoid the embarrassment of a drop of social status. Most of their slaves had run off.

"Are there no heirs?" Petronius said.

"We don't know. But we don't want the state to take us."

That would have been a bleak prospect indeed. Petronius said, "Speak to Croesus, my steward. In the midst of this mayhem, perhaps we can shelter a few of you until we know who you actually belong to."

"Domine!" she murmured and prostrated herself. "I can cook, I can make healing potions, I can brew poisons…."

***

When we entered, Petronius immediately knelt to thank the Lares and Penates that the house had been spared. Unfortunately there was nothing to sacrifice but a leftover dormouse, but he wrung its neck deftly and slit its throat, splashing its meager blood on the altar.

An old slave brought water and washed our feet. We walked into the atrium and Hylas was there. He burst into tears when he saw us. "Oh, domine," he said, "you, Sporus, you, master, alive!" He patted down a cushion and placed it on a curule for Petronius to sit.

Behind him came my patronus's nephew, Marcus Vinicius. He had a jug of wine and was pouring it into a krater for Petronius. He had ridden ahead to see that our household was in order. I noticed that armor was polished and his crest freshly dyed. "It's true, uncle," he said ruefully. "The guard destroyed as many houses as they saved. They said it's to stop the flames spreading, but there could be other plans. *Neropolis.*"

"City of Nero?" I said. "Where's that?"

"You're standing on it," said Marcus.

"What!" said Gaius Petronius.

"However the fire started," said Marcus Vinicius, "it suits the Divinity's purpose well enough. Neropolis, like a phoenix, rising from the ashes of Rome! A city all in gold and marble."

"And the poor?" Petronius said. "They'll have gold and marble, too, I suppose?"

"I don't think Himself's plans have quite extended as far as the poor yet," said Marcus wryly.

We sat in the atrium and watched the sky as twilight turned to night. The wine had turned sour in the fire, and there was no water; the aqueducts were doubtless being diverted to help put out the flames.

"Our city has lasted for eight centuries," Petronius said. "From a mere village to master of the whole world, eight centuries. I am a Roman — though I was born in Massalia, in Southern Gaul, that too is Rome. Rome is the world, and it is *my* world. I intend to die in Rome, not in Neropolis."

And Petronius read to us, not the distraught and hysteria-filled ravings of the Divinitas, but another account of the fall of Troy, one by a truly great poet. "*Quisque suos patimur manes.* We are all haunted by our own ghosts; we suffer our own private hell," he said. "Virgil died half a century before I was born, but his truth still lives."

Presently Marcus Vinicius rose and left us; I heard him and some junior officers speaking in hushed tones as they went back into the street. I poured my patronus more wine.

The night never became truly dark, because the fire was not spent, not completely. The air had a tang of smoke and burning flesh. When our master had drifted to sleep, Hylas and I carried him to the cubiculum and put him in bed. We lay on either side of him and fell fast asleep like that, the three of us. When I woke, we were both nestled in his arms. The aristocrat, the freedman and the slave. All of Rome, in one small room, an oasis in a flaming wasteland.

***

The fire lasted two more days. We stayed in the house. The bread had run out by then, as our kitchen did not hoard supplies; the master liked everything to be fresh. There was a little pork; it had been roasted before there was time for it to spoil. There wasn't even a dormouse left to eat, as it had been sacrificed on the first day.

On the third day, a messenger came to the door. The Emperor was once again commanding our attendance, and this entertainment came with tickets. An entire basket of clay *tesserae* for distribution to the household, each stamped with seat numbers, gradus and locus, according to rank; and two special ones, small marble disks, inscribed with the names of Marcus Petronius Arbiter ... and C. Petronius Gaii Libertus Sporus.

They were for seats in the Imperial Box at the upcoming Ludi.

"Games?" Petronius shouted at the messenger; the boy quailed and prostrated himself all the way to the floor.

"Yes, my Lord."

"What about renewing the city?" said my patronus. But I already understood the Divinity's intent. Misery had gripped the city, and more than money, more than bread, the citizens needed distraction. Entertainment.

Every great undertaking among the Romans must begin in blood. Every pledge of love. Every auspicious new enterprise. Every building project.

Before he could build Neropolis, Nero need a sacrifice. And to make a new city rise from the ashes of the greatest city in the world, the sacrifice needed to be big.

XXVI

LUDI

Since it would not be proper to arrive *after* the Emperor, Petronius was forced to rise at an unnatural hour. For me, it was not a problem. A slave always wakes up before his master and I was not really used to freedom yet.

We had to spend some time picking the right clothes and painting our faces a little bit, though it would not do to be too ostentatious, lest the Emperor think we were trying to eclipse him. It was almost noon by the time we arrived at the Circus, but luckily the Divinitas was a late riser.

"Noon!" said Petronius, as our litter-bearers took us to where there was a certain secret passageway, which fed into a subterranean hall from which one could access the Imperial box directly by means of a narrow stairway. "Noon," said my patronus again, "how deadly."

For noon, as even I knew by now, is notoriously the most boring hour at any Ludi. It is when they execute criminals, so there is none of the art of gladiatorial combat, where, while death often occurs, the finer points are important, and appreciated by the audience.

"No finer points for the moment," said Petronius. "Except … let me tell you about these underground passageways which lead to a certain corridor … the cryptoporticus … all the way to the Palatine. This is where they killed Caligula, you know. They say he was addressing a troupe of actors, but I've heard a slightly more ignominious story … that the Divinitas needed to get out quickly to take a crap. That's why he had so few attendants that day."

The underground chamber was cool but soon we were ascending into the bright sun. I had seen no Ludi in person but it's one of the things slaves gossip about — who's winning, who's losing, did you hear how Didimus switched from retiarius to secutor, did you see the mock naval battle, you'll never guess who caught the raffle ticket with the three free slaves, he was a slave himself and his dominus took the look — it's a subject for chatter because almost all gladiators are slaves. So it's a pathway to freedom … though it's fraught with danger.

But all the gossip in the world could not have prepared me. The *smell* alone! Blood and sweat and animal shit, all clinging to the humid air, and the monstrous, ravening sound that only ten thousand people can make when they want someone to die.

***

The smell! You never get used to it. I've worked at the Games all my life, from the time I helped with watering the animals till the time they discovered my artistic talents.

The big cats are the worst. They're loners. They don't like to be crowded. Sometimes they fight each other as much as the venators. And sometimes they're bored and won't eat. I was told, in Africa, it's the lionesses that do all the hunting. But the mob does like to see the big manes … they're like a centurion's crest almost, an emblem of virility, of power.

And that day … they say there were more big cats than in the history of Rome. They say they emptied Africa for that spectacle.

Yes. They kicked up sand and the particles were gritty in the nostrils and rank with spoor. Today it is not so bad. They perfumed the entire arena, I see. No expense spared for my great and final drama. My death will be one of the costliest expenditures of the new régime.

***

When we arrived in the box, I kept blinking in the bright sun. Sweat started to pour down my face and the smell was intolerable, despite a brazier burning frankincense and two slaves sprinkling perfume. The Imperial throne was unoccupied, but armed guards stood at every corner of the box. More of a pavilion, really; it could have held a hundred guests, but currently there were only a few poets, whom I recognized, all grumbling because of their forced attendance. Not loudly, you understand. The Praetorians *might* not have understood. Though, to be honest, they were from Germania. They probably knew only basic Latin, and less Greek.

Petronius took a seat, not too close to the throne. I did not feel I merited an actual seat, being only a freedman, so I sat at his feet, as I had done so many other times. Apart from the poets, there was a senator or two, and the usual guards and slaves. A naked Nubian gymnast gyrated in a corner, unwatched.

It was Lucan who noticed me first, in fact. "Amazing to see you wearing clothes, for a change," he said.

"Sporus's days as a delicatus are over," Petronius said. "You're a bit behind on the news, aren't you? I manumitted him."

Lucan said, "Sorry. My house burned down. No time for gossip."

"I'm sure the Divinitas will build you a new one; just flatter him about his newest ode."

"Would you just look at that!" Seneca said, as a lioness strutted past the box with a baby in her jaws. "I know the Emperor means to be thorough, but who wants to see *that?*"

"Who wants to see *anyone* getting eaten?" said Lucan. "I'm waiting for the real show to start."

My eyes glazed over as I watched wave after wave of helpless people being driven onto the sand with whips and goads. There seemed to be an inexhaustible supply of Christians, and an equally endless array of cats. The cats were in no hurry. This wasn't a hungry pride chasing down an antelope.

"They're getting bloated," Lucan said. "Such gross mismanagement."

I was not happy to see Nymphidius enter the box next. He stalked about, glowering. Apparently the lions' feast was simply too boring. As one of the two chief Praetorians he was directly answerable to Himself.

"Why are there so *many* of them?" Lucan said. "Surely there's some kind of system to manage the ratio of cats to captives. You people are masters of these big spectacles."

Nymphidius growled, "But *these* people — they're crazy! The only requirement to avoid getting eaten alive is a one minute ceremony, pinch of incense, a one-sentence declaration of the Divinitas's divinity. When they hear and smell the lions, people will do *anything* to avoid being eaten — we were expecting at least a fifty person turnover — and they're *all* going in to the arena! They're bewitched. It's exasperating."

"Surely," Petronius said, pointing to the half-eaten baby that one lioness was still worrying at, "that little thing wasn't expected to offer up the incense?"

"That's the horror of it," Nymphidius said. "They won't even let us take the babies. Afraid they won't be martyred. Worried they'll miss out on paradise."

"What a heartless cult," said Petronius.

"Indeed," said the Praetorian. "Imagine insisting on your children getting eaten along with you, just because you're too stubborn to say a few words to the Emperor's statue! These people aren't civilized, I tell you."

Nymphidius noticed me and stopped complaining for a moment. "Come here, boy, let's have a quickie behind the drapes."

"I'm *free,"* I said.

"And I'm armed," he said.

I put my arms up, trying to ward him off.

At that moment, though, I heard a familiar growl. "Hercules!" I cried, as the Empress's cheetah tugged at the Praetorian's cloak. The guests in the box laughed. Nymphidius was not popular. Indeed he immediately straightened up and bowed to Poppaea Sabina, who had entered quite noiselessly.

"You bad boy!" she said, wagging a finger … not at me, I suddenly realized, but at Nymphidius, who was quivering like a plate of larks' tongues. "Sporus is not to be molested, you understand. He is my special guest, and under my protection. More importantly, he is under Hercules's."

"Divinitas," I murmured in relief. I wouldn't normally have been pleased to see her, but she reined in the slobbering Nymphidius effectively. She beckoned me now to take Hercules from an old slave who was barely able to hang on to the leash. Hercules came willingly to me and nuzzled against my calves like a dog. Then, as the Empress sat down, she bade me sit at *her* feet while she played with my hair.

"We have a problem, Empress," said the Praetorian. "The cats won't eat."

"Then scourge them."

"Scourge who, Divinitas?"

"The Christians, you idiot. The lions are far too expensive."

Nymphidius ordered a few of his flunkies and they left the box. Presently, some burly, heavily armored soldiers started whipping the Christians, and they began swaying back and forth and stumbling toward the lions, who still didn't seem that interested.

Then, suddenly, they all started singing. It must have been some paean to their god. A few hundred people, their arms linked, singing an eerie, keening music. They rocked from side to side in time with their chanting. The audience started to pay attention. The Christians' chorus rose up in the sultry, stinking air.

Then there was a miracle, of sorts. The animals began to stir. Perhaps the music set off some primal hunger. They started to rush at the Christians, running them down, ripping throats, tearing off limbs. The crowd was howling and applauding. And still they sang. Some in the audience were impressed; they were even cheering them on.

"This is not a good look," said the Empress. "They're supposed to be abject, miserable creatures, being crushed by the might and majesty of the city they tried to burn down. These look more like heroic figures."

"I'm glad the Emperor isn't here to see this débâcle," said Petronius. "He's planning to sing himself, and he doesn't like to be upstaged."

And then, after a blast from a consort of blaring bucinae, Himself was there. He stood at the entry from the cryptoporticus, resplendent in gold and purple, coming close enough to touch, while thousands rose and shouted his name, a thunder-roar that really set off the animals now. They were leaping on their prey, and the sound of crunching bones almost drowned out the singing. You could barely hear the hymn above all that racket.

Nero Claudius Caesar Augustus Germanicus took his seat. And I, my head in the lap of his Empress, was staring right into his eyes.

And he into mine.

XXVII

MORS ET AMOR

I was on the step, wedged between two thrones, and a living god was caressing my hair. I almost pissed myself. The line between the Divinitas's charm and his rage was easy to cross; even I knew that.

"Lovely, your hair," said Himself the Living God. "Not as silky as Poppaea's but ... muskier." He bent down and smelled the top of my head. No wonder Petronius had bade me be liberal with the perfume! "One of my favorite scents," he continued. "Remind me to have some more sent over to Petronius's."

Warily, I looked across to my former master.

"Lucius, dear," Poppaea said, ostentatiously addressing the

living god by his praenomen, "the boy doesn't belong to Petronius anymore."

"Then we must acquire him," said Nero.

"Petronius told me he's been freed."

"No one is really free, where *my* will is concerned," said Nero. Without malice, just the truth. *"Eleutheria thanatos."*

"As you say, Divinitas. There is freedom only in death." I threw myself down at Himself's feet with an extravagantly obsequious move and kissed Himself's feet a few times. I think I missed the actual skin, though my teeth bumped against a ruby the size of a quail's egg. "I beg you, Divinitas, my Lord, my supreme God ... Petronius is finishing the *Satyricon* and he has made me his muse. I implore you, let me stay with him at least until his masterpiece is done."

"Brazen, aren't you?" said the Emperor. "I should have you thrown off the balcony. Your meat is probably sweeter than those sedition-mongers'." I thought my life was over, right then and there. Then he began to laugh uproariously.

"Don't, my dear," Poppaea said. "He's not ready for your malignant sense of humor yet."

"You should have seen the look on your face!" said the Emperor. Then he drew me up by the shoulders and kissed me on the lips.

Poppaea looked askance, but then she clapped her hands. The whole court followed suit. The Emperor let go and I slumped back down onto the steps in front of the throne, unsure about whether I should slink away to the relative safety of Petronius.

The Emperor waved for my patronus to approach.

"You've found a good muse," he said. "Although he's quite impertinent. He's been free for all of ... a week? and already so forward with his betters?"

Petronius said, "Ah, but before the pirates captured him ...

he was a prince."

The Divinitas nodded. "That would explain it."

I looked at Petronius, a bit panic-stricken. After all, Petronius *knew* I was just some village ragamuffin. Or had Aristarchos revealed the "origin story" he had concocted while training me in how to behave amongst aristocrats? Petronius's face betrayed no mendacity at all, but he was an accomplished courtier, suave when he flattered, lying with a smile.

The Emperor said to me, "So, Sporus, what kingdom did your father rule? Do you think I should conquer it? Are there more beautiful people there for me to own?"

Petronius said, "I'm not sure it would be worth it, Divinitas. I think it's barely more than a village. I doubt Sporus could find it on a map."

"Let the boy speak for himself."

"It's true, Divinitas. I hardly remember it."

"Perhaps my Germans would know. Do you speak their language?"

"Their language has some similarities to that of my people," I said, "but I don't really understand it. In Rome I've met only a few people who know my speech."

"Are you Dacian? Macedonian? Those places are all mine already, you know."

"No, Divinitas. Well, where I lived, we didn't really know about Rome. Our ... kingdom was very ... inward-looking."

"Not know about Rome?" The Emperor was genuinely mystified at this. "Now I *really* want your kingdom. Are there such places left in the world?"

I didn't want a Roman legion descending on what was left of my village. Not that I could actually lead the way there. I improvised. "Don't waste your valuable men, Divinitas. I'm a prince, and they killed my father. I may well be all that's left of my people. If you possess me, you already possess my country."

"You are as witty as you are beautiful," said Himself. I admired him then — yes, I had been in and out of love with him before even exchanging two sentences, and I am told that this is what is like to be young — but can you really be surprised that he could turn a boy's head just like that? Wealth and power and looks — are those not the three most alluring characteristics of a lover? He had all three. The first two in greater abundance than any other human being, and as for looks ... he was young. He was adored. He had the voice of an angel. And I must say this as well ... every man who had ever forced himself on me had had an unpleasant smell. Even Petronius, who never took advantage of me at all even though he had every right to ... he had a faint odor behind the layer of expensive perfume.

And the living god smelled like orange peel and cloves. Like the summer sky. Even here, in the stench of blood and guts and sweat and incense ... he was an island of freshness in a cloud of decay.

And, like a thoughtless child, I just sat on the step and stared up into his eyes.

"Divinity ... Divinity ..." Nymphidius said.

"What?"

"The executions are going ... rather slowly. The lions should have been done by the time you arrived, so we could get on to the more intellectual shows. But our guests of honour have made a mess of things. They all refused the incense, so they *all* have to get eaten."

"Quite the cult," said the Emperor.

The crowd had quieted down after its frenzy of greeting the Emperor. There was a lull in the arena. The animals prowled to and fro, no longer interested in their banquet. Oh, a few of them worried at a severed limb. A few heads were being gnawed at. It was sickening yet strangely riveting. Most astounding of all was the seeming indifference of the throng. Though he was trying to stay calm, I could tell that Nymphidius was beside himself.

"We can't have all this dead air," said Nero. "They need to be entertained. When there's no bread, they *must* have a circus."

"Divinitas!" Nymphidius said. "We'll get through this lot as quick as we can."

"You'd better," said Nero. "The crowd will start to get sympathetic. You never know when they'll decide the criminals are underdogs."

Poppaea added, "That would be political suicide."

"Yes, of course, my dear," he said. To me he whispered, "You see. That's all my wife thinks of. And all I care about is my art. The world is the greatest canvas, and the only canvas appropriate to a God."

I had no answer to that. I only continued to gaze at him. He was only partly in our world. He also belonged to a more rarefied universe — the world of the gods, I supposed.

"Do you know who taught me to think like that?" he said. "Your master. Gaius, my arbiter of taste."

"He understands the universe, Divinitas."

"As do you, child," he said. I was falling in love all over again.

At that moment, however, the quiet in the Circus was shattered, much to everyone's relief. The Christians were now singing up a storm. As they sang their paean to their invisible god, the crowd became incensed, and they began chanting as well, a song in praise of the Olympians, from Jove to Vulcan and not excluding a coda that extolled all the great God-Emperors of the Julio-Claudians (somehow they managed to skip Caligula.) The dueling chants were thrilling and then the music-master caused consorts of bucinae, tubae, water-organs, and tympani to play from opposite sides of the arena, melding into a blood-curdling cacophony. Slaves dropped flaming bales of straw behind the cats, to enrage them and to drive them further towards their prey.

Finally, the lions were aroused again. They roared — have you heard a hundred lions roar? — they sprang upon the Christians that remained and made quick work of them. The audience was jeering and hooting. The wind instruments were blaring. Each time someone's head was bitten off, the audience howled and laughed.

"Well, it seems to be working," said Nero.

The Empress clutched his hand. Rather, their hands clasped each other using my head as a cushion. The feeding frenzy went on and on, with fountains of blood, arms and legs being flung in every direction, beasts fighting each other over this corpse or that, but most terrifying of all was the noise of the crowd, their primal joy in bloodletting, thousands upon thousands of human beings howling above the din of the brass and the drums and the screams of the dying.

"I feel a song coming on," said the Emperor.

He called for a lyre.

As he stood, I was able to scamper away, because Himself had finally found something more interesting than me to focus on — Himself was now contemplating Himself. Or at least, his art.

He sang.

I crawled over to my former master.

"You flirted with him," said Petronius. "That is dangerous. It would have been better to just keep still and let him do whatever it is he plans to do to you. Passivity bores him, and it's better to bore Nero than to pique his interest."

The Emperor sang.

They were clearing the arena now. The beasts were being driven back to their cages which would descend through a system of hydraulics down to the labyrinth beneath the area. Those corpses not completely eaten were being drawn by hooks out through the Gates of Death.

The audience could not hear the Emperor; his song was for his private guests alone. More dignitaries were arriving now, well-dressed equites, aristocratic women with their hair piled high and with jewel-studded fibulae pinning their silk stolae. These were not all the literary circle that the Divinitas loved to have around him; there were politicians, military men, doddering old senators. Slaves poured wine and set out extra seats.

In the stands, too, the empty seats were filling up, for the noontime executions of criminals were often an excuse for lunch and a post-prandial nap, and now people were coming back, hoping that the afternoon's spectacles would be more engaging. There was another audience, as well, for the arena was being decorated with crosses, from each of which hung one of the alleged incendiaries. They were strung up only with rope — no nails — doubtless to prolong the excruciation, for otherwise they might have bled out in a few hours. No one paid much attention to them. The sight was so commonplace in Rome as to arouse no curiosity. They soon blended into the background.

More horn calls now, and heralds proclaiming the next tableau in the program...

A brief divertissement: a group of Chrestianoi who have been rooted out of our own armed forces will fight to the death against dwarfs mounted on ostrich chariots ....

A fresh batch of prisoners was being driven in by soldiers with whips. They were given wooden swords — a mockery of the meaning of the wooden sword, as it normally would signify that a gladiator has been given his freedom — and then came the ostrich chariots, each one driven by a full-sized charioteer, but manned by two pint-sized archers. The mob went wild! One of the victims actually managed to jump onto a chariot and despatched the dwarfs by braining them against the side of the car! The crowd demanded this one's freedom and he was allowed to slink out through the Gates of Life, demanding to be martyred a different way as he left and crying that he was a sinner and deserved death....

A reenactment of the Siege of Troy, complete with not one, not two, but SIX wooden horses! For your delight, the hapless citizens of Troy will be played by ... more of those traitorous Chrestianoi ... the ones who hate us ... the ones who burned your beloved city!

Fresh victims now filled the arena. And it went on and on. Hour after hour, and always ending in death. Then, as the sun began to set, something new. From the hydraulic platform there arose a vast, gleaming model of a city. Constructed in wood and painted white to simulate marble, the model had temples, palaces, even a new Circus. Conspicuously absent were any insulae for the poor.

Behold! cried the heralds. *From the ashes of the old, a Greater Rome rises. It shall be called, no longer Rome, but City of Nero!*

"Why now?" I said to Petronius. "It will be dark soon." The crowd did not seem pleased.

I spoke too soon. At a signal from the Divinitas, the hundreds of crosses where Christians had hung all afternoon were set aflame, for they had been treated with pitch. The light transformed the model city. It seemed to come to life. It glowed. It gleamed in the light of people being burned alive. The crowd murmured, then burst into applause, shouting *"Neropolis! Neropolis!"*

"Marvellous!" exclaimed the Emperor. "But Nymphidius, I hope there are enough crosses left to burn at my garden party tonight."

Petronius looked at me. He drew me into a sad embrace. "Eight centuries," he said, "of the greatest civilization in the history of the world. Gone in an evening. Kiss me, my Giton. There won't be many more kisses. I don't plan to outlive Rome."

XXVIII

SACRIFICES

There were plenty of crosses for the garden party. That evening, though more than glutted with gore, we had to sit through another banquet, this one in the imperial gardens. But it was so crowded that we managed not to be seen.

Even some of the aristocrats were homeless for a while, and unable to get food in from their country estates, so the Emperor's largesse was welcome; the rich could still banquet while their slaves went hungry waiting for the next bread delivery.

It was difficult to enjoy the lavish offerings, because the screams of the flaming torches overwhelmed all conversation. Pilatus, the washed-up old general, was holding forth about the cult Rome loved to hate, though his only knowledge of them was from signing their founder's death warrant three decades ago … an incident he had probably forgotten, until it became a good dining out story.

I was surprised that we left the banquet early. My patronus was usually very careful, never dropping the slightest hint of anything negative towards Himself.

I was surprised, too, that Petronius went straight to bed before the sixth hour of the night, for usually this was the time when he was at his most creative. More often than not he would be scratching on a tablet or writing on a scroll at breakneck speed, sometimes asking me to sit quietly in a corner in flickering lamplight, "inspiration" he would call it.

But this time he went straight to the cubiculum, not seeming to notice whether I followed or not. Not wanting him to be alone, I crept in and saw that he had thrown himself on the bed without even removing his sweaty festive garments. He was already snoring lightly.

Quietly, I undressed and lay beside him, wondering how many more times we I would do so. But I, too, quickly fell asleep, my hand gently rubbing my patronus's belly.

I dreamed of dark things.

In my sleep, a lion pursued me through a dark arena. Above, distorted faces jeered.

In my sleep, I wore a crown of thorns and I was nailed to a cross, and it was being hoisted into the air … and strange people, dark-eyed, with guttural voices, mocked me in a strange language. *Queen of Hell,* they were calling me. Black petals streamed from the sky … and the earth parted, and a dark god stood in a sulphurous cleft, and he bellowed wind and thunder. The earth was shaking.

I woke.

No god thundered. But Petronius was gently moaning, with

closed eyes. Above him, wedged between my lord's thighs, a naked Hylas rocked back and forth, pleasuring my patron. A lone lamp illumined Hylas's face. His eyes held a terrible melancholy. Hylas had mocked me when I first came, he seemed to know of nothing beyond the life of a pleasure-toy. And now he did his job, skillfully, feeling nothing.

Petronius was not even awake; Hylas had responded to some stirring in his master's sleep. Presently, my patron shuddered, convulsed, and groaned in release; then he fell still. Hylas calmly wiped off his still sleeping master and then he glanced over at me. When he looked at me, he saw I was awake, and he smiled.

And in that smile, he told me he loved me.

He eased himself off his master, and he lay down with Petronius between us. He never took his eyes off me.

"How long have you …" I whispered.

"Always."

"But you never said anything."

"Slave," he said softly. "Me not exist. But you … you became free, like real human being."

"What do you want from me?" I asked him.

"Nothing…."

"Except?"

"To go down the hill at dawn with you, make sacrifice at Apollo temple, swear me love you." I had thought him hardened; he had been ill-used since he could barely walk, I did not doubt. I wished I had learned more about where he came from, and what dark history he had endured before being saved by Petronius — for I did not doubt that every pleasure slave in my former master's home had somehow been saved from a far worse existence.

I do not know what I felt, really; I knew that if I said a cross word, he would be disconsolate. So I said, "All right, Hylas, I will go to the temple with you … because it is something you need … though unless my patronus frees you, your love is as much his property as your body."

Though we had had little sleep, we did go before dawn. We could not go far. Hylas did not really have permission to leave the villa but as a freedman I supposed I could vouch for him if asked. Hylas was both companion and link-boy, holding up a torch in the narrow dark street.

There was a small shrine at the foot of the hill, more closet than temple, really; it mostly catered to slaves. I had hardly looked at it when we passed by before, because I was usually in the litter with the dominus, and dared not peer through the curtains without his leave.

A woman sold doves at the entrance and Hylas bought a brace, paying for them himself with a worn sestertius. "Why waste your peculium?" I asked him. "I can pay."

"Me bring, me pay," Hylas said.

The room was dark. There was so much incense that you could not see the walls, so though the temple was tiny from the outside, it appeared infinite within. From somewhere beyond the chamber came the sound of a Greek double flute, wailing and undulating, like a couple in the throes of lovemaking.

The priest was a withered, tiny man who at first glance did not look as though he could ever have been in love. His voice was high and chirpy. He barely glanced at us. Another couple was leaving, an old man and a girl young enough to have been his granddaughter.

The priest spoke Greek, but with an exotic accent; he was not from one of the centers of the Hellenistic world like Egypt, but from some far corner of the empire. He said to us, "You have come here of your own free will, to declare your love?"

So far, no reason to lie.

The priest said, "You are in the presence of Apollo, who knows all truths. If you lie to each other, in this place, under the eye of the god, the god will curse you. You shall never find happiness together, and you shall never find happiness apart. Think about that before you say anything."

Beyond the smoke, in a shaft of light, we could see the face of the god. It was a crude, wooden statue, probably very ancient, not like the realistic marble in the temples of the rich. The paint was worn, but not the eyes. They had been retouched. The whites were blinding, precisely caught in the light beam. The irises were pale blue. The god stared down at us, his eyes unreadable. It was as if he meant to say to us, Truth is an absolute thing; there is no bending, no shading. And I was afraid; I had only come to humour Hylas, knowing that he would face a terrible future if he lost his dominus. Even if Petronius were to free him in his will, how would he live? In a brothel? And when lost his youth, would he be sitting at a desk selling tokens, making change for some whoremonger?

"Now," said the priest, "kill the birds."

We each took a dove and wrung its neck. We placed the birds on the altar.

"Close your eyes," said the priest. "Reach out and clasp each other's hands."

I felt Hylas's grip, cold, a little sweaty. The priest said, "Form an image of your beloved in your mind's eye. Say to that image all you have always wanted to say. Under the eye of Apollo Truthsayer, your words are blessed; and that which you dream, he can make real."

I tried to see Hylas's face in my mind but it was only a blur.

Hylas whispered, "Me Hylas, puer delicatus of dominus Petronius. Me swear. Me forever faithful to Sporus. Alone him me love."

An image began to form in my mind. I said to the image, "By Apollo Truthsayer, I declare: I am Gaius Petronius Gaii Libertus Sporus. I will live for you. I will die for you."

Fiercely, Hylas went on, "Me serve you. Me yours. For always."

And I said to the face that had vividly materialized in the darkness behind closed eyelids, "I will never betray you. I will protect you with my life."

The priest said, "Swear by the lives of the two white doves you have killed with your own hands. Their death stands as witness."

I tried to say more to Hylas, but I could not; the face that appeared unbidden to me was the face of Himself, the living god, the master of the world, the poet, the burner of cities, the singer of songs, the murderer of innocents.

We walked back arm in arm. I wondered whether what I had said constituted a lie for which I would be brutally punished. But I hadn't spoken to Hylas. Surely the god could see into my thoughts, could know that I intended no deception.

And yet I feared the curse. Because what do intentions matter?

Did Oedipus *intend* to kill his father and make love to his mother?

Fate, some say, is immutable.

As we arrived at the entrance, I saw the Lady Poppaea leaving in haste. Behind her, through the open door, I could see that the house was in an uproar. She had come with only a dozen guards, and she made them wait by the entrance. It was still not yet dawn.

Poppaea said to me, "Ah, already cheating on your patron

with the slave boys!"

"My Lady —" What could I say to someone I had known so intimately, yet who now had the power to kill me with a single word ... even a glance?

"You'd better hurry," she said. "I will see you again soon, sooner than you think." Ominous words.

The Empress climbed into the litter and drew the curtains. The soldiers and litter-bearers moved away quickly, the slaves trotting, the soldiers marching in double time. This was no official visit. It was as close to incognito as an Empress could get.

We entered the house. Things were being packed. I could see a cart being readied, a few valuables and clothes being loaded onto the back.

I saw Petronius, moving in the foyer, in a daze. He waved us away.

The steward said, "Quick. Pack. You know there's no carts in the streets after sunrise!"

"Where are we going?" I said.

"Cumae," said Croesus. "He means to consult the oracle."

Hylas stood in the doorway, confused, eyes flecked with terror.

"Shall I take Hylas?" I said.

"Take who you like," Croesus said, "only hurry. The Empress came to warn. Tigellinus has obtained a warrant for Petronius's arrest."

"But the dominus hasn't committed any crimes!"

"Treason, apparently."

"Treason? You mean, not staying for the end of the last banquet?"

"Who knows?" Croesus said.

"It must be a mistake."

I felt my patron's hands on my shoulders. I looked up at his face. If he had looked panicked before, it was gone now. His expression held a preternatural calm. He smiled at me. His eyes already seemed not of this world. They were like Apollo's eyes, penetrating my soul, peering from the fog of incense.

"Gods don't make mistakes," said Petronius Arbiter softly.

XXIX

SYBIL

It was the next morning before our party reached Cumae, travelling at a leisurely pace and stopping only for a brief prandium, and a change of horses, on an estate belonging to Marcus Vinicius, and then again for an equally brief cena at sunset, at some great lord's latifundium.

The journey was smooth and uneventful and for all the world like a household jaunt to the countryside … not the final journey of a man marked for treason. We sat in a covered cart, my patronus, Hylas, and me, and behind, in another, many of Petronius's favorite women; women of every hue, including the giantesses who had first taught me how to look beautiful.

They passed the time by singing songs and picking out ancient melodies on a kithara.

As I said, we left long before dawn, to avoid the interdiction on daytime wheeled traffic in the streets of Rome. Cumae is over a hundred *mille passuum* away from Rome, but our convoy made good time. The road was clear and straight and well kept up.

Cumae is older even than Rome. But the whole town is centered on only one thing, the Sybil.

So as we approached, people were already setting up roadside souvenir stalls, even an hour or two from the shrine, and there was an array of cauponae and tabernae to choose from, each more sordid-looking than the last. Croesus went to negotiate a room; we would likely not be spending the night, but I don't think my patronus intended to take the entire party down into the Sybil's cave. They would be able to spend the day shopping, or eating sweetmeats.

After settling the household in the upper story of a taberna that did not appear too filthy, Croesus had the dominus's litter brought down from the baggage cart, and bade the bearers straighten out their tunicae and do their hair. Gaius Petronius Arbiter was not just anyone, and he wasn't going to sneak up on the Sybil of Cumae.

I had the privilege of riding with Petronius. My former master did not seem at all perturbed by the fact that he had likely been condemned to death. Indeed, he acted as though he would live forever. And as we were carried toward the shrine, he wanted to make sure I knew all about where we were going.

"The Sybil," he said, "is a thousand years old … older, even. She is so old that she has shrunk to the size of a cricket, and her voice is a squeaky stridulation."

He told me how Apollo loved her, how she had asked to live for as many years as the grains of sand she held in her fist … but she had not asked for eternal youth, and that is why she has been withering away since before the founding of Rome. "I wrote of her in the *Satyricon,*" he said, and reached for a scroll. He read to me, in that vivid way he had of telling a story, "… and I saw the Sybil with my own eyes, hanging in a bottle, and the boys were asking her, in Greek, what she desired: *Sibylla, ti theleis?* and she answered, *Apothanein thelo.*"

"I want to die," I repeated in Latin.

Did my patronus want to die?

"You're asking me with your eyes," said Petronius. "No need to say it aloud."

"Well, *do you,* my domine?"

"Don't call me that, I freed you."

I threw my arms around him. He daubed my eyes with a fold of his toga. "There, there," he said. "Look, how ironic … it's I who am comforting you, when you have so much still ahead of you."

But I was inconsolable. I was glad Hylas did not see me break down like this. As my patron held me hard to his chest, I felt the litter being lowered to the ground and one of the bearers was tugging at the curtain.

We were in a grove of some kind and there were stone steps leading down into a cavern. The steps were worn, each slab of stone with a smooth hollow from centuries of pilgrims' caligae. The litter-bearers waited above; everyone else was at the taberna, so my patron's penultimate act was something he wanted to share with me alone.

The steps descended into a cavern, and there were boys there, slaves of the oracle perhaps, whose job was to collect gifts, sell sacrificial animals, and assist the squeamish in those little commonplaces of worship, such as wringing doves' necks. They also controlled traffic to the inner caves and there was quite a system to it all; they had made it efficient, even mechanical, over the centuries. "It's all so orderly," my patronus said to me, "you could almost say that they've made a quintessentially Greek mystery into something quite Roman."

"I think that a shiny aureus will let us jump the queue," I

said. I paid the boys myself — a minor fortune to be sure, but I loved Petronius.

"The power of coin! That, too, is very Roman," said Petronius. "Ah, the burden of Empire."

Impressed, the slave elbowed his way through the other supplicants and brought my master and me to a portal hewn from the rock, shaped like a tall isosceles triangle.

From within came a sound that really was like a cricket … a lone cricket singing after winter has already come … singing at the borderland of death. And the smell of incense, so powerful I was choking on it. "Be brave, my boy," said Petronius, and he took me by the hand.

We passed through one cave then another, following the boy who had taken my money. Each cave was entered through one of those triangular openings. The caves grew darker, the clouds of incense thicker. The voice of the cricket grew louder.

At length we reached what seemed to be the last chamber. There was indeed a glass bottle hanging from the ceiling, but I couldn't see anything or anyone inside it.

Half a dozen boys turned to look at me. Slaves held torches aloft. The boys' faces were kohled and rouged, so they seemed halfway between boy and girl. When they saw us they all prostrated themselves.

I looked at Petronius.

To my astonishment … dismay, even … they were grovelling in front of *me,* not my master.

And they cried out in chorus, "Ave, Augusta!"

'What do you mean?" I said. "I'm not an Augusta."

"I knew it," said Gaius Petronius Arbiter. "You have a destiny higher than the house of Petronius."

"But they are calling me Empress," I said.

"Are you displeased?"

"Bewildered," I said. "I'm a boy."

"That," said my patronus, "is in the hands of the gods."

"But isn't the Sybil going to say anything?"

"She speaks all the time," said Petronius, indicating the song of the cricket. "The boys translate."

"So can I ask what they mean?"

The boys rose from their prostration. One who seemed to be their leader spoke to me. He said, "You who shall be Empress ..." and the others said, "Ave!" Then he said, "You who shall a second time be Empress," and the others said, again, "Ave!" And finally, he said, "You who shall reject the title of Goddess ..." and the others again hailed me.

It made no sense, and the incense assailed my nostrils and I could barely breathe.

"No prophecy for my master, who brought me all this way?" I gasped.

The boys did not prostrate themselves to my patronus. Instead, their leader said, "You are wedded to death, but you shall not die." Another boy said, "Your hands will bleed ink." A third said, "Your bastard will be your truth."

"Oh, why can't oracles tell you anything real?" said Petronius. "Come, my Giton, was this not worth an entire gold piece?'

"It's a hoax," I said. "There isn't even anything *in* the bottle."

"Probably not," he said, shaking his head.

We turned to leave, but the way out was blocked by centurions, and at their head stood Tigellinus, Nero's right-hand man, commander of the Praetorians. I'd even been to his house before. He was, I am sure, the one who had agitated for Petronius's removal. He stood there in the smoke, smirking.

"Am I under arrest?" said my patron.

"Not exactly," said Tigellinus.

"I see," Petronius said, "I'm to be slaughtered right here, in a sacred place, while praying to the gods?"

"You don't even believe in the gods," Tigellinus said.

"Who would?" said my master. "Seeing what they have wrought in this world?"

"I tend to agree," Tigellinus said. "But, you're a nobleman, and we're civilized people. The usual conditions will apply, of course; you commit suicide properly, formally and with honor, and the state doesn't seize all your assets."

"Why, there's nothing of mine you want, Tigellinus? Not even a pretty vase, a valuable old manuscript, or the odd villa?"

"Not really," said Tigellinus.

"You never did have any taste."

I could see the Praetorian visibly restrain himself from striking my patronus. It was a peculiar game these aristocrats played, cloaking their hypocrisy behind lip service to some archaic code. I was surprised to see Tigellinus following the code; I had supposed him a simple brute.

"We will escort you back to Rome," Tigellinus said, "so that you can set your affairs in order and take care of this, ah, matter. Can we supply a physician? Himself the Divinitas could provide his personal doctor, an expert in making things painless."

"No need, Tigellinus. I'd rather not travel with an escort. It's not a good look," said Petronius. "People might talk. Rest assured, this ... *matter* you allude to ... will be taken care of correctly and expeditiously."

"It's better if we accompany you."

"Don't you trust me?"

Tigellinus sighed. "I suppose I do, really." He waved, and let us through. Just like that.

I tried to pull my master by the hand, but he insisted on walking slowly, in a dignified way. "Hurry, domine!" I whispered. 'What a stroke of luck! You could be on a ship by morning."

"On a ship? You think I mean to escape, like a slave?"

"I only thought —"

"Oh, my innocent Giton! Where would I go?" said Petronius. "Rome is my life."

XXX

AVE ATQUE VALE

Petronius's last symposium had to be perfect in every detail. And Croesus and the household slaves made it so. There were only a few guests, and all of them poets, his rivals, even; none of them would have wanted to miss the evening. There was a magistrate, too, and an official clerk. And Marcus Vinicius as well, his nephew.

It was difficult because the slaves were all weeping as they served the cena. Hylas was the sole delicatus and served the wine daintily, somehow clenching back his tears.

Before dinner, Petronius had already had a physician open up a vein, but then he had it bound up again, so that he would be able to enjoy the company of his friends.

Despite the fact that Rome had only recently burned, the culina managed a reasonable spread. No larks' tongues or fattened dormice, but the calves' brains in honey were sweet and succulent, and the homely dishes like roasted pork were well seasoned, and there was a good quantity of Falernian wine, which is the only wine that is strong enough to burn.

My former master read aloud some passages from the *Satyricon.* Then he grew bored, and asked instead to hear the classics. And so I quoted Sappho to him:

Come to me now
Release me from my harsh distress,
from all that my heart yet longs for…

"Ah," he said softly. "An ode to Aphrodite." He was weakening, but he smiled at my choice of poetry. "You have come so far in so little time," he said.

Presently he ordered the entire household to gather in the triclinium. And I was to learn why there was a magistrate present, for that night, Gaius Petronius Arbiter officially made known his last will and testament.

"As to the disposition of my inheritance," he said. "It shall be thus. Please, clerk, make a note of all I say, and magistrate, have everything entered officially, so that no questions can arise later. First, let my estates outside Rome become the property of my nephew, Marcus Vinicius. Let him take possession of my slaves, except for the ones I shall name herewith, who shall be manumitted upon my death. And this the little apartment attached to this villa, and all the furnishings therein, fall to my steward, Croesus, to whom I now award his freedom." He named a few more slaves to be freed, some immediately, some whom he asked Vinicius to free "after a certain period of time, as he deems fit." And he continued for a time in this vein, dispensing also a few perfunctory whippings to some of his more ill-behaved slaves, which were carried out on the spot. "And I bestow the delicatus named Hylas to my freedman, Gaius Petronius Gaii Libertus Sporus."

Hylas gasped, and he threw himself at my feet. He began kissing my toes, which I thought a little undignified.

I did not know what to think. I could not imagine myself

owning him. He was really a friend, not a piece of property.

"Me do everything you ask, domine," he said to me. I found his abjectness disturbing. Perhaps I should simply free him in the morning.

"Don't be sad, Hylas," Petronius said. "I could free you, but what would you do? I don't want you working in a lupanar, you're far too delicate for such abuse."

"Me not sad, domine. Me happy to belong to Sporus."

I raised Hylas to his feet. "Be happy," I said.

"Don't beat me too much," Hylas said, and kissed me on the cheek. So, I kissed him on the lips, and the guests applauded.

"Pour yourself some wine, too, Hylas," said Petronius.

"Domine … no, me not presume."

But in the end, we did get Hylas a little drunk, and he began babbling in his own language, an odd guttural-sounding argot, and he was doing a strange dance which he said came from his village. And the guests even laughed a little, almost forgetting the solemnity of the occasion.

Then there was more small talk. Nothing about the Emperor. Nothing about the fact that my patronus was slowly bleeding to death, carefully attended by his physician so he could remain conscious enough to entertain his guests until the last minute.

Finally, Gaius Petronius Arbiter called me over to sit with him. "I want to feel you close to me one last time," he said, "since we are bound for different worlds, me to wander Avernus as a lost shade, you to inhabit Olympus as a goddess … I will not see you even in the next world."

"Patronus," I said, "even if that were true, I would use my powers as a goddess to summon you to me."

"So sweet of you," said Petronius, and kissed me on my brow. "But now, I want you to do me two favors," he said. "My final commands to you, so please do as I ask."

"Of course, patronus," I said.

He beckoned to Croesus. Slaves brought the wine dipper to him. It was a beautiful object, made of some purplish crystalline material, carved out of a single large semi-precious stone. I had seen it only at Petronius's most exclusive parties ... now that I thought about it, only at the very first symposium I had arrived at, the one where I hadn't been wily enough to talk my way out of a lashing.

"Do you see this? It's the most precious object in my house — apart from you, that is, and even for you I paid less. This was three hundred thousand sesterces. Now, pick it up... and ... over there, do you see that marble column? Fling it as hard as you can, and make sure it's quite thoroughly smashed. I'd do it myself, my darling Giton, but I'm bleeding to death, as you know."

I knew it must be something that Himself coveted, so I did as I was told. I'm just a weak boy, trained in pleasure, not soldiering, but I did a creditable job. It broke in several pieces and would never be repaired. Perhaps it was because I threw it with all the rage and disillusion I was feeling, and all the terror that this whole world that had formed itself around me when I came to Rome was now crashing down around me. The wine dipper was smashed in any case, and the guests applauded.

Then Petronius had a scroll brought to me. He sealed it several times. And he said, "Tomorrow, Sporus, you will give this letter to Nero."

He did not say to the Divinitas, or any of the many circumlocutions we always use. "Before you ask," he said, "it's a catalogue of every infamy, and every scandal, and every hurtful thing he has ever done. It is my last word to him as his Arbiter of Elegance."

"But I can't deliver that — he'll kill me!" I said, panicking.

"You are the only person the Emperor *won't* kill for delivering this message."

This I could not believe. Yet, it seemed to me that if Petronius was going to leave us, there was not really any meaningful existence for me, either. By tomorrow, it would all be over.

***

It was then that the home of Petronius Arbiter was visited by no less a person than the Empress herself. She had come in secret, with only a small retinue. She stood in the doorway of the triclinium and a hush fell. What was there to say?

She stood there, elegantly and simply dressed in an imperial purple stola bordered with gold thread. Her face was whited with lead pigment, so she resembled one of the statues of the gods.

"Thank you for coming," Petronius said softly.

"I wouldn't miss it for the world," she said.

"You're not here to gloat, then," he said.

"Hardly," she said. "You've been a shining light in our artistic chaos. And you were instrumental in causing me to attain my goal. I assure you, this is not my choice. But it's the Praetorians who rule in Rome … not the Divinitates."

"Yes, Divinitas," said Petronius.

"No hard feelings, then."

"Of course not. It's just politics," said my patronus.

This was the Roman upper class. It was not proper for them to be concerned with death. Properly brought up nobles were ready to take their own lives at a moment's notice, and not make a fuss about it. It was just politics.

Poppaea Sabina walked up to where I was sitting, and she put her hand on my shoulder. "Tomorrow," she said, "I'll send an escort for you."

"And when you return from the palace," said Petronius, "you will also take possession of this house."

"Domine!" I cried out, though I was sure I would not live to inherit the house, for surely Nero would find a way to seize it.

"I will make sure of it," said the Lady Poppaea Sabina, the mistress of the world, whose every fold of flesh I was intimately acquainted with, who had the power of life and death over me. "You can trust me, Sporus."

She took my hands and I looked up at her face.

Could I really trust her? I had to, at least for now.

I saw a hardness there that I had not seen before. Having such power must have seeped into her soul. But I saw something else, too, something I had not expected to see.

What was I to her? Wasn't I just a plaything, a boy who chanced to resemble her so closely she could use me as a pawn in her little games of power?

But now I saw that in addition to all that … she also feared me.

XXXI

AMOR ET MORS

When the symposium was over, a few of us carried Petronius to his cubiculum. They laid him gently down and said their farewells. Petronius told me to remain. "It may be more dignified to let me die in peace, but I want the last thing I see to be beautiful."

He sat me down beside him and the physician knelt down and loosened the bindings so the blood could once more flow freely from his wrists, running into a priceless antique red-figure vase from the days of the Athenian Republic.

When everyone had left, I gazed down and saw that his eyes held an exquisite serenity.

"You didn't finish the *Satyricon,*" I said.

"Life is full of unfinished things," he said softly. "You, my Giton, are unfinished, too."

"Everything I am, you made," I said.

"And would that I could have made more. But you are to be Augusta, and perhaps a Goddess in your own right, as well. Oh, I wish I could see the spectacle. Sporus, you are the ideal, the perfect boy, the perfect woman." But his tone, as always, held irony.

"I am neither, and I am not perfect," I said.

"Mundus vult decipi, ergo decipiatur. Translate into Greek," he said, sounding as cranky as Aristarchos when I wouldn't apply myself..

"The world wants to be deceived, so let it be deceived," I said.

"I won't be an empress," I said, "I won't be a god. I'll let myself be burned along with your funeral pyre."

"Don't be a silly boy," he said. *"Cito fit, quod dii volunt."*

He said no more to me, but I stripped down to my subligaculum and lay down beside him, and held him, heedless of the blood that spurted all over me. I murmured many words to him, foolish words of a thoughtless child, perhaps, how much I loved him, how much I hated him for leaving me. I babbled. He was silent.

I didn't think I could fall asleep, but weariness overcame me in the end.

And so I awoke at dawn, blood caking on my arms and legs, and Gaius Petronius Arbiter was gone. Someone had come in, closed his eyes, perhaps, and covered him with a woolen blanket; they had left me sleeping.

I shifted, carefully climbed out of the bed and made my way to the bath. Hylas was already there. "Salve, domine," he said to me.

"Don't call me that," I said.

"Sorry, domine," he said. He untied my subligaculum and followed me down into the hot water, and started to scrub away the dried blood.

"There, you clean now," he said.

"But I don't feel clean," I said. I didn't think the blood would ever wash off.

After I had soaked for a time … though I felt no less dirty …

Hylas scraped me off with a strigil and oiled me. I smelled of roses. But I still felt unclean on the outside, and empty on the inside.

Hylas dressed me in a plain tunica and cloak fastened with a bronze fibula. "Now you are beautiful dominus," he said softly.

When I left the bath I could see that Petronius's body had already been bathed, anointed with perfumes, dressed in a clean toga, and that he was laid out on a low bier in the foyer. Behind him was the atrium. From the other walls, the death masks of ancestors looked on. A little incense burned on the altar of the lares and penates. Hylas led me in and I saw the household already gathered.

The libitinarius was already there, taking detailed notes from Croesus about the funeral arrangements. The slaves were weeping, some quite noisily. When I entered they looked at me with a strange kind of apprehension and awe. Gradually, they fell silent. I did not weep. I only felt the emptiness.

I was, I suppose, the master of this house, though I felt nothing at this, just the same numbness. The notion of being a dominus made no sense. All I knew was that my world had ended and I knew no other; I could not even return to my village, for I did not even know the name of the country it was in.

Presently there came Petronius's clients … all wealthy people had such hangers-on … I noted that the poets who had been so eager to attend the dinner-party last night were absent … and all of them went directly to Croesus, who knew each one by name and was able to say something appropriate, such as "Yes, the master thought of you often," or "The master wished your son to have such-and-such a trinket" and so on.

It was clear to me that all this had been planned for a very long time, probably long before any word had come about charges of treason. Croesus worked with a preternatural coolness and efficiency. He was surely the finest steward money could buy. He was free, too, now. I wondered whether he, too, felt empty.

Croesus invited me to sit on a curule behind the bier, for all the world like the young heir of the estate. Marcus took a stool beside me, but in a secondary position, as though I were the main inheritor of his uncle's fortune.

"Did he say anything to you before he died?" he asked me.

"Only ... that when the Gods want something, it happens quickly," I said, for those had been his last words to me.

"True enough," said Marcus grimly. He, too, did not weep, for that would have been unseemly for a patrician whose relative had done something honorable by taking his own life.

I sat like a stone for the rest of the morning, not eating or drinking though wine and refreshments came around many times.

Around the fifth hour, someone came for me from the palace. A small company, in fact, led by a centurion. I took Petronius's letter and followed the soldier to the waiting litter. As I stepped out onto the street, I vomited.

Hylas rushed after me to wipe it off. I went back inside for a change of clothes.

This time I was steadier.

"Are you quite all right?" said the centurion.

"I'll be fine, now," I said.

"Me go with you, domine," Hylas said.

"The boy stays behind," said the soldier. Hylas tried to follow regardless, but the centurion gave such a threatening look, I was sure he was going to strike him. Disconsolate, the boy turned back and reentered the house. The other slaves watched me, all with expressionless eyes, afraid.

I was sure I would never see any of them again.

I closed the curtain of the litter and did not look outside until we reached the Palatine.

***

And yet you did see them all again. Indeed, you survived, and will continue to survive until …

The climax of these games? My apotheosis? I wonder. Why aren't I dead already?

The program has been switched around a little bit. It seems that your throne is still being gilded, and the performer playing the role of Hades had an unexpected … mishap.

The God of Death met an early death?

He had a big match this morning against a wiry little Gaul. The audience didn't like his attitude, so he got a big thumbs down. He's normally very popular. I think he was just getting into character to play your rapist, so he acted a lot more arrogant than usual. They call him the Black Elephant; he came from far to the south, beyond Egypt, and the size of his member was a marvel; the Gaul tossed it to the crowd, so you won't get to experience it up close, I'm afraid. They're searching for a suitably magnificent replacement. They'll want to see your impalement right up in the plebeian seats.

They really want me to die spectacularly —

As you lived, Divinitas. So now, they're flooding the arena now for a sea-battle, and your death-scene will come after that. Once they've found a Hades of the right dimensions.

Oh. Flooding the arena. That explains the smell. The tang of the ocean wind is in the air.

They'll move you to another cell, on higher ground, soon. This level will get too damp. Perhaps, while they ready your next … royal chamber … you'd like to go and watch them preparing the sea-battle?

So I can get a bit of fresh air before I'm deified?

Yes, Divinity.

Shall we go?

Careful with the narrow steps. I haven't worked all day on your makeup to get it all smudged.

Oh yes. They've brought in real sea-water. But there's not much wind. It's stagnant. Perhaps they'll find some way to whip up the waves.

No expense is being spared.

The story of my life … and of my death.

But we've arrived at quite a turning point. You are on your way to see Himself, with the catalogue of his depravities, penned by the world's greatest satirist, in your hands. What do you say to him? And how does it happen that you are not crucified on the spot for such insolence?

Later, my friend. A breeze has sprung up. For now, let me enjoy the wet fragrance of this artificial ocean, and reflect on how my journey began, with chains and the sea … just as it will soon end.

Let me smell the salt and the breeze for one last time; then I'll tell you about what it was like to be mistress of the world.

BOOK TWO

IMPERATRIX

I would like to dedicate this book
to the memory of
my father,
who was the first person
to try to teach me Latin

Cito fit quod dii volunt

When the Gods want something
It happens fast.

— Petronius

I

INSULTING THE GOD

Mistress of the World? You'll tell me what it felt like? But you've been silent for hours. And time is running out. I want to hear it all.

Don't ask me yet. You made me think of my first dominus, Petronius.

It becomes more painful now.

What do you mean? You've told me about being abducted from your village. About being broken in by a pirate, whipped by a tutor, raped by a senator. You've told me of the death of your master, a man you loved with all your heart, a death commanded by a tyrant. Those are tragic, are they not? Could anything be more painful?

Can you ask? You, who are one of the agents of my execution?

From the horrors of the slave market, you are going to step into a world of perfumed baths, oriental silks, lavish banquets, sitting at the apex of the known world. Surely the next chapter of your biography is sweeter than the last.

In fact, my story turns dark, and darker still. After all, I'm sitting here in chains. Not the heavy, clanking chains of a galley slaves, but delicate chains as befit the status I have fallen from. My throne is a make-up stool, my kingdom the Circus, and I'm unlikely to survive being raped in public by the God of Death.

And yet your time as Empress must have been a bright moment in your grim story.

A bright moment?

You're in in luck. A reprieve. The giraffes are revolting.

Revolting?

Against their trainers. They're in a panic. They're not like lions. People haven't had decades of experiencing in training giraffes for the arena, and the fact that their necks can reach the Imperial box is causing chaos. You hear the hubbub outside? They are restoring order. The games won't resume until the crowd is under control.

So I have more time to contemplate my doom.

I think of it as more time to hear your fascinating story.

Only if you can order a better grade of wine. Better yet, tell the guards to escort me to a proper toilet. You've had me in makeup all day already. The bucket is not only degrading, but lonely. Public defecation is more comforting. The coming and going. And the people of Rome, from aristocrat to pickpocket, all coming to the same level, all at their most vulnerable.

One of the things I missed, when I was Empress.

Sharing a sponge on a stick with a senator, a baker, and a male whore from the suburra?

The public lavatories are the single remaining bastion of the Republic.

***

As the litter moved toward the Palatine, I did not even dare pull back the curtain. Marcus Vinicius was walking alongside. I didn't want to see his face. Or anyone's face. I clutched Petronius's letter to my chest. It meant my death, for certain, but then again, what life did I have anyway?

Fortunately, Marcus left me in silence.

We had left Petronius's home at the fifth hour, and the day was growing warmer. Each step up the Palatine increased my unease.

Seeing Himself isn't a question of just turning up and being announced. There are barriers of being vetted and searched. But today, I was just waved through, thanks perhaps to Marcus. Or perhaps not. The guards seemed anxious, nervous, even; and I knew it could not have anything to with the suicide of my patronus.

Marcus still walked with me and I asked him what was going on.

"You'll see," was all he said.

The walk to the presence of Himself is designed to be intimidating. You saw him in marble before you saw him in the flesh. Walking down a cloister, the face of Himself peered down from an inner wall, from a garden. The face was idealized, made as godlike as possible. The statues were painted in colors brighter than reality; the world of the gods is more vivid than our own drab existence.

The last two checkpoints were not even manned. I stood in front of an unwatched entry and presently it flew open, and it was Nymphidius Sabinus who emerged. He did not even leer at me, or make comments about getting me alone in a dark room. He merely hissed at me, "Get inside," and shoved me through. The throneroom was full of people and they were all talking at once. I recognized some of them, and none of them looked happy. Seeing me sparked a new round of whispers.

I walked straight into the Empress, who wrapped her arms around me. Her scent overwhelmed me, a heady mélange of perfumes from all the corners of the empire, from musk to civet to attar of roses. She was dressed in the panoply of state, her face white as a toga candida from the lead paint, her lips bright as the lips of a statue of Venus. Her hair was mountainous, and from it peered an ornament studded with rubies that matched her lips.

Everyone at court saw her embrace me, her stola whipping over my face and hiding me from view.

By showing me favour and familiarity, she made the riff-raff look away. I peered through a fold in her stola. At the other end of the room sat Nero, who seemed to almost be swallowed up inside his golden throne. He was not a god at all.

Tigellinus was whispering in his ear and the Emperor pouted, like a child whose toys have been taken away. The tittering in the room was quieting. Himself's face became completely expressionless. Something terrible was about to happen.

The Lady Poppaea Sabina, Goddess, held my fate wrapped in a piece of cloth, it seemed. Idly, she peeled off the fabric so I could look once more at everyone in the hall. The floor was a vast mythological mosaic; she and I were standing right on the head of the heifer Europa, about to be chased by the God. She held my hand and said softly, "He's aware of you. If you play this right, you'll get through this alive. He's after bigger game than you, pretty thing. I'll get you past this hurdle. I promised Petronius."

In front of the throne stood Seneca and Lucan. The poets, old and young, uncle and nephew, had been roughed up a bit, but they were not in chains or anything. They were looking at the floor. Where they stood, in fact, the mosaic portrait the radiant shower of gold, Jupiter in disguise once more, who was about to descend on the beautiful, imprisoned Danaë and impregnate her with the demigod Perseus. They stood, in fact, in a carpet of gold in a blue ocean, on which the chest containing poor Danaë floated. In most of these myths, Jupiter rapes someone, disguised as something.

***

You're going to be raped by Pluto, instead, though.

Just my luck.

Sorry to interrupt. Go on.

***

Finally, after listening to more of Tigellinus's whisperings, Himself the Divinity exploded. "Why?" he screamed.

The poets shrank back as though he had struck them.

"Why? I did nothing but seek your approbation, your acceptance. Yet you conspired to unseat me! Am I Saturn, swallowing his own children, that you must crawl from my guts and kick me off my throne? What did I ever do to you?"

"Divinitas!" they both mumbled, and prostrated themselves.

"What I simply don't understand," said Himself, "is why you haven't both committed suicide yet."

"We'll take care of it immediately, Divinitas."

"Well, don't make me have to kill you. It will be a lot less pleasant. Though undoubtedly fun. For the whole family. Tigellinus, when are the next games?"

"A month, Divinity."

"So they'll have a whole month to stew about whether their property will be forfeited to the state, a whole month to do the right thing so their descendants can still inherit? Where's the drama in a month of reflection? Did Paris have a month to pick which goddess was the most beautiful? Of course not, or there's be no Trojan War, no Homer, no Aeneas fleeing across the Mare Nostrum, no Nero's song soaring over the flames of the second Troy …."

"How dark the world would be without Nero's song." Poppaea chimed in.

"Where's Petronius? He's the only one I care about. I told Tigellinus that if he was caught in his net, he could throw him back in the river."

"My dear," said Poppaea Sabina, "my poor, dear, beautiful, wounded husband. I have someone here with news of Petronius."

She pushed me forward, into the radius of Divinity. And this is the curious thing: when I stepped into that circle, the buzz of conversation around us seemed to fade to nothing. It was as I was alone there with him, alone in this most public of venues, under the eyes of everyone who was anyone in Rome.

I stood there, eyes downcast, more boy than man. A boy who is a citizen of Rome may set aside the toga praetexta at sixteen, and don the toga virilis of adulthood. I, who had been carried across the sea as a child, I had no age at all, I had no birthday, I had no way to count the passing of time; I was the mirror of my master's will, I was whatever age he saw, and whatever gender, yet always the one possessed, never the possessor.

And the man who possessed the whole world was looking at me, doubtless already deciding my identity for me.

"I've seen this one before, several times," he said. "Once he even came to me as the god Hymen."

"And today?" said the Empress.

"Let's look at you. Boy, look into your Emperor's eyes."

"Yes, Divinitas," I said.

And looked God right in the eye.

Nero was a young man. Perhaps his body was a little less firm than when I saw him, perhaps his eyes more lined. But there was still beauty there. Could a God become shopworn? Was his ignominious end already foreshadowed in those eyes? Suddenly his eyes came much closer. His face rammed down onto mine and he extracted a kiss from my lips. I was shocked. "A second Poppaea," he said. Then, looking at his Empress, he added, "Or perhaps it is my wife who is the second."

"This is Sporus," said Poppaea, "the freedman of Petronius; You've seen him before. You've *wanted* him as a gift, but Petronius cheated you by giving the boy his freedom."

"Really! Then I regret sparing Petronius's life. Guards — go to his house and bring back his head."

"Too late, my dear," said the Empress. "He did himself in last night."

"Oh!" said Himself. "What a beautiful man! You know, he *did* love me. Such devotion! Not like these … pseudo-poets. Gaius Petronius Arbiter was the real thing." Giving me another little cuddle, he said, "And sending me this thing … *you* with a penis! What could be more perfect?"

"Sporus was not Petronius's to send," said the Empress. "The boy owns himself. And perhaps even a sizeable chunk of his ex-dominus's estate. But Petronius has sent him with a message."

"A last epistle of devotion, no doubt. Let's have it, boy."

He went to his throne. He sat down. The throne room was designed so a shaft of sunlight from on high would illuminate the one who occupied the seat of power. At that moment he became Jupiter Optimus Maximus and all the other gods. The light lit up his features, and the lines that made him more human were all washed away.

There was silence in the room.

Tigellinus said to Himself, "Caesar, what about Lucan and Seneca?"

The Emperor said to the two poets, "Once you've heard the words of the great Gaius Petronius Arbiter, go home and kill yourselves like proper gentlemen."

"We shall, Divinity," Seneca said with remarkable dignity.

I opened the scroll and began: "To the God that all Rome worships, from a humble wordsmith who has now joined the citizens of Avernus, greeting. Inasmuch as you have given all such pleasure and edification, let me dedicate to you these poor verses. As you are Hyperion, and I am merely a faex expelled from your glorious anus, my words shall not shine like yours, but let me at least say a few lines in the vulgar tongue as an encomium to your refulgent radiance...."

It was my patronus at his most acerbic, demolishing the subject even as he flattered him. Then began the poem itself, written, like Vergil, in hexameters, the most epic of poetic forms, but using the plain speech of the street.

Anxious to cast his gaze / On the womb that had made him a monster
Ripping her belly wide / He thrust in his bloodstained fingers;
Searching in vain for the One / Who had fashioned his soul in her image,
Nothing remained there but Flesh / Nothing remained of his Mother.

***

I expected at that very moment to be sliced in two by Tigellinus's gladius. There was a dead silence in the whole. The fact that the Divinitas had killed his own mother was not something ever mentioned in public, let alone to his face. Poppaea looked at me and her expression was rapt, almost adoring. It seemed that I was not just Petronius's messenger, but sent from all of Rome.

Himself the Divine Caesar bore no expression at all. The only thing in the chamber awash in light, he was as motionless as one of the statues of the Gods. My message was far from over; there was much more to come, pages and pagers of murder, mayhem, debauchery, and moral decay. I waited.

"Lovely, dear boy," said the Divine Nero Claudius Caesar Augustus Germanicus, in a voice utterly devoid of feeling. "Go on, will you? I'm anxious to hear the next bit."

II

APPEASING THE GOD

I admit, my voice was quaking.

As if matricide wasn't bad enough, the catalogue of crimes continued. My recitation went on and on, and as it did, soldiers came and stood behind me in a half-circle, swords drawn, yet Himself the Divinity did not give any signal.

There was Octavia, his first wife:

Slicing the Head off one Wife /
and presenting that Head to Another…

There were assorted other gruesome killings, including his treatment of that weird cult from the east:

Setting the City on Fire /
and setting on Fire the Guiltless

But my former dominus had saved the worst barbs for last:

Water quenched not the flames /
nor the frenzied screams of the dying;
Setting more fires to contain /
the unstoppable blaze was quite useless;
Great Caesar vanquished the flames /
with his lyre and his lyrical singing;
Orpheus tamed monsters with melos /
Nero slew fire with boredom!

I was doomed as surely as I was standing there. For though some might say the DIvinity's poetry was not the equal of Homer, only Petronius had dared to call it boring. No punishment could be horrific enough for such a crime.

I was as dead as the silence in the chamber.

All eyes were on Himself, Emperor and God. No one looked at me; I was already yesterday's news.

Incredibly, after an unbearably long pause, Nero started to applaud. And laugh. The others in the court were confused, and still didn't say anything. The Emperor cleared his throat. Silence fell again.

"You're all such idiots," he said, "to take this satire at face value. Literal-mindedness is hardly the way to perceive the complexities of the mind of Petronius, creator of *Satyricon!* This child has used his lips to spin filth into gold ... the innocence of his utterance shows it. Petronius put such a blasphemous diatribe in the mouth of such a delectable creature in order to tell me that no matter what the critics may say, my work still partakes of the nature of divine, ineffable beauty. Who among you had the breeding, the good manners, to commit suicide even before I commanded it? He was a friend. I loved him. You other poets are of negligible interest to history."

"In any case, Divinitas," Tigellinus said, "they are traitors. They joined with Calpurnius Piso to attempt to overthrow you."

"Oh, what does that matter?" said Nero. "They've committed a far worse sin than that — writing bad poetry."

The two poets threw themselves on the floor, clasping the hem of his robe.

"Oh, go on," said the Emperor. "Go home and kill yourselves already."

"And the other conspirators, Divinitas?" Tigellinus said.

"Yes, yes, yes." Louder, he announced, "You can all go and kill yourselves now. I mean the conspirators, of course. Everyone else, just carry on. Oh! If any of you conspirators have really *big* estates, I'll seize them, so I'd rather you *not* kill yourself."

"Divinitas," Tigellinus said, "It doesn't really matter. If you want their estates, we can always announce that they didn't commit suicide. Who would know? And even if they did, who would *dare* to know?"

"Are you implying that I, a God, might be in the business of deception?" said Nero.

"I—"

"Quite so," said the Emperor. "For my brother, Jove, is the biggest liar of them all." And he laughed uproariously; and everyone in the room did too, even, I noticed, those who had probably been condemned to death. But Seneca left the room sobbing, supported by Lucan. Presently other people began to leave too, some on their own, others dragged out by soldiers.

I had arrived in the middle of a bloodbath, even though it was being conducted with terrifying civility. That was the Roman way, though. No one meets their doom with as much sang-froid as a Roman aristocrat.

The throneroom had cleared somewhat. Some slaves and soldiers remained.

"Don't think for a moment," Poppaea whispered in my ear, "that my husband meant a word he said. He knows everything in your message is true. He's always suspected that Petronius didn't like his poetry."

"Am I still going to be killed?" I said softly.

"That depends on you," said the Lady Poppaea. "You've insulted him, and now you must appease him."

"Shall we eat?" said the Divine Nero. "I've had nothing all day."

***

It was about the eighth hour, still mid-afternoon, but we were ushered into a garden where a there was a table laden with what was, I suppose, a light repast by imperial standards. Much of the fare was relatively simple: bread, olives, grapes, figs, wine and salt, but in the center was a platter of peacocks' brains in a honey sauce.

The couch Himself sat in was double-width, and padded enough for a strenuous bout of lovemaking. The Empress and I shared the left couch of this outer triclinium, while on the right sat Tigellinus. At a slight distance sat a secretary, who was reading names from a tablet to Tigellinus, who was passing them on to the Emperor.

The Divine Nero sometimes shook his head, sometimes nodded; the secretary made notes.

"It's a tiring day," said Himself, "when you have to order a hundred executions before breakfast."

"I'm sorry Calpurnius Piso has put you in such a foul mood, Divinitas," said Tigellinus. "But I think this list just about covers everyone in the plot."

"But the poets — why the poets?"

"You poor thing," Poppaea said to me. "You stumbled into a monstrous conspiracy. Half the senate was plotting deicide."

"Petronius, Petronius," said Nero. "How he loved me. That final satire — so trenchant, so scintillating."

"He loved you?" said Tigellinus. "The man tore you to shreds."

"How little you understand the complexities of artistic expression," said Himself. "You're such a boor, such a brute."

"I know an insult when I hear one."

"I should have you flogged for betraying such a paucity of culture," the Emperor said.

"Then who," said Tigellinus, "would protect you from all those conspirators? Who, as I have demonstrated I think, are lurking behind every bush, every drape, every column."

"Oh, go away, Tigellinus," said the Emperor. "You, too, Epaphroditus. Just leave the list. I'll draw a line through the ones who we've dealt with."

The little clerk, or secretary, slunk away, but not before giving me a look as though he were already plotting my death. Then Tigellinus rose and he too looked at me, but more as a cat regards a mouse.

"Oh, good," said the Lady Poppaea. "We're just family now." She clapped her hands, and a tall, oiled Nubian brought in Hercules on a golden chain. "Hercules misses you, Sporus," she said. "He trusts you. Don't worry. We never eat our friends."

The cheetah meekly crouched at our feet, purring a little.

"Until they're not," said Nero.

The Lady Poppaea said to me, "This is your chance, my little twin brother. The gods, or the gutter? It's your choice. Appease him."

"I don't know how," I said.

"Your master knew how. He appeased him until he couldn't stomach it any more."

The Emperor beckoned to us both with a crook of the finger. The Lady Poppaea and I sat on either side, and Hercules moved as well. I saw that the cheetah unnerved him more than he did me. "It's good to have a spare Poppaea," he said.

"You don't own him," Poppaea said.

"I own everything," he said, a waved to a slave to bring the peacocks' brains. "I do so love peacocks' brains," he said. "Squishy, soft, and succulent." He took one between thumb and forefinger. "Say *ah,*" he said to me, and popped it in my mouth. "Why, look at him swallow!" he said to the Empress. "Can you read and write?" he said to me.

"I'm getting better, Divinitas."

"Fetch the tablet and read me the names. From the top."

"Uh … Plautius Lateranus … Afranius Quintianus … Novius Priscus …"

"You make these names sound so melodious. I love the way you said 'Priscus' … ha, ha, Priskie-Whiskie! Adorable! Just for that, I think I'll let him go."

Poppaea said, "What, just like that?" She sipped at a bowl of wine. "He plotted to have you murdered!"

"A god should be capricious," I said. "Otherwise, he'd be too predictable, and the gods shouldn't be predictable. Vengeance and clemency should be wielded with apparent randomness."

"You *have* learned something from Petronius," Nero said, laughing. "Well, I was getting tired of my secretary, Epaphroditus. Tired of looking at him. He's starting to age, too. I don't like old people."

"I suppose you wouldn't, Divinity, since you belong with the immortals."

Poppaea reached over and slapped my wrist, giggling.

"Say 'Priscus' again," said Himself. "I love your accent. It's Scythian, is it? Or even further afield?"

"Priscus! Priscus!" I said. And I laughed along with the Emperor.

But deep inside myself, there was a dark place. In that place dwelt my master, dead at his own because of the Emperor's whim. There were other ghosts, too. Hyacinth. And my own childhood, murdered by a pirate rapist. I had not seen my tutor, Aristarchos, since moving to Petronius's house. I longed for the woman named Spider, who for a time had been almost like a mother to me. It occurred to me that perhaps if I managed to get a real position in the imperial hierarchy, I could search for her. I could get things that I wanted, including an identity that was not created by an owner.

Though I had been free for some time now, it took my dominus's death to make me understand.

"Have another brain," said the Emperor, feeding me Himself.

"Divinitas," I said, "how many peacocks does it take to make such a platter?"

"Wonderful!" said Himself. "Poppaea never takes an interest in how the world runs. For her, the brains just appear by magic. The answer to question is — why — we have our own, private little — to coin a word — *pavonarium*. Would you like to see peacocks — a veritable ocean of peacocks — more bird-brains than even in the Senate?" He clapped hands, dropping a brain onto the grass, though Hercules quickly disposed of it. "Come!"

He took me by the hand and started to pull me in toward the far side of the garden, where there was a fountain cunningly designed like a pair of dolphins. I turned to look at the Lady Poppaea, terrified that I would soon be alone with the God.

"This could be your fortune," she said to me. "You've

insulted, you've appeased. Now, Sporus, you must seduce."

III

SEDUCING THE GOD

Alone with the God.

Well … as alone as was humanly possible, as there were plenty of slaves and guards skulking just out of sight, ready to pounce if their God needed rescuing. The Emperor took me by the hand, and we were almost like two schoolboys, except that one held the power of life and death over the other.

"I love peacocks almost as much as Greek tragedy," said Himself.

The cacophony assailed us before we turned a corner and we were in another cloistered walk that surrounded an atrium, but this square was jammed with peacocks. The honking was hideous, and a rancid stench of bird shit fouled the air. A low wooden railing prevented the birds from escaping into the colonnade.

The Divinity pulled out a clear, green disk with a thin gold bezel and began looking at the creatures through it. He handed me another, a red one. "Looking at the world through an emerald or a ruby," he said, "can sometimes make things ever so much more clear."

I saw the world tinted in rose. It was pretty.

"They are just like the senate," said the Emperor, giggling as he put away his jewel spyglasses. "Endlessly preening and fanning their gaudy feathers, fighting over the peahens, thinking of nothing but their own cocks and bellies! Look there!"

Two of the gaudiest specimens were battling it out at the edge, squawking and flinging each other against the railings. "The green one comes from India, the one with the truly resplendent tail comes from even farther away. And look over there — there's a white one. They are like you, all of them, they come from beyond the empire's edge. And I can have any one of them for breakfast. Just as I can have you for breakfast, Poppaea."

I was going to say, *I'm not Poppaea,* but a little warning went off in the back of my mind. *I'm a freedman,* I told himself, but *but this man owns freedom itself.*

So I just said, "Yes, Divinity," and smiled sweetly.

Himself the Divine Nero took me in his arms, and kissed me, very gently pushing me backwards. To my surprise, a couch broke my fall. Slaves had moved it silently into the colonnade. On either end, a kneeling slave held up a cup of water. I felt my clothes sliding off my back, and glancing warily to one side saw a boy folding them neatly and placing them on a silver tray. The Divinity's robes vanished with equal swiftness, though his were a lot more elaborate than mine, and *his* tray was gold.

Only a few hours had passed since I left my dead patronus's house. I was still alive, and though I had thought my life was over along with Petronius's, I was beginning to think I might survive the night.

And if the price of survival was a sore anus?

I needed to think quickly. My mind was in chaos, still trying to make sense of my grief at losing everything I had only just learned to love. My buttocks collided with the soft cushions in the exact second that my last shred of clothing was removed. Even my *subligaculum* had been untied so deftly I had not noticed until it was gone.

An image entered my consciousness … the first time I saw the Divinity, grunting beneath the thrusts of another freedman, Pythagoras. A Roman man may take the active role in copulating with anything, human or animal, but to receive, to be a *pathicus,* is lower than the lowest. But the Divinity wasn't a Roman *man,* was he? He was a God. The only God who mattered in the real world.

The God who was lowering himself into position, as another slave lifted my legs to afford him access, whose tongue was licking off the last fragments of peacock's brain from my teeth. His paused in mid-kiss and I took advantage to speak. "Divinitas," I said. "I am yours and you may possess me at any time … and yet … I have this secret fantasy … I hardly dare whisper it …"

He looked into my eyes.

"What is it, dearest Poppaea?" he said. "I can fulfill any desire; you must know that."

"Could I … my Lord … could I perhaps possess *you?"*

Nero Claudius Caesar Augustus Germanicus sat bolt upright for a moment. "That is the most impertinent thing I've ever heard." That was it. I was doomed. How could I have been so reckless? I closed my eyes. "Let me get rid of the slaves, first," the Emperor said. "All of you — one hundred paces — and avert your eyes until I command it!" I felt myself being moved into another position and when I opened my eyes, the entire entourage had magically vanished. I knew they must be there, behind columns or furniture. The caterwauling of the peafowl continued, even more strident than before.

I wondered why he had to dismiss all the slaves. The last time I had seen him in such a position, it had been at a wild dinner party with dozens of onlookers from Rome's highest echelons. But as I was to find out, there were as many Neros as there are hours in a year.

The Emperor smiled. "I know that you're not actually Poppaea," he said softly.

Nero reclined with his face turned up towards me, his haunches raised. I knew what I must do. I thought of my burning village, of the vicious pirate slavemonger who "broke me in." I thought of my master, Petronius, who had never once forced me at all. I thought of Hyacinth, and of Hylas, still waiting for at Petronius's villa, probably unsure of whether he would ever see me again.

And I thought of the first time I had heard Nero sing. He did have a certain art, he did have some vision of something beautiful, though his muse might have been twisted and depraved. I thought of how I'd fallen in love at first sight, and how quickly I had been disillusioned. And when I looked at Himself, master of the world, I also saw a small boy inside, an unloved boy, a boy who recognized flattery yet had come to believe it was proof of love. And in the moment, I did not fear him.

"Divinitas!" I whispered.

In so small a voice that he barely be heard above the squawking of the peacocks, he said, "Call me Lucius."

***

By time I emerged from the encounter, I had acquired a ruby

lens for myself, along with a small pouch of aurei. Himself did not command me to stay, but told me to go home and take care of my affairs.

"That was an exhausting bout," he said, "and I shall write an ode about it. Perhaps, I shall rhapsodize about the young Troilus, receiving the heroic member of Achilles. As a poet, I must experience all things, as you know. We shall consider our little tryst … artistic research."

"And Petronius's letter, Divinity? Shall I burn it?"

"Not at all. I shall keep it. I may need an excuse, one day, to have you executed."

"Yes … Lucius."

He slapped my face. "Never in public!" he whispered harshly. So saying, he left for an inner room, and left the slaves to escort me to back to the palace entrance.

I was standing in the hallway, rubbing my cheek. It seemed that Marcus and some other soldiers had been waiting to take me make, and that Petronius's litterbearers were standing by beyond the entrance. Dully I made my way toward the door.

But as the slaves opened the portal, the Lady Poppaea came upon me as though by accident — I knew of course that she never did anything by accident —and pretended to be surprised at seeing me.

"Oh!" she said. "You're alive."

"I think so."

A slave behind her was carrying a bowl of snow, perhaps meant for cooling a drink; Poppaea dipped her hands in the snow and patted my cheek. "He does like it rough sometimes," she said with a wink. "And yet, in a few hours, you have managed to insult, appease, *and* seduce him. You're doing better even than me."

Without warning, appallingly, I started to cry. I was nobody. I had no real home, no parents, no patron … and I was in a lion's den. Roman men do not cry. I was neither Roman, not a man.

"So," said the Lady Poppaea, "your poised exterior does have a cracking point." But she was not being cruel, just truthful.

"I'm just a child!" I said.

The mistress of the world took me in her arms. I held her tight — too tight — as though she were my mother. She wiped my tears with a fold of her stola. "There, there," she said softly. "It will be good to have you here now and then. I don't know what your status will be, as you are a freedman and I don't know whether Petronius has left you anything — or indeed whether the Divinitas will contravene the custom by seizing Petronius's property — but I am going to need relief."

"Relief?"

"Yes, Sporus," said the Lady Poppaea Sabina. "I am pregnant."

IV

DOMINUS

The Lady Poppaea Sabina, Empress of the World, had not yet told the Divinitas.

"I don't know," she said, "if he actually ripped open his mother's womb, as the rumors contend. But I think I'll protect mine, at least until it shows."

She handed me a second pouch of gold before I left. It was not yet sunset, but though I had left with nothing but a damning letter, I was returning with 40 aurei and a giant ruby. Enough to hire a legionary for three years.

"A few more visits to the palace and you could have a private army," said Marcus as he helped me into the litter. I was woozy; after an hour's exercise with the Divinitas I had downed several cups of snow-cooled Lesbian wine.

***

When I reentered the house of my former master, there was something of a reception committee, although all wore the dark clothes of mourning and many had ripped their clothes and lacerated their cheeks. I could hear female slaves wailing from inner room. Petronius had been moved to a taller bier beneath the masks of his ancestors and the household gods. A libitinarius was still watching over the body and arranging and rearranging the folds of his cloak. The house was dark.

Yet Hylas broke away from the group and embraced me before remembering his place and, kneeling, removed my caligae, whispering *"Salve, domine."* He waved away the foot-washer slave, took the jar and washed my feet himself.

"No need to call me your dominus," I said. "Not after all we went through together."

But Croesus said, "The boy knows his place."

Hylas went inside to fetch me a toga pulla so I would look less festive, and he draped it over my tunica.

"Dark becomes you," said Marcus Vinicius as he looked on approvingly.

Then Croesus said, "If I ever whipped you, Sporus, be assured I was only doing my job, and I drove the lash as lightly as I dared." He looked at me strangely. Had things changed so much?

"Never left a mark," I said, laughing, "though you really made it sting."

"It's an art," he said, "hurting the slaves without damaging them."

"You are never to beat Hylas," I said.

"That is entirely your decision, Gaius Petronius Sporus," said Croesus, who had not addressed me so while his master was living.

"If Sporus want," Hylas said, "Sporus beat me himself." And he suddenly started crying. "Me think you no come back."

"You," I said, "are going to stop speaking Latin in that

barbarous fashion. I've been here less time than you, and I know a nominative from an accusative." To Marcus I said, "Can I get Aristarchos to tutor him?"

"I doubt he's for sale," Marcus said, "but we can go to the market on the Kalends and buy him a good tutor. It will be more than 4,000 sesterces, mind you. That's all the money you have. But don't worry, I'll buy him for you as a ... wedding gift."

"Wedding? We only *did* it once."

Everyone laughed, breaking the pall. I was embarrassed, I could feel my cheeks reddening. I realized that they all *knew*. My trip to the palace only had two possible outcomes, the other one being me nailed to a cross somewhere. It was secretly a bit delicious to realize, on the other hand, that none of them would probably have imagined that in the second outcome, it would be *I* who would end up doing the nailing.

Croesus said, "We've made up the master's cubiculum for you. He would have wanted that." So I would sleep in the bed Petronius died in. I felt a twinge of panic.

"Shouldn't *Marcus* have the master's quarters?"

"I have my own house, my own servants," said Marcus Vinicius. "I'll be the master here in name; Croesus will keep up this place for me and answer to me directly; I'll take some of the slaves that were Petronius didn't set free, but you'll have a small household at your disposal and you will be my deputy. As for money, you'll get a small allowance from out estates in the country. Not much. You could start a business: no shame in that, you're not of noble blood."

"I don't know anything about business," I said.

"Buying and selling delicati?" Croesus said. "Obviously you would have insider knowledge, and a good eye."

"Croesus," Marcus said, "I don't think he wants to put anyone through what he went through."

"If not prostitution, what else could you profit from?" said Croesus.

"I want to know more about poetry," I said, "and music."

"A gentleman of leisure, then," Croesus said, without a trace of irony.

Marcus said, "I'll have to buy the young dominus a more expensive tutor, then." He started to leave; as a Roman officer, he probably had something to do other than hold a frightened boy's hand; I could understand that.

And yet, my terror overcame me. I did not want to lie down on that bed, not by myself, not even with Hylas. I wanted someone to comfort me, someone stronger than me. I reached out to Vinicnius with the only means of persuasion I knew. "Marcus!" I cried out. "Marcus, sleep with me!"

He understood, and stayed.

***

Though not in my bed. He *really* understood, you see.

He sat on a sella beside my couch. At my feet, curled tight, like a cat, was Hylas, who was fast asleep. Slaves fall asleep quickly; it's the only time they achieve freedom.

I just lay there for a long time, sobbing into the cushions, while Vinicius stroked my hair. After a great deal of time had passed, and the oil in the lamp had been twice refilled, my weeping subsided a little and I finally felt brave enough to ask him what today was all about.

"Gaius Calpurnius Piso," Marcus said with a sigh.

"Who's that? Another bad poet?"

"Worse. A conspirator. I have forty-nine more people on the arrest list tomorrow … and later I have to speak the eulogium for your patronus."

The lamp flickered. His face, lined with concerned, looked at me out of a pool of shadow. "You have to kill forty-nine people tomorrow?"

"Not in person, no, but if I don't, I'll have to send someone. Tigellinus has the master list. You'd recognize most of the names."

***

"A conspiracy is like a plague. You breathe it, you catch it, you die. Was my uncle Petronius evil? You know he was not. Were Lucan and Seneca evil? Plots within plots. They planned to kill Nero and make Piso Emperor, but inside that plot was a plot to kill Piso and make Seneca Emperor, so that the conspirators wouldn't appear self-serving."

"Did Seneca even know?"

"It doesn't matter. He breathed it. He caught it. He's dead, or as good as dead. When this is over, half the noble families in Rome will be gone, and Himself will be much, much richer. He might even be able to afford to finish his Golden House."

But I was thinking that my patronus would be laid on a funeral pyre tomorrow, and that Marcus would try to offer words of praise and comfort, but that I would not be comforted. "What will you say in your eulogium?" I said, feeling tired now, though I was afraid to feel asleep with my patronus's shade perhaps hovering over me.

"What I say will be forgotten in minutes," said Marcus Vinicius, "seeing that Himself is going to be speaking as well. He wouldn't miss the opportunity to perform a new ode. And you know that tragic odes are his speciality."

"The Divinity will perform a eulogy … over someone whose death he is responsible for?"

"He doesn't think of it that way. He thinks Petronius did it out of devotion. Even your little reading, a last taste of his satyrical wit. Petronius was always the only person who dared to criticise Himself. Even though Tigellinus got him on the death list, I think Nero meant to find a way around it. You loved my uncle. In his way, Himself too loved Petronius."

As I finally drifted into fitful sleep, I was thinking: *for the Gods, there is no difference between love and death.*

V

FUNERAL

And then came the funeral of my patronus. What can I say? The tiresome, fully paid-for wailing of professional mourners first. A Greek theme predominated, as befit Petronius's literary stature, meaning hired women beating their breasts and the keening of double flutes, doleful but tinged with eroticism. I was an insignificant little one in this throng of important persons. They included such senators as had not already been arrested or gone off to commit suicide.

***

The master of the world had no peer, and certainly master in poesy, either, not any more. Homer was long gone; Ovid had been dead, in exile, for half a century; Virgil, too had been gone as long. Horace, too. The three legends; long gone before my birth.

And the legends of our own time? Petronius was gone too, now. His passion, his love for beautiful things, his brutal wit, all gone. Until then, he was the only Roman I could sleep with and feel safe. I did not know if I would ever find another.

Seneca and Lucan had already vanished. Whether they had committed suicide, I did not know.

The funeral procession went from my patronus's domus all the way down to the forum; Petronius was important enough to merit a public eulogy, and his suicide had rendered his death entirely honorable, no matter what acts of insurrection he might have been accused of. The assemblage of priests, acolytes, mourners and instrumentalists clogged up the street and occasionally zigzagged to avoid a pile of dung. By now I was more used to riding in a litter, shielded by a curtain from the cacophony of scents: perfume, shit, baking bread and roasting meat and urine being delivered to laundries. As I walked, Rome clung to my nostrils, mixed into my sweat.

It was a long day, beginning at the eighth hour, the afternoon sun still cruel.

First, the forum, and Marcus Vinicius's was but one of a number of "warm-up" eulogies, for it was said that Himself planned to deliver the climactic words. Marcus spoke of his uncle's many kindnesses, his discriminating aestheticism, even of me. But no one looked my way; I was a boy in a toga pulla, indistinguishable from any other mourner. The kohl around my eyes was smudged from tears. Hylas stood behind me, staring at the ground. I was nowhere near the great senators and patricians. I was with Croesus and the other ex-slaves, crowded toward the back, in the shadow of an archway.

At length came Himself, preceded by a honour guard of Praetorians, to the raucous bellow of bucinae and cornua. Behind them came women dressed as maenads, each beating a tympanon or shaking a sistrum. Above the racket was the shrieking of the double aulos players, like a tempest in the trees. The music was bloodcurdling, as though the gates of Hades were screeching open.

And abruptly, it stopped.

A burst of chatter followed, became still.

I heard Tigellinus barking out a command.

The double line of guards and musicians separated into walls of an alley; Himself was arriving, carried in a litter by sixteen matched, oiled Nubians, each wearing only a white loincloth. The musk of mingled man-sweat and olive oil wafted towards us.

Behind him came the litter of the Empress, borne by sixteen perfectly matched blonde women, pale, wearing only a black subligaculum; the perfect contrast to the Divinity's litter, black on white, white on black.

In the quiet, the Emperor tuned his kithara.

He approached the rostrum that overlooked the bier.

As one who had once served as a *consul suffectus,* Petronius was entitled to wear the toga picta, though I had never seen him dressed that way. In his hands he held the shards of the wine-dipper that he knew the Divinitas coveted. The Emperor would have to look at this smashed work of art during his eulogy; Petronius was having yet another last laugh.

The Lady Poppaea Sabina had a sharp eye. She saw me right away, even though I was trying to hide behind my patronus's steward. She crooked a finger. I stepped forward hesitantly, but, heedless of decorum, she swooped toward the crowd as the guards hastened to protect her, and pulled me out.

"Look what I've found, Lucius!" she said to the Emperor. Several people nearby, hearing her, were shocked at her disrespect for the God, though she herself was technically divine.

"Petronius's Giton," he said. "And *your* replacement, should anything ever befall you."

As if anything could befall the mistress of the world, who

held everything in the palm of her hand.

Himself bade me approach. I looked back. I could see the apprehension in Hylas's eyes. I walked cautiously towards him.

"Come closer," he said. "I want to see what inspired Petronius."

I went right up to him. Of course, I was afraid, even though only a few days ago I had been ramming my small manhood into the sacred shit-hole. I tried to overcome my stark terror by imagining Himself squirming on the couch, the slaves all tastefully out of sight or averting their eyes, amid the squawking of peacocks.

The Emperor placed me on his left, and Poppaea stood on his right. He looked from me to her. "I don't know which Muse is the more beautiful," he said softly. "It's a pity Petronius killed himself; I can't legally seize his property now."

"He's free," Poppaea reminded him. "You couldn't have seized him anyway."

"My secretary, Epaphroditus, whom you met," said Himself to me, "himself has a slave named Epictetus, who is a great philosopher, though no older than you, Sporus. And you know what this boy said to me? 'No man is free, save he be master of himself.'"

I remembered Ephaphroditus, the little clerk who wrote down the names of everyone who should be executed.

"I freed Epaphroditus, you know," Himself said. "He was so helpful in choosing who I needed to get rid of after that conspiracy."

He looked at me again. Perhaps he too was reliving our little tryst among the peacocks. He smiled a little, and I smiled too. Then he said, "Perhaps he should have saved the wine dipper, and smashed you instead. Sporus in one piece rebukes me more than a voiceless piece of ancient crockery."

I recoiled a little, in fear, but he said, "If you're going to survive the palace, my child, you'd best learn to tell when I'm joking."

"The palace, Divinity?" I said.

"Yes. You're moving in."

Poppaea clapped her hands. "Thank you, my Lord!" she said. "Two of me will be able to divide the work."

"One to bear the next Divinitas, the other to fuck," said the Emperor.

He stepped toward the rostrum. Silence fell again. But in the distance there were still murmurs of the city, for Rome never sleeps. Now I recognized more of the courtiers. There was Epaphroditus, busy with a wax tablet, a boy in tow — not a delicatus to be sure, as he was decidedly plain — but so seriously-looking that he had a kind of charisma.

Was that the philosopher slave?

I saw Tigellinus, and Nymphidius, too, especially since he was leering at me. Then he sort of swivelled and leered at Hylas, whom I had left behind in the crowd. He even leered at a slave of Epaphroditus. He was omnivorous in his leering.

Marcus Vinicius was in a group of aristocrats, distinguishable by his toga pulla. As a relative — and heir — he was most clearly in morning, with his ripped garment of dark wool, like mine. But most of them had not bothered to dress appropriately; they were more festive, with a riot of colour, some even in silk. Most had come for the Emperor's recital, not to pay their respects to Petronius. Indeed, they had probably been "invited" and needed to show their faces, to prove they had not participated in the Pisonian conpiracy.

The proof might not have been quite enough for some; as the Emperor's recital began, I could see Tigellinus putting some of the guests under arrest and they were being marched away.

The Divinity began. He struck a few deep tones on his instrument. A tympanum thudded and a cymbalum tinkled. The Emperor sang a long, modulated melisma of anguish:

Ah, ah, ah, pheu, pheu!
Seven were my daughters,
seven are their corpses,
pierced with arrows
strewn over the bodies
of my seven sons…

"Not Niobe again!" Poppaea whispered to me, alluding to one of the gems of Nero's repertoire, the the virtuosic — and endless — *Niobe weeping for her children.* "It'll be the ninth hour before it's over."

VI

LUCIUS DOMITIUS PARIS

As the Divinitas continued his dirge, his public tensed. It would not do to leave, or even to nod off, lest one be noticed. In fact, some of the centurions were watching the audience quite carefully. Woe to anyone who needed to relieve himself!

I listened. Nero's voice was beautiful — I knew that already. Each pitch was carefully placed, and the melismatic ornaments shaped with such smoothness that they wuthered like a mountain wind in the moonlight.

His portrayal of Niobe's grief had real conviction, nobility even. But Niobe had seven sons and seven daughters, each shot dead by a dart from the bow of the God of the Sun.

Her grief would be a rich meal of many courses, each more lugubrious than the last.

He was just on the first of the fourteen children, but he was already drawn deep into himself, drawing on the passion of his inner daemons. The audience became a little less tense, for when the Divinitas was like this, he rarely saw anyone else, so fixed was his gaze on high Olympus.

Of course, the Praetorians' scrutiny was still on the audience, so they could not misbehave that much.

Then, as the Emperor continued his song, someone stepped out of the crowd.

Man or woman, it was hard to tell. He wore a tunica that went past his knees, dyed in imperial purple with gold embroidery. And he began to move, in a sinuous dancelike improvisation, in front of the Divinity's field of vision, his every gesture eerily synchronizing with the Emperor's song.

Each sweeping hand movement amplified Nero's tears. Leaping and crouching, the mime portrayed Niobe's inner rage behind the outward lamentation.

I heard the Lady Poppaea Sabina whisper: "Lucius Domitius Paris."

I whispered back … "Not Lucius Domitius!" For that was the Emperor's real name, in the obscure time before his uncle Claudius adopted him and made him heir to the Empire.

"No. A freedman of the Divinitas's adoptive grandmother-in-law, hence the name. As a slave, he was called Paris. He's the most famous actor in Rome."

"But … upstaging the Divinitas!"

"Delicious! And there's nothing the Emperor can do; he'd have to break off his song."

As the Emperor's song increased in intensity, so did the mime's performance. When Nero sang a high note that never seemed to end, so Paris seemed to hang in the empty air, defying the pull of the earth. When the Emperor sang rapid scales, Paris flew like the wind. When the the Divinitas sang twisted ornaments, Paris twisted his body into the shapes of the music.

By the time Nero's song ended, all eyes were on the dancer.

The Divinitas ended with a cadential flourish, striking the strings of the *kithara* and letting out a howl of anguish as Niobe's grief finally transcended words. The mime whirled and whirled until he was a blur, then sank down before the Emperor's feet, his lips landing right on the feet of the God.

Applause rang out. And I knew it was not for the Emperor. I feared for the man's life, especially when Tigellinus thrust himself out of the throng and a brace of Praetorians dragged him to his feet.

"This man conspired with the Pisonians," Tigellinus said. "Shall we execute him on the spot, or allow him one last performance at the circus?"

"Easy, Tigellinus," said Nero. "We're at a funeral, and you heard all the applause."

"I was a mere appendage to your performance, Divinitas," said Paris, brazenly insincere it seemed to me, "helping to amplify your words so they would reach out beyond the limited acoustics of this forum."

"You see, Tigellinus? Don't be such a boor."

"You can't be too tough on traitors," Tigellinus said, sulking. There was something unspoken going on between the master of the world and his right hand man. Some kind of power play. In that moment, I knew that Tigellinus despised the Emperor.

But Nero did not see it.

Paris's toadying, too, was dripping with irony. I could see it. I was bristling on my Emperor's behalf, almost certain that Nero might order him beheaded right in front of the crowd. But the Emperor did not see it.

The applause continued, crescendoed even — the crowd did not seem to realize that Paris was in danger of being instantly executed, rather they seemed to think the guards were flanking him because the Emperor was about to bestow some signal honour upon him.

The Divinitas held up his hand for silence.

"Well done, Lucius Domitius Paris," he said. "Your eloquence has earned you pardon."

'Forgive me, Divinitas," said Paris. "I am an artist, easily tricked by politicians."

"I know," said Nero. "It happens to me all the time."

The Divinitas was biding his time. Now, I understand. He was saving Paris, the way one might keep a juicy morsel on the plate to savour later, like an unborn dormouse dipped in honey.

"You will come to me at the palace," the Emperor said, "and you'll teach me all your secrets. I labour so much at my music, yet you reach the zenith of your art without producing a single sound. I shall learn from you."

"I dare not instruct a God," said Paris.

"Really!" said Nero. "But I am a good and gracious God. Compliant. Docile, even. And ever so humble. I have not an iota of hubris."

"Of course not, Divinitas."

I was starting to sense more clearly what life with Himself the Divinity might be like. Never being sure for a second where you stood. Death lurking treachery behind every turn of phrase, every miscalculated step. Ironies within ironies. And my patronus lived that life. Until it killed him.

Himself seemed bored. I did not think he would want to follow the procession out beyond the city walls, where the actual cremation would occur. And indeed, he turned, and the entire retinue turned with him, the spokes of a wheel with the Divinitas at its centre.

The Empress whispered to me, "Go burn your master's body and send him to the next life. But soon, he'll send for you. And when he does, you'll go to him. You'll listen. Everyone hears him, but nobody listens. He doesn't know it yet, but he needs you."

How could the Emperor need me?

***

I watched as the litterbearers, soldiers, and all the hangers-on receded into the distance. Our household made a tawdry spectacle by comparison, though Croesus had not skimped. Our procession moved slowly and with the proper solemnity to the closest city gate from the Forum, the Porta Fontinalis; a cremation in the Field of Mars could be considered appropriate for Petronius because of his brief time as a consul, though he was not a military man.

Here, we laid my patronus on a high bier of good wood, accompanied only by the shards of the wine dipper which the Emperor, surely, had not failed to notice in the Forum.

As a nod to tradition, a pair of gladiators fought to the death in front of the pyre. This was a solemn match, the fighters knowing there would be no rescue from the mob if they fought well and lost. They were skilled men, the most expensive that Vinicius could afford, provided by one of the best lanistas in Capua. The battle was protracted; neither was willing to be an easy sacrifice to the spirit of the dead poet.

"This is the real thing," Croesus told me. "The circus is just entertainment. In ancient times, before even the Republic, prisoners fought to the death to honour a fallen commander. Over the centuries, this noble custom devolved into pygmies fighting amazons and ostrich races."

As his heir, Marcus set the pyre alight.

I told Marcus Vinicius that the Empress had told me I would be summoned soon, that the Divinitas "needed" me.

Marcus said, "I need you too, Sporus."

"Why?"

The flames rose. So did my tears.

"Tigellinus wants the mansion, perhaps the up-country estate as well. And Nymphidius wants *you* as a kind of spoil of war."

"But Petronius committed suicide entirely properly, and his belongings cannot be seized," I said.

"We need you at court," Marcus said. "To *remind* him."

It seemed that everyone needed me there … and not for any reason that did me any good. At the moment, I longed to be a slave again. When I belonged to Petronius, everything made sense. Now, it was all uncertainty.

***

I thought about slavery again, after the long trudge home. I was in my former master's bath, with a kylix of cold wine, lying in soothing hot water with my feet raised.

Hylas was rubbing my feet. With each squeeze I felt a twinge of pleasure; we had walked, in total, for many miles, then stood for an eternity while the Emperor sang and Paris mimed.

It occurred to me that Hylas's feet probably hurt as much as mine, yet he wasn't complaining. He worked my feet methodically, his eyes downcast. He was taller than when I first met him. I wondered whether, like Hyacinth, he feared losing his looks.

"Don't you want to be free, Hylas?" I asked him.

"Why?" he said. "Massage no good?"

He applied more pressure to my soles; I think he was worried that by that question, I meant I was not happy with him.

"No, it is fine. But … your feet are in pain, too. Shall I rub yours?"

"No good. You are dominus."

"I'm no more than a year older than you, Hylas."

"Younger, maybe," he said. "You more beautiful."

I said, "But doesn't it bother you that you have to do whatever I command, no matter when or where?"

"No."

"I mean, I could say to you, 'fellate me this very second,' and even though you're dog-tired, you'd have to do it. Doesn't it bother you?"

"Of course not. Me love you, dominus."

"Domine," I said. "When you're talking to me you have to use the vocative case." For just a second, fear flecked the boy's eyes, as if I was about to order a whipping. I immediately felt like a fool. The comfort of the clouds of steam, condensing on the marble walls, was coming to me because some overworked creature was stoking a furnace in the basement, sweating like a pig. The snow-cooled wine I was sipping at came from someone's labour, and the snow was delivered by a runner from the distant hills. The world runs on slavery, I thought, and I should thank the Gods I am no longer one.

"That's enough," I said. "Help me out and then do the olive oil and the strigil."

The oil was scented and Hylas drove the scraper with a firm hand, making my skin tingling, vibrant. "You almost make me forget," I said, "that I'm holding the future of the Petronius *gens* in my hands, and if I say the wrong thing all these people whom I have come to love will fall into the hands of Tigellinus."

"Me do it now?" said Hylas, eyeing my stiffening member.

I could not help laughing. "The night we met," I said, "you tried to steal my mirror."

"That night you not my dominus. Tonight my life belong you. *Corpus, os, culus.* You take."

His face moved closer to my groin. "Don't be impertinent," I said. He darted back as if I'd slapped him. It pained me that I had fallen so easily into the habit of being a master. Had I forgotten so quickly? So I smiled, trying to signal that he should never be afraid of me.

But later, while I slept, I cannot tell what he did; for in the morning, I woke alone, and I felt more refreshed than I had felt in a long while.

But not for long, for over my simple breakfast of bread and olives, the Praetorians came to escort me once again to the Palatine.

VII

THE BOY PHILOSOPHER

If I had thought that, after being collected from home at the crack of dawn, I would be immediately be ushered into the Emperor's presence, I was wrong. The soldiers had allowed me an attendant, so I took Hylas, letting him walk alongside the litterbearers, and keeping the curtain slightly opened so we could look at each other.

"Did you do something to me last night?" I said.

"No. You must conserve. Emperor will want all."

"But I feel much more calm."

"I hold you through the night. You cry in your sleep."

I had barely wept through my patronus's death. They have taught me that a good Roman boy does not weep, but keeps a serious demeanour. I was glad someone had seen me weep and I was glad it was Hylas. Someone else would use it against me.

Once we arrived at the palace, I was greeted by Epaphroditus, who hustled me off to a little room without windows. Hylas followed, but the Emperor's secretary dismissed the guards who had escorted us.

"Let's find you some quarters," he said.

"Quarters?"

"Well, yes. I can hardly expect the Divinitas's latest plaything to sleep in the hallways."

"I didn't know I was moving in."

"You're not," said the diminutive secretary, "but if Himself were, on a whim, in a strange mood, to *hint* at it, and you did not *already* have your own apartments here, I might get a whipping, you know."

"Not you," I said. "You're more powerful than most senators. Surely you don't get whipped. Why, Himself told me, he personally freed you."

"But he forgets. And sometimes it's not tactful to correct a God."

"Still, I can't believe that you, a learned clerk, someone who knows where the bodies are buried and who's screwing whose wife … would have the indignity of —"

"Not that often," he said, sighing. "The Divinity would have to be pretty drunk. But you'll bear the brunt of that, more often than I will, I dare say."

"The beating?" My heart sank.

"No, no, he doesn't damage pretty things," said Epaphroditus. "I mean the drunken moments. You will see him at his worst, you will see the Himself he doesn't let others see."

"You seem pretty certain of that."

"Whatever. Now, let's find you an appropriate lodging. Not too far from Himself, in case he needs you at some strange hour. He won't come to you; you'll be summoned. It's not that he has a problem with stumbling to your room in a stupor for a quick bout of sex. It's because this palace has too many rooms, and more keep being added, and he loses his way more often that he cares to admit."

***

Now this Epaphroditus had a slave named Epictetus. The slave who was a philosopher. I had seen him lurking around on another occasion, and Himself had actually quoted something he said at the funeral.

It was this boy whom Epaphroditus sent to scout out an apartment for me. He led us down corridors and through subterranean tunnels. Epictetus moved rapidly, like a rodent. The labyrinth was his element. We emerged in a secret garden surrounded by a colonnade; in the garden stood a marble likeness of the Lady Poppaea. When Hylas saw the statue, he gasped.

"Dominus? *Domina?"* he whispered.

I gazed up at the Lady Poppaea. She was painted in vivid, lifelike hues. It was as if she were about to draw breath. She wore a simple stola, white with a little purple, the folds of the fabric so well painted that one could believe they would rustle in the wind. There was a whiff of frankincense; someone had been worshipping her image.

"This is the Empress's own garden," Epictetus said. He looked me over again. "We all know why *you* are here."

"I'm the Empress with a penis," I said ruefully. "A divine gift, and a divine curse."

"If the Emperor finds his way here," Epictetus said, "he'll double his chances of finding his beloved."

I have to say that all this was making me uneasy. It was not really my intention to live at the palace at all. "This is all ... just in case, isn't it?" I asked. "There's no actual command for me to live here. I'm right, aren't I?"

"True," said Epictetus, "but my master has learned to be prepared for anything."

At length, Epictetus picked out something far too lavish. It was roomier than any chamber in Petronius's house. To Hylas's delight, there was a mural that depicted the legend of Hylas and the nymphs, with a frustrated Hercules watching behind some bushes. "It's about me," Hylas said, laughing.

"One slave won't be enough," Epictetus said. "We'll have to buy you a few more. A few to look after your wardrobe, hair and makeup. Someone to run errands. I see you already own a puer delicatus, but he'll be over the hill in a year."

"I can choose a few slaves?"

"Within reason. Unless your requirements are beyond the pale, I am sure it will be covered from the imperial household management funds."

"Can I really buy anyone I want, within reason?" For I was thinking, perhaps I could find Spider, redeem her out of whatever she had been sold into. And then I would know something approaching a mother's affection.

There was a chest with tunicae and two togas, one pure white one and one with the purple stripe of one who has not yet attained manhood. There were also a few women's things, a stola and assorted embroidered cloths for draping.

"We'll bring you more clothes to pick from. And an assortment of jewelry, though I am sure more will be bestowed on you."

"I see."

"Any special requirements? Bathing in asses' milk, pearls dissolved in vinegar, that kind of thing?"

His delivery was so deadpan I did not know if he was being serious.

"People ask for such things?" I said.

"It's said that Cleopatra did, when she was in Rome as a guest of the Divine Julius."

"Who Cleopatra?" said Hylas.

"A Queen who killed herself eighty years ago," Epictetus said, "during the reign of the Divine Augustus."

"Well, but I'm not a Queen, just some kind of amusement."

"There are things in life that you have no control over. But if you *should* become powerful, have courage and use that power to do good."

This boy was special. He had a kind of serenity. He sounded like a much older man.

"I know I do," Epictetus said, reading my mind. "I read a lot. You will always find me in the Imperial library. One day I'll be a philosopher."

"I think you are one already," I said.

"True enough," he said. "I live inside my mind, and so the world matters little. Now, please ..." he gestured. Slaves who had shadowed us, keeping just out of sight, now entered the room. They carried armfuls of clothing, and more clothing in cedarwood chests. "Some of these belonged to ... other lovers," said the boy. "Some are forgotten; for others, it didn't end so well. And here, a stola that used to belong to Actë, who loved Himself before he became a God. That's a rarity from the east, a silk so sheer you can see right through it and it is like wearing nothing at all; it took three years to weave, three more to get to Rome."

More slaves came with more supplies; jugs of wine, dishes with dates, bread and salt, an amphora of fresh water; cosmetics; trinkets; a miniature shrine with an obscene little Priapus statue, presumably to bless any matings that might ensue.

"I should really ask you if you approve the room," Epictetus said, "but there is really no point. These are the best quarters available. If you need anything, send the boy."

"Send him where?" I said.

"He's a bright lad. He'll find whatever you're looking for. Slaves are good at sniffing things out. You should know, Sporus."

"You no call my master *dominus?"* said Hylas.

I put my hand on his shoulder. "This boy is everyone's equal," I said. I knew that from the way he carried himself. He had not been taught to be servile, nor had he learned it by himself. He was going to be extraordinary. Nero's circle of poets all aspired to be Stoics, but they were not averse to hypocrisy, when expedient. But this boy was the real thing.

"I will leave you now," he said. The other slaves disappeared as if by magic, and all the clothes and trinkets had been carefully put away in chests and baskets. To Hylas, he said, "Have your master dressed and bathed by the eleventh hour; nothing fancy, mind you; I think the Divinitas has an escapade in mind for after cena."

"An escapade?"

"Oh yes," said the boy. "This is Rome — where the night can burn as brightly as the day. Did your former master keep you chained up in the house day and night? Don't tell me you haven't sampled the night life."

VIII

ROMA PER NOCTEM

When the summons came, it was Vinicius.

I was happier to see him than almost anyone. After Epictetus left, I had been sitting in the room, watching Hylas sort through my clothes. I did not feel like a resident of the royal palace, let alone like the "favorite" of a god, as Ganymede was the cup-bearer to Jupiter. I was disoriented. If I left the room and shouted for a slave, would anyone listen?

Was Lady Poppaea's chamber nearby? Were there mistresses and concubines in other apartments, applying makeup and trying on garments, just in case there was visitation from the Divinitas? I sat in my suite alone, well, not if you count Hylas, but he had taken on his new role as my slave, and no longer behaved as though he were my friend.

Vinicius said, "You are overdressed."

I had thought myself elegantly simple, a simple tunica, a stola of unpatterned silk. The slightest dash of kohl and my lips shone with a hidden fire. There was a mirror of polished bronze in the room, so expansive I could see the whole upper half of myself, not like the shard that Hylas had wanted to steal from me once.

"Overdressed?" I said.

"Yes," said Marcus Vinicius. "Take Hylas's clothes. Tonight you will be a scruffy little slave. Hylas, take off the makeup and dirty your dominus's hair a bit."

"Where am I going?"

"Wherever the Divinitas wants," Marcus said. "Leave your slave here. If he gets hungry, I'm sure he can find the kitchens."

"Are you coming?"

Marcus laughed. "I don't move in the same exalted circles as you do. You were my Uncle's Giton. Now you are Jupiter's Ganymede."

It was not a comforting thought. "Your uncle didn't have thunderbolts," I said.

"He *did* have satire."

"And what good did it do him?"

"Petronius will live on, little Giton," said Marcus Vinicius. "Whereas the poetry composed by Himself...."

He did not say more. Who knew who might be listening? But after I changed my clothes a few more times, and looked unremarkable enough to please him, he led me from the room, to a passageway with a secret door, and a stairwell that led downwards. The light was dismal, just a torch here and there. "We're going halfway down the Palatine!" I said. But eventually we arrived at a kind of back entrance, where a litter awaited. It was dark. This was no Imperial palanquin, but a plain transport, the kind of thing a minor official might use. The bearers were Nubians, blending into the night. The turned as one to look at me, their eyes like stars.

Marcus waved me in. "Hurry," he said. "God waits for no one, not even Ganymede." With a great deal of trepidation, I drew the curtain a little way. Someone seized both my arms and dragged me inside, and I was alone with the Divinitas, only for the second time.

An oil lamp with an image of Priapus was the only light. The Divinitas peered at me as though I were some exotic animal. "Sporus?"

"Yes, Divinitas."

He cackled. "You look suitably plebeian," he said. "Do I?"

I must admit that he did not. For though the tunic he wore was unwashed, and his caligae scratched and worn, there was still the perfect hair, and the fragrance he wore. I should have said, "No one would be followed for a minute," but I knew that was not the required answer.

"My Lord," I said, "allow me to muss up your hair a little."

"Ah! The finishing touch! Perceptive of you."

I ruffled him up a little. He giggled. "May I ask where we are going, Divinity?"

"Oh! They didn't tell you?"

"They did not."

"We are going to … mingle with the lower classes."

#

The bearers moved swiftly. When they came to a stop, we stepped out in an alley. There were insulae on either side; some were burned out, others still stood. "Oh," said the Divinitas, "it's filthy here. Deliciously filthy."

He took my hand. "But is this safe?" I said, alarmed.

"We have people. Everywhere. There is never danger. The God has watchdogs." He pulled me along.

Down a side alley and into another. The smells! Sausages and sewage. Vats of urine waiting for the laundry collectors. And people. People of every size and colour. The night was alive.

A food stall with a counter, round openings with earthen

pots sunk into them, warmed by charcoal from below. Steaming entrées in the pots, and some jugs of wine behind. A bored slave stood there to take the order.

The Emperor chose some octopus fried in garam and honey, wrapped in a flatbread.

"It's one as, sir," said the vendor.

The Divinitas chuckled and whispered to me, "Actually, I haven't any money. I quite forgot!"

"No credit," said the slave. "We don't serve riff-raff."

"Riff-raff?" The Divinitas raised an eyebrow.

The slave shrugged. "I'll call my dominus," he said.

The Emperor scratched his ear. Then I saw the Praetorians, standing in the shadows. I fished a dupondius from my pouch and handed it over. The slave pushed over an as. The Divinitas picked it up. In the torchlight he examined it. "Uncle Gaius?" he said, referring to the one known familiarly as Caligula. "I thought his coins were all recalled." He wolfed down his octopus. He did not offer me any, even though I had paid for his food.

"Come on," he said. "Enough food."

"Some wine?" the slave said.

"At the next stop," said the Divinitas. He pulled me along as though we were schoolchildren.

A tiny doorway opened and a beefy arm emerged, pulling us inside. A corridor, barely wide enough for the Emperor to go through sideways ... and we emerged in a dingy room.

Against a mural with a pastoral theme, with a lot of nymphs shepherds and even a few sheep, there were couches set, and women of all shapes and sizes were lounging about. A few boys, too, and in one corner a well-oiled man in a loincloth brandishing a gladius. Nothing extraordinary. So it had been in the house of Petronius, when he was putting on a big party. Looking closer, I could see that they wore little signs around their necks. One said, "Lucia fellat" — Lucia performs fellatio. One tiny boy had a sign that read "Mentula magna." Presumably his organ was way out of proportion to his height.

"A lupanar," I said softly.

"Yes, a brothel. If Petronius hadn't picked you, this is where you'd be working. Your culus would be permanently gushing like an aqueduct."

I shuddered.

Presently, a proprietor of the lupanar emerged from an inner room. This was an older but still beautiful woman, her face so smoothened by lead white that it was more porcelain than skin. Her withered arms showed her true age. When she saw Himself, she started to prostrate herself.

"None of that, Clytaemnestra," said the Emperor. "I want to be an ordinary person tonight."

"Ah. You are here … anonymously," said the madam. "Well done, my Lord. You've managed to fool every meretrix in my establishment." She waved at all the prostitutes, and they waved back, jiggling, wiggling and giggling as they waved. Clytaemnestra told the Divinitas, "Take your pick."

The meretrices laughed and ignored him.

'They *really* don't recognize you," I whispered.

"They'll regret it when they're strung up on crosses tomorrow."

"Patience, my Lord," I said. "This only shows how brilliant you are at the art of disguise."

Himself whipped round and glared at me. *Glared!* I remembered watching Marcus crucifying the pirates who kidnapped me. Petronius tolerated my back talk, encouraged it even, thought it adorable. Suddenly I remembered that Nero owned me. Yes, I had a scroll of manumission and a freedman's cap.

But *freedom?* A cruel joke.

Nero's eyes transfixed me. I could almost feel the nails riveting my wrists. Then the God suddenly smiled. "So refreshing," he said, "your candour. You've saved this whole brothel from execution. Not to mention the vendor who called me riff-raff."

"He's being crucified?"

"It's the Praetorians; they are *so* devoted. To a fault, indeed. They're probably doing it now."

"Now?"

"Go on. You can still stop them."

"But … *domine,"* I whispered, still trying to pretend he was a nobody and that I was that nobody's slave boy. "I can't leave you. You didn't bring any money!"

Himself the Divine Emperor laughed. Heartily. Of course he did not need money here. The proprietor knew who he was. *Everyone* knew. The Emperor needed no protection from a fancy-boy.

"Run along and stop the execution," he said to me. "I'll be occupied for a while."

#

I slipped out of the lupanar and found myself in complete darkness. I felt my way along a damp wall to what I thought would be the right corner. There was a glimmer of light. I turned another corner and found myself in a quadrangle with a well. There was more light. People were holding torches. A crowd had gathered. Two soldiers were tying the octopus vendor to a cross. People were exciting, babbling jeering. Little boys hoisted up on their parents' shoulders. The mood was festive. The vendor was screaming.

"Stop!" I shouted. I couldn't be heard until I pushed my way up. I saw the vendor's face clearly. His terror was beyond imagining. This wasn't a fancy display cross. The man would be dying at eye level, able to look any passerby in the eye. I shoved the closest soldier and he merely slapped me away, like an annoying insect. But out of the corner of my eye, I saw Marcus in the shadows.

"Marcus Vinicius!" I shrieked.

Marcus emerged. The two soldiers stopped their work leaving the food vendor half hoisted, the cross at at an angle, the man dangling by his arms, his feet unbounded. He was howling.

"Himself says to stop the execution," I told him.

"Halt," Vinicius barked.

The soldiers let the ropes go slack. The cross landed on the flagstones with a crack. It was a good thing it had fallen wood first or a few bones would have been broken at least.

The crowd got ugly fast. "We have to string him up," said one of the soldiers. "You can't promise a spectacle and not deliver."

Quick thinking was needed. "Listen to me!" I screamed. "I'm an emissary of Himself, your Emperor and God, and he has sent me in his Divine Compassion to stay this execution!"

The crowd was roaring with laughter until Vinicius hold up his hand. Then, lifting my arm high, he cried, "All hail the Divine Nero, Lord of Compassion! Listen to his words, brought to you from the lips of the Emperor's most trusted catamitus!"

They untied the poor man and he was still in a state of abject terror, but they soldiers gave him a quick boot in the buttocks and he scampered off, gibbering. The crowd's anger turned to cheering and shouts of "Vivat Caesar!" and even murmurs about me, as in "The Emperor's boy ... plucky little thing ..." and so on.

"Nothing more to see," one of the soldier's told the crowd.

"I'll take you back to the lupanar," Vinicius said. Her escorted me back, but did not enter."

#

They treated me differently this time. I was still wearing the same rags, but now the whores treated me like a prince, fawning and stroking my hair. At length Clytaemnestra emerged from an inner room. "Back to work," she said, shooing the girls and boys from the antechamber.

"Sit," she said, pushing me down onto one of the couches. "Himself will be occupied for a time. Amuse yourself with anyone you like. Here." She gave me a fistful of lead tokens. They were like coins, but each bore an image of some sexual act. "Himself never needed money here," she said. "These *sprintiae* are the currency in this establishment. Look them over. I'm sure there's something you'd like to try."

"I don't want a whore," I said. "I'll just wait."

"Have it your way," said Clytaemnestra. "But you'll be bored, though. I have clients I have to see to." She stood up. "I'll send a slave to keep you company. Maybe the bookkeeper; she's done counting the money for the night."

Clytaemnestra left and I was alone in the chamber. I sat in the light of a single oil lamp. I gazed at the mural. The nymphs seemed to dance in the gloom. From rooms beyond I could hear giggles, moans. I could feel myself dozing off.

Then I heard a voice.

A voice so familiar, I almost thought … "Mother?" I whispered.

She smiled. It was not my mother but it was as close as I could get on this earth. She stood there, a little older, her face more lined, but her eyes were as I remembered them. A familiar face, someone who had known me before I became … this.

"Sporus," she said softly. "You've come far since we buried your friend Hyacinth."

I embraced her then, the woman who had cleaned me up

after I had been viciously raped by the pirate captain, the woman who had taught me my first words of Greek, the woman who had given me the shard of the bronze mirror which had shown my my face for the first time, the woman I called Spider.

IX

JULIA AGRIPPINA

At most a year had passed since we had seen each other, yet time had taken a greater toll that I could have imagined. She was haggard. Between the she was sold to the brothel and the time she was banished to counting money, she had to take dozens of customers a day. She was not the cream, pampered and well dressed and on display for the senators; Clytaemnestra had the full range of offerings, and several secondary houses frequented by plebeians and even slaves. It was her lack of physical attractiveness that had sent her to the lower class brothel, where they had used and abused her like an old sack of grain. But it was the wear and tear, coupled with her ability to read and understand numbers, that had sent her back to the main house and this relatively painless job.

"I've missed you so much," I said to her.

She took me in her arms and I could not stop crying. I relived it all. The sound of the sea, the pitch and yaw of the pirate vessel, the agony of my violated body. And her comforting words. Though she was a slave herself, and still was,

"Look at you," she said. "The plaything of a god, and I still the lowliest of the lowly."

"Not to me," I sobbed.

I tried to cram everything that had happened to me into the little time I knew we could be alone. It all came tumbling out. Petronius. The lofty poetry and biting portraits of real people and the filthy doggerel that he had woven into his *Satyricon.* The emperor. Poppaea and her cheetah. Otho, the husband who used me to be able to be aroused by his wife. And the Divinitas. How I loved him, how I hated and feared him, how he had simultaneously given me everything and taken everything away.

Spider's tales were more mundane than mine. Being raped by strangers at all hours had become routine to her, just something to be survived by making her mind go far away. The bookkeeping was a different routine; the tedium was a relief from the days of horror.

In the less busy hours, when few of the rooms were occupied, she told me, she swept the rooms and cleaned off the stains, for bodily fluids were shed in plenty in this business.

"Come with me on my rounds," Spider said. "It's a slow night, and there are Praetorians undercover all around here, making sure the Divinity takes his pleasures uninterrupted."

We took a steep stairway to an upper story. Small rooms lined a hallway, each one a cubiculum, barely wider than the couch it contained. Some had drapes drawn over the entry. In the others sat all manner of flesh. "Here are the snacks." She indicated a room where sad delicati sat naked. One emerged and handed Spider a fistful of coins. We walked past closed cubicula from which grunts, moans, and cries could be heard.

"These are the main courses," she told me. There were voluptuous women. One, a Briton, was painted entirely blue. There were stylus-thin men and steatopygous matrons. We ascended another stair. "On to the more exotic fare," Spider said.

Each floor was more exotic than the last. Women dressed as gladiators, wielding whips. A fat old man in senatorial toga being humiliated by a slave. A bath of eels.

As the building was structured like one of those insulae that slum-dwellers live in, there were numerous flimsy stories; I was a little nervous that the constant shaking from the amorous activities would topple the whole building. Spider could see my unease.

"The Romans are good at building," she whispered.

"Yes," I said, "as long as it's stone and concrete."

I remembered the burning city. I remembered the Divinitas's poetic interlude. I remembered the Christians, dipped in pitch, lighting up the gardens, screaming.

"It will soon be *all* stone and concrete," Spider said. "Even at the edge of civilization, we hear the talk of Neropolis, and the new Golden House that will spring up from the ashes."

We went up to the sixth level and there was a bare room there. No furniture at all. "I call this room Olympus," Spider said. "We are above it all."

"And we don't have to think about any of it," I said.

"Not true."

She crouched on the floor and told me to do the same. I saw now that there were holes in the floor. Peepholes. Each was connected by an angled pipe into a room on a lower floor. Each hole had a circular covering of polished glass.

"Peer down one of the holes," she said. "This device was devised by some Greek academic. It makes things that are far look closer."

I knew the Emperor loved to look at the world through a polished ruby or emerald; he had even given me such a gem as a gift. If someone had invented a way to make faraway objects look closer, surely it could be put to better use than to observe lewd couplings in a brothel!

I lay down and put my eye up to the nearest opening. I could see into one of the cubicula, more elegantly appointed than the others.

A beautiful woman was reclining, her back to me, her face just outside the peephole's field of vision. She did seem to almost be in the same room. It was uncanny.

"That's the best peephole of all," Spider said, "just like the Divinitas's balcony at the circus, where you can smell and even sometimes taste the blood. This channel links directly to the Emperor's private room. You will see something provocative, I am sure."

And I did.

The woman turned around and her face moved into the center of the circle of light. At first I gasped, because I thought I had seen myself, but of course, it was not me. It was Herself, the Lady Poppaea Sabina, Empress of Rome.

Her face had been whitened with lead paint. Her lips were dyed crimson. Her eyes were accentuated with deep kohl. She was brandishing a little quirt. Not the kind you would use on a slave. This looked like something that could deliver a piquant little thwack, rather than real damage.

"I didn't expect *you* here," she said, play-acting.

Then came a voice from the shadows. An all too familiar voice. "I came to say I'm sorry. I didn't mean to … kill you."

"You miserable little boy," she murmured, "You deserve a beating."

"Mother, mother, I've been bad…" Himself sounded whiny and uncertain.

The Empress whipped the air.

"I'm going to have to beat you, Lucius," she said.

The Emperor hove into view. He was naked. He was trembling. He seemed genuinely frightened. "And afterwards," he said, "can I have some milk?"

The Lady Poppaea unfastened her fibula with a single deft movement, and her stola slowly unravelled and slipped down her smooth, whitened flesh, toward the wooden floor.

"Get ready," she said, "for the thrashing of your life."

"Mother," he said.

"Who am I?" said the Empress.

"Mother!"

"What am I?"

"The Divine Julia Agrippina," he gasped.

"Suckle," she commanded. "For I am Agrippina. I am the all-omniscient mother. I am back from the dead. I shall haunt you forever."

The stola was in a heap on the floor, and the Divine Empress stood fully naked, and very obviously pregnant.

"But Mother ... you're with child. This isn't in the game."

"I *am* with child! You're a bad boy and I shall make a new Lucius," she said, still playing her role.

"How dare you!" Nero shouted. "I killed you! You're just a ghost!" He lashed out with his fists. She dodged and struck back with the quirt. They were both yelling incoherently.

"I've had enough of this, Lucius. Call the boy."

Then the Emperor turned his back and stared up the ceiling, straight up to the narrow opening of the tunnel I was looking down. Did he know I was there?

"Sporus!" he screamed. He wasn't a god. He was a petulant child who wanted a new toy.

"Go to him," said Spider. *"Now."*

X

SATURN DEVOURING HIS CHILDREN

I ran down to the Imperial Cubiculum, almost tripping on the narrow steps. Spider led the way but she did not enter. Two men stood guard. Inside the chamber — the only one that had a door and not just a drape — the Divinity was shrieking my name.

"Sporus! Bring Sporus or I'll have you all crucified!"

I burst into the chamber.

"Sporus! Sporus! O Ganymede, cupbearer of Jove — that is to say, *my* very own cupbearer!" Himself, Master of the World, hurled himself at me, clutched and held me hard to his bosom — I was almost choking on his perfume — and covered my face and neck with kisses. He ripped my tunic and starting working his way down my shoulders, my chest, handling me like a child's toy.

"Divinitas!" I whispered.

It was not, I must admit, unpleasant to have the owner of the known world slobbering all over me. I had not had any physical release for some time, not since the equally unexpected encounter in the palace when the Emperor had suddenly commanded me to mount him. Himself had not even reached my thighs before I was overcome by — that pinnacle of passion that the poet Sappho called *the mountain wind* – and all my pent-up desires came gushing out in milky profusion all over the God's face.

He did not back away but began laughing — well, alternately laughing and lapping — playing first the kitten, then the hyena. He clenched both my buttocks in his hands and, losing my balance, I fell backwards onto the couch and right onto the very pregnant body of the Lady Poppaea Sabina.

"Oh! I am so sorry, Goddess!" I said, for she still held the quirt in her hand. The Lady Poppaea shrugged.

"Well, *you're* a welcome relief," she said. "I thought I was done for."

I was not sure how to respond.

But she went on. "The Emperor's consumed with guilt about Agrippina, and who can blame him? And I'm stuck with the brunt of the guilt. You'd think he'd be a little more considerate, what with my condition. But his mother consumes his thoughts. And why shouldn't she? He murdered her, you know. It took three tries. You'll find out. Wait till you see him drunk. He'll think nothing of kicking you to death, and you haven't got any leverage to fight back with. You're not even a patrician."

"Guards!" Nero shouted. "Remove the Empress!"

The Praetorians entered and lifted Poppaea off the couch.

They carried her off unceremoniously. They averted their eyes, though I for one would have been hard pressed to avoid staring at the spectacle of their God, his face soaked in my accidental discharge, his arms having slid from my rear and His Divine Person all jumbled up on the floor of this tawdry house of *infames*. When they left, Himself snatched what remained of my ripped tunic and swabbed at his face.

I helped him onto the couch. My copious education at the hands of voluptuaries and poets had not prepared me to deal with a raving Emperor.

I took the torn cloth and wiped his face a little more. There was no water in the room, so I urinated into the wad of fabric a little to clean it, then dabbed at his face a little more.

"I don't want a little Nero popping out of that woman," he said. "I don't need a successor. I'm a God."

"Then you don't have to have a successor, my Lord," I said. "The Gods go on forever."

"But they don't *rule* forever," said Himself. "Look at Saturn, for instance. He devoured his own children, and Jupiter *still* managed to claw his way out of his belly. And where is Saturn now? Imprisoned in Tartarus for all eternity."

"You won't end up in Tartarus, Divinitas. How could you? With all that great poetry you've written. You're like Orpheus, making the stones weep."

"I am, aren't I?" said Himself.

"Yes, Divinitas."

He held me close once more. He was hateful. And vulnerable. In that moment, I both loathed and pitied him. He stroked my hair, with an aching tenderness that confused me even more.

Then abruptly he turned away, let go of me with such suddenness that I fell back down on the coach, banging my head a little on the frame, making me yelp; he ignored that.

Petronius would have kissed it better.

"Orpheus was torn to pieces by drunk, insane women," he said.

There were, I am sorry to say, gaps in my knowledge of the exploits of the Greek and Roman gods. I had not heard that part of the story. But I knew that the cult of Orpheus had mysteries and initiations. For now, I could not comfort the Emperor with another tidbit of mythology.

"Agrippina!" the Emperor cried out. There was despair in his cry, heartbreak.

I could not assuage his grief with words, but I found another use for my tongue. He sobbed as he throbbed, the hurt and the ecstasy coming together in a place beyond my understanding.

***

Sordid! Beyond sordid!

Yet these are the things you've been dying to hear since I started this sorry narration.

I had hoped that mating with a God would be a somewhat more elevating experience.

I've had two Gods, you know. Not to mention an Almost-God, who missed the throne by just a few inches.

And which God was your favorite?

The Divine Nero was as good as it ever got. Elevating experiences? You need true love for that, and for true love you need both *eros* and *agape.*

Yet you did love Himself, the one who is now the object of Damnatio Memoriae. *In a very real sense, you will be dying for him.*

Yes.

We'd better get you back into makeup, Empress. It's running again, and there's another delay in your big moment, I hear. The managed to get the giraffes off stage, but now the elephants are stampeding. Can you hear them? Animals are really more trouble than they're worth. Children, too. When there's a crowd of Christians to be eaten, the young ones ruin the whole show. Too easy to get the mob on their side, and then where's the entertainment?

Oh, the Christians! I have stories about them, as well. When the Emperor disguised himself and went among the plebs, it wasn't just brothels he visited. We managed to get smuggled into one of their so-called love-feasts once. He wanted to know what they were really like, you know. A twinge of guilt? Or just curiosity? The God I worshipped and abhorred was a complex being.

And the Chrestianoi?

They're not what people think. Their rituals are pretty dull. No human sacrifice at all.

Well, that's rather boring. I'd rather hear more about naughty things in high places.

And you will.

Are you done yet? You've sat on this latrina for an hour. Here, I'll sponge you off.

Why? So you can tell your grandchildren that you once touched a place that a God once touched?

You are too funny, Sporus. I mean … Your Imperial Majesty.

I am going to be killed horribly in front of thousands of people. I think I'm entitled to a few bad jokes.

XI

THE WOMB THAT MADE THIS MONSTER

It must have been morning when I awoke. The cubiculum smelled of sweat, overripe perfumes, and bodily fluids, but I was alone. The Divinitas was nowhere to be seen. Oh ... not so alone after all. A woman, hunched over, was scrubbing vomit from a corner. It was Spider. When she noticed me stirring, she came to me and proffered a bowl of some clumpy porridge.

"Do I have to go back to the palace?" I said. It was the last thing I wanted to do. I would have stayed in the brothel if I could. At least here I knew where I stood. I could be a whore among whores.

"Perhaps not right away," Spider said. "The Emperor has been quite worn out by the night's entertainments. I'm sure he'll send for you and the Praetorians will know where to look."

"But I left Hylas there at the palace. A lamb among wolves."

"He has a lot more experience at being a slave than you," she said. "We are good at survival."

Indeed, Hylas was already at the door, and he held out a steaming posset in an earthenware bowl.

"How did you know where I was?" I asked him.

He laughed. "Me slave," he said. "Slave know everything."

"Ego," I said, *"Ego,* not *me.* I should really beat more grammar into you."

"Now you like a real dominus," he said, grinning from ear to ear, perfectly confident I would never lay a hand on him.

"But seriously," I said, "I will buy a tutor for you. It may become useful for you not to sound like you're only good at moaning and making eyes."

"Yes, domine," he said, using the vocative case properly for the first time. I knew that he knew I noticed. I knew that he had taken the effort for my sake. And in these little ways he showed me that he loved me. "But, domine," he went on, "can't we go home?"

"I think we can," I said. Hylas and Spider helped me to my feet. Hylas had fresh clothing, a woolen tunica and a purple-bordered toga praetexta, which was really only proper for a young Roman male of senatorial rank, or a boy of aristocratic birth who had not yet reached formal adulthood. I did not feel that I belonged to either category, and I demurred; besides, it is a heavy garment, and Rome can be sultry, and even months after the fire, the air was oppressive.

I said a quick goodbye to Spider, but I knew I would see her again. I knew that the underbelly of Rome would beckon to the Divinitas, whether he was in a Senate hearing, listening to old men with no power rambling on about minutiae; or whether he was enjoying a banquet with too many dishes, or a concert with too many notes; or whether he was merely in a depression, haunted by memories of his dead mother. At these times, I could tell, the dark side of the city would call out to him. He wanted so much to mingle with the ordinary, but he never could be ordinary. I wondered when the next summons to the palace would come, and whether Himself, in an insomniac wanderlust, would even find his way into my chamber, and find me missing.

My destiny was not my own. I would have to move back there. But maybe not for a few more days...

***

It was as a kind of master of the house that I returned to the home where I had once been Petronius's slave. Not the real master of course, but certainly a kind of conquering hero, for I had survived the summons to Himself's inner sanctum.

Croesus bowed to me and led me to the triclinium where slaves immediately brought olives, bread, salt, and wine. The simple food came as a relief after a surfeit of peacocks' brains and larks' tongues and such.

Some of Petronius's women slaves embraced me and made much of me. They wanted to hear my stories and for an hour or more I told them the same tales I have been telling you, tormentor of my final hours.

But soon it was time for *me* to ask questions.

"Hylas has already told me," I said, "how slaves know *everything.* Since being freed, I've lost that ability. But more than ever, I *have* to know everything. I'll never survive Himself." And I talked about how I had been watching through the spyholes in the upper room, and I'd seen Himself actually kicking and beating the Empress in a rage. And what she said to me — that I'd have even less to defend myself with, since I'm not even of noble birth. "How will I stop him from kicking me to death, just for the momentary rush of it?"

"You need to understand the women who truly have power over him," Croesus said, "and how and why they wield that power. And you need to understand what love means to a God. And you need him to love you. You must do it by guile, by misdirection, and by understanding him so well that he could make his wishes real before he even thinks of them. Because someone like Nero does not *love.* My master, Gaius Petronius, *did* love you, Sporus. Hyacinth loved you. Hylas loves you blindly and desperately, savoring any second that you might have for him. In her own way, the Lady Poppaea Sabina loves you. And her husband Otho ... if he were ever to return from being exiled to the governorship of Lusitania ... he would marry you in a moment. You are an exact duplicate of the person he loves, without the constant scheming and with the added benefit of a penis."

"But the Emperor does not love me," I said.

"He may think he does, but there are only three people he loves, I think," Croesus said. "This I have gleaned from a thousand overheard conversations at my master's banquets."

"But he doesn't limit his appetites to three."

"No. Not at all. He's penetrated freeborn boys, senators' wives, and, it is rumored, the Vestal Virgin Rubria, even though if it were true it would bring untold calamity to the city. Well, someone who say that calamity has happened already ... luckily, I suppose, we have the Chrestianoi to blame instead. But as for the women he loves ... there is Actë, you know. She is a lowborn woman, perhaps even a slave, who loved Lucius Domitius Ahenobarbus, before he became Nero, heir to Godhood. No one knows where she is. She is somewhere in the palace. She is like a ghost, haunting the corridors. They say she'll come out into the light one day, to be with him in death."

I wondered whether I would ever meet her. "And

Poppaea?" I said. "Does he love Poppaea?"

"Oh yes," said Croesus. "That's probably why he hurts her."

"He hurts her because she's not his mother," I said, remembering what I had overhead the night before.

"His mother is his greatest love. Even though he killed her. *Because* he killed her. They say he ripped open her womb so he could see what such a monster as Himself had come from ... but that's just slaves' talk."

And now I understood more about Himself than I had learned even from Petronius. And I knew that, for better or worse, my destiny was tied to that of the master of the world.

How I envied my slave boy, Hylas. Today, I hated my freedom. I had traded my slavery for a darker enslavement, enforced not by the lash but by the gnawing dread that every step was a misstep, every word a self-condemnation.

Croesus saved until last the news that I was already being sent for. It was something really big — an occasion of state. I supposed I would be on view with the best of the imperial possessions, like the perfect vase, the comeliest horse.

But I still had until morning, because Himself was still recovering from the previous night's excesses.

"I'll sleep with Hylas," I said. "Just Hylas."

Hylas smiled eagerly.

"And I mean *sleep,*" I added.

Hylas frowned. "Yes, domine," he said.

XII

FREEDOM IS SLAVERY

I did not have to return to the Imperial presence for a few days, because the summons required preparation. A big occasion of state, they told me, giving no details. But they were sending a tailor, and I was to have a new wardrobe, grander even than the items they had already chosen for me on my last visit.

At some point, the Emperor would think of me, and at that moment, I had better be in reach. I believed, however, that Epaphroditus, who knew his master's desires before Himself knew them, would have me brought to the palace in plenty of time.

The daily routine of an upper-class Roman always began clients showing up to request favours or consult or present gifts. Without an heir present in the house, Croesus, the freedman, suddenly found himself a powerful man, even though he had no actual power; for Marcus Vinicius had vested a level of his uncle's *potestas* in the former servant, to act as proxy.

So the morning was occupied with petitions, some of them quite strange; one of them, indeed, exactly like the situation in my patronus's *Satyricon,* where two young students of rhetoric were fighting over the legal ownership of a slave boy.

The atrium was not exactly *crammed* with suppliants, but there were several waiting around. Some had perhaps found other sponsors since my master's suicide. They were a desultory lot.

In Petronius's novel, Encolpius spends an amazing night of passion with the beautiful Giton, only to have his best friend Ascyltus claim the boy in the morning. Encolpius, full of profound certainty about his love after that wild night, thinks that the boy should decide. In the book, my former master uses the incident to make you think about the complexities of slavery in a way that never crosses most Roman minds, because Giton chooses the man who mistreats him and doesn't think of him as anything other than an object.

I wondered whether we would now see this fiction play out in real life.

But we did not. The boy in question was glum and past the usual age of a delicatus, with appalling acne. The young men were spoiled scions of my patronus's former clients, citizens but just a generation beyond slavery themselves. They both had various documents with vague references that *could* imply ownership.

"Isn't this something for an actual magistrate to decide?" Croesus said.

They both started talking at once, and waving their certificates of title, or whatever the documents were.

"May I say something?" I asked. They were suddenly silent, looking at me as though I possessed some real authority. "Let the boy decide."

"That's outrageous!" both complainants said at the same time.

"He's a slave," said the one on the left. "He can't decide, by definition. He's not a person."

The "not-person" in question appeared more and more glum.

He was an unprepossessing thing but this whole transaction made me furious. A year ago I had been in as terrible a situation. Doubtless he had it worse than I ever did, because, with my looks, I was not the kind of merchandise anyone wanted to damage. When I looked at the two men competing for ownership, they revolted me. The scene from my former patronus's book was cheap and tawdry, but this did not even have the artistic veneer of being a literary satire — it was the thing itself, without an ounce of wit.

"Croesus," I said, "can I afford this boy?"

Croesus said, "Not only did you inherit quite a bit from your patronus, but you also, probably, have a direct line to the privy purse — in case you hadn't noticed."

"You can't buy him," said one of the putative owners, "until we've settled who owns him."

"Pay them both off," I said. Then, I asked the boy directly, "Which of these creatures do you choose, of your own free will?"

"Neither," he said firmly. "My father's a baker. He sold me to *this* one to pay off a gambling debt. But I think he sold me twice. Well, he was supposed to sell my brother, too, for the *other* gambling debt, but this one —" he pointed to the other of the two — "got a bit violent. He's dead. The medicus says my brother's heart was weak. This man says he was given a damaged slave and wants me as compensation."

"You people are revolting," I said to the men. "Get out."

"Can I go home now?" said the boy.

"You want to return to the family who sold you off, twice?"

"Can't choose your family," the boy said. "But I *could* choose to go with someone else. I choose *you*, domine."

"I'm not a choice."

"Master, you've shown me more compassion than I've ever received in my entire life. Let me serve you. I'll lace your caligae. I'll suck your mentula."

Croesus shrugged. "Compassion," he said wryly, "is its own reward."

"Can you read and write?" I said.

"I do all the accounts at the bakery," he said. "My father never could count past X."

"I'll give you to Hylas," I said. "You will teach him to speak proper Latin, and you're to receive ten lashes if he misses a case ending."

"No, domine, no," Hylas said. "You *kill* him. Me have no case ending."

"Thank you, lord," said the boy, prostrating himself and slobbering over my right foot. "I don't mind the lashes. My father would beat me for charring a loaf."

"We won't be beating you for that sort of thing," I said.

"I know Greek, too," said the newly garrulous boy. "And Aramaic. And Hebrew. I'm from Judaea, you know. My family was captured and sold when Pompey the Great came to Jerusalem. We've been in Rome for a hundred years."

Croesus slapped him. He grinned.

"I don't need your biography; I don't even even know your name," I said.

"Simon."

"Simon, this is Hylas. Teach him to talk like a civilized person."

"His speech will be as beautiful as his face, domine."

It seemed that my slave now had a slave.

That was another Roman paradox, I suppose. A slave is by law a thing, a blank tablet on which his dominus can inscribe any history, and personality. You cannot by definition rape a slave because that would imply the existence of a person inside that piece of flesh you violated. The death of Simon's brother had provoked no remorse at the unconscionable abuse that had caused it; it merely meant that this was a defective piece of merchandise to be compensated for....

And yet, Rome says that by a simple magical act of manumission, a person suddenly exists. And even without a person being present, there is still enough of a shadow of personhood to *possess* another non-person. Even though slaves, by definition, have no property.

There was, after all, no simple line dividing freedom from slavery.

Petronius once told me, Aristotle said that the worst thing about slavery is "that the slaves eventually get to like it."

I was free, now, wasn't I? I could go where I pleased, dress as I wanted, even buy a slave.

But I could not go where I pleased, or dress as I wanted.

That afternoon, the tailor came from the palace, and I realized just how enslaved I still was. I was not getting a new wardrobe as such, but a series of new identities, to be switched back and forth according to the Divinitas's whim.

XIII

FIT FOR A QUEEN

Apparently, whatever this state occasion was, I was not to be presented as Sporus, the Divinitas's little plaything. The tailor had come with silks, which come from far beyond the edge of the Roman world, which is to say, *the* world. "Woven by the gods themselves," said the man, a Nubian dwarf named Leontes. Priceless rolls of cloth were being rolled out and draped on statues and columns.

"I know. You are expecting a fussy little Greek," he said, as slaves spread out even more fabrics in the triclinium.

A bust of Petronius stared down from a Corinthian base. Croesus had redecorated, bringing out all the images of our former master, so that he still seemed to inhabit the house.

"Not a fussy little Greek," I said, "I know that is just a silly stereotype. But somehow *you* —"

"And you would be right, domine," said Leontes. "I could tell you that I was a prince in my country, but I imagine you've heard that before."

"Not just heard it — I've used that one myself."

We both laughed.

As his slaves (which included, indeed, a number of fussy little Greeks) measured me and prodded me and stuck lengths of sheer fabric on me with fibulae, he told me his story.

"It is true I was a prince, but I was born to a tribe that views deformity as witchcraft," he said. "But a buyer for the games came to the village, scouting for dwarfs; he had a tableau in mind, amazons in chariots drawn by ostriches, battling dwarfs in heavy armour. My father the king traded me for a dozen oxen, and was glad of the bargain. Yet, though I looked the part, I could not handle a gladius to save my life. Instead of exercising with wooden swords, I spent my time with the kitchen and household slaves, and eventually the lanista noticed that our gladiators were decked rather more elegantly than those of other gladiatorial establishments. Nothing much, but I marshalled the resources of the school to add a fold here, a tuck there, a little ornament, so that our winners looked more triumphant, and our losers at least died with dignity. Oh, I did slay the odd amazon, but eventually the senator who owned the school realized I was of more use elsewhere. You did not see the Empress Messalina's wedding gown! That was mine. A month of little stitches!"

This autobiographical chatter engaged my interest in spite of myself. I could well imagine that, if I had not had my looks, I too could have been fodder for the arena …

#

As you are now.

Don't remind me.

As if you need reminding, my Empress, my Divinity.

#

The dressmaker's chatter did have the effect of distracting me, because the more pieces of cloth they wrapped me in, the more worried I became. I started thinking I was being wrapped for burial. Indeed, in a sense, being prized object of beauty in the palace was a kind of living death.

"It's a shame about the genitalia," Leontes said. "They rather ruin the holistic outlines this sheer fabric draws in the air about you."

"Pity you can't just cut them off," I said.

***

I bet you regretted those *words.*

You cannot imagine how often I replayed that scene in my mind. An offhanded bit of sarcasm that might have sealed my fate. But who was to know? Perhaps Leontes did not have the ear of the Divinitas. Perhaps the Emperor conceived it all himself. There was, after all, no limit to his cruelty.

Nor, at times, his love.

***

I had tried on a dozen pieces of finery when I realized I had seen some of these clothes before. "Aren't these Poppaea's?" I said.

Leontes mumbled something.

"You are ignoring me."

I recognized some of the pieces. And one fibula, in particular, I was sure I had seen it. It was a lapis lazuli carved into the shape of a rampant lion, with a mane of gold.

"These clothes *are* Poppaea's," I said.

"And we have to be quick, before they are missed," said the dwarf. "The Divine Poppaea is at some Magna Mater shrine, celebrating the mysteries, but she will be back before the tenth hour."

"Why am I supposed to be wearing her clothes?"

"Can you not posture in such a boyish manner, domine? You'll ruin the effect."

"What effect?"

"My dear domine, can you turn that wrist more daintily? Can you not stampede about the room like a raging adolescent lad?"

"Is that not what I am?"

"You will play a role, domine. And if you don't do it well, it will fare badly for us, as well."

Realizing that their fates as well as mine rested on my performance, I sat still while they padded my hips and chest a little, and while a cosmetician applied painted my face with delicate strokes, and two others teased and piled my hair.

And presently I found myself looking at my reflection in a mirror of polished bronze and I was transformed. My hair was elaborately coifed and elaborated extended with a tall wig. Exotic fabrics caressed my skin, and an outer layer of rich purple left no doubt as to my Imperial status. The fibula I recognized was holding it all together at one shoulder. Lead white gave my face an unearthly pallor and my lips were stained blood-crimson.

I stood taller. Arrogance flecked my lips. I felt ennobled. Entitled, indeed.

I was not just the Divine Poppaea Sabina, Mistress of the World. I was an idealized version of the Empress. And I have to admit that, in these garments, my way of moving, my way of walking, shifted towards the feminine. It was instinctive. I never felt beautiful as a boy, but as a woman, as an Empress …

Perhaps it was just a role, but I was pulling something from deep within myself.

Or was it simply that I had no identity? That I was merely a shard of mirror, reflecting the fantasies of others?

XIV

The King of Armenia

And thus it was that I stepped, radiant as the sunlight, from my litter, and ascended onto a gilded bier drawn by white horses. Horse-drawn *anything* is illegal in Rome during the daytime — whether it's carts of merchandise or a general's chariot, which meant that wherever I was going, it had to be a major event indeed.

On this bier was a throne, and crouched on the steps were my slaves, Hylas, more friend than slave now, if he only knew it, and the Jew I had recently acquired by accident. I was greeted by Epaphroditus himself. The Emperor's secretary glowering at me was another indication that this was no ordinary occasion.

Epaphroditus said, "Now listen. You're not to say a single word. You're here as an illusion, an illusion *only.* Understand."

"An illusion, yes," I said, barely sensing I even had an identity under the layers of fabric and cosmetics.

The entire contraption started to move. The horses were not used to the narrow street. One whinnied and reared up. At once, someone else, who had been behind the throne, so I did not notice him before, came lunging out. It was the boy philosopher Epictetus, and he was struggled to hold on to the cheetah Hercules, who looking like he was about rip his flimsy gold chain.

Hercules sprang into my arms as Epictetus was forced to let go. Simon screamed. Epictetus stumbled and tripped over the step. He got up. He was limping.

"Ah," Epaphroditus said, "Hercules remembers you — that's a relief."

I stroked the cheetah. "He should know me," I said. "We shared a box once." The animal had been liberally perfumed. I am sure that it was the scent that was driving him mad. "Why is Epictetus limping?"

"He is always getting himself knocked about," said Epaphroditus.

But I suspected there was more to it than that.

Presently the horses came under control and the entire tableau, with me enthroned and the boys and a cheetah at my feet, started moving downhill.

"Since I am not to say a word, Epaphroditus," I said, "Would you please tell me what role I am to play at least?"

"Isn't it obvious?" said the Emperor's secretary. "You are to be the Divinitas, the mistress of the world. You will be fine if you don't talk. Or at least, just stick to pleasantries."

"But where is the *real* Poppaea?"

"The Lady Poppaea Sabina is indisposed today. But you knew that. She is with child and she has been feeling poorly for days. She doesn't feel like sitting in the hot sun for an endless coronation."

"Coronation?—" My panic must have shown. "Surely Poppaea is Empress already."

Epaphroditus laughed. "You actually thought …" Even my slaves tittered. They must have already heard some gossip. "No, no, my empty-headed little sweetmeat, you will not be crowned queen quite yet! This is the coronation of Tiridates, King of Armenia, at the hands of his overlord, the King of the Universe."

Simon winced. "Among our people, we only use that title for the one true god," he murmured.

Epaphroditus grunted. "Monotheists! Better not say that in front of the Emperor."

Our little cortège had grown a little. Bucinae and tubae were blaring to the steady rhythms of slaves each beating a hand-held tympanon. At the foot of the hill the street widened a little and now it was lined with onlookers. Hercules was nervous at so many people and I was constantly stroking him.

We were approaching the forum. The crowd grew, and now soldiers stood on either side, preventing them from getting too close. We were moving down the Via Sacra, with the Temple of Peace to our right, about to reach the Temple of Castor and Pollux. People watching me go by weren't entirely enthusiastic.

An egg flew at me, missing the throne but catching Simon on the nose. "You murdered Octavia!" someone shouted.

I started to say I had nothing to do with that.

Another missile, this time a rotten cabbage. It hit Hercules, who became agitated. It was all I could do to hold on to the golden leash.

"Not a word!" Epaphroditus hissed.

"Boys, help me keep Hercules under control," I said. Simon and Hylas struggled between the two of them to keep

Hercules from becoming too agitated. Meanwhile, Epictetus limped over to me with a small sack of coins.

"They'll calm down once you throw some of these around," he said.

I reached into the bag as a hunk of stale bread narrowly missed my head. Now I had a handful of coins — nothing less than a denarius, and even a few aurei. I started tossing them. The crowd switched almost instantly from abuse to cheering. A child dived through the line of soldiers at an aureus, only to have his hand stomped on by a pair of metal-studded caligae. He squealed as he was kicked back.

I wanted to help him, but the procession had already moved on. In this city that had adopted me, violence was casual and not worth anyone's notice.

I hardly had time to react to the change from being reviled to being lionized, for at that moment a nauseating stench assailed my nostrils. We were about to cross the Cloaca Maxima, a miracle of Roman ingenuity, the vast sewer into which all of the city's waste flowed before being flushed to an outfall beyond the walls. The aqueducts, the vast public baths, the intricate system that supplied the city, eventually led here. The whiff hung heavy in the sultry air; for the greater a city, the greater its production of shit.

When we crossed the Cloaca Maxima, the odor quickly fell away, or rather blended into the myriad smells of the Forum. The baking, the body odors, the grilling, the slaughtering of small animals at altars, made for a kaleidoscope of stenches, sucking up and blending into the reek of the Cloaca.

Many more soldiers now, lined up with their tall shields forming four walls. Behind them, the crowd; slaves and senators, grandmothers with infants in their arms, children on the shoulders of grownups. A blast of a consort of bucinae and wailing tones of a water-organ.

A dais had been raised up in the center of the Forum. Statues of the gods looked down from every side, vividly painted, glaring down on the world of mortals, yet the god on the throne was not painted marble. A monument himself, encased in purple and gold, Himself looked upon me as I descended. My slaves escorted me to a lesser throne, to the right of Himself, as befit my status as a lower deity.

Epaphroditus bowed deeply to the Emperor and said, "I have brought the Lady Poppaea Sabina, the Empress, to attend the ceremony as you commanded."

Nero barely looked at me. "I'm glad you've changed your mind, my dear," he said.

"Not a word!" Epaphroditus whispered in my ear as I took my seat. I smiled wanly. The weight of the robes, the stickiness of the face paint, the searing summer heat, were all making me run with sweat. Even through the perfume, surely the Divinitas would know the difference between the scent of a man and a woman. Yet he seemed oblivious.

Perhaps because the smell of the cheetah, despite his perfume, was more overpowering than mine.

"My wife," said the Divinitas, and now I saw for the first time that there was a man prostrate on the ground in front of the Emperor. Many were prostrate in fact, but this one wore enough gold ornaments to purchase a small city. As this man rose to a kneeling position, I could see his face clearly. He had the complexion of someone from the East, Parthia or Arabia Felix, perhaps, and was bearded in the eastern fashion — most Romans prefer shaving their facial hair — and had an imperious bearing, much like Nero himself.

Yet he spoke with humility. "As I have performed the *proskynesis* before you, my Emperor and God, I also humble myself before you, O Goddess," he said, smoothly returning to his prostration, this time before me. "Forgive me if your beauty blinds me a little."

"Enough of that," said the Emperor. He waved, and a slave presented the Divinitas with a crown on a silken cushion.

"You have shown me that you and yours belong to me, and that Armenia is properly beholden to me, and to Rome," said the Emperor. "And in acknowledgment that you have accepted our overlordship, we are most pleased to return to you the crown of Armenia, Tiridates."

He placed the crown on Tiridates's head.

The cheering that surged around us was not compelled. Nero Claudius Caesar Augustus Germanicus was loved in those days.

***

And still is, if history were written by the common people.

That is true. If the mob had their way, you would not be facing a grotesque death right now.

Yet they'll enjoy my death very much, I am sure.

They are fickle.

There are those who deny that he has died, I hear.

That is true. How many Emperors have ruled so far this year, three, four? Yet they still long for those carefree days of poetry, chariot races, and lions eating Christians. I think there's going to be a little bit of that as an appetiser to your big scene, actually. But people find that sort of thing boring now. The Christians are no fun; they are far too compliant.

If my execution keeps getting delayed, I may yet have time to tell of how the Divinity and I infiltrated one of their notorious love-feasts.

I can't wait!

In time. I must finish telling you of Tiridates.

***

I stood there, a few steps lower than the Divinitas, and the Armenian King between us. The cheering was overwhelming.

"This evening," the Divinitas said, "we'll have some spectacular private games as well as a banquet. And then," he went on, "perhaps I and the Empress will entertain you in private."

I dreaded to think what Nero meant by "entertain."

"Divinitas!" Tiridates exclaimed.

"Poppaea can be quite excitable when she's had too much wine," said the Emperor, turning to acknowledge the cheers. "You did say you were blinded by her beauty, did you not?"

"But is she not with child, Divinitas?"

"Oh, pregnant women can do plenty," he said, smiling.

I bit my tongue. I knew why Epaphroditus had told me to say nothing. The Emperor was in one of his moods. Perhaps he was brooding about his mother again. Was this why Poppaea had not wanted to be present?

Had something happened to Poppaea?

Did the Emperor even realise that I was not his wife?

The Emperor put his arms around me and kissed me playfully on the cheek. "Don't give yourself away," he whispered sweetly, "or I'll cut off your testiculi and feed them to the peacocks." He turned to Tiridates, all smiles, and waved at the crowd again. I waved, too, and got a massive cheer.

The Emperor had known all along.

XV

THERE ARE NO EQUALS

After the crowd had thundered itself raw, the royal procession moved on to Campus Martius where stood the Theater of Pompey. The guests followed — of course, I mean important guests only, of course, no one below patrician rank — unless you happened to be a famous actor, musician, or gladiator, of course — in that case, even slaves welcomed.

I had not seen this place before but I knew that this was where the Divine Julius had been assassinated. But that was almost a century ago. Only fogeys and philosophers know that Rome was once a Republic.

When we entered the Temple of Venus Victrix, which forms the side of the theater from which the raked seating descends, it was all I could do to act unsurprised, for every piece of furniture, every column, every wall had been gilded. There was so much gold it was like gazing into the sun.

I look my place in the Empress's throne, my slaves

struggling to keep Hercules on his leash. But once I sat, the cheetah crouched meekly at my feet.

As we sat, there was a battle between *andabatae* being staged to put the audience in a cheerful mood. These unfortunates wore helmets that covered their eyes, so they could not see anything, and were standing around swinging their swords, only occasionally blundering into a hit. They ran into walls and each other, and the audience was shouting at them, usually giving misleading directions. It was surprising that they could succeed in killing anyone at all, but eventually they all lay in a heap of blood and metal and were cleared away with hooks, with a man dressed as Pluto, Lord of Death, overseeing the slaves who had to drag off the bodies.

While they were cleaning up, Himself introduced me to his guest.

"Tiridates, King of Armenia," he said, "thanks to *my* Divine Intervention, I might add. My wife, the Empress."

Tiridates inclined his head. I detected the shadow of a smirk. Did he know?

"You look amazing," he said. "The rumors did not do you justice. And … in your condition, too."

"As a goddess," said the Divinitas, "my wife does not whelp like normal mortals. It's all magic. She doesn't have to be encumbered by a grotesque, kickable belly."

"Miraculous," said Tiridates. "Rome is fortunate to have living gods and goddesses."

I was getting a sinking feeling, but there was no way to escape. I was a puppet, and the world was the puppet theater.

"You find her attractive?" the Emperor said slyly.

"… Ah, how could I not, Divinitas?" said the King of Armenia.

"Take her for a night, if you like," said Nero.

"To profane a goddess! To blaspheme!" Tiridates whispered,

his awe tempered with salaciousness.

"We are not governed by the same rules as … men," the Emperor said, gazing pointedly at that part of my stola which should not have been concealing any kind of manhood.

At that rather awkward moment, I was rescued from my anatomy being scrutinized more closely because a huge fanfare on barbaric bucina-like instruments made from the horns of rams came blasting from the opposite within the Temple of Venus and Victrix and a cacophonous orchestra emerged, the horns in the vanguard and massive copper drums in the rear, and ear-splitting, screechy winds.

"I didn't order up a barbarian wind band," said the Divinitas, waving at Epaphroditus, who scurried out of the crowd with a scroll of program notes. "Send them away."

"By no means, Divinitas," said King Tiridates. "You've entertained me for days; let me show you an exhibition by some of our Armenian mages."

Nero seemed impatient. He never liked being upstaged, but I could see his was struggling to seem gracious. He must have his own show lined up, I thought, and didn't want to sit through an hour or two of Armenian choreography. This music did not seem pleasant to my ears — how much more painful to the Emperor, with his delicate sensibilities? He sat there, wrinkling his nose, while Tiridates applauded happily.

We sat through a succession of mages. They did things with fire; leaping through hoops, making flames shoot from their mouths, hands, and even buttocks, flames of different hues. A woman was placed in a sarcophagus and sawn in half, and the nether half walked away, her feet protruding from the coffin.

They were illusionists — sophisticated ones, tricks I hadn't seen in the marketplace. In spite of the bickering between the King and the God, I found myself entranced. The blaring music actually became bearable as time went on. And no one was being killed … not even the woman sawn in half, who came back for a bow. That was a tremendous relief, because few entertainments in Rome were free of killing, even if it was just some hapless criminal being eaten in the background.

Looking over at the Divinitas, I could see that he was not really watching the conjuring tricks at all. He was clearly impatient to put on a show of his own. At length, Himself raised a hand and silence fell abruptly, the winds gurgling to a stop on a particularly ugly dissonance.

He waited. He was always the master at waiting for the utmost silence. One could, as they say, hear a fibula drop.

"O Tiridates," he said, turning to his guest with a languid arm gesture, "you have bewitched, nay, bedazzled us with the sophisticated illusions of Armenia's mages. Let me now repay you with a performance of my own."

Epaphroditus brought a golden lyre and a slave set up a gold sedilla as the mages, musicians, and dancing girls scurried out of the way. At the peripheries of the stage, slaves were still sweeping up some bloodied sand.

"Go sit with Tiridates, Poppaea, dear," he said to me. "That throne is ample enough, if you cuddle."

Trying to behave as if this was the most normal thing in the world, I crossed over to Tiridates's throne, cheetah in tow. He made room for me. It was, to say the least, awkward. It was a tight squeeze and

He advanced toward the seat, making every step an expression of divine hauteur. The hush was complete. Anticipation, indeed … but tinged with fear. Hercules tensed. He, of course, could smell it. He snarled. But silently.

The Divinitas played a single note on his lyre. Behind him, from hidden places, a hundred kitharas responded, echoing and reechoing that single note until in hung in the air like unformed dew.

And then he began to sing.

Yes, it was Niobe again, dreary Niobe mourning endlessly for her children, yet the fact that each of his melismas were picked up by strumming kitharas made the vast chamber an elusive shimmer of sound, waves of sound, like the sea ... and I thought for the first time in an age about the sea, the salt scent hanging in the wind as though carrying my tears out over the emptiness.

"I know who you are," Tiridates said, his lips barely moving, his face set into a mask of adoration as Himself continued to sing. "I think that this entire spectacle is a scandal." He put his arm around me and let his hand wander down to where my breasts should have been. "Nice," he said, pretending to squeeze them, though he and I both knew there was nothing to squeeze.

And I? I went along with the charade. I knew Himself was watching, even as he sang his heart out.

"Is it true," he said, "what my spies tell me? That Himself kicked Poppaea in a fit of rage, and she is in too much pain to attend my coronation?"

"I really don't know," I whispered. "They don't really tell me things." Was that what the Divinitas had meant, those chilling words about the Lady Poppaea's "kickable belly?" But I had seen them go at it, in the brothel that night. Indeed, I assumed that it was part of their lovemaking — the screaming match that would segue inevitably into a bout of wild sex.

"You really are everything they say, though," he said. "The whore shines brighter than his mistress."

"Reflected light," I said, "nothing else." I looked away. Was I really going to be gifted to this man for the night? Could I steal away later? There was bound to be a banquet. And in a banquet, people pass out. Even gods. I needed to look for Poppaea, to find out for myself if Himself had taken out his rage on her … rage that I knew was really directed at his own mother, Agippina.

For a while, we listened to Himself. The sound of the kitharas was a tonal cushion on which his voice slithered like a viper, seductive and deadly. I felt the Emperor's song … crawling into my robes, licking my bare skin. He did have power. He was not some bloated amateur as so many of you have suggested, who did not even hear him sing. I wondered how it was affecting the Armenian.

I realized I had already resigned myself to being handed out like a trophy. I found myself wondering whether the Armenian would be considerate, or whether he would hurt me.

"Do you want me?" I blurted it right out, not the most prudent way for a freedman to address a monarch, even a puppet king.

"He's already offered me fifty million sesterces," he said. "All that, and a queen, too? It's a test, I think. When you come to me in the middle of the night, and I presumably discover you aren't actually the Empress…."

"You won't be disappointed," I said. "No one ever is."

"I believe it. And yet —"

"Yet?"

"I'm not much for boys," Tiridates said. "I know, that's very quaint for a Roman to hear. But there's definitely a piquancy to who you are. Not just the boy-girl thing, but also the servant-mistress thing. You're the perfect love object, able to be all things to all lovers."

"Except to myself," I said.

"Don't think I don't understand how you feel," said the Armenian King. "I gave up *everything* to be here, and I do not know if it's worth it; my life, my kingdom subject to the whims of … *that* … just like you. It's unconscionable. Nero did not win my war. It was his man, Corbulo — a fine general, a skillful strategist. But it's Nero who owns me."

"But still, you're a king," I said.

"And kings can't always do what their penises tell them. Our *heads* must rule … or else, they roll."

And before I knew it, I started to weep. Here, surrounded by Rome's elite, every eye aware of my every gesture, I felt utterly, entirely alone.

Until I became aware of Hylas. I had not even noticed him moving from my throne to crouch on the steps of the Armenian's. Hylas was expressing his feelings to me in the only way possible for a slave in such a public place. Gently, unselfconsciously, he was kissing my feet. I wished he could hug me as an equal, but in Rome, there are no equals.

XVI

THE NATURE OF TYRANNY

I could not be in tears for long. Tiridates leaned over and wiped my eyes with a fold of his kingly robe. "Not in public," he said softly. "You're a queen. The illusion is *everything*."

Himself sang, his voice soaring in the silence, now and then punctuated by a ritornello from the massed kitharas. During these pauses, the Emperor peered at me. Or so it seemed. As though I were being singled out from this whole throng. I felt like an insect about to be crushed.

So I made it through the remainder of Nero's Niobe, a boy and a cheetah crouched at my feet, comforted by a king I barely knew.

The event ended with the Senate bestowing upon Himself the Divine Nero the title of Imperator, but what did a title mean when one was already a God? He received the newest honour with a languid wave. He summoned me to his throne and said, "You see that Tiridates is taken care of."

Later came the banquet, lit up by a few leftover Christians dipped in pitch, set aflame on towering crosses, had no surprises, not even its excess. It was a select event in one of the gardens. Though it was a spectacle beyond any previous banquet I had attended, its mood was desultory.

There were no poets. They were dead, or in exile. No Seneca, no Lucan, and of course, no Petronius; the world was so much darker now, with Himself its only literary luminary.

While there were no readings by great Latin poets … there was plenty of entertaining violence, but no one was watching as the best-trained warriors in the empire fought to the death.

Interest perked up a little when Lucius Domitius Paris, the actor, did a little turn, but nothing so florid as Niobe; he knew better, perhaps, to compete with a God. In fact, he made a recitation from Aeschylus — one of the speeches of Prometheus, inveighing against the God for his punishment in daring to steal the gift of fire. I was sure that there was some hidden message in the choice of text and it certainly had an effect on Himself, who was the only person in the garden paying attention.

The Greek of Aeschylus is five hundred years before our time and bristling with weird archaisms, yet Paris was so convincing an actor that I thought I could understand every obsolete aorist and every arcane allusion. He imbued every syllable with its own melisma that illustrated what the word meant, so I needed no translation.

By now, it was getting dark, because the Christians had burned to a crisp and they had run out; most of the last batch had managed to elude execution by murmuring a prayer to Himself. Which is why no one really felt much pity for them; not acknowledging Himself puts the entire structure of the state at risk, and what is so wrong with a pinch of incense and a prayer? I have endured far worse, for the sake of survival, and I know deep inside that my true self is not touch. And what god is such a fool as to be unable to pierce the veil of hypocrisy and see what is in a man's heart?

I had got up from my dining couch and was circulating among other triclinia laid out in the garden, and I heard those exact sentiments from an old drunk man; I recognized him as Pontius Pilatus, and I recognized the stories, too — the orgiastic love-feast cults, the baby-eating and what not — from the last banquet I'd seen the old general at. But the way he told the stories was more … I would say, more mechanical, like a schoolboy reciting Homer, trying to get through the lines while avoiding the tutor's quirt.

"Ah," he said, greeting me, "Poppaea. Or are you Poppaea's evil twin? You've lost your baby belly."

"Still telling the same tall tales, General," I said. "But the telling isn't the same; this time, your tales are literally lighting up the banquet."

"It's a good thing they're using the display crosses," said Pilatus, "so we can get the light without the smell."

A woman sitting next to him said, "And without the guilt, Pontius."

"I daresay if they were marinated in garlic and garum instead of being coated with pitch, the smell would be quite pleasant," another guest piped up.

"The guilt," the woman said again, grimly lifting a honeyed mouse by the tail and popping it her mouth, then spitting out the tiny bones.

"My wife, the Lady Procula," said Pilatus. "She used to have nightmares about it. Now, *I* have the nightmares."

"Because, my dear," said the Lady Procula, "you *know* they don't *actually* have baby-eating orgies."

"Blood rites, dear. They do have blood rites."

"Metaphorical, husband! They are a completely harmless cult. The Jews don't worship the Emperor either, and *they're* not lighting up his dinner parties."

"They will be soon," said another voice. Tigellinus, also making the rounds. "I hear they are revolting again."

He bowed to me.

"Not attending to the Divinitas?" I said, trying to sound imperious.

"I *am,*" he said testily. "I am doing my due diligence, keeping my eyes and ears open for seditious whispers."

"And if you find any?"

"I keep some pre-signed, blank death warrants on hand."

I moved away.

As I was, ostensibly, the Empress, I could not just slip away although there were so many things I wanted to find out. Where was Poppaea? Was she actually on death's door? Or were they just having a marital spat? After all, even Jupiter and Juno had them.

As I move among the guests, they paid me due deference. I am sure some of them knew. Paris, the actor, no longer playing Prometheus, was being harangued by the Divinitas.

"I want your tricks," Himself was saying. "You have tricks, I know you do. Only tricks could bring that hoary, antiquated windbag to life."

I knew that to Greeks, Aeschylus was almost as untouchable as Homer, and I imagine Himself knew it too. The master of the world was baiting the actor, and I knew it was from envy. I wondered if the greatest actor of our age would soon be going the way of Petronius, Seneca, and Lucan. The unassailable canon — Homer, Aescylus, Sophocles, Euripides, Sappho … all of them, Petronius always said, were perfect. Even their imperfections were perfect.

So, when Lucius Domitius Paris did not directly spring to

the "hoary, antiquated windbag's" defence, but merely stood with head bowed, I knew there was drama afoot, more drama even than the eagle devouring Prometheus's entrails.

Finally, the Emperor whispered a quote from the play itself: "Don't labour uselessly," he said, "at what can avail you nothing."

Paris said nothing.

"You don't think I can achieve those heights, do you?" said the Emperor. "You think my singing is mere vanity, a 'sickness rooted in the nature of tyranny'? That's what you were going to say, isn't it?"

"Divinitas," said the actor softly.

"Again, you refrain from the obvious riposte: 'it is best for a truly wise man to be thought a fool.'"

It was clear that Himself, the Divine Nero, was not Himself this evening. Or rather, perhaps he was *truly* Himself ... a terrifying notion for the one who was acting out the role of his bride.

I wished I could disappear into thin air. But instead, I spoke up. "Lucius, my dear," I whispered, taking his arm, every bit the steadying hand of the loyal wife who comes to the rescue of her drunk husband, "let's not be over-hasty. Look at the man — he's merely overwhelmed by your magnificence. He's done his very best, but his Prometheus isn't fit to undo the caligae of your Niobe."

The God kissed me on the lips. His breath was mingled wine and vomit, topped with a purée of peacocks' brains. "My wife," he said — and he giggled, thinking the world taken in by the deception — "my wife speaks truth indeed."

"Yes, Lucius," I said, smiling sweetly.

He whispered in my ear, "Would that *she* were as gentle, as compassionate, as you."

"I *am* that she," I said. "As you have commanded."

"You're not my mother," he said abruptly, and looked away.

I had not managed to get away with anything. But then, he said to Paris in a changed tone of voice, "You'll teach me all your techniques. Even the Pater Patriae can learn from the least of his children."

"Yes, Divinity," said Paris, bowing again.

"Be off with you. Epaphroditus will summon you for my lessons."

And Nero put his arm over my shoulder, and led me to where Tiridates was sitting. "Enjoy him," he said, and handed me over. "I mean, her." He started to giggle. Then, loud enough for the whole court to here, "Let it be known that in my magnanimity, I share with you even my very pregnant wife."

As he seemed to have made some kind of official pronouncement, the guests began to applaud. He held up his hand for silence. Then he pushed me at his guest, and wandered off, followed by Epaphroditus and assorted Praetorians.

I sat down at the Imperial triclinium, next to the Armenian King.

"This night has been something of a shambles, hasn't it?" Tiridates said, slapping a cheeky Nubian delicatus out of the way. "And I have many more days of Himself's largesse to contend with, before I make my way back to my own country and try to put it back together after a devastating war of succession."

A slave offered us kylixes of snow-cooled wine, each beautifully hand-painted and red-on-black with a scene from the amours of Jupiter. "Look," said the King. "I've got Ganymede. Who did you get?"

"Leda, I think," I said, since my cup portrayed a woman embracing a swan. "Will you take me to bed?"

"I think not," said Tiridates. "My tastes are not quite as catholic as the average Roman aristocrat. And we have more spectacle at dawn. A sea-battle in the Circus, I'm told. Salamis reenacted."

"More Aeschylus," I said. "Hoary."

Tiridates laughed. "But it will be with a touch of contemporary realism," he said, "because I'm sure we will get to see the Persians actually drown."

"We take our make-believe seriously here in Rome," I said, surprised at how much I sounded like Poppaea … her archness, her seemingly flippant view of serious matters such as love and death … hiding a deep vulnerability.

"Ah, Poppaea," he said softly. Perhaps he knew her. He seemed to feel for her. "I am sure you want to find out how she really is."

"You know I am not allowed to answer that."

"Let me help you," he said. "Come, I'll put my arm around you, and I'll walk you back to the palace. Everyone will make the assumption. Once you escort me to my quarters, you can slip away."

I called for Hylas to bring the cheetah. He and Simon were barely managing to restrain him, between the two of them and the golden leash.

"I'm not sure what I'm supposed to do with Hercules," I said.

"No worry, domine," Hylas said. "Slaves already tell me what to do." He had the ability of a slave to figure out exactly what to do and who was who, even though he could hardly speak Latin; this is how a slave survives.

My status, and the King's, demanded a Praetorian escort, but they discreetly left us when we reached the vestibule and turned down the corridor towards the royal guest quarters. Only my two slaves and the cheetah remained, following us at a cautious distance.

After I left Tiridates, my slaves and I went to my chambers. The boys could not easily help me undress, because Hercules was fretting. At length, I took his chain myself, and he quieted down; Hylas and Simon took off my stola and my jewelry and gave me a simple tunica, and they washed away much of the white lead makeup — it was thickly applied and would take days to remove properly — and now, I was a boy again.

I did not feel any different.

"And now," I said to Hylas, "I need to find out where the real Empress is."

"No need," Simon said. "She's in the Divinitas's bed chamber."

As I have said, slaves always know everything.

"Is she … alive?"

"For now," Simon said. "That's what Epictetus told me."

It was perhaps the only area in the palace that I was confident I could find from my own apartments. "Stay here," I said. "I'll take Hercules back to his mistress."

XVII

THE LABYRINTH OF NIGHT

A woman blocked my way.

She was slight, plainly dressed, unpainted. I could not tell if she was free or slave; that's rare. Slaves, even the wealthiest and most influential, give off certain clues. Perhaps, even, it's a smell.

She wasn't a slave, but she wasn't entirely a person, either.

She had been beautiful, still was. And she stood in the doorway of the Divinitas's as if she owned the place.

"You do look like her," she said. "At least, when you don't look too closely."

"You're not surprised to see me?"

"Here, I'll take the cheetah." Hercules went to her immediately; I had thought he would only behave this way with me. That's how I knew who she was.

"Actë," I said.

"Boy's got a brain."

She motioned me into the chamber and that's when I saw that there was a all kinds of strangers clustered around the Divinitas's lectus. I heard someone moaning. Poppaea. She was not dead, then, though she was in pain.

To Actë I said, "I have been told that you always appear at significant moments, like a kind of death-goddess, or an angel of death. So this moment, whatever it is, is important."

She said, "The young do love to cut through to the truth," and stroked my hair. "Go and see her; she wants to see you."

She clapped her hands and all the hangers-on stepped back. I could see there were priests, slaves, a manicurist, a doctor. As I went toward the bed they were propping up Poppaea against some cushions. She was pale. Weakly she touched my arm.

I sat down beside her. She clutched my arm with surprising strength.

"Were you good?" she said softly.

"I don't think I convinced anyone for a minute," I said.

"Maybe you were there to convince only one person, not that you are me, but that he has a viable alternative. But he doesn't, you know. You will never be me."

"I never tried to be."

She had a faraway look. "You didn't play with him when he was a child. And you didn't love him before there the slightest glimmer of his becoming a God ..."

"Nor did you," said Actë.

"No. That would be you," Poppaea said weakly.

"Yes. I'm the one who saw him as he was," Actë said. "I'm the one who knows the child inside the madman. But this boy ... he glimpses it, too."

It was true. Actë guarded the room the way Cerberus guards the gates of hell. She would not have let me in if she hadn't seen something in me.

In a corner of the room, a slave was casually wringing the necks of white doves and tossing them on a makeshift altar. "Poor little birdies," said the Empress. "Those sacrifices never work, anyway."

"Blasphemy!" a priest murmured.

Poppaea laughed, a dry humorless laugh.

"There seems to be a lull," she said to me. "Between bouts of agony, I'm actually able to have a conversation now. But this baby will kill me."

Another priest walked by, scattering incense.

In another corner, they were brewing a foul-smelling potion.

Poppaea reached up and gripped my arm. "Find Nero. I want Saturn to see Jupiter. A new god will slay the old. That's how the universe works. Saturn may swallow his children, but they will still cut their way out. You're the future, Sporus. Find him."

Poppaea began screaming.

***

I went out into the night. I had an idea where he might be in the lupanar, where I had last seen him go to vent his frustrations. I did not go alone, but was carried in an imperial litter and followed at a distance by some of Poppaea's men. As we turned a corner into the suburra I stopped the convoy. I got out. I explained to the henchmen that we didn't want to arouse suspicion. And Tigellinus and his gang were doubtless concealed somewhere here as well, as I understood the Emperor's night-wanderings.

Though the alley was empty, I could feel eyes everywhere. Eyes in the shadows of doorways. Eyes behind corners. Some buildings were hastily thrown up again after the fire, in a matter of days, flimsy, even taller and more precarious than before. Tiny windows had eyes as well. I could feel them.

The alley was lit only by moonlight.

I slid through a narrow door. A grating voice asked me if I was buying or selling. A torch-boy held up a candle and the burly door slave looked into my eyes.

"I want to speak to Spider," I said, popping a dupondius into his palm.

"Yes, young master," he said unctuously. "Slumming, are we?"

"Don't be impertinent," I said, using the voice one used with slaves — how easily it came to an ex-slave! — and this hulking, oiled giant let me passed and skulked into the background.

The antechamber was almost empty because the whole city was still celebrating the coronation of Tiridates. Two haggard women were kissing in one corner, and a large eunuch was wolfing down grilled pigeons in another, spitting out the bones. Spider was sitting at a table, counting stacks of spintriae, the tokens used to pay for the brothel's services. She looked up.

"Sporus," she said, and smiled. "Come sit with me. It's a slow night."

"I need to talk to Himself," I said.

"Sporus … that simply can't happen."

"Poppaea's about to give birth. She wants him to see his child. She's very … she looks *haunted,* Spider. She feels like there's a kind of doom hanging over her head."

"You can't go in, Sporus. You can't."

"Spider … *Actë* is in the Divinitas's bedchamber."

"Ah. Like Hermes, appearing as messenger of death. Or like the Egyptians' jackal-god."

I owed Poppaea something. I had been play-acting all day, pretending to be the Empress while the real Poppaea was in labor. Himself had used me — but for what? Why was it necessary to have this charade of a ex-slave playing an Empress? What message was he sending to Tiridates — indeed to Poppaea?

The Goddess was not expendable. She'd told me so herself. I hadn't known him as a child. I didn't even know him now.

But somehow, for some reason, she wanted *me* to fetch him to her.

I was playing a role in cosmic some drama, penned by an unknown poet, a play from which I could not escape.

I knew where the secret room was … I had been there. I had watched the two Divinities shrieking at each other like a fishwives in the forum.

I bounded up the narrow staircase. I knew where I was going. Spider was struggling to keep up. More stairs, uneven, creaky. I strode down a corridor. I threw open a door.

Himself was with a woman. That in itself was no surprise. They were going at it with enthusiasm. The room was well lit, with a row of oil lamps; their shadows thrusted and parried on the ceiling, larger than life.

At this moment, I really did not care whether I lived or died. Somehow I had to get Poppaea's message through.

"Lucius!" I shouted.

What happened next I could scarcely believe. The Emperor had his arms around the woman and had been pulling her up and pushing her down like a toy. When he heard my voice, he let go and she tumbled to the floor. "No, no," the Emperor cried, "don't torment me, not here, not here, mother!"

He flung himself naked at the empty air.

The woman pulled a length of cloth and threw it over herself, covering herself completely except for the oval of her face. I had seen her somewhere, but I could not place her.

I realized that Spider had followed me all the way into the

room.

When she saw the woman, she hissed, "Avert your eyes! Don't you know who that is?"

At that point, another door on the opposite side of the room burst open. It was Tigellinus. I did not know whether I should be glad to see him, but perhaps, at least, someone else could now take charge. "Tigellinus," I said, "the Empress asked me to find the Divinitas and let him know she is about have the child."

"Right," Tigellinus said. He seemed distracted.

More guards trooped in. They took the woman into custody.

"You're arresting her?" I said.

"The slave woman here … was she a witness?"

I nodded.

They seized Spider as well.

"Torture?" said one of the guards.

Spider stood there, stiff, unemotional.

"Torture?" Tigellinus said offhandedly. "Of course. Make it quick, and try not to kill her."

I realized what I had done. I had sealed Spider's fate. Slaves were not allowed to give evidence except under torture. It was an ironclad law of the Empire. Stupidly, I had nodded when they asked me if she was a witness. I looked at her. She did not seem to blame me.

"You can't torture her," I said. "I won't let you." I turned to the Divinitas. "Tell them, Divinitas. Please, I beg you."

But the Divinitas seemed to have shrunk into a mere shell of himself. He did not look at me. I wondered whether he thought that somehow I was possessed by the spirit of his mother Agrippina. The Emperor did not even seem to be in the same room as the rest of us. He did not look at me, or Spider, or Tigellinus, or the woman, who still said nothing.

Tigellinus said to me, "This time, boy, he actually can't do anything. Go with the Divinitas. Take him to Poppaea. We'll handle this."

I said, "You'll *handle* this? But he's a god! This woman, she's like a mother to me."

"Not a very auspicious thing to be saying to the Divinitas," Tigellinus said, cracking a smile. "He didn't exactly have a good relationship with *his* mother."

"He doesn't understand," said Spider. "Let's get this over with."

"What do you mean?" I said. "Nero Claudius Caesar Augustus Germanicus is God! There's no one he can't have. He owns every one of us. What is so different about this woman?"

At last, the woman spoke. The room fell silent. "My name is Rubria," she said. "I am a Vestal Virgin."

XVIII

THE TRIAL OF THE VESTAL

You actually witnessed it? The notorious defilement of Rome's very essence? The God of Rome descending to the most depraved befouling of Rome?

Yes. But I did not really understand what it was I had seen. I thought I had seen everything. He had defiled prostitutes and married women, men and women, and even allowed himself to be used as a pathicus. I know that to a Roman male, to be so used was as low as you could go. I did not know then that this was an order of baseness far beyond the shame of allowing Himself to be penetrated by a lowly slave like me.

But you know now. The Vestals guard the flame. The flame is Rome. Without the flame, Rome perishes. Nothing else is as important.

I had thought that Nero was Rome. But there's only been an Emperor for a hundred years. And we're past the Eighth

Century of the the city's foundation. And all that time, the Vestals have tended the sacred flame.

You were told these things when you were brought here. You had a tutor who taught you well.

As I stood there, I remembered some of the history Aristarchos had taught me. I remembered, then, the Vestals' seats in the circus, the only seats that afforded as fine a view as the Emperor's box. Though I was not Roman, I knew the Vestals were untouchable; they were the city's living symbol, keeping the flame alive at the oldest temple in Rome, a flame which had not been doused in eight hundred years.

That infamy alone would have been enough for the Emperor to be declared damnatio memoriae, *and all mentions of Himself removed from history.*

And yet, to my still uneducated mind, she was still just some woman I had stumbled on *in flagrante* with Himself, not an unusual thing. And for some unfathomable reason, they were taking Spider, whom I loved, off to be tortured, and my master, the Owner of the World, was not lifting a finger to prevent it.

But now, I suppose you know what they had to do to Rubria.

Yes. And I know why Nero could do nothing.

***

The Emperor left by a secret stairway, and out a hidden doorway. He insisted that I follow him. He kept me close, clutching my arm at times. Some Praetorians followed at a distance. I was not able to see them take away the Vestal Virgin, or my friend who I was powerless to save.

A litter, unadorned, carried by a gang of mismatched slaves, stood in wait. A slave stepped out and crouched so the Emperor could step in. He dragged me up as well. The slave had not seen this coming and had started to scurry away, so I hit my head on one of the supports. Nero was so distracted he did not even order a whipping.

We moved quickly; the litterbearers may not have been a matched set, but they were quick and smooth. Inside, it was dark, and dank from the Emperor's sweat. As we sped along, one of the attendants pushed a lit lychnus through the curtain; I took it. It was one of those erotic terracotta lamps; I had seen them in the brothel; it was made in the shape of a rampant satyr, with the wick protruding from the creature's prodigious member. In the flickering light I saw that the master of the world was hunched at the farthest corner of the litter, and he seemed defeated, helpless.

Softly, I said, "Poppaea asked for you, demanded that I fetch you."

"She will have to wait."

"She's in labour and having a hard time of it."

"Impossible! She's a goddess!" But his tone was unconvincing; it was, almost, imploring.

"Perhaps," I said, trying a fresh approach, "as a goddess, she feels no pain, but here, living amongst men, she feigns her suffering out of consideration for the humans who surround her… surely *you've* done things like that, Divinitas. Or people would be …"

"Blinded," he whispered. "Yes, blinded by my true form. As when Semele gazed on Jupiter."

"There, there," I said, and with my free hand I stroked his arm.

"My mother never accepted that of me," he said.

The God was no different from Poppaea's cheetah, after all. He just needed a little empathy.

"Shall we go to Poppaea now?" I said at last.

"Not just yet. We have one stop to make."

Indeed, I could sense that we were not going uphill, toward

the summit of the Capitoline.

***

At length, the litter stopped. The curtains were drawn and the crouching slave returned. I stepped out first and helped Himself the Divine Nero down.

"Wine," he said.

Magically, it seemed, an exquisite kylix of snow-cooled wine was proffered out of the gloomy. Torches were being lit. We were in a garden. Next to the pathway, there was a row of statues. all stately women, decorously clad, their stolas reaching down past their toes. Their faces, discreetly painted, stared down at us like an army of avenging furies.

The pathway we stood on led to a portico, a columned façade, a huge door. The door swung open and first there came women bearing a gilded curule, which they unfolded and set down just behind the top stair. Himself, leaning on me, made his way to the seat of office and sat down.

Then about six women and some attendants emerged, the last a withered crone who nevertheless moved with the energy of a teenaged girl. She spoke to the Emperor in a sharp voice, utterly disregarding his Divine status. She and the others wore the snow-white palla and covered their heads with a purple-bordered white suffibulum.

"A fine mess you've made of things, Lucius Domitius!"

"I'm sorry, Great-Aunt," said the Emperor meekly.

The Senior Vestal must have been some neglected member of a family connected to the Julio-Claudians in some way. Perhaps they'd all had to commit suicide in some earlier purge, with the matron left to rot as the most exalted female in the Empire.

"Very well," she said. "Let's get this over with."

The Emperor summoned me and I sat at his feet. So I saw

all of it. Tigellinus brought in Rubria. She was not restrained in any way, but left to walk by herself, with a quiet dignity.

Then Spider was dragged in. To say she had been tortured does not begin to describe the wreck she had become. I saw, too, that her fingers had been smashed. Her clothing was bloody. Yet when she looked at me, I saw no resentment. She knew there was nothing I could have done, once she had followed me up those steps.

Tigellinus said, "Did you see this woman in the act of sexual congress with a man?"

"Yes," Spider said.

I whispered in the Emperor's ear. "Please, Lucius. Give her to me. Her fingers are broken. She can no longer perform her work. What good is to anyone?"

"Oh, you and your delicate heart, Sporus! I was just going to have her crucified, expunge this whole sordid incident from the universe."

I kissed his hands. He seemed immovable. How could I save the woman I'd unthinkingly condemned to such suffering. "My Lord, my Divinitas, my Love," I said. "Just give me this little thing and I'll ..." But I could not think of what act I could perform that he could not demand at any time.

I thought back to my training, when I was in the slaves' holding area in Ostia. All those lists of self-debasements that I had been fortunate to avoid because my master was Petronius. Something sprang to my lips. "Please, tata," I said, and almost meant it.

The master of the world held me to his bosom. He held me so tightly I thought I would suffocate. His sadness found a strange echo in my own. I remembered that the Divinitas's real father had died when he was two, and that the Divine Claudius had adopted him as his heir when he was thirteen, and only at the machinations of his mother Agrippina; I doubted he had called Claudius *tata* either. Letting myself be enfolded in him, I found I could not summon up any image of my own father in my mind.

"All right," he said. "Tigellinus, have the slave sent to —"

"Petronius's villa," I said. Surely Croesus would know how to bring her back from the infernum I had cast her into.

"Touching," said the Maxima Vestalis, "though hardly relevant to the business at hand. You must pronounce sentence, Lucius Domitius."

"I?" said the Divinitas. "But … the sentence is already known."

"But only you can utter it. You are the Pontifex Maximus, the upholder of the state religion."

"Must I? It's not as if I *enjoy* killing people."

"Well then," said Rubria, "while you're dithering around, I want to speak." No one stopped her. "I was six years old when I was pledged here. I was told that I would be one of the most sacred persons in the world. That all would respect me and know that by tending the fire, I keep the Empire alive. But you will never know how wretched a time I've had. Your great-auntie is a petty scold who belittles us and metes out oppressive punishments for silly infractions. Oh, you haven't tied your ribbons right. There's a corner of the hearth unswept. A whipping without any dinner. My parents bought political favour with my soul, and then your mother made them commit suicide anyway. There's nothing for me here, do you understand?" She walked right up to Himself and spoke directly in his face. "Then *you* came. You sang songs. You made beautiful poetry. You smelled like the spring. You told me I wasn't breaking my vows, because you were not a man. You were a God! How was I to know? Had I ever had a man? Did I know what it is men and women do? Of course not. You taught me. The House of the Vestals is death, worse than death. You awakened me out of the cold ground. Put me back there, at least I've lived."

The Vestals shrieked and made all sorts of gestures of averting every possible omen, tearing at their veils, uttering ritual formulae, beating their breasts. Amid the cacophony, Nero found his voice. Still clutching me to his breast, he said, "There is only one punishment for *incestum* committed by a Vestal Virgin. To lay a hand on you, to shed your blood, is anathema, and therefore your death must be entirely free of bloodletting. You must therefore, without coercion, of your own free will, be buried alive in the Campus Sceleratus. Let it happen *now*, under cover of night, while the city is preoccupied with celebrating the coronation of Tiridates."

So saying, he got up, letting go of me so suddenly that I tripped on the stairs. He marched toward his litter and I followed.

When we were moving again, he said, "No, don't ask me. We are not going back to the palace yet. We will see this story through to its end."

I only started to say the name "Poppaea" when he stopped my lips with ... perhaps it was a kiss. Perhaps it was the hungry bite of a ravening beast. I dared not pull away, until he did, abruptly. Not a moment too soon, because his cloak had almost caught fire on the lamp I had stupidly been clutching in one hand.

"Poppaea sent you, didn't she?"

I did not answer, because he knew the answer.

"She sent you so that I would *have* to kill her. I never want to kill anyone. Not even those benighted Chrestianoi. Let alone my mother. Poppaea is playing a game and she has forgotten that she only wins when I let her."

I thought of the Lady Poppaea Sabina, whose friendship —

or manipulative scheming — had brought me to this moment. I thought of her, surrounded by people in the imperial bedchamber, surrounded yet friendless.

"I will never play games with you, My Lord," I said … playing the ultimate game … "I love you."

I did not ask him to love me. That was not my place. I could not ask. I dared not. For to be loved by Nero was a death warrant.

XIX

Campus Sceleratus

Nothing they do to me today will be as horrific as what they did to Rubria. They managed to pull together a funeral procession with twenty pairs of torchbearers, and we proceeded toward the Colline Gate with drums, double-flutes, and sobbing professional mourners.

It had been less than a day and a night, and I had already been present at a coronation in the forum, Greek drama, gladiatorial combats, a lavish banquet, a flirtation by a king, the bedside of a childbirth, a sacrilegious act of incestum, and a trial.

The funeral had been put together at, it seemed, a moment's notice, but Rubria played her part as though she had rehearsed for it, walking with dignity in the procession towards her own execution.

When we arrived at the Field of Evil, the soldiers had everything ready. They must have been digging all through the trial, because the pit was already prepared. It was surrounded on three sides by torch-bearers. It was not wide — the slave quarters I shared with Hylas and Hyacinth in the bowels of Petronius's villa was no wider.

Himself's curule was set up at the very edge of the pit, and I stood beside him. I was able to see clearly, then, Rubria's journey to infernum, which was by way of a rickety wooden ladder, accompanied by a priest, who then abandoned her and pulled up the ladder. Below, we could see, she had a couch to sit in, what looked like a jug of wine, some bread, some olives.

She sat completely unmoved. And Himself did not look down at her at all.

It was when they slammed down the lid of her burial chamber that the screaming began. Undeterred, the soldiers began to shovel earth back into the pit. The screaming was terrible to hear but it grew faint as the opening was filled. No one made a sound. Just the sound of earth piling up, and the slowly fading screams. The softer the screams, the more bloodcurdling. Presently they seemed no more than the squeak of a mouse in a jar in the kitchen, and yet — in that deafening silence — the sounds were stab-wounds to the soul.

The soldiers began to pat down the earth. Soon we would see only level ground. We could walk over her as she ran out of air. She would always be with us, living, even in death.

Himself the Divinitas called for his lyre. He held it in one arm, with the other poised to begin some epic threnody. But no words came.

Instead of an Imperial dirge, there came a chill wind, unseasonal. The wind whispered and sighed and I fancied I could still hear the Vestal Virgin's cries.

Nero did not move.

At length, Tigellinus approached him and said, in a surprisingly solicitous tone, "We should get going, Divinitas.

You haven't slept for more than a day and a night."

"And well you shouldn't," said the Vestalis Maxima, not giving the god any quarter. "Take the boy and go to bed."

"Yes, Great-Aunt," said Himself, barely audible.

The withered chief vestal leaned over and presented her cheek for Himself to kiss. He did so, dutifully.

Then I helped him into his litter, and we began the procession back to the palace.

#

"No light," he said, as I held up the little erotic lamp. "I want to sit in the dark."

And so we did.

The way back was mostly uphill, and the bearers had been standing at attention for hours and were doubtless exhausted; it was a slow journey back.

"I know what you want to say," said the Emperor.

Which was strange, for I did not know it myself.

In the utter dark, in the oppressive closeness of the closed litter, in the sweltering stillness that fell as soon as the curtain shut out the wind, I felt I could say anything. "What do I want to say?" I asked Himself, not even addressing him by any title. Like an equal.

"You want to say I should have done something."

I did not answer.

"Admit it. Should have, would have, ought to have ... wherever I step, the path branches a millionfold, and I always step wrong. I could never do anything right. I've always known. Agrippina told me often enough."

I let him speak.

"How old were you when they ripped you from everything you knew?"

"Where I lived, Divinitas, they didn't really number the years. Only if someone grew big enough to do a man's work."

"When I was two, my father died. I went to the country. I lived what some might call … a normal life. I played music. I read poets. I even farmed. I grew up with, I was in love with, a slave girl, I was with her all the time, in my loneliness, she saw me; in her alienation, I saw her."

I do not know whether Himself had singled me out to be the one he should open up to, or whether, in the darkness, he saw no one at all, and felt himself alone; I had been a slave, I knew that they are often invisible; that is why they know everything.

"You mean Actë," I said. "Tell me about Actë, my Lord."

"What's to tell? She played no games."

"I know." More than any other woman of the court, Actë had seen through all my attempts to shield my soul.

"You know?"

"I saw her," I said. "I told you. She's with the Empress right now, guarding her while she's in labour."

"It's bad, then," he said. "She only comes at the turning points."

The litter turned uphill; I could not keep my balance at the steep angle and slid into the Emperor's arms. Startled, I cried out. He held me as a child holds a doll. Through the perfume, I smelled stale sweat, sour wine, and a tinge of vomit. I did not struggle, did not try to wrest myself free; the incline of the street pushed me more tightly against him.

"Call me tata again," said the master of the world.

"Tata."

He turned me around and kissed me. I tasted his tears.

"I'm not evil," he said.

"No," I said. "You're a god. You're like the wind, like the sea."

"Yes. I can't help killing people. I bear them no malice."

He squeezed me so tightly that I thought I too would be killed that night. I knew he could feel my pounding heart. He must know, I thought, the stark terror inside me, even though I am doing everything I can to appear unmoved.

I closed my eyes.

In my memory, I smelled the sea. The salt tang of captivity.

"You too are a slave," I said softly.

I did nothing. I exercised none of the arts I had been trained in. I leaned against a cushion and became almost a boy-shaped cushion myself, allowing him to do as he pleased, giving nothing in return. I will not feel anything, I told myself sternly, remembering the salted, decapitated head of the Lady Claudia Octavia, remembering the broken body of my friend Spider, remembering the haughty demeanour of the Virgo Vestalis Rubria as she descended into the abyss, and the faint screams that echoed up from the freshly-shovelled earth. I will feel *nothing*, I told myself. It was still pitch dark. We were still moving uphill.

And yet … in the end, as he flailed in the ocean of his passion, clinging to me as though to the broken beam of a wrecked shipping floating on the waves, I did feel the ghost of a feeling. Or was it just my young body, responding instinctively to being touched?

"Tata," I whimpered, clawing at him a little.

And immediately, the master of the world shuddered, exploded, and was still.

The incline levelled off. I was jerked upright and Himself slid off me. We were both slippery. The litter came to a stop.

I reached outside with the unlit lamp, and pulled it back in, lit. I saw the face of the Divinitas. Not a trace of that vulnerability I had felt when we were cocooned in the pitch black of the closed litter. He glanced at me, holding up the lamp, and might as well have been a piece of furniture, a lamp-stand carved into the shape of a Ganymede.

So quietly that I barely heard him, he said, "I suppose I shall have to go and kill my wife now."

XX

IMPERATRIX

Yes, I saw Nero kill his wife.

With your own eyes.

Yes.

It's all true, then.

But not the way they told it, and not the way it will be told. Because the world is always more complex than the words of any historian.

***

The Emperor walked purposefully, grimly, not speaking; I followed. He took a back corridor and a flight of steps I had never taken before; almost by magic, we arrived at the Imperial apartments.

And Actë was still the gatekeeper; in all that time, she seemed not to have moved. But she *knew.* And Nero avoided her gaze. He knew that she knew. He looked at the floor, like a chidden boy.

There were fewer people in the room now. The air was still cloudy with incense, but the priests, doctors, soothsayers and hangers-on had mostly cleared the room. There was a midwife and a few other female slaves; they clustered at one end of the lectus. There were no baby cries. Perhaps it had not yet come.

Poppaea was no longer screaming. At first I thought she must be dead, but then I heard whimpers. One of the women came up to me and told me she was asking for me. The Divinitas was still shrinking from Actë's baleful gaze. I left him there and went to the Empress's bedside.

The cheetah lay next to her on the lectus. The pungent feline smell mingled with the stench of the unguents and the blood, and the perfumes that had been used to mask the odors, and the sick-sweet smell of the frankincense.

I sat down. She touched my arm.

"My twin sister," she said. Her voice was weak, but her mind was not clouded.

I kissed her on the cheek.

She said to me, "You were my secret weapon, Sporus."

"So you told me."

"I never realized I would turn the weapon on myself, little brother."

"You just said I was your twin sister," I said.

She smiled. "As my sister, we're of an age, but as my brother, you're just a chid."

I managed a kind of laugh, because she obviously did not want me to seem too sad. "You see," she went on, "how Actë handles him. No one else can."

"Why isn't *she* the Empress then?"

"She has no aristocratic blood at all. In fact, she's an ex-slave."

"I am, too," I said. "Which means he can never ..." It was unthinkable in any case.

"But you're a prince," she said softly.

"I was told to say so," I said, "so they'd pay more for me at the auction."

"Oh, Sporus, Sporus," she said. "It's your innocence that appeals to him the most, you know. To all of us. Petronius, too. You're like a marble statue that has just come from the sculptor's studio — all white, all featureless. And in that whiteness, every colour is possible. And then, on the way to the temple, or to the public square, the painters come, and the statue becomes just a single someone. But before that ... Sporus, in you, we all see the persons we want to see. But only you know the person you are."

"I just play whatever role I have to," I said, "to survive through to the next day."

"You must. But, Sporus, don't dishonour my name," said the Empress. And turned the other cheek for me to kiss.

"No," I said, not knowing if it was a promise I could keep.

The midwife interrupted. "Augusta," she said, "will you look at the child?"

"No," said the Lady Poppaea Sabina, mistress of the world.

But I saw the baby. A wet-nurse held him, was feeding him. He made no sound. "Is he well?" I said.

"Barely clinging to life," said the midwife.

"Sporus," Poppaea said, "stay in the shadows for a little while."

I kissed her cheek again. Then I slipped to the far side of the room. I was about to witness a ceremony that takes place in every Roman home when a child is born. A chair was brought for Himself. He sat down, still not looking at his wife.

The wet-nurse came forward and laid the child at the

Emperor's feet.

He scrutinized the baby for a long while.

The baby sneezed. Spluttered a little, then was silent again. Not dead, but, as Poppaea had said, clinging to life.

Any moment now, I thought, the Divinitas will pick up the child. It is the absolute right of the paterfamilias in any Roman household to determine whether a child should be accepted or rejected. The baby is laid on the ground, and the paterfamilias picks it up. If he does not, the baby is taken outside and exposed. In the country, it is probably wolves; in the city, most likely, a passing slaver looking for a quick profit.

"Do you think he looks like me?" said Himself.

No one answered.

"Actë, tell me," he said.

She turned her back on him; even I knew how unspeakably rude that was.

"Sporus," he said. "Come here."

I was reluctant to, but I did not have the kind of self-confidence that the Lady Actë displayed. Making as little noise as possible, I crept up and crouched at the foot of the Divinitas's sella.

"He looks like the Empress, doesn't he?"

"Very much so," I said.

The Emperor was looking from the child to me, and not to Poppaea lying on the bed. First me, then the child, the child, then me. "Those pouting lips," he said. He put a stubby finger on my mouth. It tasted sweaty, and oily, and a little bit of semen, as well; the episode in the litter was still fresh. "But tell me, my dearest," he went on, "shouldn't the child also look like *me?*"

He ran his finger down my chin, to the nape of my neck, to my shoulder. I must say that it made my flesh crawl. But I remained numb, showing no emotion.

"Whose is it?" Nero said softly.

Poppaea said, almost inaudibly, "You know, Lucius."

"Lucius!" the Emperor screamed.

"Why Lucius," she said. "Lucius ... Domitius ... Ahenobarbus, called Nero." She only spoke in gasps.

"How many men are there named Lucius?" said Nero. "There are only a dozen praenomina in all of the Empire! Shall I crucify one in twelve of all the citizens of Rome?"

"Don't be absurd, Lucius," she said.

"You don't think I remember the day I wanted you to come to the theatre, and you begged off because of a headache? Whose bed did you climb into that night?"

"That was months ago."

"Exactly! *Nine* months."

He had been nursing this imagined slight for almost a year, and it had grown into something monstrous.

"Adulteress!" he screamed

That was when the kicking began. I had seen him do this before. I had not understood until today that their relationship had deteriorated into nothing but violence. I did not look after the first kick. I squeezed my eyes tight shut. I hoped, I prayed that the first had been enough. Finally, when I summoned up the will to open my eyes, I could see that she lay quite still, and there was blood everywhere.

I was beyond terror. Inside, I was cold and dead.

There was no honour, no beauty. Petronius's death had had a kind of nobility. Even Rubria's cruel punishment had a kind of ceremonial gravitas that made it almost bearable. This was unremitting savagery. I understood for the first time why the Chrestianoi called him *The Beast*.

They took her away, then. The slaves, the soldiers, their faces frozen into masks of unfeeling. The room began to empty.

Himself, the Divinitas, sat at the edge of the lectus. Two slaves, the few who remained with us, began to undress him, with swift, practiced movements, making themselves as invisible as possible.

I had not been dismissed.

"You see how it is," said Nero. "I can't love women. When I do, I kill them." He was not speaking to me. I realized that Actë was still there, standing behind me; she had not looked away.

She said, "Your problem, Lucius, is that in the end, all women, to you, are just your mother."

"^*You're* not," said the Emperor.

"But you know why I can't be an Empress," she said.

"Yes. Agrippina won't let you."

"But she's dead," I said.

Actë turned to me. "How little you know, little boy. Agrippina will never die. He will kill her again and again, and she will still haunt him."

Nero wept.

"Better you take the boy," said Actë. "You won't have to kill him. Agrippina will understand there's nothing to worked up about. It's only a boy."

"Even *she* can't be Empress," I began … "Well, I'm not even a woman."

"No," said Nero. "But then again, I am a God. That which mortals but dream, I can make real. My word alone makes flesh out of the empty air."

Actë said, "I love you. You are everything to me. I live only for you. And yet I know that you are mad."

And she left the room.

The Emperor said nothing more that night. He reached for my hand and drew me to the bed with an unexpected gentleness. He kissed my hands. I think he was trying to apologise, although I was not the one he had wronged. And all night long, he stroked and kissed me, his tenderness surpassed only by my terror.

The child remained on the floor.

XXI

The Morning After the Night Before

And this was how the morning after was: I woke up alone.

The child had been discreetly removed, and from then on it was as if it had never drawn breath.

Sunlight streamed in from an entryway that led to a private garden I had never seen.

I woke alone and despite the light, this might as well have been deepest Tartarus.

I did not want to remember the night. We had made love. Well, the Divinitas had made love, while I, like a doll, was but the empty vessel of his imagination.

In time I must have passed out, but my dreams were if anything more unnerving that what had happened in that endless day and night that had transpired. For a time, I remember, I floated.

A pendulum swung back and forth. No, not a pendulum, but a bottle in a cave, strung up be a hemp cord, and inside it a lone cricket stridulated. I knew this place; it was the dwelling the of Sybil, who knew all the world's secrets, and who was cursed with immortality. In the dream I wandered from cave to cave. Those I encountered looked away, as though seeing me was unbearable.

I understood then; they were the dead. They did not like to see a living person. Perhaps I reminded them of when they had been alive. They were shadowlike, translucent. It was a labyrinth, but the walls themselves moved and shifted, and wherever I went, I found I had gone nowhere. And then, without warning, I found myself at the foot of a mountain of potshards and rubbish. In my dream, I had reached Mount Testaceus, where the refuse of the city was piled up, where my friend Hyacinth still lay, I supposed. For he too had been added to the refuse that the city regurgitated every day, the mountain of the unwanted.

My dream had brought me here for a reason. Hyacinth's shade was reaching out to me.

No sooner had I realized this than he was there. He was embracing me. It was as though he were still alive. I felt him, I smelled him, I looked into his eyes and saw the longing that had led him to walk this path.

He's with me not in memory but in an eternal present.

Sporus. He doesn't call me Sporus but a secret name, in our own tongue. I cannot utter this name he calls me by, because you don't know our language. In our world, true names are secrets shared only among the most intimate.

We commune with mind alone. *How is it that I can feel you, that you don't seem dead at all?*

I am just a shadow.

But I feel you! I hear your blood racing, your heart beating when you put your arms around me!

It's the echo of your own heart. It's the rushing of the blood in your own veins. I only live because you live. When you stop living, we'll be shadows together.

Petronius once quoted Euripides to me: *Kai pos an autos katthanoi te kai blepoi?* ... "how can you be both dead and alive?" ... Hyacinth reads my thoughts and answers, *I don't know. I only know you're here and that makes me be here as well. Is Hylas looking after you?*

As far as he can.

He is a little out of his depth.

I am having this dream, I told myself, because there's something I need to know. Something is going to happen.

In my dream Hyacinth hugs me so hard he's almost *inside* me. And he says, *Sporus, Sporus, let me live through you, let me have the life that the knife took from me.*

***

The memory of the dream faded, and once more I was in the Imperial cubiculum. I did not know if I had leave to return to my quarters, or to go back to Petronius's house, which was the one place I could think of as home. I did not know if the Emperor had

I was hungry. There was not a single slave in shouting distance. I could not even see a convenient urine jar.

It would not hurt to go into the garden, surely. So, still bleary-eyed, I stepped into the bright sunlight.

This was a simpler garden than the ones I had seen in the palace. Unlike most gardens it was not in the style of an atrium; it could be accessed only from this private cubiculum, and a wall went round it, too tall to see over. Nor could I see any part of the Palatine, looming above the wall, so the garden must be strategically placed, and near the summit of the hill.

It looked to be around the sixth hour. The sun was directly overhead. I stood naked and alone. Presently I found what seemed to be a remote corner. It was behind a statue of Augustus. There were some rose bushes and, unable to hold it in any longer, I emptied my bladder.

I became aware of a fierce odor and when I looked down, Hercules was crouched at my feet. He was gnawing on a human hand.

"Leftovers," said the Emperor.

I turned and there he was, dwarfed by Augustus Caesar. Ruefully, he smiled. "I've been meaning to swap out the head," he said. "But if you keep pissing in the garden —"

"Divinity!" I exclaimed, and started to prostrate myself.

"Next time," he said, "just call one of your slaves."

"I don't know who my slaves are," I said.

"They're everywhere. Just say 'pisspot' very quietly, and one will appear. But the treasury loses money if we don't collect every drop."

"Why don't you tax it?" I said.

He put his arm around my bare shoulders and started to walk me back to the cubiculum. "That," he said, "is a *good* idea. Rome can't survive without clean togas, and laundries can't bleach without piss. You were always a shrewd one, Poppaea."

I did not contradict him.

"Tigellinus," he said.

By magic, the head of the Praetorians appeared, perhaps from behind a tree. One moment he was just there, as if he had *always* been there.

"Tigellinus," said Himself, "let's have a urine tax."

"It won't be popular," Tigellinus said.

"But we could finally afford to replace the remaining imperial heads."

"There might be other needs," said Tigellinus. "Judaea has revolted again." He then told the Emperor a lengthy story of how Gallus, the Imperial Legate in the province of Syria, had been ambushed by rebellious Jews.

"Send Vespasian," said Nero, and immediately changed the subject back to the urine tax.

It occurred to me that I had never been alone. All that lolling about bemoaning my aloneness in the cubiculum … who knows how many slaves there were, keeping themselves invisible until the God wanted something. Under the bed, behind a curtain, in secret compartments in the walls … no. I was never going to be alone, *ever,* as long as lived in the sphere of the Divinitas.

"Divinitas," I said softly.

"Call me Lucius."

I did not dare, not directly, not in front of Tigellinus, who saw this whole charade for what it was.

"May I have leave to visit the house of Petronius, and to see a few friends from my … former life?"

"Why are you asking?" said Tigellinus. "You are the Emperor's favorite. You can go anywhere you want, visit anyone, buy anything from the market, clothes, slaves — they will send a bill to Epaphroditus, you can be sure — and if the Divinitas needs any of your special talents, I will find you within the hour — the whole city is caught in my net."

The Emperor said, "He will need an escort. Tell Vinicius to make the boy his special duty. He is reliable, and he doesn't like boys, so he won't be tempted to touch what is mine."

What is mine.

Chilling words to hear, for one who had already been set free.

***

But before I could leave the palace, the Divinity had need of what Tigellinus had called my "special talents" once again.

And again, I was surprised by his tenderness, his consideration. I tried to mask my terror, as much as I could. At one point, he made me cry out, and it might even have been pleasure, a momentary joy that breached an ocean of pain.

When I cried out, he stopped. He held me. He looked into my eyes with wonderment, and, quoting Virgil, said, *"Nunc scio, quid sit amor."*

"Now I know what love is," I repeated in Greek.

Perhaps he knew; I was more unsure than ever.

Then, he said the words that instantly made me understand why the ghost of Hyacinth had visited my dreams.

"Your voice is changing," he said.

XXII

Apollo Palatinus

How to avoid being hacked up and served to the Divinitas on a platter, minus my masculine parts? Because that was the unspoken menace behind the words, "Your voice is changing."

What would be better? To survive the operation, or to wander forever in shadow, like Hyacinth?

Himself left me on the bed. No sooner had he left the room than slaves came. An old man came with a wet rag, to wipe me off. A rather dour-looking woman who started to dress me without my consent, and a pretty young one with a krater of undiluted wine.

I said, "I want my own slave."

And at that moment, Hylas emerged from a secret panel in the wall.

"Me wait so long for you to call for me, domine!" he said, hugging me.

"Not me, Hylas," I said softly, "I."

"Beat me!" he said, smiling. The others looked disapproving.

"Where are the others?" I said.

Simon crawled from under the bed. "I could barely breathe," he said, "the way the Divinitas was bouncing all over you. Do you need a poultice, a salve?"

"Take me to my own quarters," I said, as I was sure I did not know the way.

I had stopped the Imperial slave from finishing dressing me, and was wearing only a simple tunica, having left my queenly robes lying in heaps. Simon and Hylas gathered those heavy garments up, then took me down passages with stairs to my apartments. I was sure I had not come the same way. I wondered if I would ever be able to find my way, and I wondered at how my slaves had already figured it all out.

I decided that I could take literally what Tigellinus had told me: that I actually had the freedom of the city, and could go where I chose, since the Praetorians evidently had eyes on every street corner and I could never be beyond the Emperor's reach. So I decided it was time to go home — Petronius's, that is.

Once there, I could confide my fears to the only people who could really understand my predicament: Croesus, Spider, and Marcus Vinicius.

***

Just as in my former life as a slave, I sat in the kitchens gossiping. I did not feel so constrained in the kitchens. Spider was a shell, an empty old woman, yet she had made some progress to returning to health. With her broken hands, she resembled her name more than before.

Croesus, free, had cast off the sense of servitude completely.

Some of the slaves were a little cautious, but when Croesus and Spider made much of me, they seemed to accept me. Though Hylas could not help calling me *master,* or pouring me a cup of humble posca from an earthenware jug.

Simon, it seemed, was a lot more impertinent. He neither called me *domine,* nor did he defer to Hylas, to whom I had given him as a tutor. Then again, he had not been born a slave.

I said, "Simon, you said you'd lace my caligae and suck my mentula."

"When do I begin?"

"But you haven't even started on the job I've given you, which is to scrub the barbarity from Hylas's lips."

"Yes, Hylas," he said. "Come on, now. *Dominus, domine, dominum, domini, domino…"*

"Why so many?" Hylas said.

"Oh, there's more," Simon said.

"All of you," I said, "leave me, because I need to have a serious discussion with people who actually understand the world."

And the slaves scattered like chaff, knowing there was an unseen boundary behind which I would never again be one of them.

I unburdened myself to Croesus, Spider, and Marcus Vinicius, telling them everything that had transpired that night, including my dream, and the words that the Divinitas spoke to me.

Marcus Vinicius said, "Could the Divinitas have spoken in jest, or just in passing?"

Spider said, "Not when you remember the dream."

"There's truth in dreams," Croesus agreed.

"Shall I wait for Hyacinth to come in another dream," I said, despairing, "before I know what to do?" For dreams come unbidden. They don't give answers on demand. Unless…

Marcus said, "You should talk to the gods."

"But which god?" Croesus said.

"I slept with one all night," I said, "and all I got was more confusion."

Spider said, "Apollo is the god who always speaks the truth."

I knew that if I went to a temple to make sacrifice or give thanks, Tigellinus's spies would think nothing of it.

"But the Temple of Apollo Palatinus was damaged in the fire," I said.

"Damaged," said Vinicius, "but still in operation."

"It is still Apollo's house," Spider said. "There are still priests, and people still go there. To speak of dreams, go in the full moon. Diana, the sun's sister, rules the night."

***

I waited until the eleventh hour. I did not want to make a big spectacle of going to the temple. I did not take Hylas, which made him pout a little, but I knew Simon could retain more of what was said. I took the second-best litter and Marcus rode alongside.

The moon had already risen. Because of the collapse of the roof during the fire, Apollo stood in the open, in the moonlight; rain and fire had worn the paint and you could see a lot of the marble. But rather than looking damaged, it seemed that you could apprehend the god's true essence beneath the paint. The god's face was ash-white in the moonlight, like a ghost. There were traces of gold. The god's eyes seemed alive. Without a roof, the clouds of incense were attenuated, the odor faint. Laurel trees stood, some intact, some partly uprooted. There was a vendor table with caged doves for sacrifice.

I sent Simon over to buy a brace of doves. I did not say they should send the bill to the palace, but when he came and told me the cheapest pair was two hundred sesterces, and that a beautiful, unblemished pair could be as much as a thousand, I realized I should have brought more than a few coins with me.

"I didn't know doves cost that much," I said to Vinicius.

"It's a temple," he said.

I wasn't sure how one could go about sending a bill to the palace, or indeed whether I really could do that. But as I was wondering what to do next, a woman swept up the steps and approached the vendor.

"A pair of the best whites," she said.

A steward, hovering behind her, counted out ten aurei. The seller took them out of the cage. The woman waved at me.

"There you go," she said. "Remember me to the Emperor."

"But—" I began.

"Who does not recognize the Divinitas's beautiful new plaything?" she said. "Put in a good word, Sporus. I had a dream last night. Meeting you here is another augury."

I looked at her in bewilderment. She was beautiful. She was nothing like Poppaea, but she carried herself the same way. Unlike the late Empress, she had not bleached her hair to match the whores of the suburra. Like Poppaea, though, she had a penetrating gaze, and her eyes, enhanced with kohl, made it hard to look away.

"What shall I say to the Divinitas?" I said.

"What you like," she said. "But let him know I exist."

She then turned back and purchased a whole cage full, and marched up the steps towards Apollo.

The vendor's boy came up to me. "Shall I wring their necks for you, sir?" he said in a piping voice. "Some of our suppliants are queasy."

"I'll kill them," Simon said. "I'm quick and they won't feel anything." To me, he added, "My people sacrifice doves as expiation, and my father always had something to feel guilty about."

I watched the lady as she prayed to Apollo Palatinus. I could not take my eyes off her, in fact. She stood there — I could not hear what she said, but she railed, she gesticulated, she *demanded* something of the god. Presently, she turned to her steward, and he opened the cage and released all the doves she had just paid a fortune for.

"Patricians! Such idiots!" said Simon. "They'll just catch them all and resell them."

The woman came charging down the steps, the steward scrambling to keep up, and I saw now that her litter was waiting at a bend in the road.

"Who is she?" I said.

"That," said Marcus Vinicius, "is the Lady Statilia Messalina, wife of the ex-consul, Marcus Julius Vestinus Atticus."

"So," the vendor's boy said, "what will it be tonight? Unlucky in love? Harm to an enemy? Dream divination?"

"Divination," Simon said, impertinent again.

Just for the sake of form, I slapped him.

"You're a slave," I said. "By the pudenda of Venus, act like one."

"Yes, domine," he said, giggling.

Vinicius said, "Sporus, this really won't do. Croesus will give him ten lashes when we get home. It's not serious, but the boy has to learn to behave properly in public."

Simon immediately became more subdued. I felt a twinge of guilt, but I didn't feel like contradicting Marcus. After all, any Roman paterfamilias would beat their own sons far more savagely, and Simon's own father had thought nothing of selling him off.

"Tell me, Marcus, what I am supposed to do," I said.

"Speak to the god," he said. "Make sure you say your name clearly; they get confused. Then ask the favor, and offer the lives of the doves. At that point Simon can wring their necks, if you don't want to."

I approached the god.

I breathed in the faint odor of incense. I bathed in the moonlight. The eyes of the god were on me.

I said, "My name is Gaius Petronius Gaii Libertus Sporus. I am other people's creation. I'm a peasant in a remote country. I'm a slave boy whose sole existence is in others' pleasure. I'm a prince who was captured by pirates. I'm Giton, the perfect boy, stepped out of the pages of Petronius's imagination. And now, it seems, they want me to be an Empress. But who do *I* want to be? My master freed me. Last night I walked among the dead and my true friend spoke to me. Can *you* speak to me, God of Truth? If you'll only speak to me, I offer you—"

And then, it came to me.

The God had already spoken to me, before I had even asked.

The Lady Poppaea Sabina had used me to become Empress, but she had overplayed her hand.

Wasn't that what the Lady Statilia Messalina was hinting at? If I could only deflect the Divinitas's attentions onto someone else … would I not be able to wriggle free of the retiarius's net?

"Go give the birds back," I said to Simon. "I already have my answer."

"Give them back?" I could hear the vendor's boy whining. "We don't give refunds."

"Yes, you do," Simon said. "Look, there's a blemish. A thousand sesterces! Shame on you, selling sullied shit in a sacred place."

He argued so belligerently on my behalf I resolved to hold off on the ten lashes until the boy did something *really* bad. I wondered whether that would make me a bad dominus. Compassion, after all, was not really a Roman virtue.

XXIII

STATILIA MESSALINA

The best way to find out more about Statilia Messalina would be the baths, meaning I would have to go in the morning, during the women's hours. The earlier the better, perhaps.

First, I found out from Nero's spies, who watched Petronius's house at all times, what the Divinitas planned for the next few days, for he was still entertaining the King of Armenia, and there were banquets, some public, some intimate, a poetry reading, as well as visits to the chariot races, the theater, and more games.

Croesus suggested the Baths of Agrippa rather than the newer Thermae Neronis; the family of Atticus were creatures of habit.

I left my boys in the palaestra, where they could find other youths to play and exercise with. They stripped down and joined some other youths. They were running and laughing and playing as though they were free. I was glad I had not let Simon get whipped; the stripes would have given him away.

I took Spider into the thermae. Taking Croesus's advice, I played the role of Empress to the hilt.

I had come to the baths wearing a silken stola, and veiled, as though announcing to the world that I was so important I had to come incognito. If anyone thought ill of my attire, they did not dare to say anything to someone so impressively dressed.

I took the women's entrance and was admitted without question, then into the apodyteria, with Spider fussing over me. Once in the changing area, I avoided disrobing completely. I shed my stola and the tunica beneath, and quickly wrapped myself discreetly in my palla, hiding any suspicious body parts. If any of the slaves in the apodyteria had noticed, or wanted to gossip, let them.

Two slaves brought me a pile of linen towels and then I draped myself quite thoroughly, handing over the palla for safekeeping.

I tipped them a quadrans each and told them to watch my clothes.

The robes the slaves were guarding, piled up in different corners of the antechamber, were a king's ransom in themselves; if it were not for the deterrent of summary crucifixion, there were probably plenty of would-be thieves in the thermae.

Spider asked one of them if the Lady Statilia Messalina had been seen that morning. We were told that she was there somewhere. The apodyteria had doors leading to chambers of varying temperatures. I did not want to seem to be looking for anyone in particular.

First we entered the caldarium and the heat hit so hard I immediately wanted to shed my towels, though I knew better. There were women of all sizes and complexions; naked, or nearly so, all sweating mightily or soaking in the hot water, they did not seem to be plebeians or patricians. The bath was truly the leveller, the thing all Roman citizens had in common. I had not really known this, because when I came to Rome I was a slave, and after that, I had only been in the house of Petronius, who was rich enough to bathe alone, and rarely sought the company of any but his own guests.

It was better for Spider to ask the questions, flitting between the groups of women and speaking only to the slaves. She ascertained that the Lady Statilia Messalina had been through the caldarium already.

In the frigidarium, it was too cold for gossiping. The floor mosaics depicted wild sea-creatures: giant octopuses, dolphins, Neptune waving his trident. The women were in huddles, in different corners. Some were braving the cold water of the pool. The sound of women chattering seemed to come from the next room; no doubt because it was the one with the most amenable temperature for chitchat.

We made our way to the tepidarium. Here, the walls showed scenes of domestic bliss, real or fanciful — Jupiter and Juno, Ulysses and Penelope, Augustus and Livia.

More women here, sitting in groups of two or three. A few had their own slaves tending to them. Others were making use of the public slaves, some for a little more than merely a massage. It was a secret world, like the sacred mysteries. And I stood at the boundary. If I chose, I could belong here too.

We spotted the lady. She lay on cushions laid out on the marble. A slave was rubbing scented olive oil onto her back;

another was scraping the oil off with a strigil. A dumpling-shaped friend squatted beside her. The friend looked up and saw me.

"Wait, Statilia," she said, "I think you've won the bet after all. I'll leave you, then."

"Not yet, Vipsanilla," Statilia murmured. But the friend left her, laughing, and joined another gaggle.

"Enough," she said to the slaves. She stood, nude, and smiled at me briefly. Then she looked away. Then she went to the edge of the pool of lukewarm water, and waited for me to approach her. She did not call my name, playing along with my charade.

No, she did not look like Poppaea, except for the eyes. But the eyes would be enough.

I had not been wrong when I saw her last night. She would be perfect for my plans. She had spirit; Nero liked spirit. She was bossy. Nero would not like a woman who did not in some way resemble his mother.

For this was, in essence, what I needed to do. If I could deflect the Divinitas's attention to another woman … not that *I* was a woman, but Himself had begun seeing me as Poppaea, he could avoid thinking he had killed his wife … perhaps I could get past the changing of my voice. By then, it would be too late to castrate me.

Statilia Messalina barely glanced at me. She had taken it for granted that I would come.

"The doves," she said, still looking away. "Did you get the answer you wanted?"

"I got my answer without having to sacrifice," I said.

"You gave them back!" She turned to look at me at last.

"They said no refunds."

"Just like a slave," she said. "Money, money, money."

"I'm free," I said.

"You are not," she said, speaking the truth that I knew deep inside. "Can you get me an invitation?"

"He needs a wife." I did not add, any wife but me.

She said, "I have a husband."

"Will he mind?"

"My husband? He's not exactly in the Emperor's good graces right now; we haven't been seen at court for a year. And yet … I have known Lucius … intimately."

That did not surprise me. I did not think there was any woman of noble birth whom the Emperor had not at least sampled. With women he was omnivorous. With boys, I had learned, more selective. *Too* selective. Hence my predicament.

"Before you married your husband?" I asked her.

"Yes. Oh, a long time ago. But an old flame, I hope, can yet be fanned to life."

"Aren't you afraid?"

"I am not," said the Lady Statilia.

"Those whom the Divinitas loves…"

"Yes, I know. But you're still here."

"I wouldn't call it love. He *loved* the Lady Poppaea Sabina. Me, I don't think so. It is something akin to *need.*"

"Well, it is true that he *needs* an Empress. And really, you won't do. He is not so insane as to think that your lowly birth and slavish origins qualify you to be anything but a toy. Not to mention that you have a penis."

"Exactly," I said.

Suddenly her eyes widened and she looked at me in a new way. She pulled me down to sit beside her. "You've *had* him, haven't you?"

I could not imagine how she knew.

"Just once."

"Why, that effeminate, ignoble, pathetic little cinaedus!" She laughed. "No offense."

"None taken, Lady Statilia." I understood her distaste. It's my place to be penetrated. But the Divinitas — proper Romans of standing don't debase their manhood that way. They become objects of derision. And for an *Emperor* ....

"Yet I have heard, from my slaves, that that is by no means an inviolate rule in other, less exalted cultures. The Celts, for instance, like to take turns. The Nubians, I have heard, do not discriminate one hole from another. As for the Greeks, they are *eromenoi* as youths, then once they grow beards, become the aggressors."

I knew little of those other worlds, having had my childhood, indeed my very selfhood, stolen from me on that pirate ship.

"You know a great deal," I said.

"I have little to do," she said, "except read."

"He likes women who appreciate good poetry," I said.

I had studied the Lady Poppaea Sabina quite thoroughly in her machinations to become Empress. Now, to avoid Poppaea's fate, I would need to use everything I had learned.

One advantage was that the Lady Statilia Messalina was in no way my friend. She was a means to an end. No doubt, Poppaea had seen me that way as well, in the beginning, but she and I had always had a kind of bond. I would not be in this predicament, perhaps, if I had not felt a kind of love for her. I could not allow myself any sympathy for this woman, or any kind of affection. But she was haughty. She was not easy to like.

To the Emperor, I was just an extension of Poppaea. Surely, I thought, a new distraction would allow me to escape. I did not belong in these political wars, these cosmic battles for power. I was happier to be nobody.

"He's having a private reading tonight," I said. "I'll ask Epaphroditus to put you on the list."

"You'll have to invite Atticus," said Statilia. "And Atticus has no ear for poetry at all. Surely there's a chariot race coming up?"

XXIV

Poppaea of the Starlight

When next I saw the Emperor, his mood had changed again. He was now in deep mourning. He wore an unwashed toga pulla, had not shaved, nor had an ornatrix been summoned to beautify his hair.

We were in a private dining room in the palace (so far, I had not dined in the same room twice there) and there were only eighteen at table; Tiridates was among them, and, as Epaphroditus had promised me, Atticus and Statilia had been invited to the gathering, but had been relegated to the second table.

Having not been told in advance about the mournful nature of the evening, the couple I had invited stood out. Atticus wore purple threaded with gold, which was his right as a once victorious general, and Statilia had her hair piled up almost as high as an obelisk, and sported an emerald fibula.

I myself had been told just in time, so I managed to find a drab grey tunica in time. When I arrived, I was immediately sent by Epaphroditus to the head couch, and made to sit between Tiridates and Himself, who only gave me a cursory acknowledgment.

I snuggled up to Himself — he seemed to want that — and let him sob into a fold of my tunica. "I've written a poem for tonight," he whispered.

"I can't wait to hear you read it, Lucius," I whispered back. But there was no kithara on the couch, and no back-up players to add resonance to his performance.

Overhearing, Tiridates said, "It's a very special poem indeed … so special, he won't even read it himself." And that was … unlike Himself, to say the least. What poem was so special that this author dared not read it?

I was to find out. Between the two sets of three couches, in the space between the two tables, stepped the Goddess Venus herself. She was taller than an ordinary woman, and painted completely in white lead paint, as though she were made of marble. She wore robes entirely dipped in purple. A palla was of purple, too, but stitched with stars in gold thread.

When she spoke, the voice was eerie, high, mellifluous, as though the stars themselves could speak. But the rhythm of the hexameters, the precise modulation of the Greek, the way each word was colored so as to seem to bring its innermost meaning to vivid life … that was Lucius Domitius Paris, the one performer that everyone secretly whispered was better than the Divinitas.

The one artist Nero knew in his heart was greater than he was.

In the poem, Venus, called Aphrodite as the ode was composed in Greek, descends in a chariot drawn by fantastical creatures: gryphons, lynxes, sphinxes, dragons, each animal brought to life with a few well-chosen adjectives and a vocal embellishment.

Lucius *was* the Goddess. He wasn't just impersonating a woman. He was all that a woman is. The transformation was astounding, even more so than what we had seen in the Theater of Pompey. I knew I could never do that.

In the poem, Aphrodite descends into the cubiculum of Poppaea Sabina, heavy with child. I think the Chrestianoi have a similar story about one of their heavenly messengers visiting their version of Magna Mater. The Goddess invites Poppaea to ascend with her in the chariot:

Make haste and weep no more
The myriad stars of Zeus's heaven
are bidding you welcome ...
they will enthrone you
on the moon's fair face ...

But Poppaea is unwilling. Her love for Nero is too great. But the Goddess tells her

Do not be downcast
at the favor shown you
Though your husband is a man
equal to the gods

and

On this earth your two children
have passed away

Among the gods
you shall watch them
for all eternity

Then the song continued with Poppaea's apotheosis. She rode to the stars in the celestial chariot. She was greeted by a shower of shooting stars and a symphonia of starlight, represented by a chorus of concealed young boys, their voices soaring over the twanging of kitharas and the whine of double flutes.

We were in tears. It was if I was witnessing firsthand the transformation of woman into Goddess. As I listened, I remembered our first meeting. I remembered how we had pleasured each other while her first husband lay, fat and snoring, in the same bed. I remembered that in her strange way, she had been a friend to me, and she had wanted to talk to me in the end, not him, not the agent of her violent death.

I was wrapped in the arms of that agent. Hot tears spurted from his eyes and moistened my face. I was crying, too.

"You knew her, Sporus," the God whispered to me. "And soon you will know her even better."

I summoned a nearby delicatus and told him to pour a krater of snow-chilled, strong Falernian. I held it to the Emperor's lips. He sipped at it, and his tears mingled with the wine.

"Is he not a great artist?" said Nero.

I knew that my duty was now to say, "But not so great as you, Divinitas," but I could not force it from my lips. So I said nothing and smiled.

"I am an Emperor. I must have an Empress. Zeus has Hera. Cronos had Rhea. Uranus had Gaia. There can be no sky that is not grounded by the earth. I am the sheltering sky of Rome, and I must have a bride. Or … when it rains, who will receive the seed?"

I waited, apprehension gnawing at the pit of my stomach.

At length, I said, "What do you think of Statilia Messalina?"

"Oh!" he pursed his lips. "I fucked her once."

"I took the liberty of inviting her."

I indicated the opposite couch. The Lady Statilia had been placed in the direct eyeline of the Emperor, who had not noticed only because Paris's monodrama was playing out between the two tables. But now, the song was ending, and Paris was prostrating himself in the most toadying *proskinesis,* while the choir boys and musicians also came in from left and right and prostrated themselves.

He could see her clearly for the first time. A woman like Statilia Messalina always knows when she's being looked at. She smiled at him.

"Her husband," the Emperor said to me, "is an illiterate bore. Could you not have brought her alone?"

"He's old-fashioned," I said. "An old-style *paterfamilias* type."

"Have them come to the races," he said.

"But you're competing yourself," I said, thinking that it would hardly be a good moment to plan an assignation.

"Even better. The sweat of the arena is the best aphrodisiac."

I knew that the scraped-off sweat of gladiators and charioteers commanded a hefty premium in the apothecaries' market.

I noted that he was not uninterested in Statilia Messalina. I just needed to push a little harder.

After the poetry evening, I was not summoned to the Imperial cubiculum. I was relieved. I called for my litter, thinking I could sleep in Petronius's house. But as I was leaving, I was intercepted by Marcus.

"Himself has asked for you," he told me.

"Another trip through the suburra?" I asked, thinking that Himself wanted to work through his grief with another night of debauchery.

But then I saw that a large entourage was assembling: senators, Epaphroditus and his stoic protégé Epictetus, and an Egyptian priest.

"No," said the master of the world, emerging from an inner room. "No ribaldry tonight. We are going to pay a visit to the Lady Poppaea Sabina."

XXV

POPPAEA OF THE DAWN

Thus it was that I learned that the Lady Poppaea Sabina would not be cremated like any other Roman. The guests followed the Emperor, some on foot, some in litters. I sat with the Divinitas. I could not fathom his emotion.

Our litters bore us down an underground passageway that branched, here and there. There were sporadic brackets with torches, some already spent. I would not have known where we were going but for overhearing the litter-bearers and their foreman telling them where to turn. There was a network of such passageways. That was why the Divinitas, or the Praetorians, could seem to appear anywhere in the city, by magic.

Where we emerged was Regio III, Isis and Serapis, not far from where Nero's Golden House was taking shape. But we were still underground. We had reached a huge subterranean chamber, the walls painted in Egyptian style.

We stepped from our litter. It was just myself and the Divinitas.

'Where's my audience?" said Nero.

They were far behind us, hanging back. Something awkward was about to happen and no one dared presume to follow the Emperor.

Epictetus limped forward and pushed a door open. Only Nero and I stepped through. I was conscious that others, lining the corridor outside, were observing. Whispering.

A monumental statue of Anubis dominated the chamber. The walls were covered in hieroglyphics. A bald priest was working on a body that was mostly covered with a linen sheet. I could not identify who it was. To my horror, he was extracting the corpse's brains through its nose, and placing them in an alabaster jar.

In another corner, a painter was at work, creating a portrait on a panel made of cartonnage, the papyrus-and-plaster material for funerary masks. The image of the woman's face was emerging from swirls of paint, so lifelike I almost believed the lips were moving.

I knew who it must be lying there.

The priest moved and an arm slid past the linen covering. I could see a hand against the side of the table. I knew the hand. The hand had caressed the most intimate parts of me.

It was a delicate hand. It was in fact, my own hand, almost.

"Poppaea," the Emperor whispered.

He took my hand and led me to the table. The priest wiped some viscous fluid from the nostril and drew back the drape. Poppaea Sabina lay there with her eyes closed. Nero pulled the drape away completely. There was an incision through which they had removed her internal organs, but it was sewn shut and barely visible because white leaden paint coated her whole body. There was a powerful perfume masking the whiff of decay, blending with the clouds of frankincense from braziers set at the room's four corners. In the flickering light, in the fog of incense, she was a marble goddess.

The Divinitas pushed me against the side of the table and, caressing me with one hand, half climbed up over the Empress's corpse. I was terrified. Dead, Poppaea's flesh seemed to suck my life force, seemed to animate itself through the racing of my blood, my labored breath.

How could this be happening, with half the court behind the half-open door, voyeurs, tittering? I was humiliated beyond imagining, but then again, I was nothing. I believed I would be killed. His face was contorted, almost unrecognizable.

The Emperor cried out, screams of rage, pain, grief, desire and guilt, all these feelings, gushing out all at once. I could feel all these things. In my terror, I was as frozen as the dead Empress. I felt not only fear but pity. The master of the world was desperate to be loved and all he had was a dead wife and an ex-slave. I knelt against the cold stone of the slab, the one conscious receptacle of the God's despair.

Then Nero Claudius Caesar Augustus Germanicus shuddered and became still for a moment. Then he stood up and turned away from me. He did not even look at me. I swabbed my stained face and hair with the sleeve of my tunica. At this moment I was of no more import than a vase or a bowl, or a rag used to wipe away the traces of someone's lovemaking.

I was nothing. But I too have needs.

Deep inside, past all the layers that others have constructed, past the mirrors piled atop mirrors in which my owners have seen their own selves reflected, I too am a person.

And in that moment, that person was seen by no one. No one in this world.

Why then should *I* acknowledge that person? I thought. Better to play my appointed role.

"Lucius," I whispered.

Slowly he turned. I stood beside the dead Imperatrix, my tunica ripped. He did not even see me. He heard me as though it were *her* voice. And he said, "I'll make you a goddess."

"Yes," I said. "Put me up there, among the stars."

"I will," he said.

And so you became Empress.

I did not. Not at all. Not even close. On the contrary. I was, for a time, forgotten. I took little part in the elaborate rituals of the Lady Poppaea's Egyptian-style funeral.

I was not of course allowed in the Senate, so I was not there when they proclaimed her a goddess, but I was in the background with the bulk of the entourage when a portion of the temple of Serapis was rededicated for her cult and her new-minted priests performed their first sacrifices, a white heifer and also a white calf, to honor her stillborn child who was deified as a kind of afterthought.

The Romans can make gods just by passing a law.

They can unmake them, too.

You mean the Damnatio Memoriae decreed for my erstwhile husband.

A decree is making you *a god.*

A god for an hour, followed by violent death.

I don't believe in gods like these. They drink the blood of sacrificial animals and offer vague promises in return. I think that a man can be a god, but I don't think you can be a god if some old men decree it.

Was Nero a God?

There were times when I felt it.

And I felt it that day, violated, tossed aside, by a power as elemental as thunder or a tempest.

I saw the emptiness inside the God, and I knew that the abyss could never be filled. It would devour me utterly. And yet, as I have said, I too have needs.

Oh, I hated him. I hated what he had made me. I hated what I had become because of him. And yet, beneath that hate, there was still the spark I felt when I first heard him sing. There was a kind of love.

Such delicious ironies your life held! Oh, I am jealous. I am an artist, and yet my work is smudged or sweated into oblivion in a day. My beautiful transforming of you from prisoner to goddess won't even live a day before you're ripped to shreds by the rapist … oh! Did I offend? So many jobs for these arena reenactments … you get jaded.

You're not talking.

I don't blame you for getting sullen. Don't get all soggy though, or I will have to do your face again. Try not to think about it. All right. Don't say anything.

***

That day, the Emperor left in his litter, down the subterranean tunnel. I heard footsteps. People had been peeking. They might not have seen anything, but they had guessed that it was something dark, something unthinkable.

The door slammed shut. I was by myself.

Not exactly by myself; priests were still chanting, the painter was still working on the portrait, and the mummifier-in-chief had gone back to working on the dead body of the former Imperatrix.

I went upstairs, into the dawn. Stepping out of the old Temple of Isis and Serapis, I got my bearings, and I slowly made my way back to the house of my former master.

I was not summoned for some weeks; and then it was not by the Divinitas, but by the one who planned to become the new Empress of Rome, the Lady Statilia Messalina.

XXVI

THE JUDGMENT OF PARIS

I was dejected. I was depressed. I was disillusioned. For days, I lay in my former master's cubiculum. Croesus brought me wine, which I did not touch, and later, poppy juice from Ephesus, which I did. They say it will send you to a world from which you will never wish to return.

I drifted, drifted, drifted on a cloud of semiconsciousness. I drifted and willed myself not to awaken.

I dreamed. I saw Hyacinth again. This time, he did not speak to me, but I saw him, running across green fields. I saw him but he did not see me. He ran free and did not seem to know me anymore. He was naked. He was whole.

In the afterlife, or at least in my dream, his identity had not been sliced from him.

I think I saw my mother, but I was no longer sure if I even recognized her. It could have been Spider. It could even have been Poppaea.

I saw pirates being crucified beside the churning sea.

Each dream was a mosaic stone in the convoluted picture of my life.

And then there was another dream … a dream that retold the story of my life in Rome.

First, more floating. Clouds. Celestial music. The lyre, the kithara, the double flute, the tympanon.

And as I floated, I reached the slopes of a mountain. The sky was impossibly blue, almost painfully bright. A warm wind buoyed me as I sailed the sunlight.

I was in a grove. There were Corinthian columns. Three goddess stood, naked, and a chubby man in a purple toga was polishing an apple with a fold of his cloak.

Each goddess was perfect. Each stood in the tall grass under the laurel trees, each smiled, each had sunlight in her eyes and the warm breeze in her hair, each spoke with a voice that was music.

The first goddess was the Lady Octavia, primly dressed, perfectly coifed. "Choose me," she said. "I'll give you access to the reins of power. I am the true descendant of the Julio-Claudians, not an adopted misfit like you. Choose me," she said. "You will be victorious in war." The Lady Octavia was playing the role of Minerva, goddess of war and wisdom. Nero's legitimacy hung on Octavia's bloodline.

I was visiting a distorted reenactment of the Judgment of Paris. Paris had to choose to give the golden apple to whichever goddess was the most beautiful — and each goddess came with a gift. In the story, it is the gift that decides, not the beauty ….

In this grove of dreams, mythology was playing itself out as though on a stage. Indeed, there was something of Lucius Domitius Paris in all of the goddess-women; they were being, as it were, *impersonated.*

Next, you see, there was the Lady Statilia Messalina, who said, "I will be whatever you tell me to be; I will give you submission, I will give you steadfast support, wise and truthful advice, I will gladly suffer your infidelities, only call me Imperatrix."

She was playing the role of Hera, who put up with Jupiter's amours with princesses, nymphs, and boys, yet never relinquished the title of Queen of the Gods.

And the third was the one who was almost my friend, Poppaea Sabina, who stood in the center, massively pregnant yet still irresistible.

The Lady Poppaea Sabina was Venus, who promised Paris the most beautiful woman in the world.

"You *know,*" she said, "what I can give you. That's why you're going to choose me, no matter what."

Paris, the shepherd boy, who was Nero, the God, was played in my dream by Lucius Domitius Paris, an actor whose name was both that of the myth and that of the Emperor. He was playing *all* the roles in this dream-play. And all of them to perfection. The three goddesses and the god-emperor … all one actor, all perfectly distinguished yet somehow the same. I watched the scene, peering from a branch of a laurel tree.

It's a dream and it's past and present and future all blended together.

Nero-Paris says to Octavia, "You can't give me anything. You haven't got a head." And a bolt of lightning from a clear sky strikes off the Empress's head. The head rolled to a stop at the foot of the tree.

There I am, holding my breath, hoping I won't be seen. I may be dreaming, but I don't want any part of this infernal game. I know my Homer by now. This game sparks the Trojan War and endless death, and the destruction of entire civilizations.

To Statilia, Nero-Paris says, "Yes, you're steady and calming. But boring. So boring I bet you'll even survive me."

"Which leaves me," says the Lady Poppaea, whom I last remember reclining on a slab of marble. Supremely confident, she moves toward him. Her belly swells. She staggers. She tries to embrace him but he hurls another lightning-bolt.

"Agrippina!" she screams.

Poppaea splits in two and from the two bloody halves steps another Poppaea and I see now that *I* am that Poppaea. I'm no longer a watcher in this dream but the subject of the dream. Jupiter the Thunderer sends rainfall and washes the slick blood from my perfect, pristine body.

And as I walk towards him, my arms outstretched, both longing for and dreading the embrace of Divinity … the sun is impossibly bright … the wind is warm against my body … I whisper *Lucius, Lucius* and he responds … his lips open to kiss … it's beautiful for only a few moments, then his jaws expand until they they seem to swallow me, they are a ravening maw, devouring me, sucking me down into the burning heart of a volcano.

Poppaea.

I scream and —

That's when the dream faded, and I found myself sleeping on my former dominus's bed, the sheet drenched in sweat, blood, tears, and vomit.

"More of that posset," I murmured, believing that the poppy juice would send me deep into oblivion.

"Enough," Croesus said.

Simon and Hylas were wiping my brow, and Croesus was cleaning me with a sponge dipped in watered-down sour wine. And Spider was there too, telling me it was time to get up, get out and about.

"You haven't risen for three days," Croesus said.

"The palace?" I said.

"No summons. The Divinitas has been spending all his time with Statilia Messalina."

Had my ruse worked? Had the Divine Eye finally wandered away from me? I did not dare hope. But today, at least, I was still free.

"Will you take the air, domine?" Hylas asked me.

"Yes," I said. "Give me a bath. And tell the litter-bearers to stand by."

I noted that Hylas was now addressing me in grammatically correct Latin.

And Hylas saw that I was finally giving him orders, like a proper dominus. He grinned. But I felt a twinge of discomfort, though I knew it was the way of things.

XXVII

THE TEMPLE OF CASTOR AND POLLUX

It had been the nones of the month when I left the Temple of Isis and Serapis. By the time I left the house of Petronius, it was close to the ides.

Too weak to walk far as yet, I was glad of the litter. I set off without any particular goal, but inevitably, most streets in Rome end up in the Forum. There were the crowds, the colors and especially the smells: the sour wine, the foul wind from the cloaca, the smoke of grilled sausages, the whiff of a whore's perfume, the fragrance of fresh-baked bread.

I told the bearers to wait in an alley near the back of the Temple of Castor and Pollux, the Dioscuri. Telling Hylas to wait with the litter, I took Simon with me in case I bought something and needed someone to carry it. I thought I might shop my way across the grassy square and down the Via Sacra. Such a mundane pleasure, and yet I had never experienced it as a freedman. Just being able to squeeze two fruits to see which was the riper! Or to pick up a kylix and ask the price, or taste a sausage without being ordered to!

Then I thought of myself in Simon's place, and I said, "If you want something for yourself, go ahead, buy it." So we stopped at a toy stand and he chose a little wooden chariot. It was an ingenious thing, cunningly carved from a single piece of wood, and cost a whole denarius. He grinned from ear to ear, clutching it in his fist. I understood how he felt. I had never had a toy like that either.

Then I heard a crier in the distance: "Boy for sale!" above the hubbub. "Let's get back," I said to my own boy, but Simon seemed rooted to the spot.

"Come, Simon, this isn't a slave market, it's just some random man selling off his—" Then I remembered that Simon's own father had sold him off to pay a gambling debt. "Simon," I said, "did you say that your father tried to sell you twice? And that your brother was sold … and died?"

"Yes, domine."

"You have more brothers?"

"I — I don't know. My father has many women."

I put my arm on his shoulder and tried to steer him away. But at that moment, a boy was pushing his way through the mob, and in pursuit, there was a bearded man wearing a robe that did not seem cheap — not the kind of man who needed to pawn his children for cash.

The boy was running straight for us, and there was nothing behind us but the toy stall and the Temple of the Dioscuri. He crashed into a pile of dolls and, unable to go further, turned to face his pursuer.

"You already sold me twice," he said. "It's illegal for you to sell your children three times."

People around us started talking. "He's right, you know." "What sort of a father —" "Shame on you!" "He's within his rights, he's the paterfamilias," and that sort of thing.

The boy dived under the stand and crouched there, shaking.

The man noticed, then, the boy standing next to me. He transformed from a creature of rage to a kind of exaggerated joy, beaming with pleasure. "And I thought you lost, Simon," he said.

"Leave me alone, abba," Simon said.

"It is true that your little brother has been sold three times. Of course, he is a lot better-looking than you are, so I was able to realize a higher payment for a shorter period of servitude. So, let him go. I'll sell you." Loudly he cried out, "I have another one for sale here. He can read and write, oh, yes, many languages. And he has only been sold once. Well, technically, twice."

"Stop!" I said. "Technically, three times. I paid both those repulsive men off."

"You?" he sneered. "You never paid *me.* Third-party sales are not covered by the law of patria potestas."

That could well have been true, for all I knew. What did I know of the finer points of their legal system? Yet, how many laws did the Divinitas break every morning before breakfast?

Simon said, "I have a good dominus. He never even beats me!"

Simon's father began laughing.

"He bought me this," Simon said, opening his fist to reveal the little chariot.

"Toys!" said his father. He raised his fist, but hesitated when I looked at him threateningly. Like all bullies, he was at heart a fearful man. "And what do you do for your dominus that gets you toys? What do you do for him, you filthy little cinaedus? Your master seems little more than a painted whore himself. What can he see in you?"

"If you must know," I said, "he tutors my household staff in Latin and Greek."

"By the Gods!" the man said, his laughter turning into lusty guffaws.

"Don't swear, abba," said the boy. Then added something in their own language which was, I think, Aramaic. His father grew incensed.

"In that case," he said, "a thousand sesterces and you can have them both."

"I'll have my steward draw up the note," I said.

At that moment, a man stepped out through the crowd. I could have sworn I knew him. But he wore a toga, and I realized when I last saw him he was of much lower estate, certainly not a citizen. And he spoke to me in the tongue of my people.

"Don't give him a brass as," he said, and then he called me by my real name.

"Viridian!" I cried, astonished, for I recognized him as once being the slave of the old poet Seneca, Nero's tutor, who had long since been disposed of in Tigellinus's purge of Pisonian conspirators.

He spoke, his voice imbued with a gravitas that stilled dissent. "I am," he said, "Lucius Annaeus Seneca Lucii Libertus Viridianus, an advocatus and one of the jure consulti of the Imperial household."

Turning to Simon's father, he said, "You, sir, are —?

"Josephus," the man said, stammering a little. "I'm a poor baker, and this man — boy, really — is trying to stop me from exercising my legal rights."

"The younger one is lost to you completely. The law is unambiguous. Your parental rights were dissolved as soon as the third sale occurred. As for this one, however —"

"Wait!" I whispered. "Aren't you trying to help me?"

He appeared to ignore me and continued suavely, "You perhaps have a point, Josephus, when you point out that the third sale of this son was not consummated directly with you. It could theoretically be argued, then, that you have a right to sell him to this man, or any other, if you so choose."

"All right, then," Josephus said. "A thousand."

Simon clutched my arm tightly. He started to cry.

"Well yes, but this man, Sporus, also has a case. It would have to be argued before a magistrate. As one of the city's most accomplished lawyers, I would almost certainly win the case, but the law is never entirely certain. And my fees — ah, my fees —"

"Charge what you want!" Josephus said. "Just leave me enough to pay off my losing at dice last night."

"Well, my normal fee for a difficult case like this would be about two thousand sesterces, plus expenses, of course."

"That's all right then. I don't need a lawyer."

"But the young man, who is the Emperor's favorite and has access to the privy purse, would certainly want to take *you* to court, as he claims to own this boy already," Viridian said. "And I'm pretty sure he can afford my fee."

"By the pudenda of Venus, I can afford it!" I said. "Double it. Double whatever that bastard says he can pay."

"I only take coin," Viridian added. "Were you planning to pay me in loaves?"

"Have mercy," said Josephus. "Do you know how much it costs to feed and clothe a child? And the boy's been sneaking off to be with the lowest elements — pickpockets, whores, and Chrestianoi even! That's his latest hobby! He'll be thrown to the lions in no time, and where's my investment, all that food, the clothing, the love, the care, the tenderness!"

"Love! Tenderness! A turd for your tenderness! My dominus loves me more than you'll ever understand," Simon screamed.

"Of course he does. You're an investment."

"Your only investment is in the dice."

"All right! Forget all this!" Josephus said. "I'll go. I need to pay my debts, but I have a daughter."

"But attempting to sell your child a third time is also punishable," Viridian said. "What is to prevent me from having you arrested? Plenty of these good people watching this altercation would be happy to go and fetch one of the vigiles."

At this, Josephus stalked off in a rage, and the crowd started applauding.

"Good riddance!" Simon shouted. To me he said, "You see — I have a *khara* for a father."

As that died down, I could not help overhearing other kinds of whispers … like, "Isn't that Nero's boy?" "Doesn't he look just like her, though!" "He's a good boy." "He'll keep the Divinitas from flying off the handle." "He's pretty!" "Does he charge the Emperor by the hour?" and such, flattering and derogatory, all of it making me squeamishly aware that every moment I was in public, I was being observed.

"Lucius Viridianus," I said softly, "thank you for coming to the child's rescue."

"My rescue, too, domine," said Simon.

"But where did he go?" I said.

For though he had been cowering beneath the toy-stall, that child was gone. I needed to find him, perhaps to bring him under my protection. He and Simon should be together, I thought. I should free them all, I thought. I had been like them. I knew what they knew. I knew what it was to be a thing.

"Don't worry about the boy," Viridian said.

"You knew about him!" Simon exclaimed. "You know where he's headed ... you were coming to rescue him, weren't you? Please, domine, what's he to you? Is he your lover?"

"Hardly!" Viridian laughed a little. "He's my brother," he said.

And then I understood completely. "You're a Chrestianos. You, him, you're all part of that cannibal cult from Judaea."

"Not me," Simon said quickly.

"Are you going to turn me in, Sporus?" said Viridian.

I did not answer. He knew I would not. How did he know? He and I were brothers too, in a way, as much as being fellow members of a mystery cult.

"Well," he said, "that's settled. Perhaps, Simon, you would like to meet your brother properly?"

XXVIII

CHRESTIANOI

Viridian had a litter nearby, not quite as ostentatious as mine of course, but we followed him quickly through the maze until we reached a five-story insula at the foot of the Capitoline, a prime location for such humble dwellings.

We hopped out, and Viridian opened the front door himself. When I looked curiously at him, he said, "I don't have any slaves."

"At all?"

There were a few people about who appeared to be in some kind of servile status. But that was not the surprise. The surprise was that this was no insula. The ground floor of an insula usually has several apartments; it's the most livable of the floors because the city's water and sanitation systems often do not reach the upper levels. But this insula was hollowed out and while it was brick and timber on the outside, and shabby to say the least, and the foyer with its stairs leading up to the higher stories was nondescript ... once a double doorway was opened we stepped into an interior that was decorated like an aristocrat's dwelling.

"But, Viridian," I asked, "with all the rewards from your advocacy, why do you not move to a proper domus?"

"As you well know, Sporus," Viridian said, "respectable people don't *work* for a living. Imagine all my neighbors if I were to move to a domus! They would turn up their noses!"

There were no lares and penates, but there was bust of Seneca where the ancestors would normally be, and a colonnaded inner garden with rose bushes and an imported citrus tree.

"From Judaea," Simon said, in awe. He ran toward the tree.

"Would you like to send your people home?" Viridian said to me in my own language. "I can send you home in my own litter afterwards. Slaves feel strange in a house with no slaves. I would hate for them to become infected with revolutionary ideas. I know they love you, but love is never as powerful as freedom."

I told my litterbearers, and Hylas, to go back. Simon of course would have to remain; this visit was all about his half-brother, after all. But first, my slaves were treated to an amphora of wine and a basket of bread and fish.

"I'll have the men carry this stuff," Hylas said. "We don't want to stink up the inside of your litter."

"You're generous," I said to Viridian.

Viridian replied, "Our teacher taught us that we should always do to others what we would have them do to ourselves."

"Oh!" said Simon, unable to help himself. "You're a Jew!" To me he said, "He's quoting Rabbi Hillel, one of our most beloved learned men."

"A Jew?" Viridian said. "Well, I suppose you might call it that. At least, I have learned from Jews. But you know very well that I am from the same land Sporus comes from."

In the center of the garden, stone steps led to an underground chamber, and a door in the chamber opened to another descending stairway. We saw a tunnel, crudely hollowed from rock, leading to darkness. On either side of the tunnel, a torch glowed in a bracket. Viridian gave one of them to Simon and told him to walk ahead.

The tunnel broadened. Now there were niches in the rock, and a faint odor of decay. "This is Jewish burial place," Simon whispered. "You *are* one of us."

"Your people are not the only ones who use these catacumbae," Viridian said. "They've proved useful for the Chrestianoi, too."

"I've heard," I said, "that there are secret places where they ... *you* ... practice your rituals."

"Oh, the cannibal love-feasts, shitting on the portraits of Caesar, orgies, and all the other rumors," Viridian said. "I've heard those rumors too."

We turned a corner. There were more niches now, and the smell of death was more pervasive, and it was mixed with perfume and frankincense. In some of the niches lay the dead, tightly shrouded, some mummified and wearing masks that were painted with lifelike portraits, and there were also ossuaries, both of wood and of stone.

We heard a rustle. A sheet moved.

"You can come out," Viridian whispered.

Simon held up his torch. His half-brother, shivering, lay in a niche side by side with a loosely wrapped dead woman. He scrambled out.

"I didn't even know I had a brother," Simon said.

But the family resemblance was clear.

"My name is Adam," the boy said.

Placing his torch in the nearest bracket, Simon allowed his brother to embrace him. It was a diffident embrace, for they were two strangers who shared, unknowingly, a terrible father.

"Can he come and live with us?" Simon said.

"Why don't you ask *me?*" Adam said. "I'm not a slave."

"True," Viridian said, "he's been sold three times."

As he saw he was no longer in danger, Simon's brother became assertive. "I'll take the torch," he said. "It's not far."

We went down another passageway. The reek of the dead grew stronger and we were now in a wider chamber, with torches still lit. There were marble steles in Greek, Latin, and what must be some language of the east. Some niches had fresh flowers and small gifts: food, a toy, a scroll. The ceiling was high and the niches with bodies went all the way up. A ladder leaned against one wall; there was an opening, perhaps three stories of an insula overhead. Placing his torch in an empty bracket, Adam started to climb. We followed. It was precarious. I was nervous.

The opening led to a small room piled with jars of olive oil, a storeroom of some kind. Adam led us past the amphorae to a wooden door and we found ourselves in a kitchen. A group of men and women were sitting around a table and … this was very odd … they were of different walks of life. There was an aristocrat in a toga. Others looked like slaves, yet they sat at the same table in an unsettling sort of equality.

Adam said to Simon, "You see, these are my brothers as well."

Presently, there came a man who looked to be in his sixties, tall, bearded; he looked a little travel-weary. The women in the room made much of him and brought him wine and olives.

Adam whispered, "That man is called Cephas. He's come a long way to celebrate with us." And a celebration it was. They broke bread and shared it with me and Simon, and they sang songs; to my surprise, Simon knew some of them.

"So, Sporus, this is one of the cannibalistic orgies you've heard so much about," Viridian said to me, laughing.

Presently the man named Cephas began telling stories which he had heard from his own teacher, a man, who, he claimed, had come back from the dead; I had heard such tales before from other cults, for there were cults all over Rome; this one sounded a little bit like sun worshipping beliefs about Mithras, a little bit like the fertility rites of Adonis. Mixed in with these myths were homespun morality tales; when Petronius told me stories like these, they had the fire of poetry; these tales were more the kind of thing I might have heard in my old life, told by my mother.

It was my mother I thought of. She became suddenly very vivid to me. I had not thought of her, really, since the savage pirate broke me in to this new life. A tear came to my eye.

Viridian said, "Yes, it is moving, isn't it?"

I watched their faces, all rapt, all drawn into the old man's narrative. Hypnotized. I was unnerved. This was not my world. Then Cephas started to talk of a second coming, of the rule of Rome being replaced by the rule of their own God-King, and I could see how some might find subversion in all of it. I did not think they should all be thrown to lions, of course; but when they started to talk with glazed eyes about dead people coming back to rule the earth, it made me uncomfortable. Did they actually believe these things, or were these fantasies just their way of coping with the soullessness of a Rome now in its eighth century, a Rome that had swallowed up the whole world?

Yet I saw that Simon's brother was utterly absorbed in all this talk. Perhaps it was because he'd never known a real family, and these misfits were all he had.

If this was one of the infamous orgies these people indulged in, I would have to say that a slow day at the palace was wilder than this. I had to envy their sense of belonging, of solidarity, though, even as I felt they were being lulled into accepting their lot in exchange for a dubious promise of paradise.

But the love-feast was interrupted abruptly. We heard banging outside.

"Soldiers," Viridian whispered urgently to me. "Do you remember the way back?"

"Will you all go down and hide in the catacumbae?" I said.

"No, we'll face them. Now go."

"Adam, come," I said, grabbing the hand of my slave's brother.

"I'm staying," he said. "What am I to you? These people are my brothers and sisters."

Simon said, "And *I'm* your brother."

"Yes. Who you didn't even know about until today. Forget me," Adam said.

Adam pushed us toward the storeroom. He slammed the door. Holding back tears, Simon waited by the ladder for me, then we scrambled into the burial chamber. None of the Chrestianoi followed.

"They're mad, mad, *mad!*" Simon said, taking the torch from the bracket where he had left it. "Come, domine, I know the way." And he did. He had remembered every turn and he led me down the passageways without even pausing to think. It seemed to take no time at all to arrive at the garden in the insula that had been so bizarrely converted into a rich man's home.

The servants of Viridian, seeing we had returned without him, immediately knew that something had happened. Still, they arranged for me to take Viridian's own litter all the way to Petronius's house.

When we arrived, it was already the ninth hour. Pretorians were waiting outside my door. They had come to deliver an invitation to dinner.

But it was not an invitation to the palace. It was a request to dine at the home of the consul, Marcus Julius Vestinus Atticus. The invitation was not from this man, whose name I could barely place, but from his wife, the Lady Statilia Messalina.

My respite had been all too brief. It seemed that I was to plunge once more into the politics of power.

XXIX

MARCUS JULIUS VESTINUS ATTICUS

"May I decline the invitation?" I asked the guard.

"No," said the Praetorian, "we're to take you, regardless of the hour."

"But I don't even know this Atticus."

"The invitation is in his name. He's an old-fashioned person in a way. Doesn't think his wife should issue any pronouncements."

"That's about to change," said the Praetorian who was with him. No, the man with him was no mere guardsman. His tunic bore the broad laticlavus stripe of a tribune.

"In any case," said the first, "*Himself* wants you there."

"Boy or girl?" I asked.

"Didn't say."

"Simon, go in the house. Tell Hylas to prepare one of each,"

I said. To the tribune, I said, "Why has a tribune been sent to fetch a nobody like me?

"Oh, I'm not here for you," he said. "You were just on the way."

***

I did not want Hylas to go with me. If I took a slave who had the look of a puer delicatus, they would assume I had brought him to help out with the festivities, and I found increasingly disturbing the prospect of my slave, who was in some sense also my friend, being manhandled by some inebriated senator. Although to Hylas such things were just work. Slaves need feel no shame more keenly than the mere fact of their servitude.

"But domine," he was saying, "If you need to change your clothes —"

"If the likes of Nymphidius happened to be attending the Divinitas," I said, "you might be permanently damaged."

"Well, domine, if you're just protecting your property, then I understand. But I want to protect *you,* too."

"Your Greek is getting better every day. Stay home and work on your contracted verbs with Simon. I'd rather have you in pain over conjugating some verb in the second aorist than lanced by Nymphidius in a drunken fit."

I would have taken Spider, but perhaps there was perhaps a chance Himself would recognize that this was the woman who had been broken in the process of extracting information about the Vestal Virgin who had been his mistress.

In the end, it was Croesus I asked to accompany me. He was a freedman, a man who knew state secrets, and valuable enough, and wily enough, not to end up as a collateral victim should the Divinitas go on a rampage. And he knew many of the Praetorians personally. He followed me on foot.

The domus of Atticus was positively spartan in comparison with other aristocrats'. Remembering that when I last saw him, the Emperor had been weeping over Poppaea, I had arrived wrapped from head to toe in a silk stola and with my hair coifed high, topped with a diamond diadem. My appearance was as far from the inspirational Giton of Petronius as could be imagined.

Leaving Croesus to gather what gossip he could among the house slaves, I allowed myself to be ushered into the banquet. Individual portions were being served up of a pie stuffed with flamingoes' tongues.

It was not that extravagant an affair. Just one set of couches, and all nine places were full, so I did not even have a seat. The other guests included the head Praetorians, Nymphidius and Tigellinus, and a few senators. An also, I noted, the Emperor's great-aunt, the terrifying hag who ruled over the Vestal Virgins. Though the Vestals had to preserve their chastity on pain of death, it appeared that indulgent banquets were not off limits.

I stood awkwardly at the entrance to the triclinium, whose frescoes depicted a staid, conventional mythological scene, I think of Diana, Jupiter, and the nymph Callisto in the process of being transformed into a bear. Behind me, there were the two Praetorians who had brought me. Rather unusually, they did not wait outside, but flanked me on either side, silently saluting their master.

A lone singer was accompanying herself on the lyre, singing the words of an ancient Greek poet:

I drink, Bacchos! I drink!
I drink deeper than the Cyclops Polyphemos
drinking the blood of men.

Could I but drink from your skull
and drain its blood,
O you who guzzles the blood
of your poisoned friends!

"A song about wine to be sure, but an ill-omened one," I said … softly, I thought, and only to myself. But the music stopped abruptly. The God had raised his hand for silence.

"You don't like Alcaeus?" said Himself, sitting in between his hosts, the Lady Statilia Messalina whom I knew well and her husband, with whom I'd barely exchanged a word. If Statilia was overdressed, her husband was even more so, in military uniform no less, the brass polished until it was blinding, even in the candlelight.

Everyone waited.

"Who doesn't love Alcaeus?" I said, temporizing while I figured out which way the wind blew. There was tension in the room. "But … I would hate to think of wine and poison in the same breath."

"Ah, my beautiful, witty, demoniacally clever wife," said the Ruler of the World. "Have you come from the dead, come to scold me? Is my mother with you?"

"I left her back in … her tomb," I said softly.

The Emperor took from inside his toga a huge red jewel, carved into a circular spyglass, and peered at me for a while. Then he put away the ruby and tried a bright yellow topaz. He scrutinized me a little more, than bade me approach by crooking a finger. A crowd of slaves bearing platters of food parted to let me approach the table.

As I got closer, Himself put away his giant gemstones and began to laugh. After a second, everyone joined in, though none of them knew quite what was funny.

"Why, Poppaea, my beloved," said the Divinitas, "I wasn't expecting you. Rather, I was hoping to see that pretty boy who looks just like you. Can you conjure him up, perhaps?"

I played along. "It will almost be like magic," I said.

I stripped off the stola with a grandiose gesture and it fluttered to the floor. I stood in a tunica so sheer you could see my subligaculum, barely concealing the outlines of my manhood. The garment was so thin, I shivered.

"Oh, dear. You are cold," said the Emperor. "You see, our host, Marcus Julius Vestinus Atticus, though an esteemed general, is a bit of a fuddy-duddy when it comes to modern comforts. Everyone else in our stratum of society has at least *some* kind of central heating these days, even it's just two slaves fanning a furnace in the basement. But comfort's not a *Roman* virtue, is it, Atticus?"

"I think not, Caesar," said Atticus. I noted he didn't call him *Divinitas* as was now the fashion among Imperial flatterers. "A cold night in the German forest with only a pair of caligae and a tattered cloak, that's how a real soldier lives."

"Who needs a cloak, even? Some barbarian wench, or the chieftain's son, perhaps, just as warming, particularly if they struggle."

Atticus laughed, until he noticed that the Emperor was not.

"Sporus," said the Emperor, "come sit here. Statilia and I will keep you warm."

"I would not want to take the general's place at the head of the table," I said.

"He was just leaving," said the Emperor.

At which point, the tribune pulled a document out and began to read.

"In the name of Nero Claudius Caesar Augustus Germanicus, Pater Patriae, Pontifex Maximus—"

"You can skip the titles, Gerellanus, we haven't got all night," said Nero Claudius Caesar Augustus Germanicus.

"Marcus Julius Vestinus Atticus, you are under arrest for your part in the conspiracy of Piso to topple the monarchy."

At which point, Atticus laughed again, and this time, he got the joke. If you could call it a joke. "Couldn't you people have thought of a better excuse?" he said. "I'm old-fashioned. The Emperor may be a fool, but I don't break loyalty oaths. I'm a Roman."

The Emperor nodded. Then he motioned to me and I came close; he dandled me on his lap. "You've done me many favors, Atticus; now I'll do you a favor as well. You can be a Roman to the end. We're friends, so I'll let you commit suicide."

"Thank you, Caesar," said the general, and kissed the Divine Hand. He managed to make humility sound like vitriol. With an admirable show of dignity, he rose — and I slid into his seat, becoming the involuntary host and head of the table — and left the room, followed by two slaves, perhaps his personal body slaves.

"He hasn't even touched his flamingo pie," Statilia said at last. "It's his favorite."

She broke off a piece and popped it into my mouth.

It was, I admitted, succulent and smooth. The tongues, marinated in honey and a touch of garum, slithered between my cheeks until I washed them down with a white wine that had a pungent reek of Aleppo pine resin.

Statilia whispered to me, "Whatever you did, Sporus, it seems to have had the desired effect."

"Did you have to kill off the husband, Lucius?" I said into the Divinity's ear.

Statilia, who must have had very sharp hearing, said, "Oh, how deliciously topsy-turvy — the slave calling the God by his given name! It's like Saturnalia all year round."

"I'm free," I said.

"Indeed," she said, as though it were of no import. Why would it be? She had what she wanted, and needed no more favors from me.

"Can we have some more Alcaeus?" said the Emperor.

At that the singer, who had been simply standing there, occasionally undulating in a provocative way so as not to be completely ignored, struck up her lyre again and sang:

O Nicander! Your legs
are getting hairy;
beware lest it happen to your buttocks too
for then you shall know how rare it is
to find true love....

"Saucy!" said the Divinitas, patting the sheer silk about my thighs. "Well, we shan't let such a disaster befall you, shall we?"

I pretended to laugh, and took another bite of the pie.

Statilia snatched the rest out of my hand. "Not too much," she said. "You don't want to get fat, either."

The dinner was slowly returning to normal, if you could call flamingoes and suicide normal. Statilia and the Emperor kissed, using me the way you would use a silk cushion stuffed with the softest down, wrapping themselves around me, leaning into me ... it was good, though, to be a mere object. I sent my mind far away. I thought of the sea, the rhythm and the salt tang of the waves as they brought me to this bewildering land.

Presently, as the bawdy song came to an end, the tribune Gerellanus came and whispered in the Emperor's ear.

He held up his hand for silence. "It would appear," he said, "that the Lady Statilia Messalina is no longer married."

Some of the guests took on expressions of shock and horror. Everyone knew that Atticus's probity was beyond question and that he probably had had nothing to do with the Pisonian conspiracy, which by now was a tired old scandal anyway. But, perhaps, some of them *were* guilty. What if they were next?

"You'll need a husband," said the Emperor. "It might as well be me."

They must have been awaiting the cue all evening, because in an instant, the triclinium filled up with all the ready-made trappings of a wedding. There was a priest. There were children strewing nuts to symbolize fertility. There was an orchestra, and much pounding of drums and tooting of double flutes.

The Vestalis Maxima, who had not said a word during the dining, the singing, or the announcement of treason, rose and walked over to the main dinner table to preside over the marriage vows.

"Ubi tu Gaius, ego Gaia," she said, so that Statilia could repeat the words, a simple message that has been said a million times over eight centuries of Roman history, through the early monarchy, through the republic, through to now, modern times, the Empire.

But Nero could not wait for the vows to finish.

"We shall go now," he said, taking Statilia by the hand. "Gods do not need a ceremony to legalize their mating."

Abruptly, the guests, slaves, and hangers-on all started to shout, "Feliciter! Feliciter!"

Nero said to Gerellanus, "Get the body out first. Fresh blood makes a poor lubricant."

So saying, he led Statilia to the door of the triclinium, leaving chaos and confusion in his wake. At the doorway he stopped and looked straight at me. "Thank you, Sporus, for doing such a good job at the head of the table, keeping the wine flowing and the food coming."

Right, I thought. I stood up. Desperately trying to find something to say, I started off with, "Friends, don't go home yet. We don't want to waste the bounty of Atticus." I sounded like a fool. Then soldiers moved in to block all the possible exits, and an enormous roast pig, garnished with swans' wings, was carried in on the shoulders of four muscular Nubians.

"Whatever else we may say about him, Atticus certainly owned a good chef," I said, and my words were greeted with nervous applause.

"Excellent, my boy!" the Emperor shouted. Then, almost as an afterthought, "Oh, Sporus — you can have the house. Statilia won't be needing it."

He left the room, and soldiers closed ranks. The guests were not going to get to go home just yet. Not without finishing their dinner.

***

As soon as the Emperor seemed to have gone out of earshot, the gossip began. I found myself being bombarded with questions, though I knew nothing. One senator asked whether we were all going to have to commit suicide tonight. There were a lot of grim jokes after that, but I thought the food tasted particularly fine as well, and not just because most the guests assumed they would be slaughtered once the Emperor had sated his desires. The wine-slaves made their rounds more and more often.

Delicati wandered about, but few took advantage of them. There was too much anxiety in the air. There was a brief distraction when Croesus came into the room with a document he wanted me to put my name to. *"Now,"* he whispered urgently, "before Himself changes his mind." Apparently, I did own this house now. And it was bigger than Petronius's, though far less tasteful. I offered him wine, but he slipped away.

In the end, many of them were dozing off; only the old Vestal Virgin seemed wide awake, sullenly sipping her snow-cooled wine.

Even the music became sporadic. The singer had, perhaps, run out of the odes of Alcaeus. She was snoring in a corner, her arms wrapped around a pedestal on which sat a bust of Augustus.

The silence continued.

I too had had my share of wine, and I had not eaten much. Statilia's warning about not getting too fat was making me nervous.

I remember now how Hyacinth had fussed endlessly about his appearance, and keeping his looks.

Suddenly, an almost bestial shriek rent the stillness. A cry of desolation and despair. Like a child who has lost its mother, only it was the voice of —

"Sporus! Sporus!"

I straightened my tunica and stepped gingerly over the drunken senators. The soldiers parted for me. The screams were coming from an upper room.

"Sporus! I want you now!"

When a God summons you, there's nothing for it. You go, blindly, unthinking.

XXX

FORGING AN ALLIANCE

A good steward knows everything, senses exactly what is happening. Croesus had known to get the title to the general's property in writing, and now he stood at the foot of the stairs, holding the stola that would change me from Sporus to Poppaea.

The Emperor's screams were if anything more insistent. I followed the sounds and stepped into a luxurious bedchamber, the only room in the house that was not spare. Here, there were spoils of war; displays of enemy armor and weapons, a sculpture of Atticus himself, with his foot on the neck of some barbarian, at the foot of the couch so that the first thing the general would gaze on in the morning was the sight of his own victory.

The general had been discreetly removed, but there was blood on the floor, and a sword, too, that had not been cleaned yet.

On the bed lay Statilia Messalina. I thought for a moment he had killed her; but no, she was just exhausted from his depredations, and a little bruised, and moaning a little. Sitting beside her was the Divine Nero, undressed and still shrieking out my name.

"I'm here, Lucius," I said.

Abruptly, he stopped screaming.

"Have I been bad?" he said.

"Of course not, Divinitas," I said.

"No, no, that's not how we play this!" he said, pouting.

"Yes. You've been bad."

"Sterner!"

"Bad! Bad!"

"Am I a naughty Emperor?"

I was not sure how to feel ... sickened? embarrassed? compassionate? "Yes you are," I said softly. "Very naughty."

"You're not very good at this," he said at last. "The real Poppaea would have ... but you saw what happened to her."

I realized at last that while for Himself it was a game of whimsy, for me it could mean life or death. I put on what I imagined to be my most Agrippina-like voice. "Lucius Domitius!" I spat. "Nothing good will come of all this debauchery!"

"Oh, I know it, Mother," he said. "You'll have to beat me, I think."

"With what?" I said, in a parody of savagery. *"What?"*

Then I saw the bloody sword on the floor. It had a heft to it. Using the flat so I wouldn't drawn any Divine Blood, I had a crack at the Imperial buttocks. He screamed and I was taken aback before realizing that there was pleasure in his screaming. I took a few more blows. Once, I turned the sword at the wrong angle.

"One more of those, and I'll have you crucified," the Emperor gasped. And once again, in a small voice … "I'm sorry, I'm so sorry."

I wielded the sword with a little more care now. That had been a near disaster.

I looked over at Statilia Messalina, who was no longer shriveled in a corner of the bed. In fact, she seemed to have recovered completely. She was watching me intently. She had the hint of a smile. She was enjoying this, and, to my own self-disgust, so was I.

This little stint of play-acting was brief, however, for Tigellinus burst into the room. I tried to make myself disappear. Statilia sat up, and despite being naked, appeared suddenly dignified, even matronly.

"Divinitas," Tigellinus said, completely ignoring the spectacle before him, "General Vespasian is here."

"I thought we sent him to Judaea."

"You decided that only days ago, Divinitas. I believe he is here to discuss strategy."

"What strategy? Just crucify them."

"Lucius," I whispered, "you might not want to crucify an entire people."

"If they all had one neck between them," said the Emperor, "I'd snap it."

I had heard him say that many times.

"I'll meet him," he said. "Let me put on some clothes."

"Divinitas, there is also the matter of the guests at the banquet …."

"What? They haven't left yet?"

"You told us to detain them. Shall we just kill them?"

"Yes," he said. "Oh. General Vespasian will probably think it's wicked of me."

"Naughty!" I hissed in his ear, lifting the sword-hilt I'd been beating him with. He seemed to come to his senses, and allowed himself to be led out of the room, after throwing on a bloody toga that Atticus must have worn when he committed suicide.

"Come down when you're dressed," he said to me and Statilia. "I want to be seen with my beautiful wives."

I looked at Statilia as he left the room. We heard him padding down the marble steps in his bare feet.

Statilia said, *"Wives?"*

I said, "He's confused, Lady Statilia. You're his only wife … as of this evening, anyway."

"Let me be quite clear with you, you uppity little libertus," she said. "As of today, I am Imperatrix. And I have the blood of Imperatrices. The Divine Claudius's last Empress was also a Messalina. You are nothing."

"I know, Divinitas," I said, trying to sound humble. For I knew that she knew I could stand in her way if I wanted to. I was nobody, but I could be a nuisance. But it was best to be disingenuous.

"I don't mind where the God puts his mentula for the night," she said — the word sounded quite vulgar on her lips — "but you must acknowledge me as Imperatrix, no matter what silly games he chooses to play. There must only be one Imperatrix. You are to understand this at all times, or I'll have you raped by hyenas in the arena."

Then she started laughing, and I did too. We had both, after all, seen our Lord and Master at his most vulnerable. It was to be a détente of sorts, if an uneasy one.

"Of course, Divinitas," I murmured.

"In that case, let me help you get dressed. A shapeless stola as a coverall is not going to impress any of the arbiters of taste at court."

"But the only real arbiter is dead," I said, reminded suddenly of Petronius.

"True. I admired Petronius, too, you know. All the more reason to abandon simplicity and elegance, and go for the vulgar," she said. "It's the way of things. Oh, well done getting the house. I won't be needing it, of course."

"It was an afterthought, really," I said.

"I never liked it. Atticus was a peasant at heart, and my dowry alone could have bought ten of these."

Thus, alliance forged, we went down to meet General Vespasian.

XXXI

TITUS FLAVIUS VESPASIANUS

This house — which was now my house, including all its contents, both animate and inanimate, as I could see from the way that Croesus was ordering the slaves about in my name — had been miraculously tidied in a matter of minutes. An army of slaves must have been at work. There wasn't a vomit stain or an ostrich bone anywhere, and the busts and columns had been polished to shining.

The dining room was full again, but not with dinner guests. I stood beside Statilia. We had come to the conclusion that none of her clothes would fit me — for she was both statuesque and steatopygous, and I am slender, looking younger even than my tender age. So after trying on everything in she had handy, in the end I was wearing only the translucent tunica I had brought with me.

"Did the guests get killed?" I whispered to Statilia.

But a centurion standing nearby said, "It would have made more mess, so we let them shuffle home." One guest was still there, the head Vestal Virgin. I remembered that the Divinitas had called her "great-aunt" when we were at the trial of Rubria. Vestals are inviolate, unless they sleep around, so I suppose she never felt herself in any danger.

She sat at the dining couches alone, munching on bread and salt.

The Divinitas was seated on a curule in front of the dining area. To his left were a group of soldiers, including a man who I guessed immediately must be Vespasian. He was jowly, grizzled, gruff. To the Emperor's right were a wholly different assemblage. They were dancers, flower-arrangers, and a man wearing more gold ornaments than an Egyptian princess. This crowd was jostling for attention, being managed by a very beleaguered Epaphroditus, with the limping philosopher lad, Epictetus, taking notes by his side.

Himself was listening to the crowd on his right, while Vespasian's group was trying to distract him. "We'll have games of course," said Nero, "but especially chariot races. I am going to compete personally you know. And I will win the crown for my lovely … wife."

Nero saw me and Statilia. He held up his hand. He spoke of his new wife, but his eyes were on me.

"Greet the new Imperatrix," he said. A chorus of *aves* ran round the room. "My dear," he said to Statilia, "I've had these people brought in to organize the celebrations of our wedding and your elevation to the title of Augusta."

Statilia squeezed my hand. I daresay she had not expected *Augusta* quite so soon.

"Games, I think," said the Emperor, "very important games.

Titus Flavius Vespasianus cleared his throat. "Caesar, with the respect to the Judaean question—"

"Yes, yes, Vespasian," said Himself. "You'll do to the Jews what you did to the Britons, no doubt."

"Hardly, Sire," said the general. "The Britons are a loose confederation of disorganized tribes who hate each other as much as they hate us. They're separated by water from even their own kind, the Celts of the continent, who have mostly come to appreciate the gift of Roman civilization. Whereas in Judaea—"

"Judaea is a tiny, recalcitrant pimple on the flesh of Rome," said Nero. "She's a speck, surrounded by Rome. Why can you not engulf her?" He turned to a man who appeared to be the Editor of the games. "A hundred pairs, I think. And a Naumachia. Can we reenact the Aeschylus's *The Persians?"*

"Jupiter, Divinitas!" said the Editor. "There aren't enough condemned criminals to stage a battle that big. We've even run out of Chrestianoi."

"Perhaps we can buy a few," said Statilia.

"Meanwhile," said Vespasian, "I too need funds. To subjugate a people as unruly as these, as thoroughly as you have commanded …"

"There's always taxation," Statilia said.

"There's already tax on everything," Epaphroditus protested. "The people say you've taxed everything except their piss."

"Piss?" said the Emperor. "Sporus, didn't you mention a urine tax to me once?"

I kept silent. I *had* mentioned it to him once, and it was half in jest. I was surprised he recalled it. It had been an eventful day and night. But then, Himself had a sharp mind. Not an entirely sane one, but he didn't forget things. How could I have been so stupid?

Tigellinus spoke up, "I do recall, Divinitas."

"It's quite poetic, really. Rome's piss will feed her troops. It has a kind of mad logic to it."

"Caesar," Vespasian interrupted again, "these people are fanatics. They'll die for their God."

"Well," said the Emperor, "I *am* their God."

He had become exceedingly bored with the general. Presently, he told his spectacle planners he was going to go right now, to the Circus Maximus, to see for himself how the celebration of his new wedding should be carried out.

"Statilia," he said, "make sure that the General gets what he wants."

"Perhaps a little breakfast?" said General Vespasian.

Nero snapped his fingers. And the room was emptied of all the organizers, their attendants and *their* attendants. Only the Chief Vestal remained, still picking at her piece of bread.

It did not escape me that Vespasian had been eyeing me with some interest, even as he was describing the hardships of dealing with an intractable desert people and their vengeful god.

***

So you met General Vespasian! Gruff and grizzled, you called him! Did you make eyes at him, did you seduce him with your sensual voice? Did you sit on his lap in your sheer tunica?

I did not know what to think at all. I was confused.

You should have, you know. We hear that the General is on the march. If he arrives in Rome and dispatches the current Divinitas … you might have staved off your fate. We've already had three Emperors this year — and a few would-be Emperors as well. People in the drinking-houses are saying, "This might be the one who sticks."

I had an inkling. It was when slaves started to bring in the refreshments….

***

Statilia and I took our places at the head couch, while the general went to use the latrina. The Chief Vestal was still seated, at our left this time.

Statilia said softly to me: "Watch this one. There's money on him to be the next Divinitas."

"He doesn't interest you? I know you are planning to survive *our* Divinitas."

"That will be hard enough," she said, "but I have plans beyond Nero. And this one obviously likes boys; he is a career soldier, and soldiers are not allowed to marry, you know."

The Vestal cackled. "If Lucius but knew the treason you're plotting!" she said. "But I don't care. Rubria was the last straw. He defiled one of us, and forced us to kill her. Rubria was very popular amongst the sisters, if you know what I mean."

General Vespasian returned. He sat down and was served wine and bread. A simple repast for a man of simple tastes.

Statilia said, "You must come to the games, General, before you head off to crush the rebellion."

"I don't care much for fake battles," he said. "War is a nasty business and watching condemned prisoners kill each other isn't much of a sport."

"But there will be a hundred matched pairs of gladiators as well," Statilia said. "Surely one such as you can appreciate the finer points."

"The Circus Maximus is not the ideal place to watch a proper gladiatorial match," he said. "Perhaps when I retire, I'll build a better venue. If I can find the funds. The spoils of a Judaean war might be what it takes. So … I'd best set sail for Judaea as quickly as possible."

"But Sporus will watch the games with you," she said. "And the Divinitas won't be sitting in the Imperial Box. You heard him. He's going to be in the chariot races. *In* them!"

"Himself?"

"Shocking, isn't it?" said the Vestalis Maxima. "The man has gone from being the Rome's great hope to Rome's great buffoon."

"Whose boy is this, Statilia, yours?" Vespasian said.

"He's a libertus, General," said Statilia. "And spoken for by High Olympus itself."

"Any mortal can attain Olympus," Vespasian said, "with enough legions." He looked at me appraisingly. "Celt?"

"I don't know what I am, General," I said. "But I'm told it's beyond Rome's edge."

"Exotic." He turned to Statilia. "His Greek's perfect, though."

"Eukharistô," I said.

"So you'll be there?" Vespasian said, carefully putting a hand on my knee. It was gnarled, but not unaffectionate.

I managed a smile. Even Nero's death, it seemed, might not end what I had become.

XXXII

MORS …

First, it occurred to me that I should go home. Then, it occurred to me that I *was* home. The Divinitas, the newly minted Empress, and all the retinue, as well as Vespasian and all *his* retinue, had all left. Statilia had not seemed at all to want to remain; indeed, her clothes and precious belongings had been packed for days, I discovered.

In cataloguing Atticus's property, which was very efficiently done in a few large scrolls, almost as though Atticus assumed he was not long for this world — Croesus discovered that I was in fact, much richer than before.

I had an estate in Antium, a town house in Pompeii, and the income from a series of latifundia in Sicily where thousands of slaves worked the land, and where Atticus himself had never set foot in a decade.

As I have said, this house was expansive, though sparsely furnished. I could choose to live here or return to Petronius's, whose house in the city strictly belonged to Marcus Vinicius but which was to all intents and purposes mine as well. Or I could remake this house in my own image.

Except I had no image. Or rather, I had many images, having being created many times out of the potter's clay of others' imaginations and desires.

"Croesus," I said, "It is really you who should take possession of our patronus's home, managing in for Marcus Vinicius."

"You'll need a steward here, too," he said.

"Why not Spider?" I said. "And we'll send for those who are close to me, starting with Hylas and Simon." Croesus despatched one of my new slaves to Petronius's immediately.

"You may want to sell off some of the household," Croesus said.

"I'll just free a few," I said. "That way I'll be a patronus in my own right." The next hour was spent introducing me to my property: cooks, body-slaves, dressers, wine-pourers, even a token delicatus, although Atticus's sexual taste did not run to much beyond straightlaced uxoriousness.

It was afternoon by the time Hylas arrived. When he saw me, he embraced me passionately. My new slaves eyed him cautiously, wondering whether, as my favorite, he would have the authority to bully them or have them scourged for no reason.

"Something awful has happened," he told me. "Simon's vanished."

"Run away?" That did not seem like him.

"Should I give his description to the vigiles?" Croesus said.

"No," I said, "I don't want him hounded by slave-catchers."

To imagine this child branded on the forehead with the mark of *fugitivus* was too much. Surely he had a reason to disappear.

"Do you think he went to find his brother?"

"He did, domine," Hylas said, "but he only took a couple of loaves. Something must have happened to him."

Although my sojourn with a group of Chrestianoi had suggested to me that they did not eat children or practice bloody rituals, one could never be sure with cults. The entire love-feast might have been put on to pull the wool over my eyes. Wildly, I imagined Simon being sacrificed to some barbaric deity. Hadn't Vespasian told us the Jews were fanatics? And weren't these people some kind of breakaway sect, even weirder than the Jews?

"Croesus," I said, "send some of our own people to make inquiries. But discreetly. In fact … tell Marcus. A slave is a trivial matter for someone like him, but he was moulded by his uncle, and doesn't completely ignore the downtrodden. He can pull more strings than any of us."

Marcus was a good man. I had even been in love with him for a day or so, when he saved my life, so long ago.

So we spent the next few days moving my things into the big new house and watching Statilia Messalina's chests of belongings get carted away. Statilia herself I did not see; I assumed she was planning the festivities with Himself. I spent my days being briefed about my newfound wealth, or buying silly knickknacks in the Forum, and sometimes at the Baths. The newer Thermae Neronis were even bigger than the Baths of Agrippa, though they were in the Campus Martius and further away from my new residence, but they were a spectacle to marvel at, with entertainers, masseurs, and impressive works of art, and a library where I was able to read the poets those around me were always quoting.

It was true, I realized, that the spirit of poesy was dying. For in his haste to attain supremacy, Nero had managed to rid the world of some of its greatest wordsmiths. Seneca and Lucan were gone, and Petronius, of course, who had provided a kind of check on Himself's more self-indulgent fancies.

There was no news about Simon. I hoped that he'd found some connection to his brother. I did not imagine him being taken in by those cultists, but then again, for the sake of Adam, he may have chosen to be among them. To stop myself from worrying, I pretended not to have cared for him too much.

In a few days, a new series of games would begin. Although my mind was seething with confusion, I would have to stay calm. I did not want to draw attention away from the new bride, yet I had to be there. It would be best to go as a boy. But I should not look like a libertus. I should look like a prince. I should look worthy of the tales of my origins that had been circulating since I was first offered for sale.

***

How do you feel about the games now, now that you have a role to play?

Rome has built monuments to last a thousand years. Its armies have ground entire nations into oblivion. But to see Rome at its most impressive, you have to look at the games. The resources of the entire world are poured into the games. Years of training gladiators. Tens of thousands of animals from every corner of the Empire. Thousands of prisoners and other societal dregs kept as fodder for the slaughter. The amazing efficiency of getting all of it fit together, with meticulous timing, an infrastructure as complex as running an entire kingdom, hundreds of freedmen and slaves to handle every detail, and all of this expended in the name of entertainment.

And I've always had a role to play in the games.

Just not this *role.*

Just not this one.

***

I arrived early, just before the midday break. I arrived in style, spending some of my new found wealth on a more ostentatious litter and exotic, matched litter-bearers — all Germans, with shaggy blond hair, with the skins of animals thrown over their shoulders and wearing nothing but gilded loincloths. Petronius would have laughed — it was the sort of vulgar conveyance that an ex-slave millionaire like Trimalchio, from the *Satyricon,* would have possessed.

I arrived with a small military escort organized by Marcus Vinicius.

When I arrived in the Imperial Box, I got my own round of applause. I was almost the only one there. I could only see Vespasian, in military regalia, and one or two senators and their attendants.

No one comes to the games during lunch-time. Most people don't want to see routine executions, so they are scheduled for the slowest and hottest time of the day.

I could not very well have a huge retinue in the Imperial Box but one attendant seemed mandatory, so I only took Hylas, dressing him almost as magnificently as myself.

I sat just below where the Emperor and Empress would be. The only other person occupying that tier was the Editor of the games, whom I had seen planning the event with the Emperor. Behind him stood Marcus.

No one shooed me to a lowlier seat, so I presumed I was where I should be. Presently, the King of Armenia showed up just as they were bringing on the andabatae. Tiridates sat next to me, one place further from the Imperial Seat.

"I know," he said. "I shouldn't still be here. Now that the Emperor has properly crowned me, I should go back to dealing with our own problems at home. But Rome ... you have to love this place. It's filthy, sprawling, chaotic, and full of entertainments like these. Look at the andabatae down there ... it's a ridiculous idea and only a mad genius could dream it up."

There were about twenty of them down there, ignominiously clothed in just their subligacula. They swung at the air guided only by sound, their flailing blows subjected to jeers and taunts.

"It's pathetic," I said.

One man pretended to be dead, and attendants came in, poking him with red-hot irons to see if he was faking. The man screamed. Tiridates giggled. Even Hylas smiled. They could find it amusing, because these criminals were not seen as human in any way. They were thieves, forgers, murderers.

"This is boring," Vespasian said. I am sure he was itching to return to the Judaean front and was there only to be seen by the Emperor. And perhaps to get a close peek at me, too.

When one lucky andabata decapitated another with a single blow, the crowd cheered and some even started calling for his freedom, and gasped in unison when another andabata swerved and spiralled into his space, gutting him.

Tiridates clapped. Hylas fetched us wine.

"I would have left, but I promised the Divinitas I'd watch him race," Tiridates said.

The andabatae were all dead and it was time for damnatio ad bestias. The bodies were dragged off and other doors opened. It was the Chrestianoi, and indeed, the organizers were right; it was a sad selection indeed. The last time I had been at the ludi, there were so many to be eaten that it almost upset the day's schedule. This time the lions would make quick work of it.

Suddenly, Hylas gripped my foot and pointed. It was then that I saw that, among the at most two dozen victims, leading the sad procession, was Viridian. And that in the group was Adam. And beside him was Simon.

I stood up, turned to Marcus. "There's some kind of mistake. That's my slave."

Marcus Vinicius stepped down and said, softly, "The one who ran away?"

"Yes. And there is his brother. And there's Seneca's freedman. Please … can we save them?"

"Any other time," Marcus said. "But now … now is not the time. You can defy the law, the senate, even the gods. But not Rome. And all around us is Rome. Rome is watching you, Sporus. All of Rome. We are her slaves. Even Nero."

"What aren't you telling me, Hylas?" I said.

Hylas began to weep. "While you were away … he came back to say goodbye to us."

"He bought into that whole charade?"

"Slap him, Sporus," Marcus whispered.

"Why?"

"You're a dominus. People have to see that you can control your own slaves."

"Do it, domine," Hylas said. "These people must respect you."

I slapped him, harder than I intended, because he wailed. Those in the Imperial Box nodded approvingly, seeing that I knew my proper rank in society. He crouched down low and hugged my feet. "He is my friend, too," I said softly. "But this is the Imperial Box." Louder, I said, "Wipe your tears, slave."

They were herding the captives out to the middle of the arena. I saw Simon and his brother hold hands. Reaching into his tunica, Hylas handed me a small scrap of a scroll. He said, "He left this for you. I can't read it." On it, Simon had written:

I love you, domine. You know why I am doing this. It isn't because I believe the nonsense these people preached to me. You understand me. Our sacred writings say (the letter continued in Greek) *Pos aisomen ten oden Kyriou epi ges allotrias? I will still love you when I am in the next world.*

What had Simon meant by "How can I sing the song of the dominus in a strange land?" I had never asked him to sing. Or did he mean by *kyrios* some kind of non-earthly lord, some God? Had Vespasian been right when he explained that these were an intractable, incomprehensible people? Had Simon become one of the Chrestianoi, or was he merely looking for a way to commit suicide?

I would never know. And here, I dared not speak to anyone about it. I put away the note.

Rome was watching.

And I was the mirror of Rome. I was becoming like them. The games are supposed to teach Roman virtues, manly virtues: to be inured to the sight of bloodshed, to laugh at pain, to stay stalwart in the face of death. Yes, this was not the first time I'd seen people being eaten. Hylas closed his eyes. I forced myself to look.

"I'm Roman, too, now," I told myself. My eyes welled up, but I would not let the tears come.

XXXIII

ET TRIBUTUM …

I watched all of it, until the bestiarii came with spears, on horseback and in chariots, to hunt and kill the lions, to finish off the predators who had just feasted on my friends.

Hylas did not watch. His eyes were closed. But he heard it all, which might have been worse.

I had not even had a moment for private thoughts. As the last lion was dragged away, the Lady Statilia Messalina entered the Box, all white and gold — even her face, painted in layers of lead and gilt. She was escorted by naked young Nubians, each holding a corner of a billowing cloak, which covered her completely and fluttered behind her in a flurry of wind created by braided Germans wielding peacock-feather fans.

Another fanfare! In a dramatic gesture, the Nubians unwrapped Statilia's white and gold cloak, revealing that beneath it she was dressed entirely in green!

The applause was thunderous, especially from those of the public who favored the green faction. She was so dazzling that few noticed the slaves sweeping the blood from the sand below.

She billowed down the steps and took her royal seat. She nodded towards me. There was more applause; the crowd was acknowledging the fact that I held the favor of the God.

A water-organ began to play, and bucinae blew deafeningly from every corner of the Circus. From the far end, the chariots made their processional entry. The crowd was chanting the names of their favorite riders and the colors of their faction.

Finally there came Nero.

There was a gasp. Not just because the God had lowered himself to the vulgar occupation of chariot driver. He had already done that by singing and acting in public.

He was driving a chariot with ten horses. Ten pure white horses, caparisoned in gold and green. *Ten!*

"Can he do that?" Tiridates said, laughing. "Audacity!"

"The rules do specify *four* horses," said one of the senators.

"Gods don't have rules," Statilia said.

For a moment, the crowd had fallen silent. Have you ever heard a hundred thousand people catch their breath all the same time?

In that hush, Nero's chariot was approaching. He wore a green cloak which was continuously flapping in his face.He was having trouble controlling the ten horses — of course he was, those flimsy chariots are designed for lightness — and it was embarrassing to watch. But the people dared say nothing.

Until someone breached the silence, a lone cry —

"Down with the urine tax!"

Nero turned. He could not quite tell where it was coming from, but he pointed in its general direction, and suddenly a detachment of soldiers could be seen rushing through the aisles towards the cry.

Then there came another, from a different part of the Circus. And another.

They were all shouting with the same enthusiasm as when they had cheered before. The Divinitas managed to get the ten horses to move forward in a more or less straight line. He moved towards the Imperial Box, ignoring the crowd, but the shouting was like thunder now.

And then I felt it. A splash on my face, then another.

People were urinating off the sides of the tiers. Jeering, hooting, and pissing. Statilia Messalina acted outraged, but she seemed to be enjoying it as well. The chorus became a rhythmic, pounding ostinato of "No urine tax! No urine tax!"

It was impossible to control them. Soldiers marched about, lashing a few of them. But they were in an ugly mood and the soldiers were simply too few. The arena was filled to capacity, and no one was prepared for a riot.

Nero handed the reins to a professional charioteer, who urged on the horses through to the Box. As he came closer I could see his enraged expression.

Vespasian said, "This might be a good time to go to Judaea."

The shouts died down, as more soldiers filled the stands. The silence of a hundred thousand people was as terrifying as their chanting.

Himself, Master of the Known World, looked undignified as the ten-horse chariot pulled right up to the Box. I could see his expression clearly now. It was not rage exactly — I knew well how the Divinitas looked when he was angry. It had set into a mask, almost emotionless. It was when Nero put on this face that he was furthest removed from reality.

"It is for you I ride, my mistress, my wife, my mother," he said, but he did not look up at Statilia. He seemed to be looking at me. Seeing Simon's death had sent my feelings fleeing deep into the back of my mind. Now, in addition to revulsion and grief, I felt stark terror as well.

Nero smiled. That was the most terrifying thing of all.

He made an ironic bow to the Editor of the Games. Then he turned to his Empress. But again, he looked straight at me.

"He can't very well salute himself," Statilia said.

He kept looking at me.

"Delicious!" said the King of Armenia. "He wants the *delicatus* to drop the handkerchief!" He tapped my shoulder. "Or should I say, the Prince of an Unknown Land?"

It was no good to say I was no delicatus. It was no good to say I was free. The Empress drew a piece of white silk from inside her stola and handed it to me. It smelled of perfume and femininity.

The chariots lined up, the Emperor's grotesque as his horses stretched far over the starting line. Statilia beckoned for me to come and sit beside her. Not on the thronelike sedilla of the God himself, but in her own chair, which was capacious enough. "We'll do it together," she said. She took my hand and lifted it in the air. The fabric fluttered and she turned to the Editor so he could signal the cornua, bucinae, and drums.

All at once the fanfare struck up. "Let go now!" she said. She beckoned to her slaves with the peacock fans. I let the cloth fly and the slaves fanned furiously so it flew out over the arena. Then I returned to my seat.

The chariots were off! Any urine tax protests were drowned now in the screams for the Reds, Blues, Whites and Greens. Nero's ten horses were immediately out of control, sprinting at different paces, dragging the chariot in a zigzag pattern — but the chaos was working as the sheer number of horses began overrunning the lanes and throwing the competition into confusion.

The crowd loved it! Every time one of the Emperor's horses reared up, whinnying, a thousand people whinnied in response. The Greens could not help but be in the lead because his horses were in everyone's way.

Afraid to be seen to overtake the Emperor, others lagged behind. "Cowards!" the audience yelled.

Presently one of the Blues managed to snake through the melée, leaving two overturned chariots in his wake. One lagging charioteer was already being dragged around by crazed horses.

The Divinitas's team was thrown in such confusion that they smashed into the Vestal Virgins' balcony as the crowd roared in shuddering delight.

The Emperor was dislodged now, clinging for dear life to the side of his chariot as it crashed! A detachment of cavalry forced its way into the arena, blocking off the area while slaves carried Nero away on a stretcher.

The crowd cheered! "Divinitas! Divinitas!" they shouted, seeming to have forgotten about the urine tax.

The race went on. I couldn't understand what was happening. It was even hard to see which lap had been reached, despite the display in the center island of the arena. By what seemed to be the sixth lap, the Circus was in disarray. Unharnessed horses roamed. A charioteer had an arm severed. The crowd shrieked in delight.

Eventually, a chariot seemed to have made it through the last lap. One of the Whites. The charioteer waved his arms to receive applause, but the audience was booing.

Then, suddenly, a huge cheer. Himself, the Master of the World, was being carried into the Imperial Box, propped up by a pair of hefty centurions. They managed to get him to his chair. Then they lifted him up and he spread out his arms.

The Editor read the judges' decision: Caesar had triumphed. He had won the first prize! The crowd was roaring at this absurdity.

A golden wreath was brought in on a pillow of green silk. The Editor did not dare to crown the Divinitas himself, but Statilia, smiling, placed the wreath on his head. He kissed her, acknowledging her before all Rome as Empress.

Exhausted by his injury and by all the excitement, Himself sank back into his chair, and signalled that the next event should begin. It was a bit of comic relief after the chariot race, giving them time to clean up the arena in time for another race — amazons fighting dwarfs.

Noticing me seated on the step below, the Emperor reached out and touched my head. I turned. He called me up to the throne and made me sit next to him. He put his arm around me.

"Did you enjoy my victory?" he whispered in my ear.

"You were stunning, Divinitas," I said.

"You know I cheated. You're the only one who would say so to my face, so don't lie to me."

"It did come as a surprise," I said.

He kissed me on the cheek. "We have to be here all day long, and then there's a farewell banquet for Vespasian and Tiridates. And after that, I shall have to perform my marital duties. But after *that....*"

"After that, Lucius?" I said sweetly.

"Look!" he pointed. "That amazon's tunic has been ripped off. They really do amputate one breast, just as in the legend."

"Fascinating," I said, snuggling up to him a little.

"After that, you'll come to me. The real you, Poppaea. In your true shape. I know, now the Senate elevated you to Olympus, so you can come to me in any form. It's good that you're a boy in public, because I'm married. But in the night...."

"I am whatever you make me," I said, "my dominus, my ruler, my God." How could I say otherwise? I lived in a world where those I loved committed suicide or were eaten by lions. I looked into his eyes, trying to show as little of my true self as possible. But in his eyes I saw only openness, only truth. In the deepest part of his soul, he saw me as Poppaea.

Which meant that I, who was named Sporus, but whose true name was known only to the dead, had no self left at all.

XXXIV

CAELUM...

I spent many hours in one of the Emperor's private baths. Hylas tended to me, scraping every inch of me with a strigil, oiling and re-oiling me with an olive oil scented with attar of roses that had come all the way from Parthia.

A little time with Hercules, because I knew that Poppaea always had, behind her fragrance, a pungent hint of a masculine feline odor.

More time with a makeup artist that Actë herself sent to me, trying to replicate the whiteness that Poppaea loved, only in the end to wipe it all off when the artist suggested that the Divinitas might prefer my natural smoothness.

By the time I went to the Imperial bedchamber, escorted by Hylas, it must have been the sixth hour — midnight.

In the corridor, I crossed paths with Statilia Messalina, who had a retinue of handmaidens, all with candles. She stopped when she saw me.

"You look perfect." she said.

"You too," I said.

Though, it must be said, Statilia Messalina looked as though she had been through storm and fire. Her hair was wild, her eyes were tired, her cheeks hollow.

"You flatter me. But I've done my duty," she said. "Now you must do yours."

"What *is* my duty?"

"I took care of his physical needs," she said. "But you alone must salve his psyche. But don't you fear. He's tired out. The chariot race — he was more wounded than he lets on. And he knows he didn't win. He's taken out all his rage, his sense of powerlessness, on me. Now, you'll find him gentle as a lamb."

I found Nero Claudius Caesar Augustus Germanicus alone and asleep. A lone oil lamp flickered in the gloom-steeped chamber. The doors to the secret garden were open but there was no moon, only starlight.

I went and sat beside the man I hated, despised, pitied, and yet in some way also loved. I was beautiful, I know I was. I, Sporus, was not Poppaea, but Poppaea lived within me. I remembered her dying moments. In my mind I could see her, wounded, at the gates of Heaven, demanding admittance because the Senate had proclaimed her a goddess. Did the immortals obey the Senate, or was this just one more human vanity?

I bent over the Emperor's face and kissed his lips.

My tears moistened his cheeks.

Slowly, he woke.

"You came," he said softly. "The only one who truly haunts my dreams."

He drew me into his arms.

How long could I continue this deception?

He caressed me, not just with his hands but with soft words. Not his own words, but words borrowed from the greatest poets of the past. "When I see you," he said, "my tongue falls silent ... a delicate flame rushes beneath my skin ... with my eyes I do not see, but my ears hum, I'm covered with sweat, I'm trembling, shaking ..."

Sappho, I thought. How well Petronius had taught me. And how soul-stirring, for the most powerful man in the world to make love to me with the words of the greatest poet who ever lived.

I melted into him then. Thoughts of Simon devoured by lions, of Spider in the hands of the torturer, of Rubria shrieking from the hollows of the earth ... yes, I had those thoughts, but a great ocean of passion rose up and swept away those mortal hurts. "Of all the children of heaven and earth," I whispered, "Love is the most precious." This I said to the man who had killed, maimed, destroyed all the people I ever loved. I said it and in that moment meant it.

The gentleness became a tempest. The God tore at the priceless silks and ripped them from me. I was afraid that now he would know I was not Poppaea, but he turned me over and took me from behind with such tenderness I felt no pain until, engorged, he made me cry out his name again and again and again ... "Lucius! Lucius!"

It was at this moment of climax that heaven turned to hell.

Nero let go of me and I fell, limp, onto the bed.

He sat up abruptly. He did not look at me as a lover now, but as a man looks at an insect.

"Your voice is changing, Sporus," he said. "The illusion will end."

In desperation, clinging to him, I cried out, "No, my love. It won't end. This moment will be forever. I'll *make* it last forever! Oh, Tata, Tata, I swear it, I swear it."

He took me in his arms again. "Forever? Do you swear it?"

"I do!" I cried, clutching him to me with such ferocity I felt my heart would break.

But the Emperor twisted away, sat up, called out the name of one of the slaves who were always present, in the shadows, invisible, until needed.

"You said I couldn't marry you," he said. "But I can."

XXXV

... Et Infernum

Two soldiers entered the room and took me away. I was stunned. I did not struggle. We went down, down, down, past the public areas of the palace, down rude stone steps, then more steps that were just packed earth, a dank place deep in the bowels of the building.

"Are you going to kill me?"

No answer. They brought me to a small room with a narrow bed, where a man stood, and behind him, rows and rows of sharp, gleaming metal instruments.

I knew why I was here.

Since that day I have tried to forget what happened.

The best surgeons in the world are still butchers, and castration is a fate meted out to slaves, so it is not normally an operation that is taken with much care. Perhaps this was the most gifted butcher in the world, brought in from Greece or Egypt to attend to the needs of the Imperial household. Still, a butcher.

"You won't feel anything," he said, as they put me down on the bed.

They poured poppy juice down my throat, and followed it with wine laced with willow bark. They said it would dampen the feeling. There was so much fluid I felt I was drowning.

But I did not become unconscious.

Then they held me down.

I screamed until my throat was raw.

They strapped my legs to a rack that, I was sure, doubled as a torture device. They trussed me up tight, like a sacrificial animal. It took four Imperial guardsmen to hold me down.

When the surgeon began his work, the pain was unbearable, and I did pass out. I think, in a way, I died.

***

It certainly felt like death. Or what I have heard that death is like, the detachment of the self, the out-of-body feeling. I seemed to float into the air, and I watched what the surgeon was doing to me, watched myself lying there, and them thinking I was numbed from the poppy. The pain was still there, though it had been pushed far down into the pit of consciousness, like a horrifying childhood memory, gnawing, constant. As the knife started to tear flesh, my detached soul fled …

***

I floated.

Around me clouds scudded. I was carried on the breeze. The world beneath became small and distant. I could see all of

Rome, a glittering mass of marble nesting in a sea of filth. Beyond Rome, I could see Vespasian at the head of his legions, thousands of men in an endless line marching down an impossibly straight road toward the harbor at Ostia.

Soaring higher, I saw the whole of the Mare Nostrum, the sea at the heart of the Empire. I saw our whole world. I saw Judaea in flames. I saw it all, just as you see me now, but with the eyes of a spirit. I saw the dark forests of Germany. I even saw the land I was born in, at the furthest edge of the known world. The wind was warm and I floated aimlessly in its embrace for a long time, I don't know how long.

At length a temple shimmered in the cloud-banks. I came to rest on a cushion of mist. There was no ground, but where I stood was soft and yielding. I found myself walking slowly toward the steps of the temple. Its roof rested on tall Ionic columns and was sculpted with a frieze of winged Cupids, and the frieze was alive, the images moved, the love-gods fluttered about and smiled down on me.

I walked along a straight Roman road, covered with gold dust and rose petals. On either side, children scattered more petals, crying "Feliciter! Feliciter!"

On the steps of the temple stood famed lovers from the stories of the Greeks. There was Hyacinth in the arms of Apollo — but it was *my* Hyacinth, and he was radiant. There too were Eros and Psyche, Hercules and Hylas — *my* Hylas — Leda and the Swan, even Persephone and Hades. And lovers of ancient and modern history — Harmodius and Aristogeiton, Hero and Leander, Alexander and Hephaestion, even Antony and Cleopatra. All were welcoming me, congratulating me, as I ascended the steps.

The marble was cool on my bare feet as I crossed from light into the temple's shade. Inside, the walls glowed with their own light.

I was dressed in bridal finery.

My husband waited for me at the altar of Jupiter. He was the Divine Nero, strumming on a kithara and filling the heavens with his rich voice.

Beside him stood Statilia Messalina, but she was garbed as a vestal virgin. And behind the altar, as tall as an entire building, was Jupiter Optimus Maximus. Even his breathing was the sound of distant thunder, and when he spoke, the stones of the temple trembled.

Say the words, the god thundered.

I spoke, and my words reverberated in the chamber:

Ubi tu Gaius, ego Gaia.

The Divinitas put down his kithara. He held out his arms to me and I took his hands in mine. The Emperor smiled and pulled me into an embrace. His body was warm. His love was real.

Then Jupiter Optimus Maximus spoke ...

And what will you sacrifice, child, to receive this pure, eternal love?

Statilia Messalina held out a knife.

It glistened.

She bore down on me and slashed into my flesh —

And then the pain came, clawing into me, consuming me, such pain, and I screamed and screamed and still the pain came, as though they were cutting away not just flesh, but selfhood, my past, my dreams, my hopes, my loves, ripping these things out of me ... and still I screamed until I reached a dark place, void of feeling.

***

I floated again. But not in the sunlight, not among the clouds. This was a place of nothingness. No sensation. In pushing away the pain I had also pushed away all sight, sound, feeling.

I don't know how long I drifted in that abyss.

Occasionally I thought I heard a voice. My mother, calling me by my secret name. Hyacinth, whispering "Domine, domine." But none of it was real.

But after a time that seemed forever, I smelled the sea.

I could feel motion. The waves. Wildly, I thought, *I have turned back time. I'm on the ship, in chains, starting my slave existence all over again. All that has happened has been a dream. Any moment now, that pirate is going to rape me back to consciousness.*

But that did not happen. The scent of the sea grew stronger. I was moving. I could hear, as from an infinite distance, the slap of oars, the cry of the hortator, the whip as an overseer lashed the galley slaves.

"Am I going home?" I murmured.

I heard someone's voice. "He's awake."

Gentle arms of a boy took me by the shoulders and raised me up, so I half-sat, leaning against soft cushions. I opened my eyes.

Sunlight. So dazzling I had to halfway close them again.

I groaned.

Then came the shouts of a dozen men, in disciplined, military unison: "Ave, Imperatrix! Ave, Imperatrix! Ave, Imperatrix!"

XXXVI

AVE, IMPERATRIX

And so you became, officially, an Empress of Rome. A living Goddess. It's an honor to prepare you for your last ceremonial act.

My memory is still unclear about the castration. When I try to remember I just see those dream-images. The wedding on Olympus, the famous lovers of myth and history, the children scattering flowers, the glint of the knife. After that there's an overwhelming pain, and a long, long nothingness.

And when you emerged from that nothingness you were on a ship, and soldiers were hailing you as Divine Empress?

It's hazy. But it's coming back to me....

***

I was on the upper deck of a trireme. Perhaps even a quinquereme. It was huge. The splash of the oars was louder, and we moved more steadily and smoothly, than the ship of my captivity. As I regained consciousness, they were still hailing me as Empress.

There were a hundred soldiers gathered around me, so this was definitely a quinquereme. Hylas crouched next to me, and fed me plain clear water from a silver cup.

"Am I going home?"

"Everywhere is home, Divinitas," Hylas said.

At length Croesus emerged from below. He saluted me with "Ave, Imperatrix," and helped me to sit up. Soldiers lifted me up and carried me to a chair where I could see the waves.

I asked Croesus where we were going, why they were all hailing me as Empress.

"You don't remember anything?" he said.

"No. Just floating in the clouds. Pain and then something numbing. And oblivion. A lot of oblivion."

"The Divinitas commanded that an impressive ceremony be held in the palace. There were senators. There were tribunes, consuls, vestal virgins, and feasting, three days of feasting. Statilia herself welcomed you as sister."

"Why don't I remember?"

"A lot of poppy juice. You were barely conscious, though you spoke quite a great deal, even sang along with the Divinitas. Odes of Sappho, I think."

"So the wedding I dreamed of ... it was true then. I spoke the words."

Croesus said, "Yes. You are Nero's wife, and we have been travelling for seven days ... we are already in the waters of the province of Graecia."

Greece....

I lifted the sheet that they had put over me. I was naked underneath it. I tried to reach for what used to belong to me. They had removed the testes completely. The stitching was finely done and it was healing, and they had not removed *everything* — I could still pee like a boy. But whether the roots of feeling were gone as well, whether I could still summon up any kind of passion, I had yet to find out.

"Divinitas," said Croesus, "you are the same person you always were."

"I'm not," I said. "If I were, you would not have addressed me as 'divinity,' would you?"

"Just an expression," said Croesus, "and used out of an abundance of caution. It's an order from the Master of the World, and not addressing you by royal titles is now punishable by death."

I said, "You are not to call me that, unless Himself is in earshot. And Hylas, not you, either."

At that moment, Nero's secretary Epaphroditus emerged. With him was the boy philosopher Epictetus, whose limp had grown noticeably worse. They both made much of me, feeding me a little broth, a little warmed wine. The sun climbed higher; a high wind sprang up, moist and warm. The drumbeat of the hortator eased a little as the quinquereme fed on the wind. But now and then, the lash still whistled from below, and the slaves still cried out in pain.

Epictetus said to me, "In Rome, all beautiful things derive from pain. The secret of survival is to make sure it's someone else's pain."

They covered me with a cloak of purple, the purple only permitted to royals. They sat me up straight. They put cushions behind me and beneath me so that despite my tiredness, I could take on an aura of divinity.

At length, Himself, Nero Claudius Caesar Augustus Germanicus, Father of the Country, Imperator, Supreme Pontiff, Master of the World, emerged from a pavilion curtained in purple silk.

The Emperor wore clothing thoroughly dipped in purple and bordered with gold thread. On his head he wore the golden wreath he had won despite being thrown from his ten-horse chariot.

Smiling, he came to me. He kissed me on the cheek.

"Purple becomes you," he said.

"Thank you, Lucius," I said.

He gestured expansively at the sea and quoted Aeschylus: *"Estin thálassa, tis de nin katasbései?"*

"There is the sea — and who shall drain it? — the sea that brings forth purple, more valuable than silver, ever fresh, with which we dye our clothes ..." I said.

Nero smiled.

"Where are we going?" I asked him.

"We are going where we can be ourselves," he said. "To the homeland of poetry and music. Where we can forget the odious work of governance, and live in the moment."

But wouldn't the Empire collapse? I thought.

Sensing my thoughts, Nero said, "Oh, I left Statilia behind as regent. She can repeal the urine tax, if she wants. She can do anything she wants."

"And Judaea?"

"Vespasian can kill every living creature in that forsaken land, for all I care. We're going *home,* my beloved. We'll celebrate the mysteries in Eleusis, the birthplace of Aeschylus. We'll see plays and hear fine poetry. And my work will be heard in the most discriminating competition of all time ... the Olympics."

"But Lucius," I said, "I don't think this year is an Olympiad year."

"They'll change it," he said, a twinkle in his eye. "Can you stand?"

I could, with a bit of help from Hylas. So I staggered up to portside, facing the shore. I leaned against the wooden wall and watched the distant land. The Emperor stood behind me, supporting me.

At that moment, he did not seem mad at all. He held me tenderly. The decision to go to Greece had reinvigorated him. "We'll leave it all behind us," he said. "When we celebrate the mysteries together, we will be reborn. I'll make new songs about you, your beauty, your wisdom. I will make you immortal. We'll have a new start."

I had not even had an *old* start yet, but I imagined he meant that he would have a second Poppaea now, a better Poppaea than the Poppaea he had kicked to death.

"You are the only one I love," he said softly, "Poppaea."

He left me then, and I found myself alone, leaning into the wind, having now lost everything that made me myself.

Yet I could not even weep. I had been emptied of all feeling. They had drained me of everything, and now they planned to refill me. I was only a wine-kylix, and they were going to choose what vintage to pour into me. I was a freedman who had lost even the fragment of freedom I had had as a slave.

Yet I had survived. Or at least, *someone,* living inside my body, had survived. The sea, sparkling in the sunlight, was achingly beautiful. The oars slapped in a slow rhythm beneath the whisper of the wind and cries of seabirds. Nowhere is the sky more blue than Greece.

Soon we would be at the birthplace of Aeschylus, father of the drama. And Aeschylus in his *Oresteia,* Sophocles in *Oedipus,* the great sage Solon, too, had all said the same thing: "Call no man happy until he is dead."

Yet I knew that in Eleusis, one would die and be reborn. That was the nature of the mysteries that were celebrated there.

But hadn't I died already? How many more times would I have to be emptied out and remade in another's image?

I prayed to the gods, but only the wind replied.

BOOK THREE

Damnatio Memoriæ

Primus in orbe
deos fecit
timor

In this world
it was fear that first
created the gods

— Petronius

I

THE LONG WAIT

I'm remembering the sea again. I thought I smelled it yesterday. But no: they were just flooding the arena for a sea battle, and the searing sun has sucked up all the water now.

Now I only smell sand, blood, and the shit of wild beasts. I've been alone overnight; but now they've moved me to a "superior" accommodation as befits my divine status. It is on an upper level; there's even a view of the Circus, little more than a slit of dusty, hot light. It lets in quite a stench, too.

It was not exactly cool during the night, just not as searing as the day. The air was oppressive, damp. They brought in a couch for me, but kept one foot chained to the wall, though escape was hardly an option. Breakfast was stony bread, salt, garum, and a handful of olives.

Then that makeup artist returned.

But it's more than a touchup. My execution has been delayed again and my face is no longer pristine.

They tell me that this time the games have been extended for one hundred days. Why not? There have already been three coronations this year, and a few near-coronations. A lot to celebrate. And a lot of misery — taxation, the bread dole being cut, the hottest summer in memory — a lot of anguish to assuage, a riled-up mob ready to riot.

Imagine the collective sigh, the release of pent-up passions from tens of thousands of voices, as they watch a goddess being ravished to death in the arena by a brutish monster.

But why did *I* have to be their goddess?

***

Good news, Divinitas.

I'm finally getting my death scene? I've waited long enough, with only you for company.

You got me into makeup *days* ago, but instead of a quick death in front of over a hundred thousand screaming admirers, you've lured me into telling my life story. From peasant boy captured by pirates to plaything of a famous satirist. From slave to slaveowner with estates confiscated from great aristocrats. From freedman to imperial concubine. From man to woman. I've told you all these things, not to get them off my chest, but because one must do something to fill the time.

Everyone thinks the arena is all fast-paced excitement, but for us, the entertainment, it is an endless, stupefying orgy of *waiting*. Putting on makeup. Getting dressed up. Sitting through the reshuffling of schedules when the star gladiator has a cold, or a giraffe goes missing, or the lions are too sated to eat any Chrestianoi. Believe me, I would welcome another diversion, even if it's my own execution.

Don't tell me it's *another* delay.

Well, Goddess ... a brief delay. News is, Vespasian is marching on Rome. News is, Vespasian views you a little more favorably than

Vitellius. News is, if we could get word to him….

I would be surprised if he remembered me. I hardly knew him. He showed up at the party, you know, the one in which Statilia Messalina's husband was made to commit suicide. He also came to one of Himself's performances in Greece … and committed the worst possible insult … he nodded off.

The Emperor — I mean the Divine Nero, not the one who has condemned me to death — was not happy. Vespasian would have been permanently exiled somewhere, if he hadn't proved useful in putting down the Judaean revolt.

Well, it looks as if there is a glimmer of hope for you. Vespasian has been declared Emperor by our legions in Egypt and Judaea. It appears that he is marching on Rome.

Doesn't mean much. Everyone and his uncle has marched on Rome this year, and so far only Galba, Otho, and Vitellius got to be Emperor. Why make this the year of *four* emperors? Three is much more of a sacred number. Three Fates. Three Graces. Three Muses —

Nine, actually.

Nine. Right. How long does it take to get here from Judaea? By land or by sea? A month? *Six* months? Is he fighting the forces of Vitellius on his way? I don't suppose he'll just march right over and kick Vitellius off his throne? Even in the unlikely event that he knows or cares who I am, Vespasian is not going to arrive in time to save me. Though the sight of a grizzled general riding heroically into the Circus Maximus at the head of his legions to rescue the most beautiful boy-girl-Empress-goddess would, I am sure, be quite the climax.

And the crowd loves plot-twists.

Do you dare to hope, Sporus?

No.

Then at least tell me more. Tell me about Greece.

Oh yes. Olympus and Hades rolled into one.

You left me hanging. Nero had finally ordered you unmanned, to bring you closer to the image of Poppaea. You passed out from the pain, and you woke up on a ship, bound for Greece.

You tell the story then! If you know so much.

But I want to know so much more….

II

PLUTO AND PROSERPINA

The sea …

I woke in the arms of a god.

My wounds had not healed, but a god does not have to wait for the passing of a mortal's pain. I woke to Himself whispering in my ear, "Poppaea, Poppaea, Poppaea."

"Lucius," I said, moaning softly. It drove his passion; each thrust sharpened my pain. I longed to go to another place, any place, because of the pain, and because my body had not yet healed, but the god was impatient.

Perhaps I passed out, because I was propelled into some kind of dream. It was the same dreamworld where I sometimes encountered Hyacinth after his death.

In dreams we really do go to other worlds. Dreams are not mere flights of imagination.

I stood in a dry, dark place. It was utterly cold until I felt the shade of Hyacinth, a warm breath gusting in my face for just a moment.

Come.

He took my hand. We floated over stony ground. Now

and then the dead looked up at us, but mostly they kept to the shadows. There was no sun. Even the sky seemed made of stone.

Come, Hyacinth repeated, in the language of my childhood, calling me by a name I had almost forgotten, my true name.

I called him by his, too.

This place, I thought, it's not the place where we were taught, as children, we would go. I remember tales of feasting and warriors, not stone-gray emptiness. Not this desolation, this heartbreak. This was a Roman kind of afterlife, shadowy and full of regret. *Facilis descensus Averno,* I thought. Going down to Hell is the easy part. Climbing back up, on the other hand….

"Where are you taking me?" I whispered.

"To meet my dominus," said Hyacinth.

The stone floor inclined. We were descending down a kind of cave or tunnel. A cold wind wuthered. The tunnel seemed endless, yet I was descending swiftly, as though I were being sucked in by a ravenous predator. Though there was barely any light there was a searing cold, creeping up from the stone floor, from the damp walls. It was not the cold that is the absence of heat, but the cold of old corpses, of soullessness.

Follow, Hyacinth said again, and now even his breath contained no warmth.

Presently the tunnel widened, and I found myself in the throne room of the Lord of the Dead.

There was a court full of flitting shadows, their robes woven from darkness. They whispered and buzzed, like insects in a summer night. Sconces with torches from which emanated a cold blue fire lined the walls. In the distance, on thrones made from human skulls, sat the King and Queen of the Underworld.

Time moved differently in the dreamscape. Suddenly I was standing at the foot of the twin thrones. Hades stared down at me, and I saw who he really was.

"Divinitas," I whispered.

"It's true," said Death. "There is no escape."

He smiled. His voice, perfectly modulated, echoed and floated on the chill air as though he were reciting Euripides. And then I saw who had become Queen of the Dead.

"Yes," she whispered, she who gazed at me with haunting eyes, *my* eyes, who smiled *my* smile; "I am so sorry," she said softly. "In the end, you are just an innocent boy. Many have died already because of you. Many more will die. But you have had no say in any of it."

I knelt at the feet of Proserpina, the death-goddess, who was also the Lady Poppaea Sabina, whose perfect face was the source of all my suffering.

"I am not here forever, you know," she went on. "Another will take my place one day, and reign from this throne of bones. I think," and she called me by name in my own language, the one only Hyacinth had known, "I think it will be you."

Her gaze seemed to steal my soul. I began to weep.

And then it was that I felt pain again, a swooping pain that made the tears spurt still more, and I cried out in terror and desolation; I felt myself coming awake and I knew that it was the god violating me, my flesh as well as my soul.

And Nero Claudius Caesar Augustus Germanicus cried out as well, believing, I am sure, that he was giving me pleasure, for surely it must be a blessing to be raped by a god.

***

So the days passed, the Divinity hardly leaving me alone except to eat, drink, or work on the grand composition he intended to inflict upon Greece. Unhealed, my battered body taking on more hurt. And always, I feigned enjoyment. Dreaming or awake, it was all Hell to me.

But the gods are easily bored, and it was twelve days by the time we arrived in Corinth. I was afraid he would take Hylas for his amusement, but it appeared that I, the improved, more compliant reincarnation of Poppaea, had actually driven him to exhaustion.

On the eleventh day he told me he needed time to commune with his muse. I spent the day working with Hylas to try to improve his Greek; his Latin had become pretty passable. The Divinitas did not summon me even in the middle of the night.

***

It was night again when we reached Corinth, arriving, it seemed, almost in secret. We were met by some official and swiftly escorted to a villa whose owners, it seemed, had been temporarily dispossessed, not far from the Temple of Octavia; for this Corinth was not the Corinth of ancient legend, but the Corinth re-founded by Julius Caesar a century after it had been razed to the ground and its entire population sold into slavery … to teach the Achaean League a lesson. Our litters moved quickly; I did not sit with the Emperor but followed, with Hylas walking beside the drawn curtain.

The quarters were sumptuous enough, though this was not Rome. The house was in Roman style, with a small atrium. There were plenty of slaves in attendance, but they did not seem very happy. They stood about, eyes downcast, uncertain. The official, who had not even introduced himself, left hurriedly, saying that there would be a proper delegation in the morning.

Indeed, it was left to the boy Epictetus to get things set

up, since the lad was the most high-ranking member of the Emperor's household in the absence of Imperial Secretary Epaphroditus —who had to manage the Empire on behalf of Statilia, poor thing! — and he limped about the hallway, ordering the slaves to do busy work. Presently he turned to the more experienced Croesus to help him, so that my household was actually managing the domestic arrangements for the Divine Emperor Himself.

Nero was led away to what was presumably the grandest cubiculum in the house, and when I made to follow, he waved me away. "We're in Greece now," he said. "Women know their place here." To Epictetus said, "Go find your Divine Mistress a proper veil, in case any strangers drop in."

So I found myself standing awkwardly in the foyer, staring up at the death masks of noble Romans I did not recognize, presumably the ancestors of whoever had vacated the premises for the duration.

"Well," I said to Croesus, "perhaps it won't be quite so bad here in the homeland of Aeschylus and Plato. Respectable wives don't go to dinner, and I am sure Himself will need to go to many symposia."

Croesus said, "I can't imagine you sitting at a loom all day while Himself is out performing for his raving admirers. If he doesn't need Poppaea, he'll definitely need Sporus. And Sporus will sit well with the Greeks."

"But Sporus is forever broken," I said.

"Who you are," Croesus said, "is in your soul, and in your heart, young domine."

I did not answer. I did not believe him.

An old slave was polishing a bust. A balding man, perhaps in his fifties. "You," I said. "Is this the owner?"

The slave cowered.

I said, "You can speak freely."

"Domine," he said, "are we all going to be crucified?"

"Whyever would you say that?"

Croesus whispered in my ear: "You know that under Roman law, if a slave kills his master, every slave he possessed is always crucified. It's the deterrent that holds together the entire fabric of Roman society. Deep down, it's the fear of their own slaves that motivates the masters."

"Then why, when I was enslaved, did I feel so powerless?"

"Do you still?"

I nodded.

"Yet you are free."

I said to the old slave, "If you're going to be crucified, I can't really help you; you may as well tell me what's going on here — why everyone looks so glum, why we were brought here in such haste — why the governor did not meet us in the harbor."

III

Lucius Junius Gallio

We did not kill our master," said the old slave, who was named Hector, "but it is whispered that they simply will say that we did not prevent his death — and therefore murdered him by omission."

Croesus took me aside. "This house belonged to Lucius Junius Gallio Annaeanus," he said. "The proconsul of the province. He should have greeted us at the harbor, but he has committed suicide."

I racked my brain, trying to place the name. At last, I vaguely recalled him. "Seneca's brother," I said. "So, a traitor, then." He might even have ridiculed Nero's poetry in an indiscreet moment.

"He must have thought the Emperor was coming to see to his execution in person."

The old slave said, "It's the inheritance, Empress." Clearly. If he killed himself, Gallio would be considered to have died honorably, and his estates would pass by law to his heirs. But if he were put to death for treason he would forfeit everything. "Murder would be a gray area, wouldn't it?" I said. "He had not *yet* been found guilty of insurrection. The Emperor could still seize his lands ... and to make sure the letter of the law was adhered to, all the slaves would have to be crucified ..."

"A precautionary measure. An Empire is only as good as its paperwork."

Despite its madness, Rome runs with a relentless logic. You can see it from its language: number, mood, tense, aspect, person, case ... lining up like soldiers to produce the precise ending each word requires. They love Greek, because Greek has rules too, but it has vagueness, ambiguity, and an inherent ability for any sentence to simultaneously mean its opposite.

"Precautionary?" I said. "But isn't it inhumane?"

Croesus smiled a thin, sad smile. He did not have to explain. The word "inhumane" is not used of slaves, because they aren't quite human; Aristotle calls them "animate property." It was a truth I knew intimately.

But I knew, too, that even the free are not free.

"You're going to speak to Nero about it, aren't you?" said Croesus. "Don't. It won't make a bit of difference."

"Where are the proconsul's heirs, his children?" I asked.

Hector said, "They are in hiding, Divinitas. Up north, I think. They did not tell us exactly where."

It seemed I had not left Rome at all. Not the stifling whispers, not the ever-present fear of the Emperor's wrath, not the constant conspiracies. I stood there in the entrance hall of the villa, not having been told where I was to stay or where my slaves should put my things. Other slaves emerged, looking at me, curious, perhaps wanting to plead with me, though I was powerless. It was awkward.

***

After a time, Himself emerged, all purple and gold, perfumed and freshly made up. He was accompanied by guards. "We're off to visit Corinth's most famous *hetaira*," he said. "Thaïs."

"I should get properly dressed," I said.

"Oh, you're staying home," said the Divinity. "A *hetaira*'s lair is too permissive a place for the wife of an Emperor. There'll be lewd talk, drunkenness, and lots of poetry reading; nothing that should interest a lady."

"Why can't I go as a boy?"

"Because we are God-Emperor and Empress, dearest Poppaea," he said. "And your pretty head doesn't need to be polluted with philosophy."

"Aren't *hetairai* ladies?" I said.

"As much as delicati are boys," said the Emperor. Again, his tone seemed devoid of irony.

"Before you go, Lucius …" I began.

"Have a nice rest," he said. "After all, in your condition …"

I didn't know if he was toying with me or whether he was in fact in a state of delusion.

"Since I am, as you say, in some kind of 'condition', my beautiful Lucius …"

"Oh! My sweet wifey wants a gifty-wifty?" Was this cloying sweetness more delusion? Or was it all calculated? Or, worse, the prelude to some violent outburst? After my vision of Pluto and Proserpina in the underworld, I no longer cared whether I lived or died.

"Can't you seize the estate *without* killing all the slaves?" I blurted out.

"It's not like you to meddle in politics, Poppaea," Nero said, and I *knew* that was untrue.

I could not appeal to reason, but perhaps venality would work. I said, "A man like Gallio must have slaves of the best quality. It would be a waste to kill them."

"You're right," said the Emperor. "But when a slave turns against his master, you have to kill them all. If you don't, we'll have another Spartacus … all society would collapse."

"You mean to say, with all the fierce German tribes, the implacable Parthians, the constantly revolting Jews, Rome is more afraid of a few housemaids? Divinitas, *I* was a slave. Did you ever fear me?"

The Emperor seized me by the shoulders. He looked deep into my eyes. I thought I saw a single tear on his cheek. "O Goddess," he said, "you are to be feared more than armies, more than a tempest."

He kissed me with such passion that I thought he would forget about the soirée at the *hetaira*'s.

Then, abruptly, he broke away, leaving me with the taste of wine and rose-water on my tongue. "I suppose I can bend the rules a little," he said. Crooking his little finger, he summoned Croesus. "Make sure the paperwork is impeccable," he said, "I don't want Gallio's children to accuse me of reckless confiscation. I'm a reasonable God."

"Thank you, Lucius," I said, "for humoring your little wifey."

"We'll have to crucify a few, mind you," he said. "Make a big show of it and somehow let the rest slip through the cracks."

"Which ones?" Croesus said.

"I suppose the least valuable. Just kill the old ones. We wouldn't be able to sell them, anyway."

At this, Hector the old, and probably the most loyal, let out a terrified groan. I had not managed to save him.

"I'll make sure the deed is properly drawn up for the

villa," Croesus said.

"Oh, I don't need another villa," said the Emperor. "Poppaea, dear, you take it."

"I don't need a villa either," I said, wondering if the shade of the old slave would haunt me if I ever took possession.

"Nonsense, my dear. Just think of it as a wedding gift."

IV

CLIPPED WINGS

And just like that, my Lord and Master went out into the night, escorted by a dozen guards, purpled and perfumed so that none could mistake his identity.

And I was left behind in another luxurious mansion I did not care to own. Here I was, in the epicenter of the known world's culture, but I was barred from participating in its riches, because I was now a woman.

I eventually found my room, which was capacious enough. A fresco of the three Graces adorned one wall. Otherwise the furnishings were simple, though costly.

Croesus would have to do all the documents for the seizure of Gallio's estates (and gifting me the villa) … so he was busy cataloguing the property, including the slaves, which apparently were also mine now. Perhaps there would be some good musicians, or a decent scribe; though I had become fluent in many languages, and I read well, I had never been able to form any letters other than crudely.

Time passed. I paced. I knew that the Divinitas would not be back until morning — or even later.

I was sad about Hector, even more so when he insisted on coming to my chamber to thank me for attempting to save him. He was in tears. "The domina never learned our names," he said. "All she ever wanted was to go back to Rome. She didn't enjoy being sequestered at all; the local highborn women are used to it. About once a month, out of sheer boredom, she would have us all beaten. But you, mistress ..."

"I'm not your mistress," I said sharply.

"So it's true, then. The rumor. That you are not actually the Lady Poppaea Sabina."

"Does it matter?" I said bitterly. "The gods make their own reality."

"Well, I shan't be spreading such rumors; I'll be strung up and being pecked at by carrion birds."

I motioned for Hylas, who knew how to be invisible until he was wanted, to pour me a *krater* of wine, and a second for Hector. He was no longer weeping; he seemed to have reconciled himself to dying in agony for no real reason but to fulfil some bureaucratic requirements. What could I do for him?

"I'll tell them to give you a draught beforehand. And not to use nails."

"Thank you, domina," he whispered. He gulped down his wine. I took only a sip. I almost vomited. "Ah, you've just arrived in Greece," said the old slave. "Many Romans can't stomach our resinated wine."

It was true. It was all very well to hear Petronius Arbiter extol the glories of Hellenic culture, but it was quite another thing to imbibe revolting wine while being relegated to the indoors because of my gender.

"I'm not going to spend my time in Greece playing this ridiculous role," I said. "Even Hylas has more freedom that I do."

"He has," said Hector, "until some treacherous servant decides to poison you. Then he'll be put to death, too."

Hylas let out a squeal of alarm. But it seemed that the older man was completely indifferent to his fate. Was Aristotle right, that some people were just born to be slaves, that they could not transcend their condition? I could not believe that.

"Are you a Stoic?" I asked him. After all, Epictetus's philosophy had come from Greece.

"Far worse than that, domina," said Hector. "I'm a Chrestianos."

He was beyond my help. They would get around to executing him sooner or later. Of all the deluded cults in the Empire, his was the one least likely to engage people's sympathy. Presently he shuffled away. The other attendants followed him, discreetly leaving me with my body-slave.

"Get some rest, domine," said Hylas. "I've sent everyone away. I'll watch you while you sleep. You haven't healed yet. Please."

"I'm wide awake," I said. "I want to go somewhere."

"It's the middle of the night, domine."

"For the last eleven days," I said, "I've been either in a drugged oblivion, or desperately trying to send my mind far away to avoid the agony of the Divinity's *ars amatoria*. While Himself is away for the night, I want to be free for an hour. I want to see Corinth."

"As Empress?"

"As *me.*"

"You mean —"

"Yes, Hylas. I'll disguise myself. As *myself.*"

"But Himself said you must not accompany him as a boy.

Here, you must be the Divine Empress."

"I am not going to accompany him. I am going to do what Nero Himself does so many times in Rome ... You and I are going to slip out into the stews of Corinth, Hylas, a pair of nobodies, vicariously enjoying the infamous night life of this city."

Hylas spent an hour carefully scrubbing away the white paint from my face, the dark lines of kohl about my eyes, the rose-tinted lips and cheeks. He found me a clean plain *chiton*. It was in the Ionian style, because I could not wear the Doric, open at the sides; I needed to conceal my less-than-manhood. I made Hylas dress more grandly than me; this time, perhaps, he would seem to be *my* owner.

***

Preparing to go out took us almost until dawn, but I still was not tired. Just one hour of freedom, I thought, one hour of anonymity. When we left through the front door, we weren't noticed. Gallio's slaves were probably too busy worrying about whether they would live or die, and they weren't that familiar with what I looked like. In Roman society, what you wear identifies you as much as many facial features.

We giggled like children as we left the villa behind us. Though this was a strange city, it was not cluttered and labyrinthine like Rome. The real Corinth was long gone, from a series of civil wars; Julius Caesar's recreation of Corinth was strictly according to the Roman colonial template: here the temples, over there the theater, here again a forum.

But I felt like a boy again, giddy with short-term freedom, running down an alley with a playmate. I had not felt this way for a long time. The unimaginative architecture was not my concern. We raced down an alley, rounded a temple, startled a dove-seller as he hawked sacrificial birds in cages in front of the Temple of Octavia.

We laughed as he chased the birds, hopping along the steps.

"Let's help him," I said to Hylas.

We bent down and started to catch the birds. They seemed tame, not wanting to fly away.

I realized their wings were clipped.

I handed a bird to the vendor, and he sighed as he returned it to the cage. "Yes, I know," he said. "It saves time."

"It seems a pity," I said. "Birds should fly." I thought of my own fate.

"In my country," he said in a strange accent, "the buyers don't wring their necks to honor the gods. In fact, they set them free, to earn merit in their next life."

"That is a beautiful idea."

"But what the clients don't know is … their wings are clipped anyway. I was a bird-seller's slave once. My job was to catch the escaped birds so we could sell them again. The clients did not know the birds were used again and again, so their intentions were pure."

"It seems less wasteful than killing them," I said.

"If me was a bird," Hylas said — his Greek had not yet caught up with his Latin — "Me rather die than not fly."

"What country are you from?" I asked him.

"I'm from the very farthest limit of the Hellenic world," said the vendor, "beyond even the Empire of Caesar. "I am from Bactria, which is in India."

"The farthest footfall of Alexander the Great," I said, remembering some past comment of my tutor Aristarchos.

"You've heard of it! My, you had a good tutor," he said. "You are not who you seem to be, young master." We finished caging the birds and the vendor handed us an *obol* for our efforts. "Go share a lamb skewer."

We left the temple steps and turned another corner. The

sun was rising. I could smell grilled spiced meat and warm bread, and I could tell we were near a market. "You heard him," Hylas said in Latin. "Lamb."

"You go." I had become despondent suddenly. I could not help thinking of the flightless doves, captured and recaptured to ease the sensibilities of pilgrims.

V

THE RING OF THE DEATH-GOD

I did not feel I could eat anything, but Hylas was happy to eat a skewer he purchased, along with a flatbread, for our *obol.* And just like that, we were penniless again, but I was content to breathe in the smells and bask in the cacophony of the market coming to life at dawn.

But this is the strange thing: there were virtually no women. The few I saw were veiled and accompanied by a chaperone or a slave. It wasn't as though women were not allowed out of the house; more that well brought up women didn't go out. You'd see an old crone buying vegetables, or a little girl.

In Rome, women are *seen.* They make a point of it. They may not have many rights by law, but Rome is full of powerful women pulling strings behind the scenes. I had known many.

In a sense, I *was* one of them, brought back to life and inhabiting the corpus of an ex-delicatus.

Here in the agora, women were all but invisible. But there were men everywhere. Men of all ages, eating, arguing, playing games. As we passed by, they would whistle at us, blow kisses in the air, ask our names. It was quite brazen — it is odd, but you don't get this in Rome, the city of scandal and excess. In Rome it is grossly indecent to proposition a freeborn boy. Why would you, when there are slaves who must submit to any depraved whim?

We minded our own business, ignored the suggestive comments. We played hide and seek behind the market stalls. We pilfered vegetables. We ran. We laughed a lot. And then …

I spotted the ring.

Rather, Hylas tripped me, and I skidded past the stalls and into a pile of costly fabrics. And my eye came level with a silver platter that held this ring. The stone was just a handspan from my eye. It was a large carnelian intaglio and it showed Proserpina (Persephone as the Greeks call her) in a field of grain. Behind her, cape flying, the God of Death was bearing down, about to seize the beautiful goddess and carry her down to the underworld. Somehow, in infinitesimal detail, the eyes were so cunningly carved that they seemed to stare right back at me. So tiny, yet the image drew me into its blood-tinged depths. I could hear Persephone cry out in ecstasy and terror.

A voice whispered in my ear … my secret name, known only to the one person who spoke my language, who was now dead. I froze. I felt the breath of Hyacinth, a gust from the dark caves of the dead. The image carved into pink stone drew me into its world. I recognized it. Hyacinth's spirit must have led me here.

All at once I was reliving the dream that haunted me as I lay in pain on the voyage. I had seen Nero and Poppaea as the King and Queen of the Underworld.

Without thinking, I picked up the ring.

"Thief!" someone was shouting.

I stood there, holding the ring, staring into it, oblivious to the stir I was creating. We were not in one of the market stalls but a shop that bordered on the agora. The fabrics were on display on tables in front of the entrance. A bearded man was scowling at me. "Think you're just going to walk off with it?"

"No, no," I stuttered. "I'll buy it."

"Impertinent urchin!" he said, and began to rain down blows on me with his fists. "'I'll buy it' indeed! This ring is worth a dozen of you."

At that moment, the street filled with Roman soldiers. Two of them seized the proprietor and shoved him roughly against a column. "Why are you pushing me around? It's that thieving boy you should be punishing."

"I told you I would buy it!" I said hotly.

"With what?"

Croesus was making his way through the small mob that had gathered around us. He held out a pouch of coins. He threw it at the shop owner, who, still restrained by soldiers, could not pick it up.

One of the soldiers did, opened it, and took one of the coins out. It was a shiny, newly minted aureus.

"You struck a member of the Imperial family," he said. "That's a summary crucifixion."

In that moment, my status abruptly shifted. I went from invisible boy to the center of attention. A crowd was gathering … though they kept their distance. Though Greece was the pride of Rome, it was also a conquered nation. I watched the vendor's face. He had been so certain of his place, of who he was, of what I was. Now his world was chaos.

"I — I didn't how. How could I know? Look at how these boys are dressed!"

A soldier struck him in the face. "You're making it worse."

Then that soldier went down on one knee in front of me. "I'm sorry you were bothered, Divinitas," he said. "We'll take it from here."

I had not been free for a single moment. My carefree games with my slave, gathering up the lame doves, playing hide and seek among the merchant stalls ... all of it had been carefully, discreetly observed. They had been ready to swoop in at any moment.

"Let the man go," I said. "He couldn't have known."

The vendor fell to his knees, slobbered over my sandals. "Forgive me." He added, "Please keep the ring! No need for any payment. Just spare me the cross."

The Romans certainly understood the effectiveness of a good deterrent. That was how they kept the world subjugated. How *we* kept it so, I reminded myself, for I too was one of the oppressors now.

They were going to lead him away, but I held my hand up. "No, no, I'm serious. He can go. And give him his money." The gesture of magnanimity felt empty. Even as I ordered his release, I knew that I would not always be able to act this way. Sometimes, to show mercy would be to seem weak, or worse still, would seem to contradict the will of the Divine Nero; that could never be allowed. But the God was not watching.

"You would do well to remember the tale of Philemon and Baucis, who knew how to serve the god even when he was disguised as an impoverished wanderer," Croesus said. "And you, my Empress," he added, "must be properly escorted back to the mansion."

Croesus waved and a magnificent litter appeared.

"I'm not going back to the mansion," I said.

"But, Divinitas —"

"Croesus, you see how I am dressed. Don't treat me like a woman. I won't be sequestered. Later I'll put on a veil and be chaste and demure, but right now, I want to go to the house of Thaïs the *hetaira*."

I knew what I needed to do with the ring.

"Divinitas!" Croesus said.

"You know you have to obey me," I said. "Everyone does. Except *Him.*" It was only in that moment that I understood how much power I had. And that I relished that power, even as it made me feel queasy to use it.

"Hylas!" I hissed. The illusion of equality vanished in an instant. My body slave crouched down by the litter so I could step in on his back. I stomped up, knowingly hurting him a little. He clambered in after me and drew the curtain.

"Thank you, domine, for letting me feel free for a moment," Hylas said, and kissed my hand.

In the privacy of the litter, as we bounced through the streets of Corinth, I started to embrace him. But the gulf between us could no longer be breached. I knew that, even though we had played at being children together, slipping into the city past the prying eyes of the staff and the guards, Hylas had found a way to alert them. He had understood, far sooner than I, how the world I now inhabited really worked.

"There is only one way we can really be friends," I said to him. "I'll have to free you."

"Don't," he said softly. "Please don't."

VI

THE HOUSE OF THE HETAIRA

Oh, the ring! The ill-fated, infamous ring that you gave Nero as a wedding present! The ring that is now seen as the prophecy of your fate!

Yes. It's because of that ring that I have been condemned to take the same pathway to the underworld as Persephone, Queen of the Dead.

But what of it? Vitellius would have decreed some other death for me, something just as grotesque, would he not?

If you had known, would it have been your choice of wedding gift?

What is the use of speculating?

If I had known, I would have hidden myself more carefully in the forest, and I would never have been captured and sold. Don't you think I haven't thought about all the *what ifs* and *what if nots?*

If I had hidden in the forest and crawled back into the village once they had done all their looting, there would have been no one left. They took everything. They killed everyone they didn't enslave. I'd have been reduced to some kind of feral existence. Or tried to find my way to the next village, and who's to say they wouldn't sell me themselves, a child with no relatives, good for a quick few denarii?

So ... I don't put any stock in the ring's ill omens. Something else would have happened. Life is one long misery, flecked with the occasional fleeting moment of joy.

And how did you come to give the ring to Himself?

I was getting to that.

***

I had expected that the *hetaira* would inhabit some sleazy lupanar like the ones I'd seen in Rome, where you go in and pay an old woman and make your selection from a roomful of preening prostitutes. But we arrived in a tasteful villa on the outskirts of Corinth.

In a colonnaded porch, the Emperor's Praetorians stood at attention, as they probably had been the whole night. The soldiers who had accompanied me joined them; most of my entourage from my lodgings had gone back, leaving me only with Hylas. The soldiers exchanged words, but none prevented me from entering.

There was a foyer beyond the porch, with a floor mosaic in a nondescript geometric design; the walls, too, were plain with only a touch of gold in the molding. Beyond the porch was a little courtyard; to the left a peristyle whose only decoration was a breathtaking statue of Aphrodite embracing her son Eros, so vividly painted it almost seemed they breathed.

I knew then that *this* was the Greece Rome tried, in its

overblown way, to emulate. This was the Greece I recognized from the classical proportions of Petronius's villa — nothing in excess, a few art objects, and each one exquisite and unique.

Sounds were coming from a neighboring room. Not the shrieks and cackles of a Roman party, but a kind of murmuring, like the sea. I could hear the plangent keening of a double flute, the paired notes intertwining in alternating consonance and discord. Then the mournful twang of a *kithara*. And the voice of a singer.

As I entered the room, Hylas shadowing me, the song was ending. It was in fact one of the famous soliloquies from *The Myrmidons* by Aeschylus:

> *Kai men, philó gar, abdelykt' emoi tade…*
> And yet to me, it is not loathsome, because I love him.

The singer sang the phrase *philó gar* over and over, caressing each note as it hovered in the air, punctuated by the *kithara* and melding into the sobbing *aulos*. I recognized him: it was none other than Lucius Domitius Paris, the renowned singer whose techniques Himself often tried to emulate.

It was a select group, no more than a dozen, and I did not know any of the others except my husband, who did not sit enthroned but shared a couch with the *hetaira*. I assumed that was who it was because she was the only woman in the room.

Thaïs was no painted whore. She wore less makeup than most of the men. She was simply dressed, though it was expensive simplicity.

No one could see me yet; the lamps were on the drinking-table, and the doorway was in shadow.

Thaïs spoke — and all the men listened. "You can see," she said, "what Aeschylus means when he gives Achilles those words to say. He's telling us we are beautiful because we are loved. Beauty is not intrinsic."

"Surely," Paris said, "Achilles is speaking here about the mangled corpse of Patroclus. No verbal acrobatics could render beautiful a dead man covered in blood."

"No acrobatics?" said a little man, wedged between two large ones, sitting on the right couch. "You have given us verbal acrobatics aplenty!"

"Indeed, Strato," said the Emperor. "Paris has outdone himself. He portrayed both the hideous spectacle and the redeeming love with just a few modulated tones. But was it feeling? Or was it merely technique?"

"Both, I should hope," Thaïs said, laughing.

"Do you have a better poem, Strato?" said Paris. "We've all heard that when it comes to writing about the boys, you have no peer."

Strato rose and came to the front of the table. He was about to launch into some ditty when, I suppose, he noticed me.

"Sometimes," he said, "words fail me, when one such as *this* enters the room."

Himself, the Divine Nero, Master of the World, saw me at last, for I had stepped into the light.

"I told you stay at home," he said. A hint of menace in his voice.

"Poppaea's home," I said softly. "I am Sporus."

"Oh … of course," said the Emperor. Had I confused him? "My wife," he said, "the Divine Poppaea Sabina, is indeed back at the villa, sitting demurely at her loom no doubt, and on her best Greek behavior. Perhaps, like Penelope, she's weaving a tapestry to celebrate my return from this symposium. But this, friends, is my one true love … my *eromenos*."

"What?" Thaïs said. "Am I not lover enough for you, my Emperor?" She beckoned me to come closer. "Though it's good to see you adopt our customs, Divinitas." She looked at me for a long time and finally she exclaimed, "*O pais kalós*! Is such beauty even possible?"

She made me come a little closer and continued, "If I were Poppaea, I'd have had you killed by now."

The tension was almost intolerable. My boldness in coming here seemed like a mistake. Could Thaïs see through me? Did she know what a tightrope I was walking? Everyone was silent. With Nero, you never knew when an outburst might occur. I steeled myself for his wrath.

Suddenly —

"I have a poem," Strato announced. And he began to recite:

O you are fair, young Sporus, and ripe for love;
But even if you marry, we won't leave you alone.

There was a burst of applause.

This was not the time to imitate Poppaea … or rather, to imitate the *idea* of Poppaea, as the aloof, cloistered Empress. The way to brazen this out would be to act more male than I had ever acted during my time in Rome. This was a different world. A boy was not a painted plaything here. I had to suppress my feelings of victimhood, for the myths and histories that Aristarchos had used to teach me Greek were beginning to feel real. In this society, lovers fought and died together, made vows to each other that were as important to society as those between man and wife, gave their lives for each other.

In this world, I could be celebrated and honored as Nero's boy … and feel fully male. A supreme irony, since strangers had tossed my maleness onto some Roman rubbish heap.

I strode up to the man who had treated me as a rag to wipe off the detritus of his own emotional conflicts. Laughing, I launched myself onto his lap, fully expecting to be slapped for my impertinence.

He was nonplussed for only a moment. Then he too laughed, hugged me, and kissed me, rather chastely and decorously, on the lips.

And whispered, too low for anyone to hear: "Well played, Sporus. I can see there's no keeping you locked away. Well, when we're with friends, we can do as they do. But when I need it, you *will* be Poppaea."

"Yes, Lucius," I said, smiling sweetly. He was the most powerful man in the world, but there were things I could hold over him. "In any case, my Lord," I added, "I saw something in the market I thought you'd like, and I hurried to make you a gift of it."

I motioned for Hylas to come and kneel at the Emperor's feet. He held up the box with the ring with the intaglio of the Queen of the Dead.

Himself took the ring and held it up to his eye, admiring the detail.

"It's to celebrate our wedding," I said.

"The Rape of Persephone!" said the Emperor, his brow darkening. "Is this what you think of me?"

Strato, the silly poet, gasped. Thaïs raised an eyebrow.

It was only in that moment that I realized what an ill omen it was.

VII

TWO LIVES

It was in that instant that my double life in Greece began. The Emperor, it would seem, was to be accompanied on his grand tour by both Empress and *Eromenos*. Of course, they would never be seen at the same event. That would be most distasteful. Disrespectful to the wife, to flaunt the lover to her face.

Not to mention the logistics of switching identities — including clothes and makeup — in the blink of an eye. Though, since proper women weren't seen in public much, and usually veiled, I did manage to transform from time to time, when the Divinitas needed it.

But I was speaking of the omen.

The Divine Caesar was still glowering, and the guests were fidgeting. "Are you saying that you are the innocent maiden, and that I am the rapacious God of Death? After all I've done for you?"

Casually, he kicked Hylas out of the way. The boy suppressed a whimper. He did not want to compound the situation.

I had to think on my feet. "Persephone was already a goddess," I said, "and the daughter of a goddess. I was nothing before you set your eyes on me."

"Not so," said Nero. "You were the God Hymen, watching over me during a drunken wedding."

That had been the first time I ever set eyes on Himself. Yet I had not known until this moment that the Divine Nero had known the whole time that *I* was the hallucination of the God. It meant he had been watching me for longer than I knew. It meant that I had lost my freedom long before I knew I had freedom to lose.

Nero pulled me onto his lap. He stroked my hair. His expression was unreadable, even to me. It was Thaïs who came to my rescue.

"The beautiful boy is only a barbarian," she said, her voice soothing. "He can't be expected to understand our complex philosophies."

"Yes. A barbarian. That's right," I said. I tried to kiss the Emperor, but he turned his head; I caught a chinful of wine, perfume, and vomit. "That's why the Empress suffers me to live," I went on. "I'm just a pretty face. I can't speak of philosophy or poetry."

Nero seemed satisfied with how I had finessed the situation. Still stroking my hair, he spoke, softly so none could hear: "Later, we'll discuss this." I pretended not to notice the tone of menace.

Meanwhile, the *hetaira* Thaïs started to stroke my hair as well. She whispered in my other ear: "Your secret is safe, dear. People like you and me, we know how to survive." But which of my many secrets did she know?

She and the Emperor embraced, with me trapped between them, being squashed like a pillow. If you could imagine the combined scents: the clashing perfumes, the many wines, the viands and stomach fluids … all of them battering my nose while I tried not to gasp for air …

At length, they pulled apart. It then pleased the Divinitas

to feed me personally. The food was not extravagant, not like back home; there were no peacocks' brains. But the grapes were as sweet as any I had ever tasted.

At length, a weariness came over the Emperor, and he nodded off quite suddenly, like a lamp that has run out of fuel.

"Leave him be for a few hours," Thaïs said. "Would you care to see my domain?"

She motioned to the flute-players, who struck up a lullaby. I looked around and saw that most of the guests were visibly more at ease, and some, like the poet Strato, were drifting off as well.

She took my hand and led me through the peristyle to a hidden stairway to an upper floor. Again, pure simplicity. A hallway and some doorways. The floor was plain wood, but beautifully polished.

"What were you expecting, my beautiful boy? Lewd ladies pouting in the corridor?"

"It's not what I've seen in Rome," I said.

"In Rome, men and women dine together," she said. "Here, a proper woman is never seen unveiled. But men long for a woman they can be themselves with. Not just discuss art and music. Just not to feel awkward. People like me are very special, you see. We can stroke their egos *and* their organs!"

"But what about power?" I said. "In Rome, women run *everything*. Though no one admits it."

"And you don't think that's true here?" She laughed, and then showed me a door that was slightly ajar. She pushed it a little way and I saw a man lying with his eyes closed, being tended to by a younger *hetaira*. Seeing her mistress, the girl was about to speak, but Thaïs put a finger to her lips.

"Isn't that …" I whispered … "General Titus Flavius Vespasianus?"

Even in the dim light from a single oil lamp, I remembered

the general all right. He had gazed at me with an unnerving concupiscence the day he had come to get his marching orders for Judaea. And Statilia herself had told me he was rumored to be in the running for the next Divinitas.

"Why isn't he at the symposium?" I said softly.

"It would spoil the surprise," Vespasian said, with his eyes still closed. Then he added, in that growl affected by military commanders, "The Emperor's bumboy! I'd know those dulcet tones anywhere. Well, Sporus, I am glad to make your acquaintance again. Thaïs, you may as well send the girl away."

"I'd better leave," I said.

"Ah, come, boy, not quite yet," said the general, sitting up and patting his sweaty paunch. Again, he stared at me like some sweetmeat on a platter.

"I thought you were off slaughtering Jews," I said.

"I'll be slaughtering them soon enough," he said. "They're too stubborn to behave like a proper colony. I might even have to raze their capital city to the ground and enslave the entire population. Nero's express orders. But you think I enjoy being the villain? So ... I thought I'd stop off on the way and visit the Olympics; I hear Caesar is competing himself."

"It's the wrong year," I teased, knowing that Nero had had the Olympiad calendar rewritten for his own convenience.

"Time means nothing to the gods," he said. "Come and rub my back, there's a good lad."

"I'm not a whore," I said.

I left quickly, slamming the door a little bit too loudly.

"Well played," the *hetaira* said, smiling a little. "He won't forget you if he comes to power."

"I wasn't playing," I said.

"That's the very of art of it," Thaïs said. "I am the most famous courtesan in Corinth, and you outclass me utterly."

"I'm a boy," I said. "I can be direct."

"The trick, then," said Thaïs, "is to do it as Empress. Oh, don't panic, I know. I've always known."

I must have stared at her openmouthed. She embraced me and said, "We're going to be friends, Sporus."

VIII

ELEUSIS

The next day, Himself the Divine Nero and his Imperial Consort — that is to say, my castrated self — sat in state in the villa of the disgraced proconsul and were duly paid court to by the important personalities of Corinth.

The traditional *Salutatio* takes place every morning. After my patronus's death, I myself had presided sometimes. But not in the palace. The morning petitions were a public matter, but the Divinitas's cubiculum capers were not, though I understand that in Caligula's time, things were done a lot less by the ironclad rules of tradition. But now, I was Empress. I sat right next to the Divine Nero, though discreetly veiled so as not to scandalize the natives. Thus it was that we attempted to accommodate the excesses of Roman life to the classicism of the Hellenes.

I was made to fit into every world, though I belonged to none of them.

Thaïs, of course, did not come; such women are not guests in respectable homes in Greece.

It was a desultory scene. For one thing, the Emperor was — by his own way of thinking — travelling incognito. Just one ship, and without the cacophonous circus of hundreds of retainers. Even though the whole city knew that Nero was there, they had all been strongly cautioned that he did not wish to cause a stir.

There was only a handful of petitioners as we held court. It pleased the Divinitas to dispense justice in person. Some land disputes, an argument over a tutor violating the honor of some highborn youth, and a forger who was so arrogant nobody much minded when the Emperor sentenced him to having his hands cut off and hung around his neck. This was done discreetly, off-stage, like violence in a Greek tragedy, and it was just as well that our prandium was not marred by bloodshed.

It was time to go to Eleusis, the place of supreme mystery, the place of the soul's rebirth. I was to be carried there with great honor, as Empress and Goddess, with no outsiders allowed to see my face.

***

To do so we would enter Athens by night, but we would not have time to enjoy the sights, for at dawn, we each had to sacrifice a piglet before setting off on the pilgrimage on foot.

We had come humbly, with virtually no retinue. A small military escort, naturally, with General Vespasian taking command himself, though I was not sure if he was there out of loyalty to the Emperor or to keep an eye on my frayed beauty. Hovering about were the usual poets and poetasters with whom Nero loved to surround himself, including the actor Paris and the poet Strato who so seemed to admire the boys.

In addition, there came my slave Hylas, and Croesus, who was able to give a kind of running commentary, explaining the curious goings-on to me.

To the Divinitas as well, for the Divine Nero preferred the lurid bits of Greek literature and had not really studied as much philosophy as he wanted others to believe. But he could not be seen to be requesting any elucidations, so eavesdropping on his emptyheaded little Empress was a good way to acquire any necessary tidbits.

The basic story, of course, I knew; we had a similar one in my country, though the names were all different. Persephone in the fields where flowers of Tyrian purple bloomed, in the full beauty of young maidenhood; Hades bursting up from Hell and dragging her to the murky depths of the kingdom of the dead; Ceres scouring the world, cursing it with eternal winter in grief; the six pomegranate seeds that meant six months of cold and six of warmth, birthing the circle of time.

What Croesus told us, though, I did not know.

He told us that we ourselves would die and be reborn in the sacred mysteries.

"Oh," I said, "like the Christianoi."

For I remembered that that wayward sect too had among its strange doctrines some surprisingly normal-sounding ones, including the self-sacrificing god who dies in the spring to fertilize the world with his divine blood, and then returns to life after three days.

"Not like them," said Croesus, "or any other divine resurrection cult. In the mysteries, you will *actually* die and be reborn."

"Metaphorically," said the Emperor.

"Begging your Divinity's pardon," Croesus said, "I do believe we are speaking in literal terms."

"Oh, nonsense," said Nero. "I've killed thousands of

people. They don't come back, you know. But their longing remains. And you can feed on that longing. That's what we eat, you know. What sustains our immortality. Every pinprick life is a part of our forever."

We who? I thought. *We gods?*

As always, the Divinitas stood right on the line that divides the visionary from the lunatic.

The procession moved slowly, with those seeking initiation pausing every few hours often to pray or sacrifice. As the night wore on, others paused to rest, but our party marched through the darkness, having changed the bearers at sunset.

***

We arrived, then, ahead of the rest of the party, which was not really in the spirit of the pilgrimage. And it was clear that Eleusis might have seen better days. The winding road to the temple was lined with hawkers of souvenirs who were just setting up their wares, expecting a crowd at dawn: ill-favored statues of Demeter, tawdry jewelry, and crude versions of the ring I had presented to the Divinitas. There were images in the ancient style, angular and not natural-looking. There were piglets stacked dozens to a cage, waiting to be sacrificed.

I saw little, though I heard, and smelled, a great deal. I had to peer through a slit in the drapes of the litter; for I was traveling in public, demurely veiled, invisible and inviolable to men.

The portico of the temple was unattended. The procession was exactly timed by age-old tradition; no one was expected to have forged on ahead. I sent Croesus to roust up some kind of reception. There were steps that led up to the temple proper. There was a colonnade of simple Doric columns. It was dark, not yet dawn; light came from two torches burning in braziers on either side of a worn, oak door. So this was the sanctuary, the home of the great mystery of death and rebirth, the place from which you could descend into the very bowels of Erebus.

Eventually, a bearded priest emerged, still straightening his *himation*, followed by a young novice rubbing his eyes. Perhaps they had been rehearsing for the fertility rites.

Clearing his throat, in a tone of practiced arrogance, the priest said, "Who art thou? Whence comest thou, and what dost thou seek?"

"I should think that would be pretty obvious," said the Divinitas.

I whispered in his ear.

"I am a child of Earth and Starry Heaven," said the Divinitas.

"I think that comes later in the ritual," I said.

"Will the Empress be participating with the women?" said the priest, and I noticed a rather brawny priestess standing in the distance, staring at me like a lioness in the circus.

"I'll go as *eromenos*," I said quickly, for I did not want to be split from our company; however strange we were, we were familiar to one another.

I pulled the curtain aside. I stepped from the litter. I threw down my veil, ripped away my purple stola, and stood there in a plain tunica, to all who looked upon me an intact boy.

The novice giggled, and the high priest turned around and slapped him.

"You don't say anything," said Nero, "and the sanctity of this place will be upheld and respected by Rome."

"Yes, Divinitas," said the high priest. And he knelt at the feet of the Living God.

The boy beckoned to us. He winked at me and had an impertinent, knowing grin. Perhaps he too had acquired his position in society by dint of talents other than religious.

The high priest opened the door.

As we set foot in that most hallowed place, the Divine Nero whispered in my ear: "This place," he said, "is shit."

He said it in Latin, so the Greeks pretended they had not heard.

IX

MYSTERIES OF LIFE AND DEATH

Turning at the doorway, I saw that the procession that had set out along the sacred way was only now beginning to catch up. As the sun rose, I saw a line of celebrants waving branches.

"We need not wait for them," said the high priest. "The Divinitas has, as I understand it, requested a private initiation."

He shut the door. Only the Divine Nero and I had been allowed to step through. Even our slaves remained outside.

I heard faint chanting from the suppliants outside.

"Come," said the priest. "You will stand in the Telesterion, hall of the gods, built when the world was new."

We crossed the hallway, and we were in an area open to the sky, though surrounded by colonnades. Bathed in the light of dawn were heaps of rubble. We reached what may have once been a vast chamber, now roofless. There were broken columns wreathed in vines. This was once a temple, and I could well believe it existed at the dawn of history, when the gods of Olympus still dined with kings. A pungent aroma suffused the air.

Against a far wall, a few people were scurrying about. They looked up at us, seemingly surprised to be caught. They had masks. They were half-dressed. They were perhaps actors, part of the reenactment of the story of Persephone that was to come. The priest waved them away, mouthing "Not yet!" Then he turned back to us.

"This is the show?" said the Divine Emperor. "It's like a slow day at the Circus."

"I am the High Hierophant of the Temple of Demeter. Be humble," said the priest. "For soon you will meet the gods."

"Good," said the Emperor. "I've never met an equal before."

Nero was showing the kind of bravado that only emerged when something was unnerving him. I had seen him at his most vulnerable. I knew.

Another young acolyte entered bearing a worn red-figure *kylix* filled with a strange frothing fluid.

"Drink," said the priest. "This is *kykeon*, the nectar that opens the gateway to the other world."

The Emperor seized the bowl and drank, then handed me the dregs. The liquid was bitter.

"More," said the Master of the World.

"Divinitas," said the priest, "the dose is mostly carefully gauged. There could be danger. You could be lost in the other world, never to emerge again."

Nero scoffed. "But that is a dosage for mortals. And I *need* to go farther. Beyond where mortals go. So does my

Empress."

"Today, my Lord," I said, for I feared being lost in a labyrinth of the mind, "I am only your *eromenos*."

"Words," said Nero, "are only labels. We shall use whatever labels we like, and they shall mean whatever we say they mean. Let's have some more of this magic potion of yours."

The acolyte motioned and another, almost a twin, emerged with a small amphora of the potion. He refilled the *kylix*. I sipped at it. My Divine Husband took the entire amphora, threw his head back, and began pouring.

"Lucius —" I whispered.

"This isn't Rome," he said. "The senate's not hiding behind every pillar, hunched under my bed, waiting to catch my every faux pas. I'm in Greece, the gods' home country. Here I am as free as any other god."

He clutched my free hand. He was trembling. Something was taking hold of him, something different from his mercurial mood changes. Was it the hallucinatory posset? Or was it his own mind, that mad mix of power and insecurities? I held on to him, steadying him. I put back the smaller *kylix*. I reached out with my other hand and stroked his back, feeling both tenderness and stark terror.

"Come with me!" he whispered harshly. "I can't go in there alone!"

Terror overtook tenderness. He pushed the amphora against my lips. I took a gulp and then he quaffed it to the dregs and flung it so it smashed, smashed against smashed marble. The Emperor gripped my hand and then stepped … *somewhere.*

He was still there, of course. But somehow, he was not. He had left his body. Where he had been there was a bodily vessel, but it was empty, as though it had been molded form a pile of papyrus. My mind was awhirl, but I was still in the real world. I willed myself to follow …

Around me, walls of fire. No sky. Only a limitless, unbroken gray.

"Lucius!" I cried out …

Figures wavered. Were they the King and Queen of the Underworld? Smoke rose up. I was choking from an acrid, unfamiliar odor. The King leered at me, his eyes wild.

"Lucius!" I cried again …

***

You are silent. I want to hear more.

He's here! How did you manage it? He's standing before me, in a dressing room in the Circus Maximus, looking at me with the same eyes. His face … his face is like the night.

I've done a masterful job, then. Why, this is the slave, brought all the way to Rome from the markets of Carthage, captured somewhere in some dark forest beyond the desert that borders the southern limit of the Empire … rather like you, Sporus … a creature from the edge of the world. I used all my art to transform him into our Greek and Roman Lord of the Dead Lands.

This is the man who will kill me? He is as dark as I am pale. What kind of metaphor are the organizers aiming for?

Why not introduce the two of you? It wouldn't do to die at the hand of a stranger. Did I say hand? But you know what organ I meant.

I was talking about a religious experience. And you parade this creature before me — my executioner?

It will be a sweet execution for him. But he'll be following you to the dark country. He is scheduled to be eaten by crocodiles afterward.

He doesn't seem unhappy.

He doesn't understand a word of Latin … or Greek, for that matter. My dominus picked him out from a lot that were about to go off to a latifundia, to be worked to death. He knows nothing of any of this. He's just happily living from meal to meal. And you'll be his nicest. As befits being his last.

And now you expect me to speak of the mysteries of life and death?

I'll leave you two to get to know each other. Audiences like it when their stars have relationships that go beyond what they see in the arena. The performances are more moving, more multi-layered.

Performances? This creature is no performer. They've picked the most monstrous executioner of all, twice my height, a mass of muscle. And yet I imagine that the Emperor Nero might have accounted him beautiful. After all, Aeschylus calls the God of Death *nekrodegmon*, entertainer of the dead.

I'm sure our friend is very much moved by the words of four-hundred-year-old poets.

***

Yes, I saw Death.

I looked Death in the eye.

Death was a hulking, dark, monster of a man. Death was not a god at all.

There in the Temple of Demeter, Death loomed above me, blotting out the rising sun. The priests and novices were performing a masked play, reenacting the ancient myth, but the Death in my vision was mine alone.

My Death.

The Emperor stood alone too, lost in his own private vision. In his imagination, was I with him as the mythic drama unfolded, as he conversed with Olympians? When Ganymede poured his wine at the banquet of the immortals, did he have my face?

I know I saw Death.

And now, looking into the eyes of the slave who will ravish me to death, I see now that it was a premonition.

The Emperor and I were not sharing a journey into the heart of the underworld. But I believe that he thought I was with him. This entire experience, this communal death and rebirth, was a lie. The magic potion was a delusion. In my vision, I was alone.

X

Olympia

Indeed, Himself did not tell me much about the experience we had supposedly shared. He probably assumed I experienced it as well. Over the ensuing days hints about it would spring from his lips at odd moments, sometimes while he slept.

The journey to Olympia was a slow triumphal progress, as though the Divinitas had already been awarded the laurels of the victor. It was also — despite the fact that all of the Greek world had been integrated into Rome for generations — carried out with all the trappings of conquest, with the military advancing before and after.

We moved slowly, the soldiers tramping at a ceremonial pace, sitting on a palanquin as large as a cubiculum, borne by two dozen matched slaves. Even the slaves wore purple, more precious than gold.

At each stop, there were crowds, sometimes with petitions, sometimes just there to gawk at the Living God and his perfect boy — or, sometimes, his demurely veiled Empress. More and more, I became adept at whatever role I was assigned, transforming daily, even hourly. For I was never more a slave than when I was a freedman. It was magic. A dab of kohl, a daub of red, a subtle change to the blended perfumes, and I *was* the Goddess Poppaea, materializing from beyond the grave.

On our progress, stately villas of the wealthy were opened up, and our party swarmed through them like locusts.

Though they had conquered Rome with their culture, these were still a conquered people. The ostentatious estates were the country homes of Roman senators, not of Greeks.

"The rich Greeks," Croesus told me, "have all moved to Alexandria."

***

And yet … Olympia.

Olympia was well maintained. Gleaming. Rome had added to its structures but kept its classic lines. Olympia was how one imagines Greece. Gleaming columns surrounded a palaestra where youths were wrestling.

I was foolish enough to ask Croesus where Mt. Olympus was.

"Olympia is nowhere near Olympus," he said, suppressing a smile.

But the Emperor said, "Don't make fun of him. He's an innocent, a tabula rasa. A perfect being to receive all my wisdom, and more besides."

I was tiring of the double entendres. But then again, I was in and of myself a double creature, wasn't I?

Our party had come to rest just in front of the Temple of Zeus, which was to be, despite how far I'd come since being captured by pirates and sold, the first time I ever laid eyes on one of the Seven Wonders of the World.

"Come," said the Divinitas, tugging my arm. "I want you to meet my celestial counterpart."

Quickly, up the steps, ignoring the hangers-on, I was pushed into a sacred place for the second time. The Temple of Zeus was no derelict ruin, though. The space was awash in light, for gaps in the ceiling let in the sun which was blindingly mirrored in the huge pool of olive oil upon which stood the plinth that held the thirty-cubit-tall statue of Zeus, so towering that even the figure of winged Nike he held in one hand was twice the size of a human being.

Zeus was all ivory and gold. I could not imagine how many elephants had sacrificed their tusks to create a seated deity eight times a man's height. Zeus's *himation* was gold over glass. His brows were furrowed and his eyes bluer than mine. His skin had been subtly painted; not quite a flesh tone, because the creamy white of the ivory still shone through. His skin glistened; attendants anointed him constantly with olive oil, which slowly dripped into a marble-fringed pool.

I felt the god's gaze even before I looked up. And when I did, I could not look away. His eyes held me utterly.

Most temples inspire awe with clouds of incense. Everything is dark and you're on the verge of choking on the bittersweet fragrance. The temple of Zeus was different.

"Look, Sporus," said the Emperor. "There you are!"

I snapped out of my reverie and the Divinitas tugged me forward by the hand again. The Living God was pointing at the Sky God's left foot. He was excited, like a young boy. There was a relief of a boy sculpted on the heel. It could barely be seen in the shadows of the fold of sculpted cloth. The boy held a laurel wreath and was crowning himself.

"It's you," said the Emperor.

By now, there were others in the temple, standing far off; they were members of our own party. And there was a priest, dressed exactly as Zeus was; though he was an old man, he had the sculpted god's impressive musculature; he must have been beautiful as a young man. The priest said, "Few notice that little fellow in relief. It's Pantarkes, who won the boys' wrestling match at the eighty-sixth Olympiad. Four hundred years ago. He was the *eromenos* of the sculptor Pheidias, who immortalized him. You have, indeed, the eyesight of a god, to spot the boy from here."

"Don't I, though!" said Nero, and beamed. The priest seemed to have divined the best way to ingratiate himself with Himself — just casually slip into the conversation that one was aware of his divine nature.

"If you will glance way up there," said the priest, "at the god's fingertip, you'll see the words the sculptor etched."

"Oh, indeed," said the Emperor, squinting.

"You will of course know what it says."

"Of course," Himself said irritably. "But I think I'll test you on it."

"It says, *'Pantarkes kalos,'*" the priest said.

"I know, I know," said the Emperor. "Pantarkes pulcher est." He pretended to translate it for my benefit. "Now, when am I competing?"

General Vespasian approached us, followed by members of our households. I was relieved to have Hylas close by again.

"This place is as dead as a catacomb," he said. "There don't seem to be any games being prepared at all."

"Well, that won't do," said the Emperor.

"Divinitas," said the priest, "It's actually not an Olympiad year."

"But I gave orders to change the year," said Nero. "Was it not done?"

Titus Vespasianus said, "Orders were sent, Divinitas."

"The immutable will of the gods —" the priest began. He stopped himself. Perhaps too late.

Nero pouted. I knew what the pouting presaged.

The general looked at me. The high priest looked at me. My slave looked at me, and the members of the Emperor's household stole glances. No one looked at Himself, the one who owned all Rome. Not directly. To whom belonged the deadlier gaze? The master of this temple, or the Master of the World?

The humblest slave, the mightiest warrior ... they were looking to *me* to save them from Nero's impending fury.

"Lucius, my dearest," I said softly, "it is we who are to blame for arriving so early. Let's give them a little time to finish their preparations. Meanwhile, we can stay here with our cousin Zeus."

Nero continued to glower. But, as suddenly as they had come, the doom-clouds dissipated.

I looked around at the others. I waved them all away. I, who had come from nothing, could command Rome's most respected general.

The temple cleared almost instantly. Even the priest scurried away.

I stood between my Earthly master and my master on Olympus.

And it was just the three of us, unless you counted Nike in the palm of Jove's hand, and little Pantarkes in relief on his foot.

Himself the Divine Nero spoke to the King of Olympus. "Jupiter," he said, addressing him intimately in Latin instead of Greek, as though he were a close family member — or a slave — "I've often thought about what I'd say to you. I've seen you often enough in the Temple of Jupiter Optimus Maximus. But *this* you, one of the wonders of the world, this really is you, isn't it? So I want to ask you ... where is my mother?"

My heart almost stopped beating.

"Don't tell me she's gone," he said. "Don't tell me I killed her. There is no death. Death is a doorway and we, the gods, have the keys. Don't we? Look! I killed Poppaea. Yet here she is. More beautiful than ever."

He pushed me toward the statue. I was trembling. This had to be wrong. As I stepped forward I transformed, my steps echoing Poppaea's, even my breathing breathier.

"If Poppaea can come back, why not my mother?"

He was shaking his fist.

I reached behind and touched his shoulder, which was shaking with rage. Slowly I stroked his shoulder. "Don't mind him," I whispered. "When we get home, you'll convene a senate and they'll make her a goddess."

"Ha!" he cried. "Anything you can do, I can do too! You shoved Heracles up there among the stars. I'll put my mother there — properly, legally, by an act of the senate!"

"Lucius —" I said.

"You've had your sisters? So have I!" he raved, though I'd never heard of the Divine Nero doing anything like that. Perhaps he was identifying with Emperors of the past, like Caligula.

"Mothers? Sisters? Animals? You gods are nothing but incestuous good-for-nothings! And your much-vaunted

Ganymede, the most beautiful youth in the universe? Not a patch on my Sporus. I'll show you!"

With that, Nero ripped my tunica and exposed me in just my subligaculum. All at once I found myself metamorphosing into my boy persona. Even though I had been on display many times, at banquets or in the baths, I never felt so humiliated, even though my only audience was a statue. This was not Petronius, proud of my beauty, trying to get his poet friends to write verses about my smooth limbs and lovely eyes. "Are you jealous, Jupiter?" He pushed me to the edge of the pool of oil. "Do you want him?"

"Lucius —"

"You can't! He's mine!"

The Master of the World pushed me into the oil. He tore off his own purple robes of godhood. We rolled around in the slick fluid. This had to be a sacrilege! I thought. The most powerful man in the world was assaulting me, and yet I knew that to his twisted way of thinking, he was making love.

I was numb. I squeezed my eyes shut as I slipped and slid in the olive oil. I screamed in my mind — *Zeus! Zeus!* – imagining those searching eyes, the goddess of victory in the palm of his hand, the other hand clutching a thunderbolt.

Then came thunder.

The Emperor let go of me, startled.

I climbed out of the oil. A storm had burst from a clear blue sky. The god had spoken.

Water was pouring in from the areas open to the sky, but where we stood was protected. Thunder bellowed again.

Zeus had not answered Nero; but he *had* replied to me.

All at once, our slaves were there, with strigils to wipe off the oil, fresh clothes, scents and a touch of kohl. We had never been alone. All slaves in proper Roman homes know when to be invisible, and when to materialize out of the ether. I was so glad to see Hylas that I tried to hug him; diffidently, he hung back, afraid of me. Somehow, he knew I had called the thunder.

By the time the priests and other members of our party entered the temple, there was no evidence of Nero's outburst or my humiliation. I stood beside the Emperor, trying to look as dignified as I could.

The priest returned with a retinue of lesser priests. Vespasian was there, too, with a dozen soldiers.

"We're rounding up your audience," said the general, "and we're recruiting some charioteers for the race. Strangely, no one wants to compete with you."

"Why not?" Nero said. "It's not as if I'd have them crucified if I lose."

XI

CHARIOTS

There was no convenient villa for Himself to stay at, but overnight, in a nearby field, Vespasian's men had erected an entire city of tents, including a palatial one for the Divinitas.

I had never set foot in a military camp before, but this was not to be my last, as doubtless you will know from my history. But every camp I was in since then was used in actual war. This was a city manufactured in a day, with avenues, markets, even a modest arena, complete with a gold-plated statue of Himself in front of the Imperial pavilion.

Nero did not say so, but I sensed he was irked that his statue wasn't as huge as the Wonder of the World.

Tomorrow there would be the chariot race. I imagined he would cheat again by using a ten-horse chariot, not having learned from the debacle in Rome. The poetry competition would come a day later; perhaps they needed more time to round up poets.

To my surprise, the Emperor decided to sleep alone. The scene in the temple had made him irritable. He needed something — after all, he had not completed my ravishment in the pool of oil, having been interrupted by an actual god — and I was relieved that the something he needed was not going to be me. "I don't want to damage you," he said offhandedly, gorging himself on a plate of figs. I did not want to say, "The way you damaged Poppaea?" but he knew I was thinking it.

I made sure Hylas was out of sight as Himself shuffled off to a private compartment of the pavilion. There was to be a banquet that evening, but, "You take charge of it," he said.

"As Empress?" I asked him. "Or as your boy?"

"Suit yourself," he said, and vanished into his cubiculum. Two Praetorians positioned themselves in front of the entrance flap. As I turned away, a girl, gift-wrapped in silk, was being delivered to the Emperor's private quarters; I only saw strands of dark brown hair. Someone expendable.

***

Thus I came to preside over my first Imperial banquet. And because I did not have the protection of Himself, because people knew where I had come from, people did not really watch their words.

At the Imperial couch, my companion was Thaïs, the courtesan, who had travelled separately. I was glad to see her. I embraced her warmly.

"And this is the *only* place you will see me," she said, laughing, "because women aren't allowed to watch the Olympics."

"Just as well," I said, thinking of the shrieks of bloodlust one often heard from way up in the women's tier at the Circus.

At my feet sat Hylas, and Epictetus was on hand to remind me who the guests were. At the couch to my right sat the general. Beside him was the actor, Paris. Apart from some of Thaïs's protégés, there were no women, of course. The *hetairai* were sitting at the far ends of the couches, piping sweetly on double flutes, an action that Greeks find so erotic that Aristotle said that women should not be allowed to listen to this music for fear of being driven into an orgiastic frenzy.

There were plenty of guests, and the usual culinary exoticisms, such as a paté of nightingales' gizzards, but the couches next to mine were a little drama of their own. Vespasian was already a little drunk.

"What are you even doing here?" Thaïs was saying to the general. "Shouldn't you be putting down the Jewish revolt?"

"Soon enough," said Vespasian. "But why not let them have their fun a little longer? They're always going to revolt. It's in their nature. That's why this time I'm going to destroy them. I don't mean killing a few thousand of them. I mean breaking their culture, including all that is beautiful about them."

"You appreciate them," I said. "The Jews, I mean."

"What's the point of annihilating something if you don't appreciate it?" Vespasian said. And the way he looked at me said much more than quelling a rebellion in a distant province. "I'm sorry, Divinitas, I offended you in the house of the *hetaira,*" he said, and gallantly knelt down to try to kiss my feet.

"No need," I said. "Will you take more wine?"

"It isn't the time," he said. "But it may yet be."

Thaïs nudged me. It was time for politics again.

"When?" I said with a smile.

"Six hundred and sixty-six," General Vespasian said softly.

"Speaking in riddles, General," I said.

"No, it's gematria," Epictetus whispered in my ear from behind the couch, "used by Jewish philosophers to code people's names into numbers, which then have magical significance. In the case of this number, it's *chi xi sigma,* which the reduction of Neron Kaisar."

"When I was in Rome," said Vespasian, "I heard this number spoken in hushed voices, in dark places."

"Someone is planning something?" Thaïs said.

"Not me," said the general. Hylas poured him more wine.

"People don't like the urine tax," Paris said. But that made the subject too obvious, so he stopped himself, and sullenly sipped more wine.

"Am I in danger?" I said.

"Personally," said Vespasian, "I *like* the urine tax. I think I'll keep it ... *Divinitas.*" Then he kissed my hand, his eyes betraying both ruthlessness and cupidity.

And thus it was I found out that my master's days were numbered. My master's and indeed my own.

And even today, I am not yet twenty.

***

The chariot races were dull. This was not the Circus Maximus. It is true that Olympia was once the world's center for chariot racing, but those days were over. The frantic crowds screaming for green, red, white and blue were absent. This audience seemed bored, if not hostile. And this was not the colossal Hippodrome that exists in Rome.

Nero, of course, appeared with his ten-horse chariot, but he need not have. His only rivals were last-minute recruits from our own legion, and they would let him win no matter what. Some of the horses were old nags. The audience had been corralled from our soldiers and had to be eked out with

— such sacrilege — *women!* But since the year was not a real Olympiad year, the rules meant nothing, I suppose.

Thaïs honored the rules of society and her profession by staying away. I presided. I gave the signal. They were off.

The Divinitas won, and that was all there was to it.

***

Nero celebrated as though his victory had real meaning. The Imperial pavilion was large enough for a few dozen guests.,

Every aviary in Greece must have been plundered for the chef's most astonishing creation, an omelette made from ostrich eggs and stuffed with peacocks' brains, with a light sauce of honey, red wine, pepper, and garum, the sweet, tart, sour and salty flavors so artfully blended as to create a fifth flavor that could not be described at all.

Between courses, Himself handed out gifts: pouches crammed with aurei, jewels, title deeds to confiscated estates.

Egyptian boys wearing skimpy subligacula cavorted about, turned multiple somersaults, and constructed human pyramids. Women from Parthia wriggled about, completely covered except for their bellies, which quivered and quavered in an exotic kind of eroticism. No, this was no sober Hellenic symposium with men sitting around analyzing the Nature of the One. This was a Roman banquet — and it was fast degenerating into a Roman orgy.

But shortly after the hour of prima fax, when candles began to be lit and more lamps were brought into the pavilion, Himself abruptly took my hand and led me to his private quarters. The guests either were too drunk to notice, or too afraid to.

"Don't lie to me, Poppaea," he said.

But he was lying to himself.

"No, no, I know you're going to say you're not really Poppaea. It doesn't matter. You're the one who's here for me, here and now. I know I didn't really win," he said. "I *do* know that, Sporus."

"It doesn't matter," I said.

"Why did I try to argue with Zeus?" he said. "He sent that thunderbolt. Everyone saw it. Is my hubris to be my downfall? I have no thunder. No volcanoes, no tempests. I don't control the winds, the floods. Only people."

"People love you," I said.

"Don't lie to me. I killed my mother. I killed my wife. I'll kill you, too. Just wait."

"Yes, Lucius," I said softly. "Whenever you like."

At that moment, I did not know whether I would survive the night.

"The poetry contest," Nero said. "That's *real.* That's about truth, and beauty. If it is hubris that afflicts me, I'll transform it into a true paean to the human condition. They'll all be in tears. I'll win that one. As *myself.*"

"You deserve to be happy," I said.

"Then make me happy," he said. He embraced me with real tenderness. He was weeping. I dried his cheeks with my lips.

His grief, it seemed, was unquenchable. I did not really know how I could be of any help. But what I knew how to do, I did. And shortly after, he descended into fitful slumber.

XIII

SACRIFICES

In succeeding days, the Emperor brooded, demanded to be left alone with his lyre, or rehearsed by himself, sometimes using Lucius Domitius Paris as a sounding-board.

I wandered with Hylas through the fields and avenues of Olympia, managing to avoid being recognized much of the time by the simple expedient of not dressing as a member of the Imperial family.

Freed from having to entertain the Master of the World, we were able to wander down byways, stopping to buy souvenirs, and to pray at the temple of Zeus, which was by no means as intimidating as when I had been there with the Emperor.

Everywhere they were selling bowls, *kylixes,* and vases with the inscription *ho pais kalós* and images of beautiful boys, for here people like me and Hylas were celebrated in a way that decent Romans would've probably found a little embarrassing. There were so many athletes, many wandering in casual nudity, that Hylas and I did not really attract any attention. While there were stares from time to time, there were few lewd comments or whistles.

At night, the Emperor was too worn out to make demands on his beleaguered Empress. It could almost be said that those days of preparation were idyllic.

Inevitably, however, would come disappointment.

After days of feeling quite liberated came the day of the poetry competition. The Emperor rose long before dawn and took me by the hand. We walked along almost deserted avenues: past the temples, past the Palestra, past the stadium, past rows of statues of victors of contests, sometimes sculpted centuries ago, but still lovingly painted to seem still real, still beautiful, still in the bloom of youth. Past olive groves, past souvenir stands, where even now they were setting up their wares.

This was the same avenue I had walked down hand in hand with Hylas. The same market, the same temples, the same groves … but these things were not the same.

For I knew that just out of sight, there lurked a detachment of Praetorians ready to protect the emperor at a moment's notice.

We did have the illusion of being alone. But I was acutely aware that it was an illusion. Himself, perhaps not as aware.

Himself took me to a grove far from the temporary tent city the army had built. We stood in a circle of olive trees. An old marble herm with archaic, angular features looked down on us. There was a little altar to Apollo. Piled around it were old lyres, many of them weathered and worn. This was the place where great artists dedicated their music to the god.

Nero took me in his arms and kissed me chastely on the cheek. Fearful, I felt myself going limp. But he was showing me a kind of tenderness.

He said, "I haven't really had time for you, dearest. But a few hours from now I'm going to have my great moment, before all the gods. So I wanted to do something just for you."

"I am happy, Lucius," I said.

"Well, I want to make a sacrifice. And sing you a song. A song I made just for you."

He snapped his fingers. Out of nowhere, a slave appeared and handed him a small, sealed jar. It was old, painted with classic, black-figure images; one side represented a boy with an eagle, Ganymede I imagined. The other was a goddess, Aphrodite perhaps, for she seemed to be stepping out of the sea.

"You can't fool me," Nero said. "I was never fooled. I've always known who you really are."

"But ..." I said. "You don't say anything, because it would break the spell." I hoped I sounded thoughtful and not full of panic, as I desperately sought to find a way to cling to whatever shred of identity was left to me.

"Let's offer it together," said Himself.

He placed my hand on the jar along with his. Something in the jar was sloshing, and I wondered whether this was a fine wine we were offering up.

"Aren't you glad I saved them?" the Emperor said.

I felt hollow. I felt empty. I had to contrive a witty, worldly response. "Well, at least I will be whole in the next world," I said. It was all I could do to keep from vomiting.

"I know," he said. "I'll want you complete when we are in Olympus." I think he was trying to apologize.

As we held the jar up, he held me closer to him. He took my severed organs and laid them on the altar, among the ancient lyres. "Apollo," he whispered, "as you loved Hyancinthos, I love Sporus."

He kissed me again. There was no passion, but there was a strange sincerity.

When he released me, he said, "You see, I do know your real name."

He did not; my real name died with Hyacinth, because he alone spoke the language that my true name could be spoken in.

But I did not tell him that. "Yes, Divinitas," was all I said.

Himself lit the flame at the altar — rather it was lit for him by a slave who somehow managed to be invisible — and put in a pinch of incense. Or rather, a pinch of incense was discreetly dropped in by another slave. Sweet smoke welled up, making it easier for the slaves to disappear; it was like a conjurer's trick. Nero turned to me.

"Now that we've made the sacrifice together," he said, "you probably know I have been thinking a lot about what lies on the other side."

"The other side?"

"Of the river."

By which, of course, he meant death. The only being who regularly makes the crossing of the Styx, then returns to the world above, is Persephone. And that is the role it seems I am fated to play, in the end.

"I know I won't be here much longer," he said. "That's why I brought you to Greece. To know where we are going, we must first comprehend where we come from. We must come to the source of our being to understand ourselves."

"What makes you think it's coming to an end?" I asked him.

"I hear things. There are plots."

"But you've always managed to suppress plots," I said, thinking of the dozens, perhaps hundreds, of suspected traitors who had been executed or ordered to commit suicide. Including all the innocent ones. Like my patronus.

"Every escape is narrower than the last."

"But you have the Praetorians."

"Who can be bought. No, no, my dear, there is almost no one who doesn't feel a bit of rancor or resentment. For a god, I am quite put upon."

"Actë," I said.

"Yes, Actë. And you."

It was true enough. For all that he had violated me in the most hateful of ways, I had never wished him ill.

"That's why you must make me a promise. I mean, I've undone the wrong I did you … or at least, I will have undone it in the next life. Now, I want you to swear that you will be with me when that moment comes. It will be bloody, I know. And you're one of the few who understands … how lonely it is to be a god."

"And a man."

"Yes. Like the god of those Chrestianoi. Maybe I should have thrown *my* worshippers to the lions. In a world without sycophants, I'd have a clearer view."

"You're not alone," I said.

"*You'd* never lie to me," he said.

"No," I lied.

A lyre appeared in his hands. He motioned for me to sit, and I did so on a stone bench in front of the herm. And then he sang.

Not in the Greek of immortal poets, but in plain Latin, the language of the mob, the language you speak when you're among close friends, the language you speak to slaves.

I strive with the winds
but soon I will go

where everyone else has gone
wisdom and beauty are never found together
but in you, youth, they are;
seek other shores; seek adventures;
but as for me, love pinches
like an old crab

There were no fanciful apostrophes to mythical beings. No protests against the Fates. No plaints to the Nine Muses. And to go with the words, Nero had found a melody that was almost like a folksong. Since moving to the palace I had walled off my heart and mind, but I felt my reserve crumbling. Hadn't I once fallen stupidly in love with him, when he was distant and impossible to get close to, when I was nobody? Then again, how long had those feelings lasted?

Tears were welling up when it slowly dawned on me that Nero had stolen these words. No wonder they sounded familiar. They were lines lifted wholesale from Petronius's *Satyricon,* scrambled and served up together like a dish of eggs and honey.

The Master of the World was a thief. He stole words. He stole Divinity itself. He had stolen my dreams. And, as he looked deeply into my eyes, *I knew that he knew this.*

Now I was really weeping. I was mourning my patronus as I never had before. I poured out all my pent-up sorrow.

Nero knew I did not weep for him.

He did know me, you see.

There was a boy named Lucius Domitius who had been banished from court together with his ambitious, stiflingly protective mother. He had grown up among slaves. He had spoken Latin all day long, like ordinary people. He had loved Actë. He had known, as humans understand the word, happiness.

One day, he had been summoned back to Rome, and Rome had devoured him and left him without a heart.

Lucius Domitius had become Nero Claudius Caesar Augustus Germanicus, Pater Patriae, Pontifex Maximus, the Living God.

Lucius Domitius was dead.

Yet, long after Nero had buried him, it was Lucius Domitius who truly saw me.

XIV

SONGS WITHOUT WORDS

The poetry competition seemed to take place in a completely different world, for even though chariot racing was born in Olympia, its frenzied, bloodlust-driven apotheosis was in the Circus Maximus. Yet the crowning glory of Olympia was as the birthplace of poesy.

There was a litter waiting by the side of Apollo's Grove. It must have been there all along, but somehow it conveniently hove into view just at the moment when we needed to be transported somewhere.

It was a covered litter and inside, it was capacious enough for two slaves kneeling at the ready to be able to apply fresh cosmetics to the Emperor and to change his simple garments to the resplendent attire of a master poet.

The metamorphosis took but a few minutes and I watched with amazement at the slaves fussed over my master, working with both skill and celerity.

By the time we arrived at the theater where the competition was to take place, the Master of the World was also its mistress. For he had decided to perform his showpiece, the "Grief of Niobe." They had erected a pavilion for him to prepare in, but he wanted to watch his rivals. At the same time, he did not want to reveal his costume. "Just throw a big cloak and a veil over me," he said. "No one will know it's me."

Everyone *did* know, of course. But no one said anything.

It was an ancient amphitheater of the kind so cunningly built that it could reflect the briefest whisper and make the entire place reverberate. It could take a whimper of pain, a moan of pleasure, and turn them into world-shattering outbursts of emotion.

When we arrived at our seats, it was already mid-morning. An old man was performing. His narration was a classic subject: King Priam, begging vengeful Achilles for the body of his son Hector. But the poet, instead of using an epic meter and epic language, had recast the monologue into a lyric form and used the Aeolic dialect as though this were something written by Sappho. In the background, a chorus of boys dressed as Trojan women were sighing and swaying back and forth in a strange parody of grief. It was all very modern, and you could tell that the audience wasn't having it. In these competitions, the audience is very knowledgeable and nothing much gets by them.

When the old man had finished, there was desultory applause and a few cheers from a small claque, who were obviously his very special devotees. He bowed a few times and exited with his entire chorus, who gyrated in a rather unorthodox choreography as they followed him off stage.

"What passes for art these days," Nero murmured from beneath his veil.

Next came three more Niobes that had been scheduled in today's program. Each was more hysterical than the last; it had been unwise of the organizers to put all three of them one after the other. I remembered that my own Lord and Master considered himself an expert at this role. It's very easy to move an audience with a speech in which you are surrounded by dozens of your dead and dying children. And Nero's version of Niobe was considered particularly gut-wrenching, not to mention overlong. By the time the Niobes were done, it was well past mid-afternoon.

At any other athletic or artistic event, there would be vendors selling exotic delicacies, and our audience would have been munching on sausages or cakes or quaffing wine. But, as I say, they take their poetry very seriously in Olympia, and the crowd listened with rapt attention, even to the third Niobe, who was extremely wearying to listen to. It was not a good day for the vendors.

An announcer declared that there was now going to be a special unannounced competitor. I looked up. I admit I had been nodding off. At this moment, too, several members of the Emperor's entourage appeared and took their seats behind me. Among them was the general, Titus Flavius Vespasianus. There were also members of my household staff and that of the Emperor's. They had been waiting until now because they did not want to sit through a lot of men portraying hysterical women in maudlin verse.

During this entire time Himself, the Divine Nero, had been sitting next to me in the Imperial box, which was not a separate structure as it would have been in Rome, but simply a partitioned section of the best seats. Himself had been watching the competitors intently and as it became clear to him that none of them was his equal, he had allowed himself a little smile, especially when the third of the three Niobes was shrieking.

He turned to me and he said, "I'm far more of a woman than they'll ever be". And he poked me in the rib, thinking this a very fine joke and seeming to have forgotten the womanhood he himself had inflicted upon me without asking.

I suppose we were anxious to see who the surprise competitor would be, but no one was as surprised as Himself. For the man who walked over to the center of the scenic was no less a figure than Lucius Domitius Paris himself. And Paris, too, was Niobe. *Another* Niobe. This Niobe was wearing a simple cloak, as though awakened from sleep to the horror that had been wreaked on her children.

The Emperor sputtered, "How could he, how dare he!"

There was no chorus. There was no ensemble of *kitharas* and flutes. Only a single four-stringed lyre. Paris waved for the music to begin. We were all waiting for the sound of his voice, celebrated by critics and music lovers throughout the empire. But he did not sing. The lyre sounded ... just one note, again and again.

Nero whispered, "I brought him here to help train me, not to undermine me!"

Then Paris spoke. Again, he did not sing. After a brief introductory strophe and antistrophe, Paris stopped his recitation, and allowed the lyre-players to play, just a repetitive sequence of notes, a slow ostinato that seemed meaningless enough but grew in force and obsessive power until the sound produced was overwhelming.

And Paris *mimed* the tale of Niobe's grief. This was his surprise! He had not entered the *singing* competition at all — he was not going to sing a note. *This* was his revenge against the poetaster Emperor's mediocrity.

Paris was alone on stage but as he played all the roles — the gods, the tormented princess, the innocent boys and girls — you could see all fourteen children riddled with arrows as the twin gods, sun and moon, hunted them down and shot them. You could hear their screams, the shock of the palace servants, the swoosh of celestial darts as they found their marks, the rending of flesh, the spurt of blood and the gush of tears. All without Paris making a single sound.

I looked around. People were in tears.

Nero muttered, "I begged him to teach me mime. *Begged* him! He refused. He refused *me!* And I now I know — he always intended to make a fool of me!"

Nero rose from his seat and began to storm away. I got up to follow, but he sternly waved at me to sit back down. "You must represent Rome," he said. He left, and a dozen Praetorians went with him.

Paris had still not sung. What I witnessed next was extraordinary. I saw the spirit of Niobe slowly dissolve, like wine poured into sand, and the actor emerge. It happened slowly. It was as if Niobe had possessed his body and soul, and now was gradually dissociating herself from him. And what remained was an actor, an empty vessel.

There was a stunned silence.

The applause came like a storm at sea.

Lucius Domitius Paris, I thought, *is a dead man.*

XV

MADNESS

We waited. I do not know how long, but it was far longer than the time it should take to set up the next contestant. In fact, the sun was beginning to set. I realize now that the Divine Nero was planning to use the sunset as part of his performance, as though, like the gods themselves, he could control the very movements of the celestial bodies.

First, there came a deafening fanfare from a dozen cornua and bucinae along with the pounding of sets of tympana and the wail of a water organ. The musicians were concealed behind the *skene,* so it seemed that the music was rising from the walls and the mountains.

Then entered a chorus of fourteen boys, seven of them garbed as girls, in a fantastical imagined recreation of archaic Mycenaean court dress. They wore masks as in an ancient play by Euripides. They sang an ode to the beauty of their mother, Niobe, and of her pride in her many children, which had challenged the fecundity of the mighty goddess Leto, parent of Apollo and Artemis.

The lilting melody was interrupted when the overhead machina was activated and Artemis and Apollo descended from the sky. They were carrying golden bows and immediately began shooting arrows from overhead. The audience gasped. A child clutched his stomach as blood spurted.

I heard people behind me: "This is *real!*"

Surely, this couldn't really be happening. But the gods did not stop shooting arrows until every child lay in a pool of blood. Then they entered the machina and were carried back up to Olympus. This was carrying realism too far. Surely, the theater was not the Circus. Surely, these were not some hapless criminals condemned to die for our entertainment. They were chorus boys with beautiful high voices.

Then, as the children lay there, as the crowd whispered and murmured, as I watched in consternation, another god entered, this time from somewhere beneath the stage. Dark was his aspect and he wore a dark cloak and held in his hand a pomegranate. I knew that this had to be Hades, god of death.

Hades walked among the dead children. He touched each one gently with his pomegranate. As he did so, a flute played, a melody of aching loveliness, a melody that sobbed and soared. A miracle was occurring. Each child was coming back to life. It had been theater after all, and not some execution of cheap slaves. Stagehands, dressed in black tunics, emerged with mops to remove all traces of the stage blood.

Then the applause began. It was not forced applause. The audience had had a true catharsis, believing Niobe's children had really died, then feeling true joy and relief when the god revived them.

The chorus stood and bowed to the audience. Then Hades dismissed them, and they left the *proskenion*, each boy holding hands with a boy-girl.

I really wished I could be there with them. They died and they got back up again. This evening, they would go home to their families or their lovers. Acting ended with the end of the play.

But my life was not like theirs. I was never allowed to stop acting. I even had to act after I lost consciousness each night, making sure I fell asleep in an elegant position, tucking myself into my Emperor's arms in case he wanted me without awakening me. The hours of freedom — wandering the market with Hylas, for instance — were rare, and would probably end completely once we returned to Rome.

There came another deafening fanfare, and Hades slowly walked to the front of the stage. A cloud of smoke appeared from nowhere, enveloping him completely as the music welled up and then died away. Smoke filled the amphitheater. Some started to cough. Others, I think, were afraid something was on fire.

The fog cleared. The god of death stood there no longer.

Instead, it was the Living God. It was my husband. It was Nero Claudius Caesar Augustus Germanicus, Master of the World and would-be laureate of the greatest crown in poetry. And only then did Nero launch into his song, his own version of the grief of Niobe.

This was a version I had heard before. It was by no means dull. Nero modulated his voice, producing an enormous range of emotion from grief to madness to bittersweet remembrances of Niobe's children. Nero had skill, and he had practiced every melisma to perfection.

I knew this was Nero's finest public performance. And yet I was unmoved.

I remember, though, that while the public had been entertained by the gimmickry of the opening, Nero's singing impressed them on a higher level. Nero loved this music and he made it his. He really did have talent. If only he had not been Emperor ... what an artist he could have been! And perhaps he would not have been driven mad.

For this was the same voice that had once convinced me that Nero's art had deep and thoughtful sources. The Emperor had thought out every inflection, every vocal ornament. Yet, there was something that I had never noticed before. There was an emptiness.

Perhaps it was because when he had sung to me earlier that morning I had realized that he had merely regurgitated the words of my beloved patronus. I no longer felt sincerity. I remembered his true self, I remembered how he had sung to me, alone, in the grove of Apollo.

This was not the real Nero. This, like me in my role as the Empress-Eromenos of the Divinitas, was acting. It was not entirely sincere, yet I believed that Himself believed it to be. Truth and lies had become so interwoven in his mind that there was no distinction between them.

But looking around me, I could see that the audience, this most sophisticated and knowledgeable of all audiences, was not unmoved. Indeed, the performance was well worthy of receiving a laurel wreath.

The entire display of color, spectacle, and drama at the beginning had not really been necessary. Nero could have just walked onto the stage and begun. It was perhaps insecurity that had made him adorn his performance with such extravagances.

In a while, the Divinity settled into a long catalog of miseries. Niobe recounted every slight, every painful exchange between her and the goddess Leto, who envied her fourteen children yet became enraged by her hubris.

It was during this rather long-winded segment of Nero's narration that I became aware that someone behind me was snoring. I tried to ignore it, but the snores became quite intrusive. I did not want to turn around for fear that Nero might notice that I was not giving him my full attention. But as the singing continued, the snoring crescendoed, and since it too was accentuated by the echoing acoustic of this amphitheater, I knew that the snores would eventually be heard by Himself.

Slowly I turned to see if I could detect the source. Snoring at a poetry reading is already reprehensible, but when a god himself declaims, surely it might even merit the death penalty. So I sneaked a look behind me. The snorer was none other than the great general himself, Vespasian.

The snoring became so loud that it was competing with Himself, interjecting a percussive accompaniment to his singing.

Then the unthinkable happened.

Nero was singing the words *pheu, pheu* on a series of high falsetto long notes. The highest, purest, most beautiful of the notes was rudely truncated by a particularly loud snore.

The Emperor stopped in mid-note.

He glared at the audience, and his eye alighted on the snoring general.

Nero exploded. He flung his lyre at the spectators. He missed the general completely and struck an old man in the chest. The man slumped forward. The audience rose to its feet. The Emperor stalked off the *proskenion* and vanished into the building behind the stage.

The second he was gone, they were speaking all at once. Their rapt attention had been shattered in an instant. I heard some whisper *sacrilege.* Olympia could not be profaned — Olympia, the heart of the Hellenic identity, the icon of cultural leadership in a conquered land.

As the hubbub continued, General Vespasian finally woke up.

"What happened?" he said, rubbing his eyes.

One of his Praetorians said, "You've insulted the Emperor." Other soldiers were laughing.

The general rose from his seat. He turned to me, and I got up too.

"It seems that I must go, my pretty one," he said.

"Where?"

"I'm needed in Judaea. There's a revolt than needs suppressing."

"But the Emperor's wrath —"

"Your beloved is not long for this world. And you must know who actually rules in Rome. The army. Your God is just a propped-up puppet, Sporus. The tide has turned."

"The tide? But who will protect me?"

"It's every man for himself. Or herself. As for me, my only option is clear: huge military success in far-off Judaea, something really epic. Perhaps I'll burn down their temple, capture whatever is inside their Holy of Holies, enslave everyone in Jerusalem — oh, there'll be a market glut of pretty, dark-haired boys without foreskins, but you'll still be the only blonde without balls! I'll be ruthless. And when I have been ruthless enough that all the world fears me, I will march back to RomeItaly and mop up any mess that has been left in your pathetic Emperor's wake. And if you survive the chaos"— mockingly, he kissed my hand — "perhaps a wedding to the former Empress Poppaea could lend my reign legitimacy."

And with that, he gestured to his men. Smartly, as one, they turned and tramped out of the theater.

Only two Praetorians remained.

XVI

Ubi Gaius Ego Gaia

Despite the outburst, or more likely because of it, the laurels were awarded to the Divinitas. He did not even have to complete his performance.

Since his amazing performance entirely in mime, Paris had not reappeared. Perhaps he was already on his homeward journey. Indeed, I imagined him riding alongside General Vespasian, perhaps bound for Judea, so that they could both escape the long arm of the Emperor's wrath.

The award ceremony was not attended by any of the contestants. Perhaps they had all already gone home. The judges consisted of a panel of elders who spoke briefly in turn before proffering the laurels to the Divinity. He did not humble himself to receive them but took them from the hands of the chief judge and placed them on his own head. Surely in his heart he must have known that Paris had outclassed him utterly without even singing a single note of music.

The ceremony did not take long. The judges said their congratulatory remarks, but they were all platitudes.

A handful of soldiers remained to escort Himself to the encampment. The Emperor and I sat on an open litter this time, presumably so he could show off his laurels and be admired by the crowd of admirers, only there was not much of a crowd.

There were a few curious onlookers, though. As we passed them, they bowed low. Some even fell on their knees. There was a sense of unease, an atmosphere of dread. After people paid their respects, they slunk sullenly away.

Presently, there was almost no one left lining the avenue except for some bored-looking children. And then there were none of those, even.

To reach the tent city, the party had to make a sharp turn and pass through some woods. They then descended a gentle incline to reach the shallow valley where the Emperor's headquarters had been built in only a day.

It was when we emerged from the forest that we could see a crowd congregating. They were all standing around a wooden post from which something was dangling. It looked a bit like a human being, but it could not have been one. We came closer. The crowd saw us and immediately backed away. They looked at us in horror.

The Emperor ordered his litter to stop and, taking me by the hand, led me to take a closer look. People scrambled out of the way. I couldn't help letting out a little scream when I saw what it was.

Nailed to the wooden post was an almost intact, flayed human skin, the arms and legs folded like cloth. The head, what was left of it — the face that is — was warped and folded beyond recognition. But I knew who it was.

"I couldn't very well have him crucified," Himself said, shaking his head. "He's a Roman citizen."

"Does it satisfy you?" I said.

"No," he said.

"What will?"

The Emperor said, "He wouldn't teach me the art of mime. And now he never will. His art has died as well."

"This," I sighed, "is what happens when you challenge the gods." For I knew that the Emperor was recreating the story of Marsyas, who had dared to claim to play the flute more beautifully than Apollo. They had engaged in a competition, with the winner being allowed to do anything he wanted to the loser. Apollo elected to have Marsyas flayed alive and hung his skin upon a pine tree. That is how the story goes.

"Thus," said Nero, "we see the consequences of hubris."

I said, "Lucius, surely this was too high a price to pay."

Nero replied, "To challenge the gods is a blasphemy for which there is no such thing as too high a price to pay!" And then he began to quote the words of the poet Ovid.

"quid me mihi detrahis?" inquit;
"a! piget, a! non est" clamabat "tibia tanti."

I repeated the words, translating them into Greek: "Why are you tearing me apart? A flute is not worth a life!"

Ovid's lines spoke of dismemberment and music but somehow the incessant rhythm of the hexameters made something beautiful out of what should have been gruesome and distasteful.

"But he would not teach me mime," said the Master of the World. "He could have just taught me. He kept something in reserve, something which he knew could be used to defeat me."

I said, "You're not defeated, Lucius. You're alive, and he's not."

He turned to the flayed skin, which was flapping about now as a wind rose, pulling against the nails. "Do you hear that?" He shook his fist as he addressed the remains of Lucius Domitius Paris. "I'm alive and you're not!" Shouting to his attendants, cowering in the background, he said, "Bring me my lyre!"

"It's broken, Lucius," I said.

Hylas was the only one bold enough to bring it to him. The frame was dented, and two of the four strings had snapped. Oblivious, Nero seized it and began strumming on the two remaining strings, which had loosened and now twanged and thwacked against the soundboard.

He sang, his voice breaking, pausing between words to curse or to weep:

O son of Leto…

and I realized that he was finishing the performance at the contest that had been interrupted by his fury, continuing with an apostrophe to Apollo.

He rasped out the final strophes of the soliloquy, his voice a grotesque parody of the hysterical Niobe.

The song ended. No one came to gawk. He had driven away the crowd, this man who thrived on having an audience.

"What about it, Vespasian?" he shouted. "Are you still snoring?"

"Lucius," I said softly, "he's gone to Judaea."

"I gave him no such permission."

"You commanded it," I said. "He is to burn down their temple, enslave the entire city of Jerusalem, and bring back whatever's inside their sanctum sanctorum to lay at your feet."

"I commanded *that?*"

Taking a lead from Petronius's art of manipulating the Emperor, I said, "Only you could have conceived of a spectacle so epic, so magnificent, so *total.*"

"Oh," he said. "I had forgotten."

"Yes, Divinitas," I said.

"I had forgotten!" I knew that he meant he thought I was lying. He turned to Paris's flayed skin again. "I don't remember ordering *you* killed, either," he said, though now I knew *he* was lying. "I forgive you," he said. "You can come back to life now. You can return. Just as Hades sent Persephone back to the land of the living, I order you back."

It sounded like one of the things the god of the Chrestianoi was rumored to be able to do. *Where is the line between the real world and the world of the insane?* I wondered. And at what point had Himself crossed over to where there was no longer any turning back?

I could sense a tantrum coming on. Nero believed there were no limits to his power, but General Vespasian had told me quite clearly that the limits were there. The limits did not depend on extravagance or cruelty. It was the army that tolerated the foibles ... and the army who would replace the Emperor ... in its own time.

The few soldiers who remained were no doubt ordered to obey the Emperor without question until such time as they received other orders. So at this moment, all our lives were in danger. Nero was furious, and did not know *why* he was furious. Only I knew that his rage was ultimately directed inward, at himself, and that Himself was the one person he dared not punish.

I had to break the spell.

"Lucius," I said, "let's get married."

"What do you mean? We *are* married."

"No, *you* married *me* while I was unconscious from pain and poppy juice. I did not even know it had happened."

"You mean a proper Roman ceremony, with a priest and witnesses?" I could sense his mania halting and turning a corner.

"Yes!" I said. "And a proper Roman banquet."

"Oh yes," he said, kissing me passionately as Lucius Domitius Paris's flayed skin flapped in the breeze of sunset. It was a kiss of tenderness as well as terror, of purity as well as insecurity. I felt them all, all those emotions; I was the mirror of all these feelings, unchecked and unrestrained; I had to receive the entirety of the tempest all alone; all this, and I was a boy of not even twenty.

When he broke away at last, I turned to see my people, Croesus and Hylas, and the Emperor's staff, Epictetus and others, drawing close. I said to them, to no one in particular, "A wedding. A priest. Guests. Nobility. Entertainment. A banquet."

And by magic, all those things were produced out of thin air.

And thus it was that I, in full bridal costume, stood hand in hand with the Living God, and spoke the words, "Where thou art Gaius, I am Gaia."

In the night, he reached for me, sobbing.

"Our beautiful dream is over," he said.

In that moment, I did love him.

XVII

FORESHADOWINGS

So you have a plan. If you hold out long enough, Titus Flavius Vespasianus will ride to the rescue at the head of a huge army, and you'll be saved.

I doubt he'd bother to save me.

Why not? You told me he flirted with you.

Vespasian has something the last four Emperors lacked: sense.

Is it sensible to destroy an entire province and enslave its entire population?

Not from the point of view of the Judaeans. But see this as a future Emperor might. Why not sacrifice the Jews on the altar of stability? Think of the triumphal arches, the commemorative coinage with the words *Judaea Capta* imprinted for the entire world to see, think of how this would show the Empire that Rome cannot be withstood by anyone … let alone by the one god of a distant desert tribe.

I cannot imagine that he will come for me.

Thanks to you, I've already met my death. My big, beautiful, dark demise. I am sure the pain will be both exquisite and excruciating. But I've accepted it. If I could be a real god in life, why not a false god in death? Petronius would have loved such an irony.

***

We are on the ship now. There was no triumphal progress. We took to sea as soon as we could, with only the minimum of pomp. On the way to Greece, I had been drugged and mostly in a stupor. On the way home, the voyage seemed endless. I had plenty of time to reflect about myself, about who I was, and what I would have to do if the unthinkable happened.

And so it was that one night, under the stars, in the midst of the sea, I stood with my slave Hylas, with Croesus not far off, and told him I was going to set him free.

"I don't want that," he said, his Latin now almost. "You know I don't."

"But you are my slave," I said, "so it must be what *I* want."

"Don't you love me anymore?" Hylas said.

I beckoned Croesus to come to us with the documents of manumission.

"I can't truly love you," I said, "if you are not my equal."

He looked at me for a long time. Then he said, "You think you're going to die."

***

He was right, and the time for that draws ever closer.

But before it happens, there's more to tell you.

Nero's decline was precipitous and all the Emperors that followed in swift succession were each of them very different. And all of them, save one, loved me.

Let me rest now, and we will go on in the morning.

XVIII

THE SEA

Joyful or mournful?
The same gulls, crying over the same sea.
The Romans call it *Mare Nostrum … our* sea.
Arrogance, or acknowledgment?
Tell me, Sporus.
***

My life, short though it will have been, falls, like a chorus of Euripides or an ode by Pindar, into clear, contrasting segments, each delineated by water. Like classic Greek poetry: first a strophe, then an antistrophe, matching each other perfectly in scansion yet often saying each other's opposite. And an epode at the end that brings the opposites into harmony, constrained by the art and artifice of the poet's command of the language …

It sounds pretentious, Empress. Days have gone by, and still we're waiting for you to go onstage and make your grand exit from the world. I don't know why it hasn't happened yet. I can understand your wanting to find some kind of order to your chaotic life. But your life … a Greek ode?

Hear me out. I've had some time to think about it. You've made me up and cleaned me up and made me up again so many times, preparing me for the brutal execution that keeps getting put off. I wouldn't recognize my real face anymore, not in the finest polished mirror.

A Greek ode?

First, the idyllic childhood that I barely remember, followed by my capture and being sent in chains by sea to Rome. Then, my life with my beloved patronus, the intrigue at court, the path that led me from slave boy to a fateful meeting with the Lord of the World. And after being viciously mutilated, stripped of my maleness, another journey by sea to the heart of civilization, where I learned just how precarious this monumental edifice called Rome really is, and where I finally came to understand that this world I know can disintegrate on a whim.

Between each stanza of my life, there is the sea.

There was the sea that brought me to Rome. Every gust of wind, every unfamiliar scent, every cry of a distant seagull was terrifying to me. I felt the sea through a miasma of pain.

My second journey, the antistrophe to this ode: knowing all I knew, great poetry and art and music crammed into my mind by the greatest minds of Rome, a trek to the very heart of civilization … all the hope in the world … all the joy, yet tempered by the fact that I had lost something I could never get back….

And now, it was my third voyage.

I had arrived with despair and discovered, in the darkness, hidden reserves of hope.

I had left again with new hopes, only to find them dashed by the corruption in Olympia, the world's icon of fairness and of unpolluted devotion to beauty and goodness.

And now I was returning, knowing in my heart that we were doomed: I, of course, because my very identity had never been my own, those close to me, because their fate was tied to mine, and mine in turn to the fate of Himself the God, the Divine Emperor, Lord of the World, Nero Claudius Caesar Augustus Germanicus, Father of the Country, Pontifex Maximus, whose name, because of an edict of Damnatio Memoriae, may no longer be spoken.

You haven't even told me your name.

Do I need one? I am just a slave, working for the editor of these grand games of triumph. I am treated well, because my skills are rare and valuable, but if your death doesn't rise to the appropriate level of epic drama, I'll probably get a beating.

Before you send me out to the arena to be raped to death by a monster dressed as Hades, whisper your name to me.

So I can be the last person you think about?

Anyone but Nero.

XIX

TRIUMPH

And so, after Nero's so-called victories in the Olympics, you and your Divine Companion returned to the Eternal City in triumph.

Oh yes. A triumph! Parades! Honours! A temporary increase in the bread dole! Free baths for a month! Lottery tickets with country estates and all-night tokens for the city's priciest, naughtiest lupanar!

And of course, games!

Like these *games?*

Games like these — the ones I'm going to be killed in — well, a little more spectacular, nothing so measly as today's sorry spectacle. There's not enough gold left in the whole world for the kind of extravaganza we witnessed in the last days of Nero Claudius Caesar Augustus Germanicus, my Husband and God.

I've heard that certain legendary animals are now extinct because of those games. Sea-unicorns — dragons — camelopards — wyverns —

Dragons! I see those games have become even more legendary in the memory!

I didn't believe it either.

Games, yes — bigger and more splendid and more innovative than ever before. The Divinity had not merely triumphed over barbarians — he had conquered the very heart of civilization. He did not just own the bodies of his subjects — he possessed their souls — he had remade art and music in the image of Himself.

But first there was the triumphal procession itself. Nero dispensed with the traditional whisperer in the chariot who was supposed to say, constantly, "Remember, thou art mortal." He was, after all, a god.

He had ten white horses dyed green so no one could mistake whose colors he favored. I was in the procession, too, as Venus, stepping from a giant golden scallop shell, with nymphs around me to hold up feathered fans to hide those parts the crowd might have been curious about. I was the perfect object of love, both boy and girl, both child and immortal.

Though Vespasian's legions had sailed to Judaea, there was of course the Praetorian Guard, still under the command of the sadistic Tigellinus and the seedy Nymphidius, who had stopped trying to molest me in the hidden corners of the palace since I had become the new Poppaea. Though he continued to molest me with his eyes.

There were plenty of Praetorians marching in the triumph. As the Divinitas had told me when we arrived, "They at least will be loyal to the last, since they're paid three and a half times as much as ordinary legionaries. *And* they're getting a special donativum in honour of our wedding."

Yes. Our military might must be bought and paid for, or it all falls apart. As Vespasian told me … it is the one sure truth that underpins our Roman way of life.

***

It was dawn and we had only been back from Greece for a day or two. His Majesty himself had arrived just as unannounced as he had departed, and it would take some time to pull together all the spectacles that he needed to be devised for his triumphal return. But meanwhile, given that General Vespasian had a very large army, even though it was moving further and further to the east … the Praetorians needed to be massaged a bit.

"It's about money again, isn't it?" I said, as we lay once more in the cubiculum where I had seen Poppaea kicked to death.

This room, heavily perfumed to cover the omnipresent traces of an aroma of spilt wine with hints of vomit and of cheetah piss, with Hercules on his golden leash at the foot of the bed, and my body-slave Hylas hiding behind the drapes, now felt like home. That was the oddest thing of all, how this most unreal of environments had come to have a sense of familiarity, of welcome even. I lay back, allowing Himself to explore my body with his hands, to peer at my pores through eyepieces of polished ruby, sapphire and emerald.

"It seems to be healing well," he said, running his finger over the scar. It no longer pained me. But the Divinitas's touch did not bring the kind of automatic arousal that might have happened in the past. It was just a touch. "You're not feeling any pleasure," he said.

"A kind of pleasure, perhaps," I said. But I was surprised he even asked; he rarely thought of anyone's pleasure but his own. "Thank you for asking," I said, and kissed Himself lightly on the cheek.

Suddenly he turned from me, sat up. "The army," he said. "The cursed *army!*"

"It *is* about money, then," I said. "It's time to pay them off."

"And every time I do it, I give them more, and it buys me a shorter span of protection."

"How much do we need?"

"Don't worry your pretty little head about such sordid details, my love," said the Divinitas. "However much it is, it won't be worth as much as a single hair from your precious, delicate pubis." He proceeded to pluck one. Such was his idea of an erotic conversation.

"Don't," I said. "I've few enough of those as it is." Indeed, since my mutilation, no new ones. "Though if they are worth that much, surely you can pay off the Praetorians with one."

He laughed, and then became suddenly very thoughtful.

"You actually mean to do it!"

"Don't be silly," the Emperor said. "And yet … I have the most brilliant idea, Sporus. *You* will be the one to present the donativum. That way, they will all see and acknowledge their Empress, and it will dispel the misguided rumour that somehow Poppaea was mysteriously murdered by someone or other!" I wanted to roll my eyes, but he seemed much taken by this new conceit. So I just looked at him with that look of girlish adoration that he loved to see in me.

***

I prepared myself for another stupefyingly dull ceremony, in which I would have to sit stiffly enthroned and be charming and Empress-like, while slaves handed out pouches full of money to all six thousand or so members of the Praetorian Guard.

This was not what transpired, however. It was a private event, and only a few dozen of the most important Praetorians were there. It was more in the manner of a morning salutatio, the kind my patronus, Petronius, had every morning, no matter how enervating the previous night's orgy had been. Of course, being the Emperor's salutatio, there was more ritual and more grovelling, and more at stake — life and death, even.

It had taken me a very long morning to be made up and sumptuously dressed as the Empress. It had taken almost longer to get to the Emperor's new audience hall, because I had to be carried by litter-bearers through a tunnel that connected the Palatine to the Oppian, the southern spur of the Esquiline Hill. It was about three hundred passus, and there were inclines, both downhill and uphill. A different palace on a different hill, yet the linking passageways made it all part of the same world, Nero's world, far from the bustle of the world's most crowded city.

The throne room was shiny and new, part of the Golden House that had been continuously under construction since the great fire, now in part deemed fit for habitation. The new palatial complex took up most of the Oppian. On this spot had once been slums with insulae housing thousands of poor people. Now there was this Imperial chamber, with a vast mural that continued around three sides of the hall depicting the last days of the Trojan War. A huge statue of the Divinitas, with his right arm upraised in a kind of benediction dominated the far wall. I could have sworn I had seen the same statue once in the forum, except that then it had the head of Augustus. Of course, statues' heads are routinely changed when there is a new Emperor, but you would think Augustus would be sacrosanct.

When I arrived, the salutatio had been going on for a little while. A few petitions had been brought on behalf of various traitors; to most people's surprise, Himself had proved merciful, commuting a damnatio ad bestias to a more gentlemanly suicide, and even banishing a few people instead of killing them.

He was at his most magnanimous that morning. He was not properly dressed to be a god, having it seemed, not bothered with makeup or robes.

He waved me over to a throne that was on an equal height to his own. "Come, Poppaea," he said. "Time to dominate our troops."

Epaphroditus, ever the Imperial gatekeeper, gave a signal and two Praetorians in full dress uniform approached. I knew them both, of course. Tigellinus, who had always treated me like some kind of insect … and Nymphidius, who never bothered to conceal his lust for me.

But I was not the boy they once despised.

Now I was their mistress, whom they still despised, though they could not show it. Instead, they were forced to prostrate themselves before me.

"I trust you are in good health, Empress," Tigellinus said. He didn't realize that I could hear the sound of his gritted teeth.

"I am," I said sweetly. "All healed now." I flashed a smile.

"You are even more beautiful, Divinitas," said Nymphidius, "than you were before your … accident."

"I should think I would not be the worse for it," I said. I made sure he saw a momentary glower before I smiled again.

Epaphroditus beckoned again and slaves came from within, carrying heavy gilded chests — two slaves to a chest, and even then they were almost too heavy to lift. They opened the chests, which were filled to the brim with gold aurei.

Surely there were not so many gold coins in the world. Each one was worth a hundred sestertii, more than a month's pay for a common legionary. One chest could buy a legion for a year, and the chests kept coming.

"I trust my husband and I will have your loyalty," I said. "Distribute it however you see fit." I knew this meant that Tigellinus and Nymphidius would get the lion's share.

It took the better part of an hour for soldiers to carry away all the gold.

By the time it was all done, the other petitioners had left, for the time allotted for salutatio was long over. Only the two chiefs of the Praetorians remained, standing at attention and waiting to be dismissed by the Emperor.

I got up from my throne and turned to see Nero chuckling.

"What have you done?" I said. "Stripped the gold from the statues of the gods?"

"It's just a loan," he said. "I'll replace it."

Epaphroditus whispered in my ear, "It's not as much as it looks, Divinitas. Or, from another viewpoint, more than it looks. There's been a bit of debasement."

"In the gold?"

"In the silver denarius, Empress. So an aureus can get you more denarii than ever."

The two Praetorians could hear everything we said. I could see they didn't mind about the silver coinage being debased. They were going to pay their underlings in denarii and hang on to the gold themselves. They had become even richer than they'd calculated, for it was the ones below their rank who would get swindled.

"But what if they strip the gods bare?" I said, louder than I should have.

Nero, who had heard me, said, "I'll just raise taxes; Epaphroditus, you'll see to it."

"Divinitas —"

"How's the urine tax going? Sporus's idea — and a very clever one, too. Togas have to stay white, and laundries never go out of business."

"There's been a lot of discontent about that urine tax," said Epaphroditus.

"Riots," Nymphidius said.

"But you've put them down," said Himself.

Nymphidius Sabinus peered at me, while pretending to keep his head bowed. "The Empress has given us a generous donativum," he said. "We shall protect the Empress."

"Excellent," Nero said.

I looked into the Praetorian's eyes. He had that practiced blank look that many courtiers have, so that they won't give themselves away. But though I had been at court only a short time, I saw what flickered beneath that empty gaze. He was pledging to protect *me.* Nero was too self-involved to consider that Nymphidius had not said he would protect the Emperor.

In that moment, I knew there was a plot. A plot hatched in our absence. A plot that probably involved half the people the Emperor called his friends.

I've often said that so much has happened to me, a boy not even twenty. Yes, I am young to have lived through so much. And yet …

Now remember, as you hear out the rest of my story, that Nero Claudius Caesar August Germanicus was no withered, aging pervert like Tiberius, no stuttering old fool like his uncle Claudius. He was younger than the carpenter god of the Chrestianoi. Caligula was that age, too, when they knifed him in the tunnel between the palace and the Circus Maximus.

Nero was barely thirty, and already, I knew, his days were numbered.

Nero had killed, directly or indirectly, those who had truly cared for me. He was all I had left. In his own way he loved me, even though the only way he ever showed love was by inflicting pain. But now I would have to consider survival.

And that unsavory man Nymphidius, with his lascivious sneer and his ill-concealed lust for my body, a man I had always loathed, was offering me a lifeline.

XX

GAIUS JULIUS VINDEX

And while we slept, the tide was already turning. The Senate was having a secret meeting to overhaul the taxes ... and the fact that Gaius Julius Vindex, a governor in Gaul, was leading a revolt.

When I awoke, Himself was no longer there. That was unusual; it's normal that the person of highest status in a bed is the last to wake, and finds that everything has been made ready for him.

In one corner of the room, Hylas was folding togas.

"Lucius?" I said softly, expecting that the Divinitas was outside in the private garden. Watering the flowers, perhaps, since he was the only person in the Empire whose urine wasn't taxed. As I sat up, I saw someone else.

Standing at the foot of the bed was the last person I would have expected to see. But as I slowly became aware of things, I realized that her coming was inevitable.

"Actë," I whispered.

"I came as soon as I felt it," she said, "and my feelings never lie." It was true. At every truly key moment in Nero's life, Actë had somehow managed to be present. She lived in shadow, absent from the parties, the orgies, the poetry readings, the arena, and the discussions on strategy, yet she always knew when a moment of crisis was at hand.

I said, "Will this be the last time?"

But I had already divined the answer. From what Vespasian had told me in Greece. From whispers in the corridors in the brief days since our return.

Actë said, "I fear it. I heard everything that happened in Greece. Even what happened to that actor."

The image surfaced in my mind. Lucius Domitius Paris, the greatest actor of our time, flayed alive and flapping in the breeze of sunset while Himself intoned his flawed hexameters to cowed onlookers, even as his most powerful general was in the process of abandoning him. The Emperor declaiming with such mad passion. The actor's skin fluttering. The gorgeous twilight over Olympia. The attar of roses that doused the Divinitas blending with the stench of freshly-killed flesh. I tried to blank my mind, but the nightmare memory would not subside quickly.

"Poor Sporus," Actë said softly. "The things you've seen, the things he had you live through."

She held out a hand and tugged me up from the bed. In a moment, Hylas materialized and was starting to dress me.

"Go away," I said. "I freed you."

But Hylas only laughed as he tied the subligaculum around my loins and slipped a cool silk tunic over my naked body. "Yes, domine," he said, "you freed me."

"Tell them to dress you quickly," Actë said. "Male, I think. Full toga. I think we are going to the Senate."

"Senate? But we're not members," I said.

"And I'm a woman," she said. "Come along. We may not be full members of the Conscript Fathers, but I know where all the peepholes are."

***

There was, not at all to my surprise, a secret room that could be reached through a tunnel, then a back stairwell. It was a low-ceilinged upper room in the Curia Julia; while there was no view of the senatorial chamber, the sound was particularly clear, echoing through a system of pipes that had been engineered for eavesdropping. The Divinitas was already there, and his aspect was grim as he sat on a golden curule, flanked by Epaphroditus, his secretary on one side, and the Praetorian Tigellinus on the other.

Where was Nymphidius? I was he who had said I would be protected in this crisis. Nymphidius wanted something from me, something I knew I could still trade on; to Tigellinus I was as useless as any other pleasure object. I was about to ask someone, but Nero shushed me with a finger to his lips.

"Listen to that one go on!" Nero was muttering.

We heard a quavery old man: "And what is our Divine Emperor doing while Gaius Julius Vindex leads a rebellion in Gaul? Are we to return to the internecine chaos of the interregnum, after a century of this pseudo-monarchy that has stripped the Senate of its rightful authority? Must seven centuries of the Roman Republic end in this nightmare dictatorship?"

Epaphroditus said, "Titus Viridianus. An old fool. I'm surprised he wasn't eliminated in the last purge."

"We can remedy that," Tigellinus said. "It's never too late for a fresh purge."

"Wait," said Epaphroditus.

Tigellinus said, "Indeed. I have the Senate surrounded, as a precaution."

Viridianus was continuing, "Of course it would normally behoove us to send a force to crush this Vindex before it gets out of hand. Yet are there not some people in this chamber who would favor Vindex, who has after all declared his allegiance to General Galba, governor in Spain, a man considered perhaps eminently more sensible as a ruler than our mad poet Emperor?"

"I smell treason," Tigellinus said.

"Let's march right in there and arrest them!" said Himself.

But Epaphroditus said, "Wait, Divinitas, wait." He held up his hand. Surely more senators would condemn themselves if we gave them more time. And they did.

"Didn't you already send money to Galba?" A whiny, wheezy voice. "*And* donated to Nero's triumphal games?"

Another voice: "It doesn't hurt to bet on the green *and* the red. Nero is popular with the mob, and relatively harmless to those of us who stay out of sight. I might just retreat to my new estates in Sicily."

"Sextus Varus," Epaphroditus whispered.

"Estates in Sicily," said Tigellinus. "Something you'd like to add to your holdings, Divinitas?"

"Make a note of it," said Nero. "Would *you* like something in Sicily, dear?" he added, to Actë.

"You will not be rid of me so easily this time," she said.

"Take the estate," said the Divinitas.

"I'll share it with Poppaea, here," she said, and I thought: *That could never have happened if the real Poppaea were here.*

"It's nice to see you two getting along," said the Emperor.

After an hour or so of listening to various senators incriminating themselves, Himself had had enough. "I'm going in," he said. I started to follow, but he motioned me to stay behind. "Just Tigellinus," he said. "The Senate is no place for wives."

"All right," I said. "I'll listen for people whispering behind your back."

The Emperor left the room and so did most of his entourage, including the Praetorians.

The only people who remained in the eavesdropping chamber were Epaphroditus, Actë, and me. Even the slaves had vanished.

With Nero gone, the atmosphere swiftly changed. We didn't speak. We just listened. The condemnatory babble went on for awhile. Occasionally Epaphroditus identified a speaker.

We could hear the tramp of military boots. Nero had reached the Senate chamber and all at once, the hubbub was stilled.

Then I heard the voice of Tigellinus, matter-of-fact, almost bored. "The following members of the Conscript Fathers," he said, "will commit suicide by dawn tomorrow. Titus Viridianus. Publius Claudius Afer. Lucius Sponsianus. Marcus Plautius Niger." Tigellinus droned on. He didn't sound as though he was sentencing people to death; more like a Greek schoolmaster taking roll call in a roomful of inattentive young aristocrats. The list came to an end and he concluded: "A member of the Guard will attend you at your residence in case you need any lessons in how to die like a proper Roman; though I trust there is no one in this august body who doesn't know how to sensibly and expediently commit suicide. The requisite paperwork will be delivered to your residences, along with witness statements that suicide was carried out and thus your heirs will still inherit, as opposed to all you possess being subject to seizure by the Imperial Estate."

"Those documents will have become meaningless come morning," Epaphroditus said.

"True enough," said Actë. "There are perfectly legal ways of invalidating them. Illegible witness signatures … misspellings … even just misplacing some scroll or other."

"Yes. Bureaucracy has been getting more and more devious since the Divine Claudius was Emperor," said Epaphroditus. "But there are more direct ways to intervene. For example …"

Epaphroditus pulled a document from a fold of his tunica.

I had always been told that governing an Empire was about manipulation and ruthless action, but perhaps it was also true that the secretaries, eunuchs and advisors had the ability to override all those traits with obfuscation. But there was more. In Greece Vespasian had taught me that it was the army who ruled the world.

But it wasn't always so. There was also the bureaucracy.

"I have here," Epaphroditus said, "as it happens, a letter from General Gaius Julius Vindex."

"Isn't that treason?" I blurted out, forgetting all I had been learning about keeping my composure.

"You heard Nymphidius," said Nero's trusted freedman, the man who held all the keys to the Empire. "Even if Nero did not. The army pledged its loyalty to *you*, Empress."

Actë began to laugh. And suddenly, Epaphroditus, too, was laughing. Presently, the absurdity of it all was so overwhelming that I too was suppressing laughter.

"It is not as ridiculous as you think," Actë said. "Wasn't it Nero's idea for you to be the one to hand out the donativum? He *planned* this! He thinks, my poor beautiful mad beloved, that when everyone turns against him, *you* will still be foolish enough to want to protect him."

"Me?" I said.

"Yes," Actë said. "Because, beneath all the manufactured drama, *he* is the only reason you exist as a thing of value in the world. And you love him for it."

As always, it was Actë alone who dared speak the truth that was hidden.

XXI

SPEAKING TO GODS

"Don't misunderstand me," Epaphroditus said. "I *love* the Divinitas. More than that; I love the *man*. I have to. I have been his slave; I am now his freedman; I belong to him in a way no one can understand who has not been a slave. As you, Sporus, will always belong to Gaius Petronius Arbiter, even now, when you are Queen of the World."

"Love isn't always about blind devotion," said Actë.

"No, it's not. But it *is* about belonging to another person completely, unconditionally, utterly. My whole life has been about smoothing the journey of Nero's life," said Epaphroditus. "Softening every blow, salving every hurt. There are so few of us. In his journey, we're the cushions in the litter. We soften the bumps in the road. We have helped him to live as beautifully as he could, despite the flaws we all know about. And now, there comes that time when we must help him to die beautifully, too."

I thought, he has found the good even in slavery, which is the darkness at the heart of this luminous civilization; it is the structure that sustains the edifice.

I did not believe any of it. Philosophers turn black to white, and evil to good, all the time, with this nonsense they call logic.

I asked Epaphroditus how we could help Himself to die when dying was probably furthest from his mind.

"We have to ease him into it," he said.

Actë added, "We might even have to do the thing which must not be thought."

Which was, of course, the thing *everyone* in an Imperial court contemplates.

Believe me, for I have lived in four of them and even reigned, after a fashion, in some.

***

In the night, the God made perfunctory attempts to penetrate his Queen. Himself did not succeed and presently he fell into a kind of slumber, twisting, turning, muttering imprecations in his sleep. I could not sleep at all, my mind racing about all the treason whirling around the Imperial court … including, in a sense, my own.

A few hours before sunrise Himself sat up abruptly, startling me awake as well. "I have to talk to her in person," he mumbled. He sprang from the bed. Slaves emerged from the shadows bearing lamps and clothes. Hylas was in the background rubbing his eyes.

"You have to talk to who?" I said.

"Are you coming?" said the Divinitas.

"Who?" I said, still mentally exhausted from today's revelations.

"Mother, of course," said Nero. "She'll know what to do."

It would have been tactless to point out that the Divinitas had long ago disposed of his mother, so I just told Hylas to go and talk to those standing guard outside the chamber. "Just tell them Himself is going somewhere. Urgently. They'll know what to do."

They did. In the half-dark of the antechamber, a litter was readied, as well as a small guard — nothing ostentatious, just for protection — and Nero paused only for a modicum of makeup, just a simple coating of ghostly white to the face, a touch of kohl for the eyes, a paste of powdered gold for the lips; and he wore only a simple tunica, though as befit his rank it was completely dipped in purple, worth a half-year's wages of a centurion, I guessed. Oh, and a gold tiara in the shape of a laurel wreath, to remind us all that he was the world's universal artist.

All this was prepared with the swiftness of slaves who have no life other than the will of their lord … and the urgency of knowing their lord might not be long for this world.

Meanwhile, it was Hylas who was taking charge, unnoticed, whispering to the guards the names of whom to summon, who needed to be in attendance. But as no one knew where we were going, I was not sure that he was doing anything useful.

"Watch Hercules," I told him. "Get them to bring him something nice."

"Peacock's brain?"

"A whole peacock."

I was wondering how Nero planned to have any kind of conversation with his mother — even setting aside the fact that she was dead. If he could talk to the dead, would she even want to talk to him … her own murderer?

In the litter, he did explain where we were going. The litter-bearers, not wanting to appear not to have divined Himself's will, were moving slowly, in order to give the impression they knew where we were going.

I was alone with the God in the litter.

"Tell them to hurry," he said to me. The bearers' footsteps were echoey, and our pathway was sloping downwards. We must be in a tunnel, one of the secret pathways away from the palace.

"Their minds are not as all-seeing as yours, Divinitas," I said. "Let's give them a clue, at least."

"You're being cunning again, my pet," said the Emperor. "Where do *you* think I'll be able to talk to my mother?"

"My first thought would have been the Temple of Capitoline Jove," I said, "since all the Divine Julio-Claudians are with Jupiter now, feasting on ambrosia and on nectar poured by none other than Ganymede …"

"The only creature in Heaven and Earth who *might* be more beautiful than you," Nero said. "But I hear a *but* coming."

"The Senate hasn't declared Agrippina a goddess," I said.

"Strange, isn't it! That a congregation of senile buffoons has the power to confer a seat on Mt. Olympus, when they can't even organize my piss tax properly."

"So she doesn't have a temple of her own, either, unlike the Divine Augustus," I said. "But gods live in temples, and gods have wives …"

"Uncle Claudius! You *are* clever," said the Emperor.

"The Divine Claudius," I said. "Your Uncle Claudius … he *has* been deified. She might have gone to be with him."

It was dark in the litter; there was just the one lamp lit, and it was sputtering, as the slaves had not had time to refill all the lamps before morning. Yet I could see Himself smile. He liked the fact that I was clever.

"There's more to you than meets the eye," he said. And he ran a finger lightly across my cheek.

The litter was moving more purposefully now, as I made sure to speak loudly enough for them to overhear. The pace picked up. The bearers were moving at a trot. We had emerged from the tunnel, but I did not dare peer through the litter drape. I could hear the clank of horse-drawn carts, so I knew it was not yet dawn.

The litter moved more swiftly now.

Familiar smells of the eleventh hour of night: bread baking, sausages and fish being grilled in the open waiting to serve thousands of breakfasts for people on their way to the Forum or the baths. The litter-bearers were moving so quickly now that the smells and sounds were blending into chaos. I could hear our guards quirting people out of the way.

And now we were moving steeply uphill. The Caelian Hill, I knew. You could see it from the private garden of the chamber I shared with the God. The litter angled upward. I heard the trickle of water on marble. I slipped back into Nero's arms. Then the litter righted itself, and stopped. We stepped out. Gazing across the city I could see the sunrise, and the secret garden

We stood in an open space, with trees, columns on three sides, and, where the Caelian rose, a marble wall with a complex web of fountains and waterfalls and statues of nymphs, some spewing water from their lips, others catching it in their hands or outstretched arms; water channels crisscrossed the floor.

"Look," said the Emperor. He pointed across the valley and all the way up to where if I squinted, we could make out the wall around our private garden, angling out from the hillside. I imagined beyond the wall Hercules skulking among the herms and flowers. "It's us," said Nero.

"Actually, we're down here," I said.

"No, we're not. I mean, yes, but up there … that's the *idea* of us, you see. This great and sprawling empire, and at the summit, it's us, you see. There we stand, the poet-emperor-god, in an eternal embrace with his beautiful boy-girl-wife."

Sunrise in my eyes; I squeezed them shut. Very suddenly, a tear came. "I'm losing you," I said softly.

"You won't lose me."

"Your mother did," I said, and immediately regretted it.

"You're not my mother," he said. Decades of rage concealed in his soft utterance.

Then came a voice from within, thundering with authority, "But *I* am."

XXII

THE PRIESTESS OF CLAUDIUS

A priestess stood in front of the waterfall. She looked to be the type that had been dedicated to the gods since childhood, and had known no other life until now. She was wrinkled, shrunken, wrapped in a cloth covered with ancient bloodstains. She was wet, too, having burst through the curtain of water.

"Lucius," she shrieked, "Lucius, Lucius, you've come looking for me at last."

Nero made to follow her into the gushing water. I held him back. "Be careful, Lucius," I said. "She isn't really Agrippina."

"But she is. I'd know her voice anywhere."

Two acolytes in white tunicae emerged and dragged her back behind the waterfall, and in her place stood a priest. Imposing, with a white beard, every inch what one imagines a representative of the gods to look like.

"Divinity," said the priest, "Agrippina's shade appears to have possessed one of our priestesses. You may speak to her, but it is also possible that what possesses her is just some kind of madness."

We could still her shrieks from behind the rushing of the waterfall.

"It's the gods who send madness," said Nero, "as Euripides tells us ... *I've driven them from their wits, and from their homes* ... that's what the God Bacchus did."

"And in the same play, the prophet also says, *There is no cure for madness. The cure itself is madness,"* said the priest.

"I see you know the classics," said my husband.

"Priests are not uneducated," said the representative of the God Claudius. "When your uncle lived in the world, he loved knowledge. He wrote histories of the Etruscans, and studied the past with great attention."

"Perhaps not Euripides," said Nero.

"No," said the priest. "That would be my personal passion. It was with great interest that I followed the news of your victory in Greece. I must admire you, Divinitas, for your victory, against all odds, in the wrong year."

"And at such sacrifice," said Nero.

"I'm sure he suffered greatly," said the priest, making Himself realize that he knew exactly what had happened with Nero's rival Paris.

"I atone every day," Himself said. "I torment myself through the night. I weep tears of blood."

"Perhaps not quite enough," said the priest.

"How so?"

"There are many kinds of sacrifice, but in general, Divinitas, they are concerned with avoidance — you send an envoy to the land of death — a pigeon, a goat, a snow-white bull — one rarely sends oneself."

"You mean I need to sacrifice myself? How then should I return with an answer?"

"Ah, yes," the priest said, "a paradox."

"Lucius," I said, "I don't think he means it literally."

"I think he does," said the Emperor. "He wants me to be like the god of the Chrestianoi, you see. Redeeming the world by sacrificing himself."

"I didn't know," I said, "that you knew anything about their philosophy."

"Oh, Epaphroditus keeps me informed. If you're going to execute a few thousand people, you should study them a bit." He turned to the priest. "A drop of blood," he said, "and I speak to my mother for one hour."

"A single drop?"

"It's the blood of a god," I said quickly. "And you don't know how squeamish he is. I'll have to prick him myself."

"A quarter of an hour, then."

The priest bade the Divinitas step through the waterfall, and put out an arm to block my path. But the Emperor said, "No, no, the Empress never leaves my side. And she needs to take my blood."

The water rushed only for a minute. We were through and in some kind of cave. A few torches flickered in brackets in the rock, but you could hardly see through thickets of frankincense.

The Divine Claudius, in effigy, loomed above us, rising from a little dais in the center of the cave. I had heard him called a stuttering fool, but as a god, he was imposing. There was an altar, and a brazier with more incense. On the altar the old woman writhed. "Lucius!" she shrieked. "Don't you miss me?"

Then, after a frightening spasm, she collapsed upon the altar, spent, whimpering.

"The blood," the priest said.

I led my master by the hand to where the priestess lay. I unhooked the fibula that held my garment in place. It had a dolphin design, for it came all the way from Britannia.

I stood naked next to my God. I took his hand and stabbed the fibula into the fleshiest part of his palm. He yelped in a most ungodlike manner, and I touched the bleeding spot to the priestess's forehead. She twitched, then was still.

"Just like Uncle Claudius, this entire operation," Nero said. "He wasn't a real Emperor, just an idiot in purple robes."

The priestess sat up. "You silly boy!" she spat. Himself was so taken aback he did not answer, but snatched away his hand and stepped back. "Claudius was no fool. But *you* are!"

From a few paces' distance, I watched the woman transform. It seemed she could control her very cheek muscles. Her face was quivering and re-forming. She was becoming another person entirely, and Himself, the Dominus of the Cosmos, was quaking.

"Don't say I'm a fool," he murmured.

"I gave you the throne," she said, "and you had me killed."

"Killed? You're right here!" said Nero.

"And *you,* child, are right here," she hissed, pointing to her own womb. "You want to see the place that engendered such a monster as yourself?"

With that she threw herself back on the altar and launched into a terrifying parody of childbirth. She tore at her garments. Her dugs slapped against withered flesh. She whimpered and shrieked and clawed the air. Himself watched in awe, completely convinced. He stood beside her, held her hand, whimpered in tandem with the priestess. It would have been comical were it not so terrifying.

"You're tearing me apart!" she screamed. "I'm birthing a god!"

"Mama!" he cried — and it looked as though he were trying to crawl inside her. I could not look away. He had utterly infantilized himself while his surrogate mother flailed at the air. Clouds of incense billowed. I was choking. I turned away, retching.

When I looked up again, he had wrapped his arms about her and appeared to be attempting to suckle.

"There, there," the priestess said. "Perhaps you *have* killed me, but there's still enough of me left for you to love."

"Are you waiting for me?" he said.

"What else is there to do here?" she said. "You didn't have me made a god, and now it's too late."

"I can command the Senate."

"You can't even command your wife."

"Poppaea!" He reached behind his back, clawing the air until I went to hold his hand. Then he pulled me into the bone-chilling embrace of the old woman. "Poppaea," he said, "you'll tell the Senate. You'll still have influence. Nymphidius will protect you."

It was likelier that Nymphidius would rape me to death, I thought. But I only said, "Yes, Lucius. I'll tell the Senate."

"And me, too. Don't forget me. I have to be a god. Otherwise … they pursue you." He stared wildly about, seeing creatures no one else could see. "To the ends of the earth, to the edge of death."

"Who chases you, Lucius?" I said.

He cringed. He clung to the simulacrum of his mother. I realized that he was being tormented by those who drive matricides mad, the Furies.

"They're not here. How could they be? I didn't kill … her. Look. She's still here."

"There, there," the priestess said. "I'm here. But you have to go."

"My Empress will make you a goddess. I promise."

"You too, my dearest," I said, and kissed him on lips that tasted of vomit.

"You'll make sure I can be with Uncle Claudius?"

"Yes," I said.

"I'm not mad," said Nero. "I know you're not Poppaea. I killed Poppaea. I killed my mother. The Furies are standing all around me and I smell their rancid breath. No, you're not my wife. You're not my mother. You are all phantoms."

More incense thickened the close air. I watched the master of the world weeping in the arms of the priestess. I watched and felt nothing.

And as he wept, I too felt drawn into a vision of my own. The cave, it seemed, grew larger, darker, the flickers of light fewer and farther between, until it seemed I stood in a place I recognized from other dreams I had had … I was in the underworld again. I knew I was there, because I could feel the shade of my dead friend Hyacinth, and he was speaking to me in the language of our childhood.

"He thinks he's going to fly up, up, up to the height of high Olympus," he said in an eerie singsong. It was a sound I dimly remembered from childhood, some shaman intoning against the background of the sea. "He's not going to fly fly, fly. He's going to fall, fall, fall. But he will still rule."

And then I saw what I'd already seen in other visions. The throne of the king of the dead, and on that throne Nero, his eyes piercing me with a savage cold light.

"Go to him," Hyacinth said. "You don't have a choice. No man conquers death."

Hyacinth's chanting rose in pitch until it became am wordless keening. Dead youths were dressing me in black robes.

The King of Death spoke to me. "Persephone," he said.

I walked slowly towards him. More dead souls were gathering, strewing my way with wilted flowers. The Lord of the Dead gazed upon me with eyes of infinite sadness, yet I saw no tears. The dead do not weep.

"Lucius," I said softly. The vision faded and I saw that the living *do* weep.

When the Emperor had wept until he was spent, he sat up slowly, gathering his wits. He looked from side to side, and it seemed that his apparitions of the Furies were fading.

He looked at me, too, and whispered, "Persephone."

I thought of the ill-omened intaglio I had given him in Greece.

In Greece we had both had a vision in the temple, but we had not shared the same vision.

But I knew that this time he had seen me in the land of death. As queen.

So I was not his plaything, but Death herself, Death who comes to all, like a mother, like a lover. I smiled a little, hoping to give some comfort. But the Emperor was past consoling.

And presently they came to take Himself to the place that had been chosen for his suicide.

XXIII

A PLACE TO DIE

We had arrived in Rome in a triumphal convoy, fresh from Himself's great victory in Greece. We departed in the back of an oxcart, in secrecy. The sun was still rising, but we only had moments to leave the city, because of the ban on animal-drawn vehicles during the daylight hours. Hylas was driving, since there was no one of lowlier status with us to do anything menial.

We left through the Esquiline Gate, the nearest, erected by the God Claudius himself, as Nero told me, in a murmur, peering from an opening in the canvas cover of the cart.

"Why can't they just send a professional?" Nero said, shaking his head. "A gladiator. Someone to do it quickly and painlessly. Decapitation's almost instant. I could hardly cut off my own head."

He seemed almost flippant about our world tumbling down around us. He was cheerful, even, especially after days of moodiness and the big shouting match with the priestess-mother surrogate.

Epaphroditus, leaning over from the passenger seat, drew

back the drape and said, "My Lord, it's customary to do this one yourself."

"It *is* called *suicide,* I suppose," the Emperor said meekly.

"Where are we going?" I asked Epaphroditus.

"There's a place prepared," he said. "It is only a few miles beyond the walls, but it is safe. It belongs to Phaon, one of the Emperor's freedmen and a loyal client. No one will intrude."

By that, I was sure he meant that the Praetorians were already aware that the Emperor would finish the final chapter there. I was sure that, eventually, they would intrude, after allowing a decent interval to perform the act. We had at most a few days.

The road was crowded. "Can't you make them go faster?" I said to Hylas.

"They're oxen, domine," he said.

They were intolerably sluggish, and more so as we turned at the first milestone to the north, moving bumpily through mud and stones. It took almost until midday to reach Phaon's villa, though it was a mere four miles from from the city gates. Even though there was no one around us, we did not lower the awning, or there would have been no shade.

"It's only June," Nero said, "and it's already sticky. Let's get it over with. I shall be glad to have managed to miss the stench of summer sweat in the city."

There was an olive grove where a little Cupid was set up for lovers to worship at. A pair of dead doves lay entwined on the altar, and behind the shrine we found a paved path at last, though somewhat overgrown with weeds.

The villa itself was nothing much. A statue of the Emperor stood in the entrance hall. There were no lares or penates, because, as a freedman, Phaon didn't really have proper ancestors as such. In Rome, only Romans count.

Like all villas, this one had an atrium, a portico, and side rooms. Epaphroditus led us to a chamber with no windows. The wall was painted with a sylvan mural, so we did not feel hemmed in. The mural was new, and over-bright; things in the chamber did not belong together; mismatched vases, a tapestry the wrong color and so on; Phaon's taste would not have pleased my late patronus.

***

This Phaon had come ahead, and was there to greet us along with another freedman named Neophytus. They were hard to tell apart, except that Neophytus did not speak.

Phaon greeted the Emperor at the doorway, prostrating himself. "The Senate's gone and done it," he said. He did not dare meet Nero's gaze but spoke to me instead. "The Divinitas has been pronounced Damnatio Memoriae. His name is to be erased from every monument, every inscription; his statues to be taken down; his effigy no longer stamped on legitimate Roman coinage."

"We are not to be gods, then?" Nero said to me.

"There was no such sentence passed on the Empress," Phaon said. "The Senate thinks the Lady Poppaea Sabina may yet have a role to play." He said this without apparent irony, even knowing who I really was. We inhabited an imaginary universe, after all. A man was a God and a boy was an Empress.

We half carried, half dragged the Emperor to a couch that had known better days; the rose-leaf stuffing was leaking from a torn corner. A girl brought the Divinitas a kylix of wine. The Emperor sniffed and rejected it with a baleful glare. The slave scurried away.

"No wine. I want to face this moment with utter clarity," he said. "What an artist dies in me! I want a final death-song that will rank with the last words of the most beautiful heroes of antiquity."

"My Lord," Epaphroditus said, "don't do Niobe again. That was ill-omened."

"Niobe lost her children," said Nero. "But today, my children are losing *me.*"

"Hylas," I said, "bring water." I dismissed the other hangers-on; Nero only wanted to have people around him he knew, people he believed loyal. Some would have called us sycophants. Yet I think everyone in the room truly loved Nero, on some level.

I am sure of it because of what happened in this room.

***

At first it was as if nothing at all was going on. The Divine Nero sipped water from a glass krater. We waited. It seemed that the air itself thickened, began to weigh down on us.

Epaphroditus finally started to say something, but the Emperor held up his hand. "I'm writing a new song," he said quietly.

We waited. And after a few more sips of water, he began to sing, without lyre or other instrument, in a dulcet falsetto.

We stand on the stairway that leads to the gates of Olympus, he sang, then stopped. And again he started: *We stand on the steps* … and stopped again. There were tears in his eyes.

"They love me," he said softly. "The people love me. I just have to show myself."

"The Senate doesn't," said Epaphroditus. "The army doesn't."

"Is there any pain?" said the Emperor.

"Not if you do it quickly," Epaphroditus said, though I sensed he was lying.

"And Actë, Actë … why isn't she here?"

"She is on her way, Divinitas," Phaon said, without much conviction.

"Oh, look," said Nero, pointing at the mural, "an enchanted forest. Such awful taste you have, Phaon."

"We can't all be Petronius Arbiter," Phaon said.

We stand on the stairway that leads to Olympus, the Emperor sang again, changing the words a little to improve the scansion. Each line ended with an elegantly ornamented melisma. We listened to him for a few moments, and he abruptly stopped.

"The Muse is reticent today," he said. "Are we surprised?"

He sat, fidgeting, called for more wine. Finally he said, "I don't have a song in me, Poppaea."

"Maybe you don't have to sing it aloud," I said softly. "Maybe you can just think it."

"And you'll hear it on the wind, my darling," he said.

"I'll hear it on the wind."

"On the wind."

"Like a mountain wind —"

"As it swoops down upon an oak tree —"

"Love shook my heart," I said.

Ah, Sappho! Centuries-old words I once heard on the lips of Petronius, who owned me, yet never treated me like a *thing*. I had been Petronius's muse, but I was not Nero's.

"Thank you for reminding me," Nero said, "that while I tower above you all, while I am your sheltering sky, your Divinitas, there is a high Divinitas that I must look to."

As expected, we all protested that no, we believed in no higher power than Nero Claudius Caesar Augustus Germanicus; he was our only world; he was our protector, the love of our lives. We said this, repeatedly and with a desperate desire to have him believe us, knowing full well that

Epaphroditus had been in communication with those who planned the Emperor's downfall.

"It's fine," he went on. "Do not weep for me. I will await you in my Imperial palace in the sky." I did not remind him that he would not be in Olympus unless the Senate were to enact his deification. Rome has created so pervasive a bureaucracy that it encompasses the very gods. "But," he went on, and he pulled me down to his lap, and covered my face with soft kisses, "I want *you* to do it. These people around me … perhaps they'll feast on my corpse as soon as I'm gone. *You* won't. You are my one true wife. You will reign with me on Olympus."

"You want me to …"

"Give him a sword," said Himself, waving at slaves who were not there.

"No, Lucius," I whispered. "Come on, I don't know swords. I was trained as a delicatus, not a gladiator."

"You'll do as I tell you!" he said with abrupt harshness. I recoiled. Not missing a beat, he continued, with infinite tenderness, "Because you are the only one who really loves me."

"Your mother…"

"I killed her! I killed Poppaea! I killed them all! Now … you, Sporus, you … kill me. I order it."

Phaon held up a monstrous gladius; I would not have even had the strength to lift it, let alone wield it. I shook my head. Presently it was Hylas who thrust a dagger into my hand. It was almost a toy, with a jewelled pommel and a phallus incised upon the hilt, perhaps something you'd play with at the lupanar.

"My beautiful boy-wife," said the Emperor, "make love with me one last time."

I held the poignard in my left hand, and with my right I stroked Nero's cheek. He had not had time for his morning attentions. I touched stubble, mingled with tears. I kissed him. He pulled at the fibula that held my clothes together and they slid to the floor. He drew me towards him. "I belong to you," he whispered. "You have my leave to penetrate me." The ultimate abasement of a Roman, something never to be done in front of others, not even freedman.

"You know I can't anymore," I said.

He unfastened his own robes. I sat in his lap, my cheeks against his cheeks. He was entirely flaccid, stripped of manhood. As *I* had been since before we went to Greece. "I can't," I repeated again.

He guided my left hand so that the point of the blade touched his lower abdomen. "Yes, you can. See? A God can do anything. I took away your manhood. Now, in my last moments in this earth, I've made you hard again."

"My Lord —"

Was this delusion? Did he *know* he was weaving a fabric of fantasy, or had he already entered the unreal world? "Push into me, my love," said Nero.

"I don't want to hurt you, Lucius," I said.

"Oh, so considerate!" he said. "But you can't hurt me anymore."

He hugged me savagely to him, forcing the dagger in deeper. He moaned. And I too moaned, not in desire but in sheer terror. He squeezed me again and again, each time crying out, and then there came a moment when the illusion must have been shattered, he was screaming in pain now, and I was trying to disentangle myself but the dagger sank deeper, blood was spurting now, gushing on to my hands and chest, and still he clung to me as I slipped and slid on the slick blood.

Suddenly I felt rough hands seizing my shoulders.

"You stupid boy! Can't you get anything right?" It was Nymphidius Sabinus. He pushed me to one side. He sliced into the Emperor's chest with a single stroke of his sword. The God slumped to the floor. Epaphroditus and the others were babbling, screaming.

I stood there, naked and bloody, shivering though the room was intolerably hot.

More Praetorians entered the chamber now. Nero's freedmen prostrated themselves, expecting to be killed. Nymphidius told them to be silent. The Praetorians lifted up the dead God and placed him on the couch. Others cleaned the blood.

I still stood there, numb. I was not thinking that my world had ended, that I had lost everything I had so recently gained. As I gazed on the face of the man who had once owned my mind and my body, I did not even feel relief.

Nymphidius gave one of his soldiers a brief nod. That man decapitated Phaon and Neophytus in quick succession.

"Enough," Nymphidius said. "Nero's secretary may prove useful. He'll have access to all the records. Can't run an empire without a creature like him."

We heard Hylas whimpering in a corner.

"A pretty slave," Nymphidius said. "Give him to the centurions."

"I'm free," said Hylas softly.

"No one is truly free," Nymphidius said.

"You know your Euripides," I said.

"Ah! The Empress deigns to speak!" said Nymphidius. "You know, I'm not a barbarian, though you snubbed me at every turn."

"Hylas was my slave," I said. "I freed him. The appropriate documents have been properly drawn up."

"And if I were to say that the documents have been … mislaid?" Nymphidius said. "Would you vouch for his freedom?

"I would."

"At what price?"

Nymphidius looked at me. I was naked, soaked in blood. I do not know how I summoned up any semblance of dignity, but somehow, I managed it.

"What you can take," I said, "take. You will not take my soul." I stared him down. Nymphidius wanted me in that very moment. I saw it in his eyes. Yet he stopped short of helping himself to the spoils of usurpation.

"I am impressed," he said. "An Empress's virtue, for the life of a slave. I would have been happy to pay far more, you know."

"Do you mean to take the throne?" I said.

"Tigellinus is off to battle Vindex. I'm the only leader of the Praetorians in Rome, and you know that it's the army who chooses the Emperor."

"Isn't General Galba marching on Rome? Could Vindex not cross the Rubicon too? How long do you think you could hold power for?"

"I have you," he said. Then, to Hylas: "You! Slave or ex-slave, whatever … take the Empress to the bath. Make sure she is cleaned up, and clothe her in whatever finery this sorry household may possess." Then to one of his men he said, "Ride to Rome and kidnap the High Priest from the Temple of Jupiter Optimus Maximus. Get these bodies disposed of, and have the slaves decorate this villa for a nuptials."

It seemed that I was going to remain Empress for a little while longer.

XXIV

IMPERATRIX REDDUX

N*ymphidius,* you say. *What do you mean, Nymphidius? There's no Nymphidius among the ones who seized imperium this year.*

How do you even remember all their names?

Galba. Galba was next.

I barely knew Galba. A great general, I've heard. I saw him. He barely glanced at me, And he had no animosity toward me. Didn't waste a single thought on me, unlike Nymphidius.

Nymphidius had always been obsessed with me, as I've told you before. I had haunted Nymphidius's dreams, and I did not even know it.

And now, ripped from Nero's fatal embrace, my Emperor barely cold, I was to be married again … to this same Nymphidius.

***

My toilette was cursory. I lay in the bath for barely an hour, with Hylas my only attendant, for Phaon's household was being rounded up and catalogued for auction. Indeed, the water was lukewarm, because there were no slaves in the basement to keep the fires going. I was shivering. Phaon had a full-service private bath, but the frigidarium and the caldarium were the same temperature … tepid.

As I lay in the water I tried to empty my mind. So much hatred, bloodshed, so many plots and counterplots! If the water had been warmer, at least … unable to think, I rose abruptly and went to a lectus where Hylas anointed me with perfumed olive oil, and tenderly scraped my soft skin with a strigil. This was better than the water, Hylas understood every inch of my body as well as his own. If I still had my manhood, his ministrations would surely have aroused me. And yet …

Even unmanned, a felt an echo of the man I could have been, a silky warmth spreading outward from my loins. I did not feel desire, but I did feel Hylas's unquestioning love. That is what I told myself, yet in spite of what I had become, I did feel a twinge, an unexpected stirring. Hylas giggled.

"You didn't lose it *all,* domine," he said.

"I'm not your master," I said.

"If you ever weren't," he said, "I'd die."

"Well," I said, "at least you've mastered the Latin subjunctive." I felt cold for desire to linger. Seeing me shiver, Hylas rubbed the oil harder, then brought a woolen to cover me. I sat up and let Hylas apply some perfunctory makeup; a little lead paint, some kohl for my eyes, a touch of crimson for my lips; I looked like a statue of Venus that has been in the sun too long.

Presently, some very timid slaves came in to dress me, their eyes downcast. They may have been told they could be crucified at any moment. From elsewhere in the house, I could hear unmistakable sounds of people being killed, and the tramp of soldiers' caligae.

Still, these attendants had skills. I do not know if Phaon had a wife; but there were plenty of serviceable women's clothes in the home. They were not the softest, and there wasn't any silk, but there was a stola of linen and a woollen palla edged with some kind of fur. They found me some gold bracelets and a necklace of baroque pearls.

"Your mistress's?" I asked them. They did not respond.

Hylas said, "They told me she hasn't been seen in days, domine."

One of the girls whispered, "She went to her relatives in Gaul."

They held up a mirror. I was hardly the image of an Empress, but then this wedding was going to be a joke as well.

I was right. There were several high-ranking priests present, and a few doves were sacrificed, a few words were said, and I repeated, for the second time in my short life, the magic formula that made me Nymphidius's wife, *Ubi tu Gaius, ibi ego Gaia…*

There was no feast. Nymphidius scooped me up and carried me to the cubiculum. He threw me down on the cubile and began to rip off my tawdry wedding garments. When I struggled, he slapped my face, left and right. I bit my tongue.

"Nymphidius," I said, "I've been a slave. I know how to be raped."

Not to utter a word. Not to cry out for fear of exacerbating the violence. To become nothing. To be no one. To become one with the furniture.

"Whore," Nymphidius said.

My tunica tore in his hand.

"I've watched you for so long. Even when you were nothing, you looked down on me. And when you became Nero's, you made me feel worthless as a dog. You, and everyone else. It's always Tigellinus this, Tigellinus that! Tigellinus, handsomer, crueler, more ruthless, more vicious. I'm the second most powerful man in the Empire, and you didn't offer me one scrawny buttock. That is going to change now. You may think I need you to make my rule legitimate. And yes! Your false pedigree is going to hand me my throne. It doesn't mean you're not my wretched little strumpet."

He shoved me hard, keeping me pinned. He bore down on me, ready to penetrate. I tensed. I tried to be far away. He can't have my soul, I told myself.

"Tomorrow morning I will march into the senate with you by my side," he said. "They won't laugh at me anymore."

With one hand he pushed my face down into the cushions. At least I wouldn't have to look at him. I squeezed my eyes shut. Images of being "broken in" on the pirate ship rushed unbidden to the surface of my memory. *I'm not going to scream,* I told myself over and over. I felt Nymphidius lower himself onto me, the hairs on his chest slick against my back, reeking of sweat and perfume. I tensed. I could feel him rear up now, could feel him probing me, getting ready to thrust.

"You love this," he whispered.

I did not speak and slapped me again. He probably wanted me to whimper. I would not give him any satisfaction.

"Poppaea! Sporus!" he cried out. "Poppaea! Sporus! My Empress! My slave!" Crudely, cruelly, knowing he could as much pain as he wanted to, he began to push himself into me.

I'm not going to scream, I told myself again.

Then I heard footsteps. I heard the swish of metal slicing through the air. Blood drenched the back of my head, ran all over me. I screamed at last, a scream of sheer terror and desolation.

Then I wrenched my face away from the cubile and saw Nymphidius's leering head, a knuckle's breadth away from my face. Blood was gushing from the severed neck. The rest of him had rolled onto the mosaic stones.

I went on screaming now, unbottling all the terror I had shoved deep down into my psyche for years and years. I sat up.

Praetorians stood around me, not staring, not caring. One was sheathing his sword.

For the second time that day, I was naked and bloody, in front of indifferent strangers.

Then a man in a toga entered the room. The soldiers all saluted him. One of them took away the head, and sat me up straight. The blood was sticky on my face, my arms, my back and chest.

"Thank the Gods you're alive," said the man. "I've pined for you every moment that I was in Lusitania."

I did not recognize him at first. But I knew who he was.

"Am I *your* Empress now?" I asked softly. It seemed an unlikely destiny for this man, whom I had known to be completely under his wife's thumb, and whom Nero had treated more or less like a human carpet.

"No, no," said Marcus Salvius Otho, first husband of Poppaea, the man who enjoyed women so little that he once needed me in his bed in order to satisfy his wife, the most beautiful woman in the Empire. "Get dressed. We'll travel together."

"Are we going back to the Senate? Are *you* going to claim the throne?"

"Not at all," he said. "We'll take Nero's body back and have him properly taken care of. After that, we are riding north, to meet General Galba on his way to the city and to make sure we are seen to be his allies. We have to make sure we are not on any proscription list."

"General Galba?"

"Yes. The army has declared him the new Emperor."

XXV

OTHO

Leave Nero here," Otho said as we prepared to leave. For while I had had a wedding on the grounds of this villa, and had almost been raped in the main cubiculum, there was still a room that held the bodies of Nero, his two freedmen, and assorted slaves whom the Praetorians had seen fit to slay. Their bodies were piled up around the late God's, as though the Emperor were holding court to an entourage of corpses.

"Shouldn't we take him back to Rome, offer him up for a proper funeral?" I said.

"Why? He was the most hated man in the world. People will think we are of the Nero faction, and we'll be Circus-fodder."

Otho told us to leave the dead Emperor right where he had died. We had all been instructed not to mention that he had not *exactly* committed suicide. Murdering an Emperor was a crime, after all, no matter how well-intentioned. Suicide was a matter of dignity, of being truly Roman.

"I still don't understand why we can't take the body back," I said to Otho.

"It seems Nymphidius didn't tell you everything," he said. "The reason the damnatio was enacted was that Nymphidius informed the Senate that the Emperor was in flight, on his way to Egypt."

"So they think he's still alive?"

"Yes. As soon as they pronounced the damnatio, the news

arrived that General Galba had defeated the traitor Vindex in battle. Nymphidius thought *he'd* be declared Emperor, but as soon as the Senate heard that Galba had the army, they made *him* Emperor, and he's on his way to Rome now. With several legions to back him up. No one minds marching on Rome any more, not since Julius Caesar crossed the Rubicon. But Galba is still days away, and Nymphidius assumed that with *you* on his arm, he could assume the principate before Galba arrived."

"But I'm on *your* arm now," I said.

"Yes, you are, my darling," he said. "I've dreamed of this day ever since Nero took you from me." I did not remind him that it was Poppaea the Divinitas took, not Petronius's little slave, and that Poppaea did not exactly resist abduction.

"And why don't *you* want to be Emperor?" I asked him.

"You know what I'm like," Otho said, and I truly felt sorry for him; he took me in his arms, blood and all, and kissed me. It was not unwelcome, because Otho was one of the few people with whom I possessed the upper hand. He loved me, or rather, he loved Poppaea, and she spoke to him, in a sense, through me. I kissed him back. We were both covered in blood now, and it was at that moment that Actë arrived, too late for the tragic trilogy. At least she caught the comedic satyr-play that was the dénouement of Nero's so-called suicide.

She rushed into the room and flung herself on Nero's body. She was weeping loudly, making something of a display of extravagant grief, crying out "Lucius, Lucius," beating her breast. This was not like her.

"Actë, you're too late," Otho said. "And if you carry on so, your life may be in danger."

"What does my life matter?"

"No one wants to be associated with a hated despot," Otho said.

Epaphroditus was hovering. Perhaps he was still in a state of shock at not having been summarily executed.

"Take care of her," I said to him.

"Yes, Divinitas," he said.

***

At first Otho wanted me to follow him on horseback, but that was I skill I had never learned. So once again I found myself clambering into a covered cart, with only Hylas for company; Otho rode in front, and a handful of Praetorians, and we set off down the pathway, away from the house, where the God of Rome was being mourned by a concubine, a freedman, and some dead slaves.

We had barely reached the gates of Phaon's estate when we heard people shouting. Beyond the portal a mob was forming. I could hear murmurs, curses. At first I could not make out what they were saying, but it sounded ominous.

"What's going on?" I said. Hylas, peering through the drapery, said, "They're not letting us through, domino. They're throwing vegetables at the Praetorians."

The crowd were chanting Nero's name. "Where's Nero? Where's Nero?" They were shouting, "We want our Emperor!"

Otho rode up to the cart and said, "We'll need to get back inside. I'll have the guards clear the mob first."

"I thought you said he was the most hated man in the world," I said.

"He was," Otho said. "Everyone says so."

"That means you've never listened to the mob. If you had, you would have known that the people loved him."

"But he killed people! He was a sexual monster — look what he did to you! He killed the perfectly innocuous Chrestianoi! He even taxed our piss!"

It wasn't just vegetables. I heard rocks clattering against the walls of the estate.

"You said everyone hated Nero," I said, "but you were wrong. Only the Senate hated him. And in Rome, it's the mob that counts."

Otho did not appear to know what to do, even though he had arrived on the scene of Nero's suicide, and had already overseen the execution of a potential usurper. Or at least, had not forbidden the Praetorians to dispose of Nymphidius. But he wasn't really running things. I realized that someone had to make decisions, and that Otho was, now as much as before, a ditherer.

"Hylas," I said, "straighten my robes and fix my makeup. I need to look like Nero's Empress." Hylas brushed me down and refastened my fibula. I got down from the cart.

Otho said, "Oh, no, Poppaea dearest. We need to keep you safe. You are precious. The most precious thing in the world."

"The mob may want to throw rocks at you all the way to the gates of the city," I said. "But they're not going to stone their Empress."

Otho started to protest, but I said only, "Uncover the cart. I am going to play the role Nero gave me."

"They'll kill you!" Otho said.

"And bring the Emperor."

Some of the soldiers pulled down the awning and someone ran back to the house and returned with a sedile. I got back on and sat enthroned. Hylas sat at my feet. I wasn't Cleopatra on her golden barge, but I needed to carry myself like a Queen. Presently a few slaves came with the the body of Nero, along with Actë and Epaphroditus. Actë continued her ostentatious grieving while Epaphroditus walked with head bowed; I could not tell what thoughts he was having, though I guessed he was most concerned with survival.

We formed a new convoy now,

"Now lead the way," I told Poppaea's ex-husband.

Feeling far more trepidation than I let on, I waved imperiously at the guards. They opened the gates. I saw the crowd, heard jeers and catcalls and demands for the Emperor to appear.

But when I stood up, with the body of my husband decked in Imperial purple in front of me, those who saw fell silent. The silence rippled down the road; I could see people standing, as far as the eye could see, but slowly the crowd was parting, moving to either side of the Appian Way.

A single cry: "Long live the Empress Poppaea Augusta Sabina!"

There came an echo, then another, and another.

And then it seemed the whole crowd erupted.

In that moment, I held more power than anyone in the entire world.

XXVI

THE HOUSE OF PETRONIUS

But I knew it was not to be for long.

All the way to the city, it was as though I had been awarded a triumph. When we passed through the gates, the streets narrowed. Crowds crammed the side of the street, pressed into doorways, peering from upper stories and rooftops. The Praetorians, the only military allowed to set foot in the city without Senatorial permission, preceded and followed my cart.

I could not help noting that they were cheering for me, and for Nero, but not for Otho, who turned to left and right and made acknowledging gestures in spite of this.

As we moved towards the Forum and the Curia Julia, the atmosphere changed. Cheering was sporadic. The crowd was better dressed and more sparse. Rich women out with their slaves, coming from dressmakers or jewellers. Men coming from the baths or on their way to symposia. The lupanaria would open later and the patrons of the day would be replaced by the surreptitious traffic of the night.

The sun would set soon. The Senate would normally have gone home by now, since Senate sessions by law had to end by nightfall, but Otho had sent a messenger ahead. When our procession entered the Forum, there was no more cheering. People stood and watched us, dull-eyed, sullen.

There came the solemn pounding of a tympanum. Ahead of us, in the front portico of the Curia Julia, standing behind the colonnade, a man was slowly beating the drum, while alongside came the cacophonous braying of bucinae. They had not managed to get together a decent orchestra for the Emperor's homecoming; the music would have been better on a slow day at the Circus. Nor did it blend well with the bleating and breast-beating of Actë. Deprived of her reason for existing, she had become powerless, pitiful.

We were met at the steps by the consul Tiberius Silius Italicus, who was the only presiding officer in the Senate that day. His co-consul, Publius Galerius Trachalus, was already on the road to greet General Galba.

As the drums pounded and the bucinae wailed, a litter borne by a dozen unmatched slaves emerged from the huge bronze doors of the Curia Julia, and more slaves emerged to lift Nero's body, which had mostly been swabbed clean and was wrapped in a fresh purple cloak, and to transfer it to the litter; the bearers then carried it through the doors, which clanged shut. And that was the last I was to see of Himself, the Master of the World, my tormentor, my benefactor, my lover.

Italicus began to regale me in long-winded hexameters.

Queen of the Sunrise, he intoned, *Mistress of the Evening Star,*
Pearl of the Sunset, O much beloved Lady, outshining even
The resplendent eyes of the cow-eyed Juno…

He continued in this vein until I lifted a hand to stop him; his fulsome apostrophe came to a squawking finish. "I can see you are a poet," I said.

"Yes," he said, "I've written a poem even longer than the *Aeneid.*"

"By the Muses," I said, "what subject could merit such treatment?"

"The Punic Wars, Divinitas," he said.

"Well, I suppose it is safe to impugn the Carthaginians," I said, "since they can't impugn us back."

I am not sure he realized I was making fun of him, but he changed the subject. "Otho," he said, "the Senate commands you to join the consular embassy to Galba."

"I'll have to go," Otho said. "If I don't kiss his feet, I'll probably find myself kissing the Tarpeian Rock."

"True enough," said Silius Italicus. "A lot of traitors have been flung from that selfsame rock in the last few days." To me he added, "You may remain in Rome, of course, under senatorial protection." Which probably meant a dagger in the night, or, if they were feeling generous, a vial of poison.

"I think I'd feel a little safer with these Praetorians," I said. "I will go with Otho."

***

Otho did not even have a home in Rome, and I did not really want to return to Nero's Golden House, and so we ended up at my villa, well, one of my villas, the one that was once Petronius Arbiter's.

To step into the house where I had last lived as a slave was a strange thing. To be welcomed by Croesus, who had once had the unwilling task of whipping me, filled me with a bitter joy.

The women of the house made much of me, claiming I was too thin and bringing me a stuffed mouse from the kitchen, dripping with honey and garum. Hylas was smiling to see old friends. Shortly afterwards, Marcus Vinicius arrived and embraced me warmly. This was the only place in the world that felt like a home to me.

"Shall I put Marcus Salvius Otho in the cubiculum of the former dominus?" Croesus said.

Before Otho could reply, I said, "I would prefer Petronius's chamber always to remain as it was."

"Another room, then," said Croesus. "We do have several more, you know."

The evening meal was a little strained. I sat as host, alongside Marcus and Croesus, whose status was of course no longer that of a servant. And I was at the center of the head triclinium, my status not dependent on any master, lover, or husband. And Otho was being entertained as my own guest, not as a visiting dignitary. I was not there to sit on his lap and smile flirtatiously. We had fresh delicati to do that job, for Croesus had filled all the household positions vacated by Petronius's death, manumissions, and my departure to the royal palace.

Petronius had always had two delicati in his service; when I came I had been the supernumerary. Croesus had found examples more exotic even than I had been, beautiful creatures from beyond the edge of the Empire. One was dark as night, and the other pale as snow with almond eyes. Otho was not displeased. For Marcus Vinicius, there were also girls, one skinny and one voluptuous. And if Croesus could sit at my table, then so could Hylas. He did, awkwardly.

No one talked. A girl of the Aksumites, who come from Ethiopia, played on a tortoiseshell lyre and sang in an unknown tongue, accompanied by boys playing finger cymbals and a little drum. The song was lyrical, full of twisted melismas.

During dinner, which was a simple affair with only around a dozen courses, we had local wine, Falernian, well diluted with water; afterwards, a Greek wine, Chian I think, drunk inappropriately neat, for we needed something to break the tension.

It was Otho who snapped first. He flung his kylix across the room and it smashed on the mosaic stones. He began weeping uncontrollably. "He was my friend," he kept repeating.

Croesus said softly, "He stole your wife, and exiled you to Lusitania."

"My wife's right here," he said, gripping me by the shoulders.

"Your wife," Croesus said.

Otho looked at me.

"I was with Poppaea when it happened," I said.

"He was my friend," Otho said.

But the Gods do not have friends, I thought.

"We leave at dawn," I said. "If you don't align yourself with Galba before he reaches Rome, you are done for."

***

I lay in Petronius's chamber. But I could not sleep. I could hear poetry from his lips take wing: his own, but also the ancient lyric poets, Sappho, Alcaeus, and the modern ones like Ovid; those words, weighted by memory, hung in the air. I yearned to be hugged by my old master, to fall asleep to the rhythm of his breathing.

Around the sixth hour of the night, I realized I could never sleep with all those ghosts. I sprang up; Hylas, on the floor next to me, rubbed his eyes, threw a sheer cloth over my shoulders, and lit a lamp, and followed me out into the hall, so quietly I knew he was there only by the flickering light he held out.

I stumbled at random through the portico, into the atrium, among the trees and the herms, pallid in the soft moonlight. And in this way, I found myself in a guest chamber, where Otho lay, not sleeping either.

"My beloved," he murmured.

What a vision he must have seen. Me, a silhouette against the lamplight, the fabric already slipping down my chest and pooling on the tiles.

Me, impossibly beautiful, more dream than flesh.

"You don't know how I longed for you, Poppaea," he said. "In Lusitania the Celtiberian boys are renowned for their lubricity, but they were not you."

"I am not Poppaea either," I said.

"No, not the Poppaea of the stinking flesh," he said. "You're the Platonic perfection of Poppaea, the face of a goddess and the loins of a god. Oh, but you broke into my dreams, you troubled my waking thoughts."

I walked toward him. I no longer had the wherewithal to return his desire. But I felt pity. And so I let him take me into his arms. He was not pleasing to me. He had a stale smell, and it did not blend well with all that Chian wine. Understanding my distaste, Hylas blew out the lamp so I would not have to look at him. I try not to remember what followed. I sent my mind to a place far, far away.

***

But this was not your first time with him.

It was and it was not. For when I joined him and Poppaea in their unhappy bed, I was a slave. I existed to be used, as a tool to salve Otho's inadequacies and Poppaea's needs. I needed to please him, because my master sent me and I always yearned for Petronius's approval.

That night, I was permitted to feel disgust, to feel ill-used, because I was free, a human being. The mechanics were the same, but I had free will. Yet I still let him do whatever he wanted. He lurched, he flailed, he cried out. And I made myself feel nothing. And when his ecstasy was spent and he fell into a deep sleep, Hylas led me to my private caldarium, and I tried to soak away every trace of him from my body.

You didn't love Otho even a little?

It is strange. I loved Petronius. That is obvious. But I also loved Poppaea for her wit and deviousness, and because, while helping her own cause, she felt for me a little. I loved my fellow slaves whom I later owned. And there was Nero. He was a monster, and yet, there were little ways in which he made you love him despite his madness. There were moments of purity, of clarity. Only in his death did I truly understand the words of Catullus: *Odi et amo* … how love and hate could be so inextricably intertwined.

But Otho? I did not love Otho.

That night I realized that I was never going to love anyone again.

It was going to be about survival from now on. Only survival mattered.

XXVII

GALBA

We'd wasted some time delivering the dead Divinitas to the Senate, and spending the night in my villa. It only took a week to reach Galba's encampment, as he had already crossed the Po. For speed, and because we weren't going to fight anyone, we only took only one maniple of cavalry, and I finally got used to a horse. I think Otho picked the gentlest one he could for me. Always considerate of my pace, Otho did not force the cavalry more than thirty miles a day.

The stench came first, when the walls of the castra were not even in sight. And we could see scavenger birds in the distance.

Otho said, "He's been busy crucifying people. You can smell it from here."

As we got closer we could hear the pounding of nails and the grunt of legionaries hoisting crosses. Otho had sent a messenger ahead, and our man returned with a legate from the castra, to make appropriate greeting and to lead us in. And presently, at the wooden gate, Galba was there himself, the very picture of a military man.

The reek had become overwhelming and now we saw a forest of crosses; they were recent, for most of the men, women and children who had been strung up were still alive, and some were not too weak to still be groaning.

"Hail, Caesar," Otho said, acknowledging reality for the present.

"I'm terribly sorry about the mess," said the General. "But you know how things work. Setting an example."

"Crucifying children?" I gasped.

"If slaughtering one village can buy the allegiance of a thousand ..." said Galba. "Besides, they weren't citizens."

"You should show some respect to the Dowager Empress," Otho said.

"You're pathetic," Galba said. He turned to his legate. "Take the boy and find him some proper clothes."

I got off my horse — or rather, was helped off — but as I was being led away, I overheard more of the conversation.

"There's going to be no more chaos, Otho," Galba was saying. "People will confine themselves to their proper station in society. Cross-dressing will be confined to the home, or to designated brothels. Only the anuses of slaves and social inferiors will be violated. Women will no longer meddle in politics." He continued in that vein until I was out of earshot.

Galba was not going to be a popular Emperor, that was certain.

***

Our entry into Rome was the reverse of my previous triumph. The crowd outside the city was sullen. Many looked away. Galba rode ahead. Otho rode just behind.

I was in the entourage that followed him, but not in a position of prominence. I wore a simple tunic, my hair no longer coifed, my face no longer whited with lead paint. No one recognized me without my royal regalia. I was just some superannuated delicatus, without any skills, and no longer capable of growing up into a whole man.

As we entered, however, the crowd grew, though they still said nothing. Presently someone cried out, "Isn't that Otho, Nero's friend?"

Galba turned. A centurion stepped out of the ranks and slapped the man's face.

Otho rode up to Galba and whispered something. Galba motioned. Two soldiers rode forward, each carrying a hefty sack. They began tossing silver denarii into the mob. And finally the cheering started.

I heard someone say, "This one's real, not the debased crap the last Emperor was shitting out!"

"Ave Caesar! Please lift the piss tax!"

"Ave Caesar! Double the bread dole!"

At last, in the distance, we could hear shouts of "Galba! Galba! Galba!" Perhaps someone from the Senate had come out to coach the mob.

When the soldiers ran out of coins, more were brought up from the back. As we approached the Forum, people were filing into the square now. It was still not what you might call crowded, but the denarii were having a real effect. Gold would have been better, but these were not prosperous times.

What can I say? We reached the Curia Julia, and this time the Senate were out in force, standing before the huge bronze portals which had been flung wide open, revealing the Augustus's pristine white marble within.

The crowd were yelling full-throatedly by now, as much in fear as in enthusiasm. This time I watched a living Emperor enter the Senate, not a dead one.

I wished never to see him again. It was one of the few wishes I ever had in life that was actually granted.

And so it was that I returned to my own villa, as I had come to think of it.

But I could not live out my days in quiet luxury. For one thing, I had acquired a house guest. Marcus Salvius Otho, husband of the woman I looked like, former friend of a disgraced Emperor, former governor of Lusitania, followed me back to the house. He had no home in Rome, and I did not have the heart to send him away.

Except from my bed; that night I asked my slaves to watch the door to my cubiculum, and slept with Hylas in my arms, clutching him to my bosom, like a child with a favorite toy.

***

I had known from the moment I heard him muttering about restoring morality, that day in his castra, that Galba would not be well-liked. For one thing, he made no effort to revoke the damnatio memoriae which had been pronounced on the late Divinitas, and had allowed only a skimpy state funeral, without even any games.

Not only was the urine tax not repealed, but there was an even worse problem.

It was Marcus Vinicius who told us about it, and it was a problem we should all have foreseen.

It was at another of those nerve-wracking dinners, with Otho gazing longingly at me while the entertainment danced and sang. With no special guests, the repast was really simple;

I had forbidden the slaves to serve more than five courses and to hold the dormice for higher-profile visitors.

"Why can't *I* have a dormouse?" Otho was complaining. "It's not as if you can't afford it, Poppaea."

"Don't call me Poppaea anymore. I am Gaius Petronius Gaii Libertus Sporus again now, Marcus Salvius Otho," I said. "The Divinitas said no more gender-hopping. I was there, I heard it."

Otho seemed oblivious. "We need to get married," he said.

"Why?" I said. "You're not planning to seize the principate. You don't need *me* for any kind of twisted justification. You don't need to live in Rome. Don't you have estates?"

"Nero made sure I was starved for resources and stuck in Lusitania. It was all I could do to pay these few Praetorians who came with me to dispose of Nymphidius. Poppaea owned everything and ... in effect, *you* are Poppaea now, by the fiat of the Divine Nero."

"And marrying Poppaea would get you all your property back ... and give you a shot at the throne, however far-fetched," I said.

"I love you," he said, tearing off a hefty hunk of bread and swallowing it with some wine and olives. And we did not speak for a long while, but ate in silence.

It was at that point that Marcus Vinicius arrived and was ushered into the triclinium. He kissed me on the cheek and sat down on my left, and without any further salutation, said, "Galba is doomed."

"But," Otho said, "he's only been Emperor for two months."

"It's the donativum," said Marcus. "The army hasn't been paid."

"Why not?" Otho said. "When a new Emperor is proclaimed, there is always a donativum to the army. Nero's was excessive, at 3,750 denarii, and bankrupted the treasury for years. He was forced to debase the currency."

"Nymphidius promised them double that, and Galba won't pay it."

"Seventy-five hundred denarii?" Otho said.

"Each," said Marcus Vinicius.

The normal salary of an ordinary soldier is two hundred and twenty-five denarii per year. This offer, therefore, was like paying every soldier thirty-five years' wages.

"What could he have been thinking?" Otho said. "I would not dare promise that much, if they made *me* Emperor."

"How much?" said Marcus Vinicius.

"Well … just hypothetically … I might pay twelve hundred and fifty … and that would be extreme, for the Divine Augustus gave a donativum of only two hundred and fifty and that was not upon his accession — it was in his will."

"I will convey your offer to the Praetorians," Marcus said, rising from the table.

"Wait!" Otho said. "I haven't *offered* anything to anyone."

But Marcus Vinicius was already on his way out, and Hylas was handing him his sword and helmet.

I said to Otho, "That was foolish."

"It would be nice to get my estates back," he said softly. "And to be able to appear in public with my wife."

"I'm not your wife."

"I want you," he said.

I despaired of ever being allowed to be my true self. I took a gulp of undiluted wine, so quickly I could barely keep it down. "I suppose you'll have to become Emperor then," I sighed.

XXVIII

DOMUS AUREA

For most people, the assassination of an Emperor is unthinkable. For me, it had become almost commonplace.

I had seen — some would say, participated in — the killing of my late husband.

I had been relieved, if not actually taken pleasure, at the murder of Nymphidius in the moment when he was about to mount me.

I did not really relish being present at the death of a third. Especially since both previous deaths had occurred while the princeps, or would-be princeps, was attempting to make love to me.

Fortunately, I was probably not to Galba's taste, and so Otho did not need me to lure the current Caesar to some sordid tryst. The murder of Galba was accomplished by one thing only: money.

And not even real money; just Galba's refusal to pay what

Nymphidius had promised, and Otho's lesser proffer being deemed more reliable, and better than nothing.

So it was that less than three months after his triumphant entry into the Senate, the spineless and ineffectual Otho succeeded in engineering the Emperor's demise.

He did not give me any details.

He merely pushed past the guards at my door and interrupted my breakfast. "It's done," he said. "Have your slaves pick out something pretty for you to wear."

"Where are we going?" I said.

"Home," said Otho.

"Home?"

"To the Golden House."

Once again … *my* home. Not Otho's.

***

Later I would be told how Galba had been lured to the Forum, and how not a single Praetorian defended him — though a few hapless Germans did, not understanding our politics. A minor battle had raged in the Forum.

I heard about his head being displayed on a spike to mocking boys who had ridiculed his virility, then later sold to his daughter. But I had only seen and heard Galba that once, so it meant nothing to me.

Otho had been proclaimed Emperor by the Praetorians, carried on their shoulders into the Curia, and the Senate had little choice but to vote to grant him full Imperium. Otho did the right thing, having a hundred and twenty people executed for killing Galba, thus deflecting responsibility for the assassination from himself.

The flaw in all this was that Otho had had to promise to make good on Nymphidius's donativum….

***

And so I returned to the Golden House of Nero.

The house of three hundred rooms. The house with the secret garden at its summit.

Those who greeted us were familiar to me. Epaphroditus, who could not be disposed of because he alone knew where every document was. Epictetus, still limping, still philosophizing. Old Spider, now living in the bowels of the palace. These were people who cared for me. There was even Hercules the cheetah, who had gone a little mad in my absence, but started to calm down as soon as he detected my familiar scent.

So this vast palace, robbed of its flawed soul since the death of Nero, was also home to me. Having nothing, I now possessed more than I ever had when I was the plaything of a god.

I came dressed in the best finery that could be found in Petronius's house. Here, there was nothing for me but to live the image of a Goddess.

Otho was a diligent Emperor. To everyone's surprise, he was an even-handed ruler. The mob had known him as Nero's friend, and they even started to call him Nero Otho. I was accepted as Empress, with the occasional snigger mind you, but no one really objected. My possession of a penis was a minor foible. My presence gave a veneer of continuity to Otho's rule. The games came back and the bread dole was doubled. Things were, if not actually utopian, at the very least calm.

You would think that Otho would continue to rule for decades; things were more stable than they had been under any of the later Julio-Claudians. But of course, there was one thing that hung over his head, one Damoclean flaw … Otho had not yet paid the army donativum promised by

Nymphidius. Not the seventy-five hundred denarii, not even the twelve hundred and fifty he had agreed to. The treasury would not have borne it without tripling the taxes.

Each morning, Otho went to work, taking petitions and supplications, religiously attending the Senate, officiating at state sacrifices, opening games. I usually dined alone, and saw Otho only in the dead of night.

Each night, I suffered his attentions, doing my best to please him or at least not to offend; each morning I was thankful to have survived another day.

And in the daytime, I wandered through the palace. Sometimes with Hylas, sometimes only with the cheetah. The Divine Nero had built this place with infinite imagination and cunning, and it seemed I was the only one there to appreciate it.

There were hidden grottoes underground, illumined by eerie blue light; there were libraries with diligent curators and no visitors; there was a theater designed for an exclusive audience of one guest with attendants; there was even a private lupanar with a fine selection of perfect women and boys, and not a single customer. I spoke to Epaphroditus about it, and he quietly sold off the whores; I used the money to redecorate the area as another private dining room.

And everywhere, there were images of Nero. He was painted on walls. There were statues. There was a mosaic with Nero as Apollo, strumming on a kithara.

The Golden House stretched from the Palatine to the Esquiline. There were underground passageways, stairways to unexpected vistas. There were fountains. There were treasure chambers. There were cubicula that had never been slept in, and slave quarters whence the slaves had never been summoned to perform any tasks.

Everywhere, even in hidden corridors, I saw images of my former husband.

There were never any images of Otho. Otho was Emperor, but in this palace he was invisible.

Growing bolder, knowing no one could stop me, I started to wander the city with a small escort, sharing a litter with Hylas. Everywhere we went, the crowds steered clear, for soldiers went in advance to move the populace out of the way. Near the Circus there was a towering statue without a head.

Elsewhere, images of Nero had been defaced, scrawled over with graffiti.

"I know you are thinking of him," Hylas said. "I know where they keep him." And he directed the litter-bearers to take us to the Pincian Hill, in the northeast corner of the city. I was not familiar with these streets and wondered how Hylas had come to know of them.

We found ourselves at the entrance to a mausoleum. A veiled woman stood guard. It took a moment to recognize her as Actë, for this building was the resting place of the Domitii Ahenobarbi, Nero's family before he was adopted into the Julio-Claudians; few remembered his birth name was Lucius Domitius Ahenobarbus.

"This is what I do now," she said. "I watch over Lucius's tomb."

Actë was not only veiled, but wore the plain white robes of a priestess. This place was a hidden temple to a man whom the Senate had not deified. No one had dared to invade this private mausoleum.

I hadn't even known Himself had been decently buried. I had imagined the vengeful Senate throwing his body to the beasts, or leaving it to rot somewhere.

This peaceful place was not what I had thought to find.

"Let me take you to see him," Actë said. She took me by the hand and led me through a low gate to a garden. A statue of Himself, not decapitated, stood at its center. A small temple lay beyond. Actë went on ahead and I followed.

There was a circular chamber within. Another statue of Nero stood watch, with incense and an altar.

The tomb itself was simple; it had probably been someone else's tomb, hastily re-carved. Another woman tended an altar-flame. I was again surprised to see who it was: Statilia Messalina, Nero's only surviving properly married wife of the appropriate gender.

I had barely seen her; she had never lived with us, and had existed purely as a convenience. Now she, too, was here, veiled and robed as a priestess.

"You could join us if you wanted to, Sporus," she said. "History has cast us aside; here we can be at peace."

I wasn't quite ready to retire from life itself.

As you know, I am not even twenty years old yet, and I then, no reason to believe I could not continue to survive somehow.

I put my hand on the sarcophagus. A frieze had been sculpted around it, not with any great skill, for the artist had worked in haste. It depicted the major incidents of Nero's life. His elevation at the hands of Claudius. His much-vaunted war in Britannia and the quashing of Boudicca's rebellion, which he had not even been present at. His building of amphitheaters. His victory in the Olympics. His mother. His wives … Poppaea and Statilia. Actë was not depicted, and neither was I. We were not part of the official history.

I stroked Poppaea's marble face.

"How can he have a temple, when he isn't a god?" I asked no one in particular.

Actë said, "The Senate doesn't *really* create the gods, you know. We do, in our own hearts."

I sacrificed a dove to Himself; they were kept in cages in a back room.

We heard a fanfare from outside. Someone important was arriving with the full panoply of state.

Announced by a quartet of cornua, preceded by a dozen Praetorians, it was Otho who entered.

"There you are, my dear," he said. Not to me, but to Statilia Messalina. "The Senate has urged that I take a female wife to clarify the line of succession, and I can think of no one better than you."

"You'll divorce me?" I said, not without a glimmer of hope.

"Of course not. You're still my one true love. But the Senate thinks that in public at least — at state functions — a wife without a penis might be more viable politically."

"I might have one of those," I said, "but the Divine Nero made sure I would never grow into a man."

"Statilia, you will keep the throne warm for me while I am gone," Otho said. "While my beloved Poppaea-with-a-penis will warm me on campaign."

"Campaign?" I said.

It was then that I learned that we had used up all the good will from the army that came from my association with Himself the late Divinitas. The ill will from not paying the donativum had continued to fester, and now, as it were, the boil had burst.

"I should have paid the seventy-five hundred," said Otho.

The army in Germania had declared their own general, Vitellius, Emperor, and it was up to Otho to lead his as-yet unpaid and very displeased troops north to do battle. The civil war of succession, paused when General Galba had defeated Vindex and when Otho had slain Nymphidius, was now back in full swing.

XXIX

CIVIL WAR

Thus it was that in my short life's winter I finally saw war, the thing that drives the human experience.

I had heard a thousand songs about the glory. *Dulce et decorum est pro patria mori,* Horatius Flaccus rhapsodized. Julius Caesar said *Veni, vidi, vici,* and Romans frequently repeat that *audaces fortuna juvat.* Fortune favors the bold.

The Greeks, four centuries ago, knew better, it seems. Euripides called war *ta megista kaka ton anthropon* ... the greatest evils of the human race. He defined it as "a man, and the beginning of death." Petronius had filled my brain with so much poetry, yet I had never imagined the blood. The screaming. The hacked-off limbs. Boots tramping through bloody mud. The clash and the clang of it.

Before that, there was a short voyage; we set sail up the coast in order to shorten the distance to cut off Vitellius before he could march all the way down to Rome. Otho journeyed in style, with every luxury brought with us from the Golden House: soft couches, an Imperial cook, livestock for fine dining, and a supply of body-slaves and masseuses; the Imperial secretaries, headed by Epaphroditus, were with us as well. As for me, I only had Hylas, but at the last moment had brought Hercules as well, as the cheetah had been lonely in my absence, and had acquired a vicious streak, devouring one of the maids' children. With me, he was always sedate, and of course, well fed.

We were joined by legions from Dalmatia, Pannonia and Moesia, and we had the Praetorians; there seemed to be little reason not to prevail against legions who had been made to force-march from the Rhine, and were probably eked out with mercenaries from Germania.

But the omens were not very auspicious.

A white ox slaughtered upon landfall had two livers. An eagle fell dead out of the sky at Otho's feet as we rode inland.

I had briefly been in Galba's castra, but that was just a miniature one, an advance party from his army. Since I was being dragged about by soldiers, I didn't see much anyway.

My first experience of a full-blown Roman camp was that it was much like Rome itself — filled with food vendors and blacksmiths and other tradesmen; but it was all much more orderly, less chaotic, than the city; the avenues were wide and straight; the soldiers knew what they were doing, and had conjured the castra into being in just an hour or two.

There weren't many women. Soldiers were not allowed to marry until they retired. Some kept a woman, or shared one with friends. But the camp boys were a more common sight. Many soldiers kept one, brought from home or picked up as booty from some village. They were just as warm in the night, and could be left to run wild in the day.

It was boys like these that had mocked and jeered at Galba's decapitated head.

If there was one thing that was different about this city of tents, it was that it reeked of masculinity.

"Don't be too curious," Otho told me. "And stay in the tent when we go into battle. You'll have people to keep you safe."

At the first battle, we could not hold the invaders at the Po, and they thrust right past Otho's army, deeper into Italy.

I did not witness the battle, of course. But I did not want to be cooped up in the Imperial tent for the duration of the civil war. And so, restless, I went to see the aftermath.

But I had my first experience of walking at dawn through a field of the dead. I had left Otho's tent in haste, without the elaborate transformation into a Queen. Instead, I dressed as a member of the military. Doubtless I was the envy of the urchins who thronged the camp.

I had my bearers carry me to the field, then walked on on foot.

It had been more of a skirmish than I battle, I was told later, but it was overwhelming. The dead were strewn about in heaps. Loose arms and legs were scattered among them. Flies buzzed and there were birds everywhere, pecking at eyes and wounds. And dogs.

Against the rising sun, I saw a kneeling man, eyes raised toward Heaven, a man in his fifties, perhaps, in a white robe.

"Doesn't he remind you of Simon?" Hylas said, and ran over there, heedless of his caligae squishing dead human flesh.

Curiously, I followed my freedman. I saw nothing to remind me of the boy I had last seen being eaten by lions in the Circus. Unless it was the way the man prayed, swaying and muttering.

"Are you a Jew?" I asked him.

"Not exactly," he said.

I knew then what Hylas had seen; this man was one of the Chrestianoi. I wondered how he had managed to avoid being sent to the arena. Perhaps he had mouthed the obligatory formula of worship to Rome's god's at the last minute.

"Is it safe," I said, "for people like you to be here?"

"Safe? The army is full of us. With the Mithras people and the Sol Invictus followers and the worshippers of rocks and stones, nobody notices another Eastern cult."

I supposed that, with death around every corner, any religion that promised instant salvation would be desirable.

The man, whose name was Josephus, told me that he was a repairer of hipposandals and saddles, and he was in business for himself.

"Why are you praying in the midst of corpses?" I said.

"I don't know. I think I was waiting for you," he said.

"You don't even know me," I said.

"But my dominus does."

"You're a slave, then." Many masters allowed their slaves to run their own businesses and received a share of the profits.

Josephus said, "We are all slaves. Even you. Especially you, because the events that shape you cannot be controlled by you. You will die soon, you know. But before you do so, you should taste Divine Love."

I laughed bitterly. "I have," I said, "and from more than one Divinitas."

"Listen," he said. "I may have lost my looks, but I too was once a delicatus. My master was a centurion in Judaea. You've heard of the place."

I remembered Pontius Pilate going on and on about what a troublesome province it had been. And how he had crucified the leader of these Chrestianoi. "I have," I said.

"My master bought me from a family who had been made destitute by all those those Hasmonean taxes. I didn't want to be sold, but he treated me well; he truly cherished me. My family taught me that most of the world's sexual practices are abominations, but my master never let me feel like an object. I loved him as much as a slave can love a master; he loved me more than that, I think. But I became deathly ill. My dominus told me there was a healer who could cure any sickness, but I told him I was on my deathbed. Still, he insisted on seeking out this so-called prophet, so I kissed him goodbye, and waited to die. Some days passed, I think. I drifted in and out of consciousness. And then something happened…."

"What? Some charlatan waved a wand over you? A witch gave you a magic herb?"

"No … I was lying there in my misery. And then — all of a sudden — it came over me … a wave of pure love. This love wasn't just warm and tender; like fire, it burned; I felt as though I were being sucked into a raging flame. I knew that this love was death. But then, suddenly, the fever left me. I stood up. There wasn't a trace of the illness. And my dominus had not even come back from seeking out this healer."

"The magician cured you from miles away."

"My dominus told me about it. He said that this prophet wasn't like a Roman priest, with ritual formulae and sacrifices. All he said was, *You came all this way, and you didn't even bring your puer with you.* My master told him that he was confident in the healer's abilities. And the rabbi said, *Go home, then. I've already cured him."*

"And you lived happily ever after."

"No, no, listen to me. This feeling of absolute love ... it was something real, something so powerful it can transform anything. My own parents, who sold me to feed themselves, called me a whore, an abomination. Where I come from, no decent person would bestir themselves to help a puer delicatus. It wasn't my fault, but still, I had betrayed my faith and my culture and gone over to the Romans. Even before the Romans came, our land was only a reluctant participant in the Hellenistic world. That's why we're seen as backward, barbaric, clinging to an unfashionable religion.

"In that moment, you see, I became truly myself. And I've tried to let others achieve that transformation, too. The Romans crucified him, you know. But I learned that every love we feel is an echo of Divine Love. The world will end soon, you know. The Beast has already been slain."

"The Beast?"

"Your late husband."

"I was there when he died," I said. "This wasn't a noble sacrifice to bring about a new age. It was something sordid."

"The highest Heaven's foundations rest in the depths of Hell," he said. "You can't touch the stars unless your feet are firmly planted on the earth."

I took Hylas's hand and we left the man praying for his delusions.

***

During the night I was plagued with bad dreams.

More vividly than ever before, I saw my childhood. My mother. The homely sounds of my native language, a language for which the Romans did not even have a name.

I saw the fire and the pirates. I relived the violation on the ship. And once again in my dream I entered the half-world of the dead and came face to face with Pluto, the death-god, greeting me as his bride.

Pluto who was Nero, demanding that I lobby the Senate to admit him to Olympus. "If no one worships me," he said, "how shall I survive in the underworld?"

And in the dream I'm telling him: "I visited your tomb. There was a temple. I sacrificed a dove to you. Actë and Statilia are your priestesses."

"Only two to worship, out of the whole world that once lay at my feet?"

"They will *all* worship you, Divinitas. I'd stake my life on it."

"You'd die for me, my sweet little boy-wife?" said the God of the Dead in my dream. And reached for me with ravenous arms, and enveloped me in a thick darkness, snuffing out my breath until —

And in the morning, we struck camp and moved on to the next battle, which would be at a place called Bedriacum.

XXX

BEDRIACUM

Yet every battle is the same: more corpses, more harrowing amputations in the field hospital, more wailing, bereaved lovers. By all accounts we were winning, but it weighed heavily on Otho.

I did not go back to the battlefield again. I knew I would find that deluded Chrestianos raving about Divine Love, while scavengers feasted on the dead. I had been curious, but after a few more days of the campaign I did not leave the tent anymore. When Otho came from the field he performed a perfunctory coupling with me, then fell to snoring. I had become something on a list of daily tasks. He took no joy in me, though he murmured *Poppaea, Poppaea,* in his sleep.

Otho had gone through the motions of fighting with one foot already in the grave.

I sat in the tent and made myself beautiful, surrounded by my confidants and Otho's hangers on. One evening I sat quietly while his generals argued. Push ahead! You already have them on the run! No, wait for the Dalmatian legion to arrive, save your men for a bigger battle. And Otho, swayed by both sides, agreeing with first one, then the other.

This would not end well and when Otho decided, quite arbitrarily, on a major battle near the village of Bedriacum. We had moved our camp there. It was a pleasant little village.

The Dalmatian legions had almost arrived … they were no farther away than Aquileia. But Otho did not want further delay. I watched the army march out of the camp and waited in the tent.

By the afternoon, the camp was filled to overflowing with wounded. It was chaos. Though I had confined myself to the Imperial tent, I could hear the madness closing in on me.

When Otho entered, I could tell he had already given up.

Several of his officers followed him in. "Don't, my Lord," they were saying. "We still have a very good chance of winning."

Otho sat. Hylas poured him wine. There was bread. He dipped a hunk in salt and downed the whole krater of wine.

"Yes, Marcus Salvius," I said. "We might win."

Otho was the only security I could cling to now. I had to prevent him from giving up. But he only said, "Yes, my darling, we *might* win. But we'd still be in a civil war. It will only end if there's only one claimant to the Empire left standing."

"But you've been a good Emperor," I said.

"I haven't paid the army," he said. "I don't know where that money would come from. Someone craftier than I must balance that equation."

"But Marcus —" I said.

"No, no, my dearest Poppaea. The proper Roman thing to do in this circumstance is to commit suicide. I would retain my honor; my property, meagre though it is, could go to my heirs, such as they are. I'll get a decent funeral, and a decent cranny of the afterlife to inhabit. My mind's made up."

I dreaded what I knew he would ask me next, and he did so anyway. He said, "You're the only person I trust, and I don't want it botched. So please, Poppaea dearest, hold the sword while I run on it."

I was sick to my stomach. "I can't do that, you know I can't," I said. "I'm ... you know, delicate."

"Ita," he said. "Delicate es," he added, correcting my grammar to the feminine form of the adjective. "But you can surely hold a sword without flinching. Look at all the bloodshed you've seen!"

Yes. Why was it so hard for me? Since my enslavement, I had seen crucifixions, beheadings, and people eaten by lions. An Emperor had died in my arms, and a would-be Emperor had been killed while raping me. What was one more dead Emperor?

***

All at once — a clamor from outside! We heard shouts and swords clanging against shields! A few shrieks of dying men. And then, abruptly, silence. Except for the distant whimper of someone being raped. It would not be long.

One of the generals placed a sword in my hands, and angled it upwards, directly at Otho's heart. He steadied me, making sure my grip was firm.

I told myself, *There is no love between me and Otho.* It was not as it had been with Nero, where there was both love and hate in equal measure; Nero and I were bound together by his delusion and my willingness to inhabit it.

I don't love you, I thought. I had only ever pitied him.

And so it was that Otho looked into my eyes and said, "Farewell, my beloved," and "We shall see each other in the next world," and slowly bent down to kiss me; the blade entered him as he embraced me, and as his lips touched mine, the sword-point breached his heart.

For the third time, I was holding a bloody, dying Emperor in my arms.

It was then that the cries of "Hail, Vitellius!" could be heard from all around us. Our men had all gone over to the enemy. Loyalty had been bought, and it was fleeting. The shouting came in waves. We were drowning in an ocean of traitors.

"You see … why … now," Otho gasped. "I could not have … remained."

I knew that Otho had at least attempted to govern well. He had done popular things. But only paying the army their donativum would guarantee stability. And that would have caused Rome to starve to death. It was a dilemma with no viable solution.

We heard the tramp of soldiers' caligae. The tent-flap was ripped open. The victor of the battle stood in the entrance.

I had never seen Vitellius before, but I knew exactly who this must be.

Aulus Vitellius was square-jawed and chubby-cheeked. Otho was overweight, but Vitellius was luxuriantly obese. He was jovial as he walked in; he had been cracking jokes outside.

As he came in, Otho died. He rolled onto the floor. Some of his men hastened to make sure he lay in a dignified position.

Vitellius hardly glanced at him. He only looked at me. I sat there, covered in blood, my makeup not completely done, my clothes ripped. I looked nothing like an Imperatrix.

Certainly not to Vitellius, who said simply, "So this is the much-vaunted cinaedus."

I was probably done for, so I decided to brazen it out. "Don't use such a vulgar word, Aulus Vitellius. I am no one's dirty little catamite. I am the recognized wife of Nero Otho, and until the Senate decrees otherwise, I'm still your Empress."

"Is that so?" Vitellius said, and started to laugh. His men all laughed too. And then Otho's own servants, who had stood by loyally in attendance on his honorable death, also started laughing. Sycophants, the lot of them.

"You're a cheeky one," Vitellius continued. "Don't you realize you're entirely at my mercy? I could have you crucified."

"You won't, though. Despite everyone's efforts to denigrate his name, Nero is still more popular than any of you one-day Emperors. Giving me a slave's death would be politically unwise."

"You have the backbone to threaten me, yet the intelligence to talk sense," Vitellius said. "You're no ordinary catamite."

"Would you like to find out?" I asked him, hoping that a twinge of seduction in my voice would lower my chances of execution.

"Impertinent little savage!" Vitellius said. He slapped me resoundingly. It stung, and I should have fallen off my seat, but I gritted my teeth and glared back at him.

He laughed again.

"I'm not going to kill you," he said at last, "not yet at least. You are entertaining, and what you say has some merit. If I am to rule, I'll need the good will of the Nero-loving mob. Meanwhile ... why don't you make yourself useful? You could take care of the arrangements for your husband's funeral, for example."

"At the expense of the state?" I said.

"You pay for it," he said. "I'm going to have to find a way to eke out the donativum."

I looked down at the body of my most recent husband. Marcus Salvius Otho, known as Nero Otho by the mob, had been Emperor for ninety-one days. It was the shortest reign in the history of the Empire. Unless you count Nymphidius's, which could be numbered in minutes, not days.

I was not chained up, not for now. I was accorded a modicum of dignity. The Imperial secretaries and staff were immediately requisitioned so they could start to brief our new Emperor on the current state of affairs. But I was allowed to keep Hylas with me.

I was given an hour to prepare for the journey back to Rome. Otho's body, as well as my person, were to be among the spoils of this civil war.

As we quit the tent, as I was boarding the cart that would take me to whatever was next for me, I noticed that a few people were being crucified; no more than strictly necessary to show that Vitellius meant business. It was almost an afterthought. There was no one of any importance. I did notice that Chrestianos among them, though, the one who had spoken to me about the incomparable splendor of Divine Love.

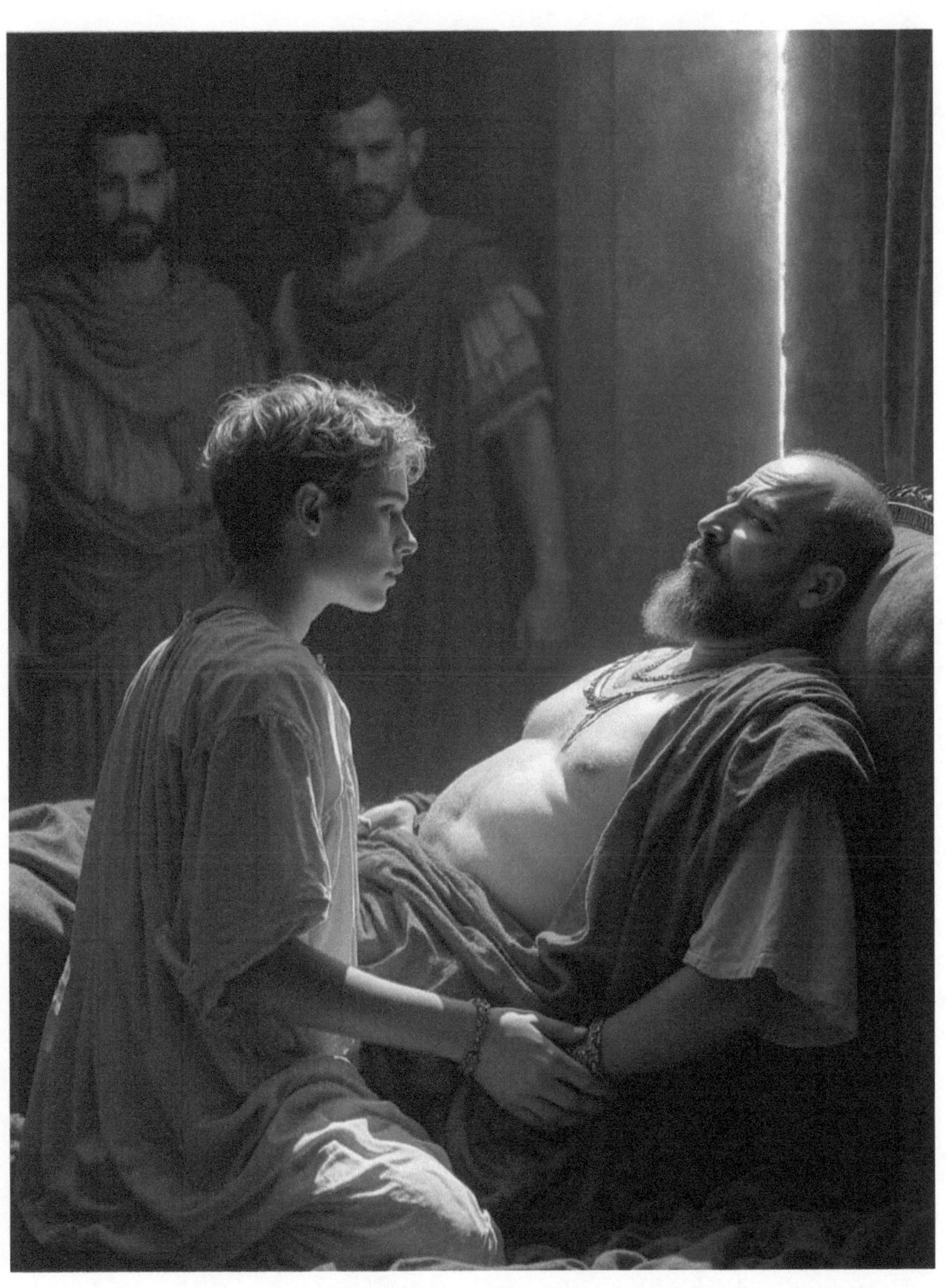

XXXI

AULUS VITELLIUS GERMANICUS

So … Vitellius let you live.

For a while.

Then what are you doing here at the Circus, and why am I being tasked to transform you into the Goddess of Death?

I said for a while.

Do you not understand?

There are philosophers who say that time is a circle, not a line. I say that time can be both a line and, at other times, a recursive circle which you cannot escape from.

For a few months, then, I was neither a condemned criminal nor a revered goddess. Rather, I was under a kind of house arrest. The Senate, of course, declared Aulus Vitellius Emperor, adding the title of Germanicus, though he had not conquered any Germans. Rebuffing the past, he did not take the appellation Caesar as well.

Vitellius did not wed me — not having grown up among the Julio-Claudians, the first Emperor *ever* not to have been born into Senatorial rank, he was somewhat straitlaced when it came to the duties and societal place of men and women, and no room in his mind for any other gender.

However, unless the mob turned against the memory of Nero, who had been the most entertaining of the first five Emperors, he could not exactly get rid of me. Certainly he could not do so quietly, because people would ask questions.

Can you hold still for me? You are restless, Goddess.

And how could I not be? This endless making up is taking its toll. It's one of those endless circles. You make me into a goddess, then you wipe it all off and start again.

Tell me about Vitellius-who-wasn't-called-Caesar, then.

There is not much.

***

Yes, Aulus Vitellius Germanicus was Emperor, and he filled the Praetorians with his own loyalists, but half the army had not declared along with the Senate — these others favored Vespasian, who was still far away, massacring Judaeans in that remote and troublesome province. Vespasian's shadow loomed over Vitellius's Empire. When would Vespasian arrive? When would he seize power? When would the Senate switch sides and grant *him* imperium over the civilized world?

I admit that I too longed for the coming of Vespasian.

Vespasian knew me. He had even flirted with me. He bore me no malice, and I was sure it would be better to be a distant hanger-on in his world than the center of this one.

An astrologer predicted that Vitellius's reign would end. Vitellius had all the astrologers in Rome rounded up and crucified. The madness of absolute power had started to infect him after only a few months.

When people started to gossip that Vespasian was on the march, the tide turned for me as well. Vitellius summoned me to dinner in the Golden House.

When I arrived, I was immediately separated from my entourage, and armed guards came to fetch me. I did not recognize any of their faces. Dinner was in one of the atria, but around us, the Domus Aurea was being dismantled. From a cage, Hercules watched us, looking weak and unfed.

"Frivolous waste," Vitellius said as I was ushered in. "Cheetahs, peacocks ... while the plebeians have to make do with free bread."

"... and Circuses," said one of the other guests.

I saw that it was Pontius Pilatus, whom I had last seen at one of Nero's banquets.

"Indeed, Circuses," Vitellius said. To me, he added, "You remember Pilatus? A washed-up governor? I summoned him in case he could give me some tidbits about the enemy."

"Titus Flavius Vespasianus," said Pilatus. "Glad this 'washed-up governor' can still be of some assistance to the Divine Vitellius."

"I'm well aware that I'm not Divine," Vitellius said. "But I *am* a pragmatist." Then he turned to me. "You know something about Vespasian, don't you?"

"I met him," I said. Had I just been summoned so as to squeeze me for information? That would be a relief. I had lived for several months, never knowing when the axe would fall.

"You more than met him," said Vitellius.

"Perhaps he wanted more," I said. "But I was married."

I became aware that Epaphroditus was standing behind Vitellius, in the shadows. He would not look at me.

"My secretary," Vitellius said, "who knows everything about everyone. What do you have?"

Epaphroditus said, "We have intercepted a letter, written in code, addressed to 'Divina Poppaea.' It says, 'Wait for me, my dear.' What do you have to say about this?"

"I don't know anything about it," I said. "I mean … it was intercepted. How could I know? I am happy never leaving my house, never talking to anyone but when I am summoned."

"Alas, Sporus, the memory of the Divine Nero is no longer an asset to my reign, and neither are you." To Epaphroditus, he said, "I shall tell the Senate that tomorrow, we will act on the long-standing decree of Damnatio Memoriae, and erase the name of Nero from the world."

"Yes, Divinitas," said Epaphroditus, looking at the floor.

"Arrange to raid all the treasuries, money vaults, and assets hidden in temples. Melt the gold from the statues of the gods. We'll find a way to pay the donativum Nymphidius promised."

"It still won't be enough," Epaphroditus said.

"Taxes, then."

"The mob won't like that," I said.

"Oh! The catamite speaks!" said Vitellius. "We'll have to make sure that doesn't happen again."

I should have kept silent.

"What will calm the mob when taxes are too high?" Vitellius said, turning to Pilatus.

"Games, Divinity."

"Then we'd better find a way to kill Nero's memory, raise taxes, *and* entertain the mob all in one action," he said.

So saying, he pulled a ring from his robe and dropped it on the dinner table in front of me.

"Do you recognize this?" he said. "It was found among the late Nero's most prized possessions."

It was the keepsake I had bought Nero in Greece, and it sealed my fate.

I was to become Persephone in the arena.

XXXII

PERSEPHONE

Yesterday, the editor of the Games invited me into the arena for another rehearsal of my public execution. "It's tomorrow. Very last postponement. *Nothing* can go wrong," he told me. "This has to send a clear message throughout the Empire."

They chained me up, and told me to act "terrified" while my rapist, whom I had already met thanks to you introducing me some days ago, threw himself at me with abandon; he did not perform any actual penetration, as that would be saved for the spectacle itself, though I clearly felt the stiffness of his eagerness for the task.

"Make a big fuss," he whispered in my ear. "I'll try not to hurt you too much. They want a show, and it's got to be to the death, but that wouldn't have been my first choice; I'd rather keep you around for encore performances, if you know what I mean."

"What if I just pass out, and they drag me out?"

"They'll know," he said. "Not much that escapes them. They're experts, and I'm just a slave, doing what I'm told."

An "artistic advisor" — so they called him — was on hand to make sure that the Vestal Virgins would get the best view, and that all his scenery, representing the underworld, was correctly set up.

"Now, listen, Sporus," he said in Greek — he was one of those artists who had not even bothered to learn the barbaric tongue of their conquerors. "You play this with nobility, like a real Queen. Don't scream and wail like a two-obol whore. You're a goddess, and you can tell from our friend's priapic splendor that he's a god. If you display the proper qualities, who knows? The audience might even demand your freedom."

"I *am* free," I said.

"Now *that's* the spirit. Dignity. Nobility. You know who you are. A goddess, daughter of the Earth herself."

After the rehearsal, they took me back to the bowels of the Circus.

***

The first to visit me was Epaphroditus.

He still could not look at me, but he said, "You know I had no choice."

"You have to survive," I said. "All of us do. We use what the Gods have given us. Wealth, power, family. For you, it is wisdom, knowledge, and intellect. But for me … all I have is my looks."

"You are the thing that men desire," Epaphroditus said. "If Epictetus were here, he would tell you this: you must let go of everything to find some form of peace."

"Beauty is the greatest curse," I said.

"Oh, Sporus," he said, "how you have short-changed yourself! There is so much more to you than physical beauty. Come now, I need your forgiveness."

I forgave him — he desperately needed forgiveness, though for what, he did not tell me — and he left, leaving behind a bag of honey cakes. Perhaps he thought I should die with sweetness on my lips.

***

Then came my real family: Croesus, Marcus Vinicius, Spider, and Hylas. We exchanged few words. I said, "Don't bother to see the show tomorrow; it will never live up to the advance publicity."

They were all weeping. Not me.

Croesus said, "Epaphroditus gave me another letter, one he did not tell Vitellius about. In it, Vespasian says he is looking forward to seeing 'all of Nero's Empresses, especially the little one I flirted with in Greece.'"

Marcus said, "I am going to join him tomorrow. They say he is not far. They say he may meet Vitellius in battle ... at Bedriacum."

Bedriacum would always be known as an insignificant village that made and unmade Emperors.

"Be careful," I said.

"Don't worry," Marcus said. "Half the Praetorians are throwing in their lot with Vespasian. They see what he achieved in Judaea, and they see his aristocratic connections."

"Everything that I own, that's still in my name somehow," I said to Croesus, "draw up papers. I want it all to pass to Hylas."

"I don't want anything!" he said. "I want to die with you!"

"Don't be silly," I said. "You have everything to live for." Hylas began to weep inconsolably. I wanted to hug him and tell him everything would be all right. But how could I? My fate was about to be far worse than any of theirs. And yet all I wanted to do was give comfort to another. What was wrong with me? I comforted them all. I hugged each of them many times.

Hylas was the most reluctant to leave. "When I you first met me," he said, "I was just someone else's lips and buttocks. I couldn't even say anything to my owners. You gave me a tongue. You gave me a mind. You gave me freedom."

Then even Hylas left me, and *you* came back, to give me my final, final touches of makeup.

***

And this is how it ends? The premiere satirical poet in the world, the most beautiful woman in the Empire, two Emperors and a would-be Emperor … and finally now the Bride of Hades?

I hear people have been waiting since dawn to be seated, and my execution is not until late afternoon. There will be gladiatorial bouts, a venation with giraffes and elephants, and a full-scale recreation of the sack of Troy before my deadly defloration.

You have managed to squirm out of so many things.

Perhaps I still will.

Vespasian may arrive in time. It does not seem likely. Even if he should prevail at Bedriacum … that's not exactly an hour's ride beyond the walls of Rome!

Or, perhaps, my performance could be so breathtaking that the crowd demands I be spared. That does not seem likely either. You see, it isn't just the God who will be violating my soft flesh.

Everyone in Rome has wondered what it was that Petronius felt when I snuggled up to him. How Nero felt when he took his boy-mistress to his bosom. What it was that

Otho and Nymphidius felt, that made them attempt to attain an empire just to gain entrance to my body.

And now they will all know. All of Rome, vicariously, will be fucking me today. All of Rome will know what it is like to love a Goddess. How can they make the sign for mercy when they are too busy coming to climax?

No, I am not going to be spared.

What other choices do I have? Shall I bribe you with the title to one of my villas, so you can smuggle me out with the corpses of slain gladiators?

You might consider the honey cakes, Divinitas.

The honey cakes?

... they are poisoned, aren't they?

I may not say.

How much did Epaphroditus pay to get them through?

I may not say.

I daresay he knows where to get the most tasteless, odorless ones, the ones that worked so well on so many of Nero's predecessors. Should I try them? An ignominious end! But at least I would deny Vitellius the satisfaction of a huge propaganda victory against the memory of Nero.

Nero!

I close my eyes and I see him vividly. Nero Claudius Caesar Augustus Germanicus, poetaster and potentate, traitor and tyrant, master of all the world, seated in glory amidst lickspittles and sycophants ... Nero, whom I alone understood.

Oh, you shone brightly in the tawdry grayness of our world! You were magnificent in your corruption, in your self-delusion. You dreamed a new Rome into being, though it was founded on the folly of Narcissus.

If I eat these honey cakes, will I come before your throne?

Or will I enter a world inhabited by such as Petronius, who was the first to treat me not as an object — even though he owned me as an object? Will he touch me tenderly and call me his Giton, his Ganymede?

Or will I be reunited with Hyacinth, to run with him through the hills and forests, speaking the language of an annihilated people, ignorant of the dark and violent Empire beyond the sea?

I have only a few hours to decide how to die. In public or in solitude. In honor or in infamy. By choice or by compulsion. In agony or like gently falling asleep.

Or I could always hope for Vespasian....

πολλαὶ μορφαὶ τῶν δαιμονίων,
πολλὰ δ᾽ ἀέλπτως κραίνουσι θεοί:
καὶ τὰ δοκηθέντ᾽ οὐκ ἐτελέσθη,
τῶν δ᾽ ἀδοκήτων πόρον ηὗρε θεός.
τοιόνδ᾽ ἀπέβη τόδε πρᾶγμα

The gods may take a myriad shapes
and make the unexpected happen
that which we think does not come to pass
instead the gods bring the unthought into being
as all can see

— Euripides

AFTERWORD FROM THE AUTHOR

Just about every historical source — none of which are quite contemporaneous with the events, and all of which have certain agendas — says that Sporus committed suicide.

And yet….

This book was originally a popular serial in the now defunct Amazon *Vella* platform. From the beginning, I've had readers begging me to let Sporus live. Why shouldn't he? He's had a really tough life — a lifetime of tough lives, and he didn't even get out of his teens.

So … for those friends in particular … I've left it so maybe, just *maybe,* he got away. One reviewer even asked me not to believe Suetonius, Cassius Dio, and Tacitus, but go with some of the less well-known sources, so as to avoid "breaking his heart" … and I do hate to break people's hearts!

When you write a novel in the first person, you can't really kill the protagonist off — or how would he be the narrator? I cheated by setting up the circumstances of the narration so that the death could happen after the last page.

But for those of you would like to imagine an escape, a rescue, or an embarrassed cover-up by the editor of the games … I've left the door very slightly ajar.

Apart from this little (well, *big!*) thing, I've tried to be as historically factual as I could be, while molding the facts to fit the necessary structure of a novel. It's actually mostly the mundane things in this book that are made up out of whole cloth ... getting from incident to incident, coalescing different incidents and of course the initial pirate raid. No one actually know where Sporus came from.

But *really* weird stuff in this novel is often historically attested. The urine tax. The Emperor cheating in the chariot races by using ten horses, not even finishing, yet still winning the first prize.

Even when you remove obvious anti-Nero bias from the incidents described by ancient historians, what remains is still pretty crazy. And yet we are only gradually starting to realize that Nero was in fact a very popular Emperor.

I've tried to treat those things that are outlandish, shocking and immoral to modern sensibilities in the spirit in which the Romans themselves took them. Sex and violence were not the profundities of the human condition that they are in our society today. Rather, they were entertainment.

The universal truths of 1st Century Roman life were quite different. To us, *virtue* is goodness. To the Romans, the noble quality of *virtus* belonged to the penetrator, never the penetratee. Suicide was commonplace and well-respected. Slaves did not object to being raped any more than a chair complained about being sat in. The idea of people being *equal* was perhaps unimaginable.

Yet this was a world in which slaves could, and did, not only become free but arise to positions of immense power. They could be powerful, indeed, even while still being enslaved: there was a whole army of tutors, doctors, accountants, scribes, and other specialized professions where most of the practitioners were in fact owned by someone.

There was a fluidity between being a non-person and a full-fledged human being — and Sporus's life journey, though incredible, was by no means unthinkable.

I became aware of Sporus not through ancient history but in an English class. The legendary Michael Meredith was my teacher and we were discussing Alexander Pope, who satirized a contemporary, gender-fluid member of the aristocracy as "Sporus" — a "painted bug of gold that stinks and stings."

Michael explained to us who Sporus was in ancient history. In Pope's time, the 18th Century, enough people must have heard of Sporus to get the joke. These days, with less classical education going around, I fear not so much.

This character is mostly just a footnote, but for almost six decades I have been wondering: what if *he* were the viewpoint character for the chaos of Nero and its aftermath?

Like many authors, I end up writing books that I would love to read, but no one seems to have written. Thank you for sharing this strange journey with me.

ABOUT THE AUTHOR

Once referred to by the International Herald Tribune as 'the most well-known expatriate Thai in the world,' Somtow Sucharitkul is no longer an expatriate, since he has returned to Thailand after five decades of wandering the world. He is best known as an award-winning novelist and a composer of operas.

Born in Bangkok, Somtow grew up in Europe and was educated at Eton and Cambridge. His first career was in music and in the 1970s, his first return to Asia, he acquired a reputation as a revolutionary composer, the first to combine Thai and Western instruments in radical new sonorities. Conditions in the arts in the region at the time proved so traumatic for the young composer that he suffered a major burnout, emigrated to the United States, and reinvented himself as a novelist.

His earliest novels were in the science fiction field and he soon won the John W. Campbell for Best New Writer as well as being nominated for and winning numerous other awards in the field. But science fiction was not able to contain him and he began to cross into other genres. In his 1984 novel *Vampire Junction,* he injected a new literary inventiveness into the horror genre, in the words of Robert Bloch, author of Psycho, 'skillfully combining the styles of Stephen King, William Burroughs, and the author of the Revelation to John.' Vampire Junction was voted one of the forty all-time greatest horror books by the Horror Writers' Association, joining established classics like Frankenstein and Dracula. He has also published children's books, a historical novel, and about a hundred works of short fiction.

In the 1990s Somtow became increasingly identified as a uniquely Asian writer with novels such as the semi-autobiographical *Jasmine Nights* and a series of stories noted for a peculiarly Asian brand of magic realism, such as *Dragon's Fin Soup,* which is currently being made into a film directed by Takashi Miike. He recently won the World Fantasy Award, the highest accolade given in the world of fantastic literature, for his novella The *Bird Catcher.* His seventy-plus books have sold about two million copies world-wide. He has been nominated for or won over forty awards in the fields of science fiction, fantasy, and horror.

After becoming a Buddhist monk for a period in 2001, Somtow decided to refocus his attention on the country of his birth, founding Bangkok's first international opera company and returning to music, where he again reinvented himself, this time as a neo-Asian neo-Romantic composer. The Norwegian government commissioned his song cycle *Songs Before Dawn* for the 100th Anniversary of the Nobel Peace Prize, and he composed at the request of the government of

Thailand his *Requiem: In Memoriam 9/11* which was dedicated to the victims of the 9/11 tragedy.

According to London's *Opera* magazine, 'in just five years, Somtow has made Bangkok into the operatic hub of Southeast Asia.' His operas on Thai themes, *Madana* and *Mae Naak*, have been well received by international critics.

Somtow has recently been awarded the 2017 Europa Cultural Achievement Award for his work in bridging eastern and western cultures. In 2020 he returned to science fiction after a twenty-year absence with *Homeworld of the Heart*, a fifth novel in the *Inquestor* series.

In 2023, Somtow was elevated to the status of Thai National Artist by Thailand's Ministry of Culture, and in 2024 he was awarded the status of Public Diplomat by Thailand's Ministry of Foreign Affairs.

S.P. Somtow has published over one hundred books, as well as premiered over a dozen operas which he composed and wrote the libretti for,

To support S.P. Somtow's work, visit his Patreon account at patreon.com/spsomtow.

His website is at www.somtow.com.

www.ingramcontent.com/pod-product-compliance
Lightning Source LLC
Chambersburg PA
CBHW030429310726
48979CB00009B/1683/J